Praise for *Cards of Identity*

"One of the three or four most mercurially alert, unnervingly funny books to have appeared in the twentieth century."—*Sunday Times* (London)

"A novel of fiendish ingenuity. It will make you laugh, it will make you wince, and it may just possibly make you crawl under the bedclothes forever. . . . *Cards of Identity* may be remembered and read for some time to come."—*New York Times*

"*Cards of Identity* is the most considerable attempt at a serious and sizeable satire that we have had for some years. It is witty, full of comic invention . . . and it is packed with fundamental brain-work. There is the added pleasure, too, that Mr. Dennis is something of a literary virtuoso."
—*New Statesman & Nation*

"*Cards of Identity* unfolds as a succession of brilliantly ingenious vaudeville turns. . . . There is much in Mr. Dennis's nightmarish entertainment which is both blazingly funny and savagely penetrating."—*Atlantic Monthly*

"The writing itself is distinguished: Nigel Dennis's style, urbane and precise, is a perfect vehicle for his wit."—*Commonweal*

BOOKS BY NIGEL DENNIS

A Sea Change

Cards of Identity

Two Plays and a Preface

August for the People

Dramatic Essays

Jonathan Swift: A Short Character

A House in Order

Exotics: Poems of the Mediterranean and Middle East

An Essay on Malta

CARDS *of* IDENTITY
NIGEL DENNIS

DALKEY ARCHIVE PRESS

Originally published by Vanguard Press, 1955
Copyright © Nigel Dennis, 1955

First Dalkey Archive edition, 2002

Library of Congress Cataloging-in-Publication Data:

Dennis, Nigel Forbes, 1912-1989
      Cards of identity / Nigel Dennis.— 1st Dalkey ed.
        p. cm.
      ISBN 1-56478-319-7 (alk. paper)
        1. Psychologists—Fiction. 2. Theater—Production and direction—Fiction. 3. Congresses
and conventions—Fiction. 4. Identity (Psychology)—Fiction. 5. Brainwashing—Fiction. I.
Title.

PR6007.E55 C37 2002
823'.914—dc21

                                2002019290

Partially funded by grants from the Lannan Foundation, the National Endowment for the Arts, a
federal agency, and the Illinois Arts Council, a state agency.

Dalkey Archive Press books are published by the Center for Book Culture, a nonprofit organization
with offices in Chicago and Normal, Illinois.

www.centerforbookculture.org

Printed on permanent/durable acid-free paper and bound in the United States of America.

To

THE OLIVERS OF NORRIS WOOD
with thanks and gratitude

PART ONE

'WILL you be back for lunch?' asked Miss Paradise, clipping each word like a bean. 'I am not going to walk miles in fog to get you sausages, to find you have preferred sandwiches in a pub.'

Her brother began slowly to drum his fingers on the breakfast table and stare out of the window, evading the question by seeming to be groping for an answer to it. But as he had been doing this every morning for a week his sister became impatient at once. She repeated her question, as he had feared, in a form which showed that she had not intended it to be answered at face value in the first place. 'Do you know what you are going to do now?' she asked, clipping her words more than ever. 'Have you any plans at all? You knew Sir Malcolm was going. Did you, in advance, think of someone to take his place? Have you tried Admiral Blair at Wickington? They say he's a great rider. What about the new people at Little Hall? Don't the girls want ponies? Don't you keep up with the times? Every fishmonger's daughter is a horsewoman. Perhaps you have lost your go. Having Sir Malcolm so steadily all through the war has robbed you of go. I spoke of your sausages; it was your character I meant. And by your character, I mean the bills. They are straining my nerves. Another bill and I shall snap.'

He looked at his pepper-and-salt jacket, his cord breeches, his leggings, and felt that he might never have bothered to put them on, so naked was his sister making him. But he again played for time, looked out of the window, and answered lightly: 'As a matter of fact, I've not got a horse I can lay my hands on at the moment.'

His sister looked very angry. He knew as well as she did the law of question-and-answer – that it is dangerous to turn the first question, fatal to turn the second. Mr Paradise, hoping desperately to evade this law, tried to save himself by reverting to the question in its first form and saying: 'Forget the sausages, my dear. It's hard to get good ones, anyway.'

This made her much angrier. While he peered miserably out into the fog, she dug deeper. 'There was a time when you were *younger* and had more *spirit*, when you got the rich person *first* and the horse *second*.

Often you found that the friendship could be made and kept without the help of a horse. Did Mr Truter, your bosom friend, have a horse? No. He had a Rolls. Did old Miss Mallet ride? Only in a bath-chair. But you wheeled her in it. Have you become a coward? Or will you get on your bicycle this very morning and broach the admiral?'

'Really, dear,' he said, 'you talk as if it were my nature to be a kind of parasite.'

This shocking word caused Miss Paradise to burst into tears. 'I hardly know you any more,' she cried. 'I ask myself: who are you? Are you my brother? Or have *I* changed into someone quite different? Something has happened to one of us, and I'm sure it's you. Why, there's nothing to recognize you by any more! Everything about you seems to belong to another person. It's like living with a stranger.'

He was badly frightened by these remarks, which cast doubt on his very existence. To make certain that he was all there, he gave his knee a sharp pinch and let out a hacking cough.

His sister's sobs were unaffected by this, but the fog responded immediately. It flew right out of the garden of the little lodge, split in two to reveal, a hundred yards away, a huge oak in the centre of the park, and finally, with a flourish, uncovered the middle of the roof and front of the mansion of Hyde's Mortimer itself.

'Nobody has any money any more,' sobbed Miss Paradise, 'or so they say. Then why is it that every tinker is a steel master, every brick-layer an architect, every taxidriver a garage king? Why do I feel that the very air is reeking with money and that we are the only ones who don't seem able to grasp it?'

Her brother gave a roar and jumped from his chair. '*It's the breakfast-room!*' he cried. 'What the devil can that mean?'

The strong, eager tone of his voice – so familiar, so *like* him – brought Miss Paradise to her feet with a bound. Her wet eyes, following the trembling pointer of his finger, saw that though fog still lay over the wings of Hyde Mortimer, the central clump of tall chimneys was in evidence and that from it, cutting a tunnel into the sky, rose a splendid pillar of white smoke.

'Nine o'clock,' said Mr Paradise, looking at his watch (a farewell present from Sir Malcolm when he took the remains of his capital to Australia). 'Why, that was breakfast-time in old Miss Mallet's day!'

'But that was twenty years ago,' said Miss Paradise. 'Are you sure it's the breakfast-room?'

'My dear,' he replied, drawing himself up haughtily, the better to enjoy revenge; 'I may be frail on bills and horses, but credit me with knowing every major chimney within twenty square miles. . . . No smoke, I note, from the drawing-room. Perhaps he is not married.'

'That would be useful.'

'Or else the wife is an outdoor type. . . . Alas! fog still hangs over the nursery.'

'A widower, perhaps.'

'Don't build castles in the air. I have often heard of widowers; I have never met one.'

'That's what Mr Truter said of blue-eyed poets.'

He opened a drawer and took out an old-fashioned pair of binoculars: he had chosen them when asked by the widow of one of his patrons what he would like 'to remember him by': the choice had not been large. Grasping an extensive wheel between the lenses he wound away until the apparatus thrust forward like twin cannon. His sister having opened the lattice window, he held the monster steadily to his eyes while the little room filled with wet March air and heavy breathing. Miss Paradise took position behind her brother and did her best, as she peered over his shoulder, to check the pictorial envy that the user of binoculars provokes in those who have but eyes. Hopefully, she magnified her vision to match his: she saw the tight, pitted, mortared texture of the red-brick façade, the sparrow perched on the fold of roof-lead, even the python line of a bell-rope glimpsed at the edge of a tall window-frame. Then, in a burst of hallucination, she created the perfect image in her mind's eye and set by the breakfast-room window a fine old gentleman of the old school, plastered with shining decorations (he was going to a levee) but glowing still more with the generous dignity, the matchless dawn-colour, with which a large bank balance suffuses the complexion. In her heart she gave little cries, in tones that matched the hues she had conjured up: 'a little tucked away', 'a nest-egg', 'something for a rainy day'. Aloud, she cried impatiently: 'Well? Can't you see *anything?*'

Her brother, bound closer to reality by his use of a machine, replied carefully: 'The maids' rooms appear to be empty. But the blind is up in the butler's pantry. The Blue Room is definitely in use; someone has left a towel right on the bed. The shutters are still nailed on most of the other windows, including the kitchen: it is all very odd, as if they were sure of a butler but had yet to find a cook. I wonder if it's not some agent or auctioneer temporarily camping.'

'You must go and find out, mustn't you?'

'Of course. It might be somebody who has absolutely no right.'

'Exactly. Burglars on our doorstep.'

'I shall say something to that effect if it turns out to be a real owner. That I dropped in because I know the old place so well and would hate to see it a den of thieves.'

'How clearly you see things! Now, let me see *you* before you go.'

He stepped back with a tolerant smile, and she ran her eyes – quite dry now – over his small, neat face and brisk little moustache. Now that he was going into action they had exchanged roles: she was a fussy old lady again, pulling at a corner of his coat, conning him for soup-stains, giving his sword and armour the last rub-up. He, for his part, had assumed the stance of a modest officer and gentleman; his sister noted with pride that even after a patronless twelvemonth his old clothes looked trim and clean; he was not the kind to respond to hardship with buckled trousers and slopped foods. He was really, after all, the good, dear, brave little brother with whom she had lived for thirty-five years, a man who had borne excruciating humiliations and always exacted a good profit from them. 'Look what I've saved for you,' she said with a burst of tenderness, producing a Woodbine from a cupboard. 'Light it up and have a good puff.'

He had to punish her for the doubts she had cast on his identity before the fog broke, but he did it gently and correctly. 'Naturally, I can't be sure about lunch,' he began, blowing out a plume of smoke.

'Of course you can't. Your work must come first.'

'And don't indulge in hopes; that's always a weakness of yours.'

'I'm afraid it is. I'm a woman, I suppose.'

'Often a man is most himself when he least appears to be.'

'I tend to forget that.'

'You yourself are not always the same person.'

'One always imagines it's the other who's changed.'

Honours now being even, a pause followed to allow the new stability to take effect. Then Miss Paradise said: 'Will you go on your bike? It always looks so clean and sets you off.'

'I think I'll walk. Then I can take my riding-crop. It never looks well across handlebars.'

'Yes, yes. Foot and crop; very nice.'

She would have liked a parting hug from her knight, but of course he was too much a man for that. One of the many sad things about living with a man was that one had no wish to hug him when he was in flight and he had no wish to be hugged when he had faced about. She gave a large sigh.

'So settle yourself comfortably until I return, my dear,' he said with grace. 'Worry and anxiety are a woman's worst enemies. If I am not back by one o'clock . . .'

'I shall know . . .'

'I should think . . .'

He moved out into the garden, and Miss Paradise, after hesitating a moment, called after him: 'You know, coal is high and the evenings still chilly. One quite small load of wood, just to start with . . .'

'We'll see, we'll see,' he called back.

*

He hoped he would not be rusty in today's approach. How, he asked himself, had he broken the ice on entering his previous anchorages? What had he said? What had they replied? Mr Paradise had a perfect memory and as he now flashed over his first meetings with Sir Malcom, Theodore Truter, General Pugh, Sir Thom Browne, and the rest, he recalled with interest that the first conversation in each case had been about *money* – how much the Government took and was wasting, how much was getting into the hands of the wrong people, how much it was to be desired but how small was its purchasing power, how spendthrift of it were countless people the speakers could name (this led to many harmonious anecdotes). But the point, above all, to be reckoned with in this first conversation was the near-penury of the patron himself. Mr Paradise would always remark, when poverty came up, that he, too, was pretty well penniless; but having thus shown, as it were, that his hands were clean, he would withdraw from any further competition, allowing the distressed magnate to assume the whole title and freehold of poverty and range into the most cruel details of his taxation and penury. The rich had a grudge against people who claimed to be poorer than themselves: they were generous only to those whom they believed secretly to be doing very well. So, on reaching the first shrubberies of Hyde's Mortimer, Mr Paradise had his notes well in order: (1) Am here to prevent theft. (2) Jest about worst thieves being in the Treasury nowadays. (3) Pleased surprise at seeing the old place in good hands again, a circumstance almost miraculous in view of Government's desire to destroy rural this-and-that by taxes. (4) His love for, and intimate knowledge of, Hyde's Mortimer. (5) A friendly warning that all the local shopkeepers, without exception, were swindlers.

He emerged on to the broad carriage sweep before the front entrance. Two pretty iron-railed flights of stone steps, very delicate in comparison with the grossness of the mansion, led to a small balustraded terrace on to which the door of the breakfast-room opened – or rather, had once opened, for no one in Mr Paradise's memory had ever used this big door. For this reason, he was making his way to the side entrance when he heard voices and saw three figures standing on the terrace, looking out over the balustrade.

They were a middle-aged man, dressed in a purple dressing-gown whose knotted waistband fell in thick golden hanks almost down to his furred slippers; a handsome woman in a sable coat of which the collar, turned up all round her head, made a pretty frame for her white skin; a lounging youth, dressed elegantly but very lightly in comparison with the other two and braving the chilly air by leaning the fingers of one hand on the cold grey stone of the balustrade. A pale sun – which presumably was what had brought them out – lit them as with a soft spotlight, throwing a sheen over the lady's complexion and fur and lighting a small blaze on the gentleman's golden tassels. The three of them were watching the fog's efforts to resist the sun in the impersonal, detached way that aristocrats have when confronted by natural elements: Mr Paradise was impressed.

Suddenly the young man spoke, in a low, amused tone. 'Father,' he said, 'I *think* the butler's come.'

The older man appeared not to hear. Reaching into a deep pocket he produced a small object in fine leather, like a diary, turned a few pages in it, and announced in a deep, clear voice: 'In ten days' time it will be National Savings Week. Let's celebrate with an orgy. Three thousand pounds of reckless fun.'

'Beaufort is right, dear,' said the lady, still staring into the writhing mist. 'I have noticed him myself.'

Still the older man appeared to hear nothing. Raising his head, as one who is floating up into a dream, he said: 'To me, such an orgy should have an air of profound *mystery* about it. It should represent a large sum of hard cash wreathed around with mists of ethereal unreality. There should be about it the sense of combined wizardry and substantialness that one feels on hearing the phrase "invisible exports" – an expression whose impressiveness is in no way lessened, but rather increased, by seeming to be a form of intangible profiteering performed entirely by ghosts.'

'Father,' said the young man, suddenly looking at Mr Paradise, 'here's a visitor. Do pay attention.'

At this, the lady, too, turned towards Mr Paradise; and so at last did the father, slowly bending his head sidewards until his eyes were wholly absorbed in the visitor. After a moment of this, he uttered merely one word: 'Yes?'

Mr Paradise, poor man, had no idea what to say. It was impossible, with three such figures talking at such a distance in thousands of pounds, to hurl back a quip about burglars or income tax. Moreover, to be scrutinized as through three sets of lorgnons embarrassed him violently, the more so because it was being done from a point fifteen feet above his head. He began to advance across the neglected gravel, but not only were his legs weakened by the mention of so much money but his head was quite out of joint; the closer he drew to this splendid trio, the higher he was obliged to tilt his face. By the time he had dragged himself to the base of the terrace he felt every inch a beggar; even his riding-crop, far from inducing confidence, only emphasized the inexcusable lowliness which any horseless person feels when he advances on the mounted. All his secrets, his greediest intentions, his devotion to making one penny grow where none had grown before and then to eke it out in exciting farthings, seemed to be reflected in the six great eyes that looked down on him. Fortunately, he observed, the eyes' owners did not appear to be enraged by what they so clearly saw; on the contrary, they observed his corruption with the friendly curiosity of scientists. Possibly for the same reason they said nothing to untie his tongue, as if they had expected him and made jovial bets as to what his first words would be.

At last the lady came to his aid. With no effort she rearranged her face into the time-tested lines of feminine invitation, drawing Mr Paradise forward by sheer suction. Into her eyes she injected vapour of a kind Mr Paradise had not seen since his mother bathed him on her knees. It was remarkable that though enveloped in a sable coat she could convey a sense of warm bath-towels and hissing gaslights shining through clouds of steam, intermixed, strangely enough, with the warmth which the round legs of chorus girls fill the air with in their passage. Hers was, in short, an appeal to the lost identity of his child-hood and youth, and it was out of these years that he croaked in-nocently:

'I love the old place.'

She answered immediately: 'Of *course* you do!' and sent him a sparkling flash of congratulation.

'So I just came to see if you were all right,' he continued, fragments of his adult plan tumbling back into his head.

'To see if we were all right,' the man repeated slowly. 'I see.'

'There being burglars . . .'

'Ah, yes. Well, as you see, we *are* all right.'

There was another painful silence, until the man said, quite sharply: 'Won't you come up?'

Mr Paradise mounted the steps, dragging his crop like a tail.

'Is your horse quite safe, sir?' asked the younger man politely, 'or shall I take it to the stables for you?'

'Frankly,' croaked Mr Paradise, missing the top step and all but fall-ing on his face, 'I have temporarily no horse.'

'Only the crop is permanent,' suggested the lady, smiling.

'Exactly, madam,' said Mr Paradise, 'by force of habit, I suppose.' Suddenly recovering his wits, he made a grimace and added: 'With taxes what they are, my few poor steeds have had to seek other pastures.'

'Doubtless you miss them dreadfully?' she asked sympatheti-cally.

Their language, he felt, was becoming rather old-fashioned, so he replied more lightly: 'Oh, I still manage to pick one up here and there,' and proceeded to do as much for his legs.

'You must tell us your name, sir,' said the older man, examining Mr Paradise from head to foot.

'Henry Paradise is my name. My sister and I have lived in the South Lodge here for many years.'

'Ah! Then you knew my old aunt, old Miss Mallet?'

'Very well indeed, sir. And her father before her.'

'Well, well! You are virtually a member of the family, it seems. Are you also familiar with this house?'

'I know it from top to bottom,' said Mr Paradise, feeling jaunty again and giving his knee a slap with his crop. 'I might say there is hardly a draught in it that has not played on my neck.'

The man seemed gratified. He gave Mr Paradise another close examination, actually stepping aside, at one point, to see how Mr Paradise looked in silhouette. Then, he asked abruptly: 'Do you always have a moustache?'

'*Really*, Father!' said the young man. 'What a very rude question!'

'*Much* too personal,' said the lady; 'you have not even introduced us.'

Mr Paradise, delighted by their support, smiled tolerantly and said: 'I really don't mind the question. As to the moustache, I have had it for years, though, like most people with moustaches, I have shaved it off from time to time to see what's underlying, if you know what I mean.'

'I know exactly,' said the gentleman: 'that was just the reply I expected.' Giving Mr Paradise a final glance over, he said to his companions: 'Exactly the man we want, no?'

They both nodded.

'Would you by any chance,' the gentleman continued, 'have an hour or two to spare this morning?'

'Is it quite fair to ask that?' said the lady. 'Mr Paradise probably has many things to do.'

'*Most* inconsiderate, Father,' said the young man, giving a sigh which suggested that he and the lady had suffered from this selfishness for many years. Mr Paradise suspected a not unpleasant pattern for his behaviour in the future: he would serve his new patron with smiling amiability and the other two would marvel at his unselfishness. 'Whatever my business,' he said, 'I find it hard to refuse my help when it is asked.'

At this all three of them nodded with such enthusiasm that Mr Paradise was very puzzled.

'Well, that is admirable!' said the gentleman in a loud voice, as if suddenly everything had been settled. 'Now let me introduce us. I am

Captain Mallet, nephew, as I mentioned, of the old Miss Mallet who was so dear a friend of yours. This is my son, Beaufort; and this is his wicked stepmother, my present wife. Where his *real* mother is, it would be safer not to inquire. Parenthood presents many complications nowadays and most of them are not fit for public discussion, even with an old friend of the family.'

Mr Paradise thought this introduction had been very late in coming and very improperly performed – exactly what one expected, in fact, from a very rich person. 'It is most courageous of you, Captain,' he said, 'to open up this fine old place again, with taxation what it is.'

'Oh, you think so?' said the captain, with surprise. 'Personally, I cannot think of it as much of a place to live in – rather a *den*, I would call it, compared with some of our other places. We just happen to need it, at the moment. As to taxation, I never have anything to do with it at all. I prefer, in fact, never to have the subject mentioned by anyone in my hearing.'

'Very rude, Father,' said Beaufort with another exasperated sigh. 'Can you never tell when people are trying to say a friendly thing?'

'Mr Paradise has already been kind enough,' said Mrs Mallet, 'to ignore my husband's recurrent rudeness.'

Mr Paradise responded with a smile of ineffable servility. He saw it all so clearly now and knew he could slip into place like a king-pin.

'Shall we go in?' said the captain, crossly. He opened the big door, and then turned abruptly on Mr Paradise. 'You have not become another person suddenly, have you?' he asked. 'Perhaps you would rather not come in at all? After all, you haven't the slightest idea what sort of people we are or what you are in for.'

Again Mr Paradise gave the gracious, accommodating smile which, though he had only used it twice before, seemed already to be an established part of his life. 'I am at your service, Captain,' he said.

*

Miss Paradise's cuckoo-clock, gift of Alfred Truter, cuckooed one o'clock. As the jaded bird popped in again, Miss Paradise gave a groan of joy. Sitting down to the kitchen-table, which she had already furnished for the worst, she looked at her brother's empty place and gratefully murmured: 'Well done, thou good and faithful servant' – adding, as she returned his sausages to the larder: 'I was an-hungered and ye took me in.' He was splendid, really splendid, her brother was: who but he, with his sharp eyes, his trim moustache, his stiff little breeches, his robin-like brain and look could poke his nose in on people just rising from their first breakfast and be asked to lunch? When she imagined how furious she would be if someone's brother tried to play such a trick on her; when she pictured the speed and hostility with which she would bundle the wretch out of doors again, she was thrilled by her Henry's audacity and thanked Heaven for having given her such a brother. His absence would give her a chance to give the whole lodge a tremendous sweeping and dusting: it would delight him to see everything spick and span when he returned, probably a little tired. First meetings were always tiring for Henry: there were the words to be chosen with such tact, the visage to be torn from the shape it had kept from the last patron and rearranged to fit the new one, the whole self to be adapted to unfamiliar usage in the space of a mere morning. But he would manage it: when she next saw him he would be quite another person, and it would be her duty still to recognize as her brother a man who would in fact be someone quite different. She would know it was Henry because he would know her and would sit in his favourite chair unconscious of having changed, expecting the same things in the same order in the same surroundings.

So she threw herself into the housework, faintly singing and talking to herself and trying to anticipate the story he would tell when he returned – always such a thrilling return, the first one, with the new yet always familiar tale issuing from the new face, accompanied by mannerisms and little gestures new-born that very day like lambs. At last, like any other housewife, she happened to glance at the bedroom clock – and lo and behold, it said five o'clock, and the evening fog was closing in again on the latticed windows. 'Why, the naughty boy!' she exclaimed with a gasp, 'he has managed to stay for tea as well. Surely that's a little risky on the first day?'

She unwrapped her head and made tea. When the cuckoo sang six, she began to listen for her brother's step, confident that she would know it no matter how much it might have altered since breakfast-time: some patrons were halt. But when it was eight o'clock and pitch dark, she began to worry. Surely no man in his right mind, she asked with a burst of practicalness, would keep Henry for dinner as well? On the other hand, one must never forget the extraordinarily temperamental behaviour of the rich, to say nothing of Henry's amazing talent for distorting time to such a degree that one hardly knew whether it was past, present, or future – in particular, how he could prolong a conversation that was slipping away by hitching its tail to the head of a new topic and starting out afresh as if no change of subject had occurred. And then there were his countless anecdotes, some of them quite technical and of real interest to men of affairs – terrifying, almost morbid tales of fortunes imperilled by inefficiency, taxation, wastage, recklessness. 'I am sure,' Henry had once confessed to her, 'that they often have the feeling, once I have gone, that I stayed much too long; but I am equally sure that they feel that this was because they selfishly refused to let me go.'

But when eleven p.m. came, and still no Henry, Miss Paradise's feelings began slowly to change. She didn't dare put on her coat and go up to the big house: she had done so once on a similar occasion and disturbed her brother at a crucial moment of the budding friendship: his rage had been terrible and he had said that her impatience had cost him weeks of effort. So now she went slowly to bed, sulky, but trying hard to remind herself that she had spent many a night alone when Henry was sitting up with a sick cow of Sir Malcolm's or resolutely sticking at the bridge-table of the gayer General Pugh.

But when she was half asleep her thoughts began to wander. Say something had happened to Henry; say he had been drowned in that flooded bomb crater in the middle of the park? I would never get over the shock, Miss Paradise said to herself, starting to cry; with Henry gone I would be another person, a sort of ghost. She cried until her grief had been eased, after which, like any bereaved person, she half-shelved the dead and half-opened his bank-account. Even for the best of legatees this is a painful moment of emotional readjustment: woe must still be conscientiously sounded with the left hand, while the right is shaping a melody quite out of keeping with moral harmony. But at least the moment of reading out the will is one of the few occasions when capital drops its striped trousers and reveals itself as none other than naked cash. Yet only for a few exciting minutes – for Miss Paradise found, marvellously enough, that no sooner had she transferred the dead Henry's hard cash to her own account than it instantly resumed its trousers and became capital once more – godlike, interest-bearing capital of far greater stature than it had been prior to Henry's death; exactly twice the size, in fact, since theirs had been a joint-account and death had thus no option but to be a tidy carver. Indeed, Miss Paradise, suddenly possessed of exactly twice the capital and exactly half the dependents on it, now began to take over the sole share of worrying about it – was it happy as it was; could it not be made happier by being shifted to more interesting quarters? She at last decided that she would take this question up with Henry, having quite forgotten by now that he was no longer the other half of the joint. When, abruptly, she realized what shocking tricks her mind had been playing, she was more than horrified, she was also confused and exhausted. For, in those exciting moments of put-and-take, she had so rearranged her world that not only had Henry's identity been allowed to dwindle, but her own had proportionately doubled. Now, back in reality, she found it painful to divide her new self, swollen by its new capital, in two, and restore Henry to his rightful half. In consequence, though she struggled for many more minutes to listen for his dear, returning steps, she was harried by the suspicion that the ears with which she was listening were attached to a person who no longer existed, and that the sound for which they were listening had long since ceased to be.

*

Crunch, crunch – here he was! She jumped out of bed – what a sunny morning! how late she had slept, in her grief! – and hurried to the casement window. But there, below, was not Henry but their joint nephew, a character so undesirable that his uncle and aunt had had to insert special paragraphs into their wills excluding him from all postmortem benefits. What distinguished him from them most sharply was his absolute disrespect for property and corresponding vacuum of interest in people who possessed it. Industry of any kind he abhorred; yet to say this was to depict his character too vigorously, since he was one for whom the abhorrence of anything would demand more energy than he had to give. Where his uncle and aunt, aided by the turns of two world wars, had raised themselves several notches in the social scale, the nephew, seemingly deliberately, had descended in inverse proportion, finding his friends and his livelihood in strata that made no demands on his lax character. His habitat was the fringe of the machine-shop and garage; his income came from a string of purely secondary transactions such as re-sales of old motor-cycles, spare parts, tyres, petrol, anything that was rationed or in short supply. And since the garage had now replaced the old market as the point where town and country met, Lolly Paradise's dealings also included commodities which, in other days, would never have come together – disparate things like lengths of pipe, squares of turves, gravel, old batteries, spirits of salts, roofing-felt, dung, and margarine. In all such deals, Lolly was the go-between, the one who exacted the lowest price from the seller and the highest from the buyer, a method of business that respectable people such as his uncle and aunt believed to be a shameless innovation, unknown to society before the war. Lolly had heard of cheques, and even seen them; he had glimmerings of the great credit system on which usury and society are based, but he himself refused to fiddle with such matters, conducting all his transactions in currency notes and silver. The very thought of writing his name openly on a cheque, where all might read it, struck him as an act of folly that might be all right for some people (though he could hardly say why) but would be, for him, as senseless as leaving a record of all his transactions with the police and the town council.

What also shocked his uncle and aunt was Lolly's indifference – indeed, absolute ignorance – in matters of social class. Descriptive terms such as 'gentry', 'middle-class', 'squire' were, to him, the equivalent of 'sith' and 'eftsoons' to the student of purely contemporary literature. Lolly did cash business with anyone, and it no more occurred to him to consider their social status than to open a bank account or make an income-tax return.

He stood, now, on the gravel, with his greasy shoes, his hollow trousers, his imitation leather jacket scored with scratches. 'Hello, Auntie!' he called in a high voice, smiling winsomely on one side of his face. 'Nunky home?'

'No,' said Miss Paradise.

'Thought he could help me.'

'Why? He has never done so before.'

Many nephews would have winced at this snub, but Lolly was unmarked by what he considered a simple statement of fact. 'When'll he be back, Auntie?' he asked.

'I have no idea. I am not one to pry.'

20

"'Cause if it's going to be long, I'd just as soon drop the whole deal,' explained Lolly, his eyes glazing – and he spoke nothing but truth, for if any transaction threatened to be laborious, Lolly just discontinued it, without mentioning his withdrawal either to the prospective seller or the prospective buyer. 'Where did he go?' he asked, summing-up a faint revival of interest.

'He is engaged at the Hall,' retorted Miss Paradise with lordly triumph, quite forgetting, in her eagerness to give this snub, that Lolly would not understand its social implication at all. Indeed, he now looked curiously interested, as if she had told him that someone had dropped a load of old batteries in the park.

'Up *there*?' he asked with some surprise, heaving a wavering thumb in the general direction. 'People moved in there? What's it? School, now? Ministry?'

'I am going out,' replied Miss Paradise sharply, regretting her folly and withdrawing from her loop-hole to dress. 'You may as well go too.'

'You bet,' he said affably. Then, after a pause, during which she heard his feet shuffling meditatively in the gravel (he always left a cleared circle in any space where he had stood), he called: 'They got cars an' things up there, Auntie, or just horses?'

'I have no idea,' cried Miss Paradise, pulling on one of Mrs Pugh's old corsets.

'Think you could ask Nunk for me?'

'No.'

'Well, all right.' He added in a cheery, friendly tone: 'Well, I'll be going now, Auntie. I'll drop in and see you again, if I have the time. You ain't worried, are you, Auntie?'

'Do I sound worried?' roared Miss Paradise from the back of her bedroom.

'I thought you did. If you're going to the village I'll wait for you if you like. It's a lovely day.'

Miss Paradise made no answer. At last she heard Lolly move slowly off down the road, not exactly whistling but emitting feebly a tooth-strained string of sibilants. She went to the window and peeped out to make sure he would not hide behind a tree and see which way she went – an act of guile which would never have occurred to Lolly. But, from down the road, he saw her head immediately, gave her a friendly smile, and waved his hand. 'Don't worry, Auntie!' he cried. 'Only makes your hair grey.'

A few minutes later Miss Paradise left by the back door and, staring like a Roundhead at any tree that might be harbouring Lolly, took the way across the park that was best hidden from the road. It brought her on to the main drive, and no sooner had she begun to follow this up to the Hall than she heard the roaring of an engine and a large sports car came racing up behind and stopped beside her. At the wheel was a handsome young man, excellently dressed but attractively tousled – all legs, langour, and devil-may-care, as a youth in a sports car should be. He gave Miss Paradise a delightful smile, superior in every way to one of Lolly's clove-hitches, and cried with boyish eagerness:

'Are you going up to the house? Can't I take you the rest of the way? Such a fag.'

'How very thoughtful of you,' answered Miss Paradise. 'Are you by any chance . . . ? I suppose you are . . .'

'The new people? Yes. Beaufort Mallet is my name.'

'How nice to hear that old name again! Well, Mr Mallet, I am Miss Paradise.'

'Paradise,' he repeated gravely, turning his blue eyes into the sky and looking more attractive than ever. 'I seem to recall the name, but I cannot remember in what connexion.'

'Perhaps the old Miss Mallet who once lived here mentioned it. Or perhaps you saw my brother yesterday.'

'Oh, that's not likely, Miss Paradise. Yesterday was our first day here, so nobody would come to call, would they?'

'Of course, Mr Mallet, I know nothing of my brother's affairs, but I remember when he went out he said something about just seeing if there really were people at the Hall and not, well . . .'

'Not people who had no right to be there?' cried Beaufort. 'But how clever of him to know that there was anyone here at all! Do you think the milkman told him?'

'It would not surprise me.'

'You don't mean,' exclaimed Beaufort, his face becoming worried all of a sudden, 'that your brother hasn't come back?'

'So it seems, Mr Mallet.'

'But "seems" is surely not the right word, Miss Paradise? After all, if your brother *had* come back, you would be the first to know. He

22

couldn't be two persons at once, could he, any more than he could be in two places at once?'

'I would think not, Mr Mallet.'

'Then you must be terribly worried, Miss Paradise! And here I stand talking! Do jump in immediately and we'll rush up and see.' And he packed Miss Paradise into one of those deep bucket-seats that lower the whole horizon of the world and instantly induce a sense of helplessness in all but the driver. 'It's quite possible,' he went on, churning the engine into a fine roar, 'that he saw my father, or even my stepmother. Are you very upset? Yes, I can see you are. Let's go full speed. A minute saved often makes the difference between life and ... well, life and great discomfort. Was he your *only* brother?'

'Yes, and there's an old bomb-crater in the park,' cried Miss Paradise, falling to pieces. 'I fear he's in it.'

'You must see Father at once,' said Beaufort, driving at terrifying speed. 'Father can do *anything*.' He took one hand from the glistening wheel and gave her knee a chummy thump.

'You are really a very kind young man,' sobbed Miss Paradise at the top of her voice as the rain-puddles rent under the furious wheels like ripped silk. Though pleased to have his hand on her knee, she would have preferred it to be on the steering-wheel. The next second the car made a frightful semi-circular turn and stopped with Miss Paradise's door exactly at the foot of the stone steps.

'So you have opened this door?' asked Miss Paradise, curiosity breaking through her tears like sunlight.

'Oh, Father would never hear of a *side* door,' said Beaufort, his voice very grave. 'Now, Miss Paradise, do come along quickly. I hope to heaven we've not missed him.'

He hurried her up into the breakfast-room and instantly left her, shouting breathlessly: 'Father! Father! An emergency, Father!'

By now Miss Paradise was convinced that Henry's whereabouts did amount to an emergency; but even as she was trying to find the proper response to loss of something priceless her eyes were roving round the breakfast-room with astonishment: it looked absolutely palatial with its deep carpets, tall curtains, and golden ancestors – had they done all this in one day, or had they been secretly preparing for weeks? She heard Beaufort still shouting excitedly down the passage: 'Father! Father! Wherever are you?' and suddenly, from far away, a deep voice

replied slowly and incredulously: 'Is it *me* you are calling so hysterically, Beaufort?' The poor boy's tone became flustered at once: she
heard him say, almost pleadingly, 'Well, Father, it's an *emergency*, you
see; a man has disappeared.' 'Then, pray,' replied the deep voice, drawing closer, 'compensate for his absence with presence of mind.'

Miss Paradise barely had had time to adjust her look to the awe-
someness of the voice when Beaufort threw the door open and his
father came in. What an entry; what a man! – a full-length portrait
stepping slowly out of an Edwardian picture book, so beautifully
dressed and blending so many time-honoured characteristics: the
carriage of a duke, the perspicuity of a great surgeon, the courtesy of a
sultan, the steel of an imperial governor. And what a sheen on his fine,
mature features and on his good boots – real boots, not shoes: the sight
of it all struck Miss Paradise as forcefully as if an undertaker had come
in. 'You may go, Beaufort,' the vision boomed, looking first at and
then quickly away from Miss Paradise with princely tact. 'Yes, sir,'
replied the breathless boy, withdrawing immediately with an ashamed
expression. Oh! how quaint! how charming! how different from
Lolly! 'She is Miss Paradise, Father,' he panted out, as he disappeared.

The father waited to hear the door click. Then, without hesitation,
he advanced across the carpet, extended the polished white fingers of
his right hand and felt Miss Paradise's pulse. While he listened, his head
slightly cocked, to the beat of that sundered kettle-drum, he expelled
from his face all such feeble answers to crisis as worry, doubt, even
sorrow: in their place he set placid but inexorable stringency of attention, and his brown eyes, directed full upon Miss Paradise, shone with
such a walnut finish that she could see herself reflected in them – thin,
concave, a mere petal.

'Kindly sit down, Miss Paradise,' he said, gently exchanging her
pulse for the sort of chair in which a woman can sit without having to
be eternally pulling down the front of her skirt or keeping her knees
braced at right angles. 'Be so good as to tell me the story, as briefly and
clearly as your condition will permit.'

Miss Paradise told him what she had told Beaufort.

'So you are a very, very anxious woman,' he said when she had
finished.

'Well, shouldn't I be, don't you think?'

'You have telephoned the police, of course?'

'No, I haven't. Thinking he was *here* . . .'

'I can see what a shock you have received,' said Captain Mallet. 'In your normal state you would never for an instant suppose that your brother could pay a formal call on total strangers and stay with them for twenty-four hours. However, since the alternative seemed to be his having stayed in the bomb-crater over a similar period, you decided to come straight to the house. You could not face the crater. You are hoping against hope. Forgive my grimness. I do not blame you.' He went to a table, raised a speaking-tube and, when a gurgle came from it, said sharply and simply: 'Drag the crater.' Then he returned to Miss Paradise, saying: 'I am deliberately assuming the worst. There is no reason whatever to believe that it has happened.'

'The police . . .' said Miss Paradise.

'That is the next step, of course. Unfortunately, our telephone is not connected yet. But my son can carry any message in his motor-car with equal speed.'

This made Miss Paradise smile. 'He *is* a nice boy,' she said.

The captain started, as if she had irresistibly diverted his train of thought. 'He is a *likeable* lad,' he answered slowly, pride and disappointment mixing in his eyes.

'So thoughtful, so kind.'

'You find him so?' asked the captain, bending on her a look of deep interest. 'One so easily forgets that one's children's manners improve in proportion to the distance they are from their homes. I imagine that in our daily life, particularly when we are young, the recurrence of the same problems, the same routine and habits, causes us to show impatience, even rudeness, to those we love. We who are more mature expect, and consequently demur to, the daily frictions of domestic life. Do you not find it so?'

'Indeed I do. My brother and I always rub along.'

'Exactly; that is just the phrase. And, consequently, of course, we easily mistake youthful vitality for bad manners – though, I must say, the two characteristics are often hard to distinguish.' He added, after a pause: 'The boy has lost his mother.'

'You have done wonders without her,' said Miss Paradise, unable to resist another quick look round the splendid room.

'Thank you. And yet, he needs more than either I or his excellent stepmother can provide. An overwhelming love; something all-embracing and tender: if I could find it for him, in one form or another, I would welcome it with open arms. However, I shall tell Beaufort that at least one discerning person has shown approval of him.'

They exchanged warm, understanding looks, as befits people who are sharing an excursion into the deeper elements of living. Indeed, Miss Paradise was by now wishing that this lovely, old-fashioned chat could drag on interminably – that at nightfall a butler would enter and draw-to the heavy curtains, shutting both her everyday self and the outside world out of existence. At that moment the captain bent forward and felt her pulse again. 'Our little moment of distraction has done you good, I think,' he said, as if he had cleverly planned the whole direction of their conversation. 'The police must, of couse, be informed, but perhaps are you now in a state to give me a few details about your brother. Meanwhile, a little tea would soothe both of us, I think,' and he pressed a bell. 'Is he a tall man?'

'Oh no: quite short. Not a dwarf, of course.'

'Ah. Not a dwarf. And dressed, you say, in riding-clothes? A horse?'

'Not actually with him, no.'

'He could not have fallen off it?'

'Impossible.'

'Ah. Clean-shaven?'

'To a large extent. There *is* a moustache, but he keeps it cut so flat and allows it so little spread that it is easily overlooked.'

'Ah. Now, what about moles or birthmarks?'

'No birthmarks and few moles – not where a stranger would notice them, anyway.'

'Ah, well. We can pursue that point later should any question of identity arise. Ah ... What kind of *manner*, may I ask? Vigorous? Apathetical? Nondescript?'

'Both vigorous *and* nondescript, I would say.'

'I think I know. Friendly? Fond of visiting?'

'He chooses his friends carefully, but once he has done so he sticks very closely to them.'

'Ah. Is he *inclined* to absence and disappearance? How can I put it without being rude? Do nights pass without him? Is he, shall we say, not always quite *there* after a convivial evening with friends?'

'Sometimes it has seemed so to me. He is always *there*, of course, I'm sure; just absent from me.'

'Yes, yes. It is hard to know exactly, isn't it, who is and who isn't? Is he by any chance a little free-handed with money?'

'Oh, never that. Never, never.'

'Ah. Inclined rather the other way?'

'Much more.'

'What people who didn't understand him might call close-fisted? Tell me now, if I am not impertinent, have you on account of this thrifty bent of his ever had *differences* with him? I find that so many tussles between people who otherwise love each other dearly can be traced to money. It is astonishing when you think of it how much people will put up with in the way of duplicity, disloyalty, even broken-heartedness, and yet become most unforgiving where a banknote is in dispute. Do not hesitate to silence me, my dear Miss Paradise, if you find I am too personal.'

'I am finding it most helpful,' said Miss Paradise frankly. 'The only thing that is troubling me is that I have never thought of my brother in the way I have described him. He seems like two persons now, and I'm afraid that you would never recognize the real one if you saw the described one. Or do I mean it the other way round?'

'We are trying, you see, to *discover* which is the right way round, Miss Paradise. If we hit on the right way, we are pretty sure to find the right man at the end of it, regardless of any wrongness that may have crept into his description en route. I'm sure you see that. Now, here is a very blunt question indeed which may take us a step farther. Has your brother, despite the fact that you "rub along", ever suggested breaking off connexions? To put it cruelly, have you ever thought that he might suddenly walk off, taking the cash-box with him?'

At this, Miss Paradise turned quite faint. 'There have been times,' she said at last in a cracked voice, 'when we have quarrelled and . . .' But she said no more: panic was making her eyes bulge.

'Of course, were he to do so,' said the captain easily, 'the tragedy would be purely an emotional one. A little loose cash would be neither here nor there, since your *capital* would be safely in the bank.'

'No! No!' screamed Miss Paradise: 'not safely at all! It's a joint account!'

'Good heavens!' exclaimed the captain, quite losing his calm. 'Now that is *quite* another matter!'

27

'I am destitute!' she screamed, filling her lungs to the full to give her emptiness true measure.

'Not as long as I live, by God!' he answered, suddenly striking his fist on his knee.

But Miss Paradise had ceased to be impressionable. Not the captain, not the palatial room, not the fairy-dream of having escaped from her ordinary self were as horrifying as the sudden conviction that reality had escaped from her. Seizing her bag, she made a rush for the door.

'Miss Paradise!' cried the captain, springing after her.

'Bank! Police! Let me go!'

'Not in this condition! Why, none of this may be true of your brother!'

'It *is* true! Some sixth sense tells me! I know! I know!'

'That your brother is a thief?'

'Yes! Yes! Instinct tells me! He is *worse* than thief! He has murdered me! He has always wanted to. I have always known. Let me go this minute. I will see him in prison!'

'Let Beaufort drive you,' exclaimed the captain, gripping her wrist. 'Don't you see it will be *quicker*?'

'Then *get* him, *get* him!'

The captain released her and ran to the speaking-tube. As he raised it, slow, steady footsteps sounded outside the door.

A butler entered with a silver tray. Gently, he advanced across the room, and with each step he took, Miss Paradise's frantic face drew tighter and tighter. When he was past her, she gave a plaintive, incredulous cry: '*That's* him, isn't it? Henry?'

'Tell Master Beaufort to bring the car round immediately,' said the captain into the speaking-tube. 'We are going after a bank-robber. No delay, please: he is probably miles away already.'

The butler, having laid down his tray, turned and began slowly his march back to the door. Clearly, he was well-fitted for his office, for though Miss Paradise's eyes ran up and down him madly and one trembling finger pointed straight at his face, he continued his sober walk unmoved.

'Who are you?' screamed Miss Paradise suddenly.

The butler halted, as if such a question was more than flesh could bear, and looked hopefully to his master. 'A little sal volatile, Jellicoe,' said the captain in a low voice. 'Just knock on the door and leave it outside.'

The butler bowed. 'Beaufort will be ready in five minutes,' said the captain to Miss Paradise; 'then we will scour all England.' He rubbed his hands briskly.

The butler again passed before Miss Paradise, moving to his exit like a ghost who has played its part. As a ghost she saw him, and her own fingers stretched out to take him by the shoulder. But she was no longer able to judge his distance from her, so that he passed a full foot beyond her reach; nor was she able to encompass his whole name, and could only say: 'Hen. . . . Hen!' She saw the door close behind him, and the captain standing out in front of her: she heard his voice say firmly, but pleadingly, 'Miss Paradise! Try to listen! Try to be yourself!'

'But it was Hen. . .'

'So will everyone be Hen, Miss Paradise, till we have tracked Hen down. Here now, this deep chair.'

'Have I lost my wits?'

'Only the outer eye, Miss Paradise – the unimportant eye.'

'I know *you*; I can see *you*.'

'Because you trust me, Miss Paradise. You trust I am not Hen.'

'Don't speak of him! To think I gave him a Woodbine to cheer him on! Oh!'

'Can you see this cup?'

'Yes.'

'Then drink it up, Miss Paradise. We have a long way to go and you must be strong and well if you are to perform your proper duty.'

*

'Dear Florence,' said Mrs Mallet in her soft voice. 'Our one and only Florence. Do you feel any more yourself? I am going to draw back the curtains, so you must tell me if the light is too blinding.'

She drew half the curtain back, revealing a comfortable, homely room. Miss Paradise's cuckoo-clock ticked on the far wall; on her dressing-table lay her brushes, comb, and pin-bowl. On the wall at the foot of her bed was her favourite photograph of Henry, pointing his stick at one of Sir Malcolm's cows. Miss Paradise surveyed it all with the equable look that marks lunatics and the newly-risen: the world (her look said) is furnished with many sightly shapes; it is not for me to try and name them.

'See, here,' said Mrs Mallet, pointing, 'your own little clock, Florence, to tell you the time as it has always done. And your pretty own things, to use every day, to tell you where you are. And your pretty old mirror, to see yourself. We have brought them all here.'

'You talk too much,' said Miss Paradise crossly, vexed by being urged to leave the restful state of non-recognition.

'Oh, Florence, I am sorry!' said Mrs Mallet. She took Miss Paradise's hand, squeezed it gently and said no more.

'So, it's me, Florence,' said Miss Paradise in an aggrieved tone, after a long pause.

'Yes, you are Florence,' replied Mrs Mallet gently, giving her a look of congratulation.

This look had a strong effect on Miss Paradise. Though almost all her mind was still dead, one faculty suddenly became shrewdly alive – that of how to win compliments. 'That's my clock,' she said pointing.

'Oh, yes, Florence, you clever dear; it *is* your clock!'

'An' 'at's my brush an' comb an' whatsisname.'

'Right again, Florence, dear!'

''S my brother an' cow on th' wall.'

'How fast you are coming back!'

Vanity having thus led the way to the surface, towing behind it the faculty for recognizing any object that would please it, Miss Paradise might now be said to be conscious. But she was still rebellious, she still required to be self-convinced, and Mrs Mallet seemed to know this. 'I have been asked, Florence,' she said, 'to remember to give you all sorts of messages from downstairs. The captain, of course, sends his love, and says that nothing will induce him to let you start work again until you are absolutely yourself. Master Beaufort sends you a big hug: don't ever tell him I told you, Florence, but he went to his room in tears, when he heard . . . And Jellicoe presents his compliments and wishes you a quick recovery: "The best housekeeper in England, madam," he said; and there were tears in *his* eyes, too.'

Miss Paradise gave an approving grunt. Rivers of tears, explosions of love; this was life as it should be. 'He brought me tea on a silver tray,' she said, giving Mrs Mallet a shrewd look.

'You even remember *that*, Florence? But that's wonderful.'

'I remember *everything*,' said Miss Paradise boastfully.

'*Everything*, Florence?'

'Why not? I wasn't born yesterday.'

'But Florence, dear, the doctor said it might be weeks before your poor mind began to grasp things again.'

'Doctors! What do they know?'

'Do you remember the old lawyer who tried to be so sweet to you?'

'Certainly.'

'And how we fetched you from the lodge?'

'Everything.'

'You know we didn't mean to be unkind?'

'Of course.'

'Well, you *are* a marvel, Florence. But then, of course, you stood up to everything so wonderfully at the time that nothing about you can surprise me any more. I think that if they hadn't pushed you just a bit too far by reading the will you would never have collapsed at all.'

'That's just what I think,' said Miss Paradise in a resentful voice, not minding her perplexity so much, however, on learning that another was responsible for it.

'The captain understood at once. "A brave soul," he said to me afterwards, "can endure any loss without flinching. What brings its collapse is to learn that, as a result of loss, it has obtained material gain." '

'Henry's gone, hasn't he?' asked Miss Paradise suddenly.

'That's what I meant, Florence, dear. The thought of benefiting by his going . . .'

A hammering began in Miss Paradise's chest. She would have liked, without knowing why, to burst into tears, tears of mingled loss and ignorance. But, having proudly laid claim to perfect remembrance, she could not bear the thought of renouncing it. And as she lay, tormented by sadness, curiosity, and conceit, there was a light tap on the door and a boyish, handsome face popped through.

'Beau! You are a naughty boy!' said Mrs Mallet sharply.

'I simply *had* to come,' he answered simply, and crossing the room with quick steps he bestowed on Miss Paradise the sweetest, most loving smile she had ever received. Then, bending down, he slipped one arm under her neck, gave her a passionate buss on each cheek, and muttered: 'Hurry up and get well, Florrie-Porrie! This old barn is like the grave, without the sound of your keys.'

'*Beaufort*,' said Mrs Mallet, biting her lips at his tactless mention of the grave.

But he was out of the room immediately: the two women heard his footsteps running quickly down the passage.

'Poor boy!' said Miss Paradise in a gratified tone. 'His eyes are full of tears.' What pleased her about her situation was that although she couldn't understand it, it was so sensible and right. Her feelings of loss were matched at every point by all manner of reward: certainly, she never remembered being loved so much by everyone. And as she had always believed she was the most lovable of women, the present situation, however puzzling, seemed to fit her so well that she was in no mood to question it.

'May I come in?' said a gruff, gentle voice, and there stood the father, power and tenderness struggling for mastery in his face. 'Dear, brave Florence!' he said, standing back simply and surveying her with awe. 'What a character! What a soul! What a *lesson*!'

'And she remembers *everything*,' said Mrs Mallet.

The captain was astounded. He exclaimed: 'But the doctor said . . .'

At this, Mrs Mallet and Miss Paradise looked at each other and began to laugh. Their amusement perplexed the captain: he scratched his head and walked up and down like a clumsy puppy, muttering: 'But, bless my soul . . . I don't see . . . Really, it doesn't seem . . .'

'Florence and I have talked it *all* over, dear,' said Mrs Mallet, touching his arm. 'We have decided that doctors don't know everything. There is nothing more to say.'

'That's right,' said Miss Paradise.

'Then . . . then, what happens next?' blurted out the captain, bereft of all his normal poise and command.

'Why, dear, we wait patiently now for our splendid Florence to get on her feet again.'

'And that won't be as long as you think,' said Miss Paradise, re-membering suddenly that she had feet and studying with interest the bump they made under the blankets.

'Well, by Jove, then, I simply don't know what to say,' the captain confessed. 'I have never known anything like it in my life.' Suddenly, unable to restrain himself, he said furiously: 'We've filled that devilish

crater up, Florence: yes, by God, we have! It will never claim another
life.'

'You are opening old wounds!' cried Mrs Mallet. 'See, now, you've
made her cry! Oh, you tactless men! I wish you would all go away.'

Miss Paradise now wept freely for Henry, the more freely because
she could hold the captain responsible for her weakness. Fixing her
eyes on Henry's photograph, she not only wept for his dear memory
but out of a vague feeling that, though dead, he had somehow not
gone in the way she had supposed. 'We know where he is!' she exclaimed aloud.

'We do indeed,' said the captain loudly. 'Where all men are when
they have fought the good fight!'

'I hardly know how I will look after myself, alone,' said Miss
Paradise.

'You will never be alone, Florence,' said Mrs Mallet: 'not with three
people who love you as we love you.'

'But I am destitute!' cried Miss Paradise, suddenly recalling a word
that had been eluding her.

'Oh, no, Florence!' boomed the captain in distress. 'He has left you
everything, the savings of a lifetime! It is a considerable nest-egg.'

'Oh, my dear!' said Mrs Mallet very crossly, 'if you cannot understand better, do leave the room! It was *spiritual* destitution that was
meant.'

'He meant it kindly, madam,' said Miss Paradise, and wondered
what on earth had made her say 'madam'. She added: 'Do you know,
I thought I saw him again? Carrying a silver tray.'

'Was that when the will was being read, Florence?' asked Mrs
Mallet. 'In the breakfast-room, in the morning? After we had brought
you from the lodge in the car?'

'Yes, it was then.'

'Yes,' said the captain, pacing the floor: '*Sometimes we think we see
them*. And we ask them: "Who are you, vision of one whom I loved?"
And they can vouchsafe us no answer, since they are not walking before
us but are in our mind's eye. They carry a silver tray: it bears the hearts
of those they have left behind. They are taking these hearts away for
ever.'

This sounded reasonable enough to Miss Paradise, so she went on
crying quietly, shoring up the image of her disappearing heart with a

picture of a nest full of speckled eggs. 'Good, good Henry,' she said. 'He wasn't a wicked man at all.'

'He was one of the best,' said the captain. 'That, doubtless, is why he has been taken. Or so they tell us, anyway.'

'I think Florence has had enough for this morning,' said Mrs Mallet, rising and drawing the curtain again. 'I shall go and make her some soup. All the maids have gone, Florence, in a sudden panic.'

'Well, bless my soul!' exclaimed the captain indignantly. 'You accuse me of tactlessness and then you say the one thing that you know will upset Florence beyond everything!'

'No, sir, I am proud to hear it!' said Miss Paradise truthfully.

'Of course you are, Florence,' said Mrs Mallet. 'You know there is more in you than in the whole tribe of men.'

'Even sturdy little Agnes went,' said the captain ruefully. 'But you, Florence, always said she would.'

'Indeed, I did,'

'The older I get, the less I seem to know,' said the captain in a resigned voice. In the half-darkness he took Miss Paradise's hand and said gently: 'I shall go now, Florence. Words cannot express my admiration. The day you again take your seat at the helm of our household will be one of the happiest we have ever known.'

'But I have never been anyone's housekeeper!' cried Miss Paradise with resentment.

'She has forgotten her promotion,' said the captain, drawing the curtain open again and smiling proudly at Miss Paradise. 'How proper for the humble heart, to recall everything except a matter for pride!'

But Miss Paradise no longer was sure that she wanted further contact with this strange new world. She had no wish to deny her familiarity with it: puzzled though she was, she had already decided that she must have been on intimate terms with these affectionate people for many years. But now, following so many elevating compliments, she was being told that she had come down in the world, and this did not please her at all.

'Florence, you remember old Mrs Jellicoe, don't you?' asked Mrs Mallet.

'Of course,' said Miss Paradise. 'Jellicoe's wife.'

'Jellicoe's *mother*, that's right. Who was so sweet to you when you first came, when Beau was a little boy.'

'Yes, yes. I remember *everything*.'

'Well, then don't you remember stepping into her shoes a few months ago, and how naughty you were and kept saying you didn't want a rise in salary . . . ?'

'But we insisted,' said the captain, 'and we carried the day.'

'I don't know that it happened quite in that way,' said Miss Paradise gloomily.

'I think I can explain the uncertainty,' said the captain. 'In the violent upheaval that poor Florence has experienced, many fragments of her past have been dislodged. She remembers all the pieces, but she cannot be too sure where they fit. This is not her fault: it is because she remembers them, one might say, with such a marvellous brilliance, that a shadow is thrown by the substance upon its relevant position.'

'You will exhaust the tired mind with such conundrums,' said Mrs Mallet.

'Madam, I understand perfectly,' said Miss Paradise.

'Of course you do,' said the captain. 'Now, what has happened is that, in the general confusion, the bottom has been put in the place of the top. Florence knows that her self has undergone a recent change of position; but whereas she has in fact been raised up in the order of things, she feels, on the contrary, that she has been cast down. This is something that only happens to very modest people; for modesty, always yearning towards humble things, never feels more humiliated, as it were, than at the moment when it is lifted up. You, Florence, you who have experienced this paradox, think you are not worthy of your new station. Nor are you, of course – in your own incomparable eyes. But in *our* eyes, my wife's and mine, which dwell in a region so far inferior to yours, not only are you supremely adequate to the role of housekeeper but, indeed, fitted for far, far higher things – if such there be. That you should choose to serve us when your soul is as far above us as the stars – this has always puzzled us and always will. All we can say is that, for our part, we believe you have given us the privilege of serving *you*.'

This was not Miss Paradise's idea of the relation between employer and servant, but she did not object to its being held by employers. Moreover, the captain's description of her selfless character was not one which any sane woman would deny. Apparently, over her strongest, most-ethical resistance, she had been promoted, given more

35

salary and left a nest-egg. This in itself was reward enough, but what made it even better was the fact that to the reward was added a sensitive recognition of elements in her that others, so far as she could recall, had overlooked. All she had lost, it seemed, was Henry, and she could shed tears for Henry. She began to do so, murmuring: 'He was a good man, wasn't he?'

'No woman ever had a better husband, Florence, as you yourself often remarked,' said Mrs Mallet.

Husband? This was a shock, but a pleasant one. So he had been her husband; then she must give him more tears, tears of even greater intimacy. She fixed her eyes on his photograph and marvelled at the sight of him – so trim, so debonair, so priceless a husband. 'He loved horses,' she said.

'He loved everything, especially people,' said the captain.

'But you came first,' said Mrs Mallet.

Who was the man in the photograph with her husband? A trouble-some memory began to spin in her mind but she had no wish to whip it up: the situation was already so right and complete. She felt every inch a saintly widow, inspired by tragedy, ethics, love, and capital. 'Well, well,' she said with a sigh and a smile, 'I think I am better now.'

'Ready for another good sleep,' said Mrs Mallet, smiling.

*

The captain and Mrs Mallet descended to the breakfast-room, where Beaufort joined them immediately, asking: 'Well, all ship-shape?'

'*Most* satisfactory,' said the captain, collapsing onto the sofa. 'We left her snoring like a pig. But how my oratory has exhausted me! Open *The Times* and lay it over my face like a good boy.'

Beaufort obeyed, and then came up behind Mrs Mallet, who was leaning back in a chair, and gently turned up her face. He kissed her lips and murmured: 'And you, my darling stepmother? Has oratory dulled your tiny tongue? Do you love your handsome stepson?'

'You little beast!' she said, letting out a sigh of exhaustion and turn-ing her lips away, 'I suppose while we were slaving away at that harridan you were jazzing about in the car.'

'I got up much earlier than either of you,' answered Beaufort, clos-ing Mrs Mallet's eyes and rubbing them gently with his thumbs.

When I came bursting in to buss our Florrie I was straight from a good morning's work.'

'Was it really good?' asked the captain, his voice hollowed by newspaper.

'Sheer joy,' replied Beaufort, removing his thumbs and kissing Mrs Mallet slowly, first on one eye then the other.

'Stop it at once, please!' cried the captain from below his canopy. 'What would Jellicoe think, may I ask, if he came in and found my son making love to my wife?'

'I don't know why you should be so exhausted,' said Beaufort. 'She was not very difficult, and you said that her brother had been quite an easy job.'

'I did,' said the captain, sliding *The Times* down. 'It was having to sit up so late with him that tired me. And, as always, it was only when the last nail had been driven home that I realized how much my arm ached. His character was not strong, but he had been using it for a long time. It was quite rusted on to him. Why he wanted this identity so much, I cannot imagine. It was two a.m. before I convinced him that it was entirely his own invention.'

'I hope you have supplied him with a rich, full past,' said Mrs Mallet.

'Everything a respectable steward could want. As a lad, I decided, he ran away to sea. Twenty years of drink and women followed in all parts of the world. Now, at last, he is going straight and though we cannot *quite* assure him that he will ever atone for his sins we can at least assure him that he is no longer trying to escape reality.'

'Has he been with us for long?'

'A good many years. He came straight here from the Navy. I found him, dead-drunk, in a Portsmouth gutter.'

'I suppose he is still dreadfully ashamed.'

'Wouldn't you be? He owes me a debt he can never repay.'

'Does he still drink?'

'We stumble on him sometimes taking a secret pull.'

'He took well to a watery past, did he?' asked Beaufort.

'He couldn't resist it. The internal struggle of it all fascinated him. I mean, the long healthy hours at sea, followed by the revolting excesses of shore-leave.'

'And he likes his name?'

'He took to it immediately. Would you care to construe?'

'I should love to. We begin with the premise that every butler believes he was born to command a fleet.'

'That is correct. Go on.'

'But Nelson, you felt, was too common a name. Howe and Hood might be a pair of fishmongers; Anson and Camperdown are excellent names, but can one be sure that they suggest admiralcy nowadays? I am sure you thought of Beatty, but decided it was too rowdy for a butler. The same of Mountbatten. But in Jellicoe you found *everything* – a bellicose, echoing, challenging suggestion discreetly balanced by an opening syllable indicative of a nature congealed and wobbly. In short, though he is for ever partly something pink, shaking guiltily on a plate, he has, in whole, the stuff of leadership.'

'That is first-class, Beaufort. Thus it was, exactly. Incidentally, it may interest you to know that at first I toyed with the idea of an identity from the race-course. But when I put out a few racy feelers, he shrank in horror. That is an important thing to know, by the way. Never, except in rare cases, build on the existing disguise. Imagine the horror of this wretched man if I had taken up his crop and cord breeches and named him Donoghue.'

'And *too* Irish,' murmured Mrs Mallet sleepily. 'Not the streak we want here at the moment, with so much to do.'

'While we are on the name matter,' said the captain, 'here is a résumé of our attitudes. First, Mrs Paradise. The hideous abbreviation "Florrie" may safely be used by you two, on account of your being creatures of tenderness, jollity, and enthusiasm. To me, however, as master of the house, she must always be Florence, no matter how deep my feeling for her may be. The reason for this double-approach is that while Florence is fraught with grave, inhibitory influence, Florrie is suggestive of loose hair and even misappropriation. Thus, it will be for me, as it were, to suppress her rogue instincts with Florence, and for you two periodically to detonate the overcharged cannon with sparks of Florrie. It is a simple matter of balance, and if she shows signs of getting out of hand, you two can always start sticking in a few restorative Florences. . . . Now, her brother. He is to be Jellicoe at all times to all three of us: his is not a name to conjure with. To make Jelly out of it, for instance, would be fatal. It must always be uttered gravely and deliberately – dwelt upon, even: in short, treated as the outward and audible form of his inward and spiritual grace. It must be remembered that he has spent his whole life in the role of an unscrupulous steward, just as his sister has always been a receiver of stolen goods. Since his was the more active role, we cannot afford to relax our nominal pressure for one moment, though in her case we can safely give her the illusion of being human as well as honest. This, I must say,' concluded the captain, 'is a great deal more than most people have nowadays.'

'The religious aspect is going to be a nuisance,' said Mrs Mallet.

'Not if you keep out of deep water, my dear. Don't try to be profound about it; try and make it chime with Florrie, if you see what I mean. I shall supply the heavy Florence metaphysics. How interesting it was, by the way, to find the withered old habit still latent in her!'

'It puts *me* on the rocks, rather,' said Beaufort. 'I shall find it hard to be both devout and sporting, reverent and naughty.'

'Quite so: you are too young for Friar Tuck.'

'And too good a figure, thank heaven!' said Mrs Mallet.

'I suggest a bolder course,' said the captain. 'You are the apple of her eye, are you not? She has mothered you ever since you were a baby. She knew my first wife and, at heart, I am sorry to say, still feels that my second marriage was a betrayal of that dear memory, of which you are the sole fruit. But who are you, a thoughtless boy, to be aware of the tragic loss you sustained in infancy? As far as *you* know, you are perfectly happy and are merely amused by her efforts to consider you an orphan. Her religious views strike you as somewhat comical – the comedy of those we love. Your attitude to her deepest feelings is one of sceptical, jesting irreverence. Laugh sardonically, though in a kindly way; enough to shock her into worrying about your wild character. She will give you a long, grave, muddled lecture on Christian principles, to which you will say something like: "You're a good sort, Florrie, you really are," and give her a hearty kiss. She will love you far more if she feels that it is her duty to reform you: that's only human. I am sure you will do it very well: I don't want you to become merely a man of action: I think of you, in full maturity, as comparable to one of our generals, earning his living by bloodshed but convinced that he is at heart a student of poetry.'

'You don't think Jellicoe will want to marry the widowed Mrs Paradise?' asked Mrs Mallet.

'I think there will be too many obstacles. There is the religious barrier, for one thing. He has not her faith. There is his past. He probably went through ceremonies of marriage with at least two women. He is certainly an absentee father.'

'In brief, poor Mrs Paradise is too good for him,' said Mrs Mallet.

'And, I suspect, too fat. He is a neat man.'

'She is to retain the name Paradise, is she?' asked Beaufort.

'I think so. The addition of "Mrs" is change enough. Jellicoe will assume the Christian name Henry, one which Mrs Paradise greatly esteems.'

'What a lot of nostalgic memories she is going to have!' said Beaufort. 'Does she know how different they are from Jellicoe's?'

'He is too polite to speak openly about them. But she knows – or will know after we have dropped a few hints – that he was only just saved in time.'

'You don't think he should have a dead wife?'

'No. Two living ones are quite enough. I don't want him to feel like a murderer – which is what all widowers feel sure they are.'

The captain got up, paced the floor, and looked at his watch. 'Two in two days,' he said; 'that's not bad. The President will be impressed. But we must work very hard if we are to have not only a staff but a steady, stable staff when the Session opens. What have you to report, Beaufort?'

'Promising stuff. Last night I lay awake wondering *where* I could best find, collected together, the largest and most varied number of local people. What, I asked myself, is today the most popular social resort? I thought of the cinema; but it is too dark inside; I thought of the local auction, but it is too distracting. Suddenly, I saw it in a flash: the doctor's morning "Surgery".'

'Bravo!' cried the captain, gently clapping his hands.

'I got down there sharp at opening-time this morning. To my delight I found that no less than four doctors, all in partnership, plus a nurse, cater for Hyde's Mortimer and its environs. Their ages range roughly from twenty-five to seventy-five: all are in an unbecoming condition of intense hysteria. This condition is not shared by the patients, of whom, this morning, there were twelve men, fourteen women, and six children. Save for hacking coughs and muted whispers to the children, all sat in relaxed silence in an ante-room, on close-set chairs that followed the walls round in an eternal square with an occasional gap for a door. Old papers, which the children love to tear, stand on a central table; a large filing cabinet in a corner, with one drawer always dangling out, contains the visitors' Health dossiers.

'What impresses one about this "surgery" is that it seems perfectly to realize and to blend two old and popular dreams – the pub-keeper's dream of a respectable clientele and the parson's dream of a happy congregation. The ritual sense is over-poweringly strong, particularly as all visitors to "Surgery" keep their eyes closed, cast-down, or fixed in lively expectations on the narrow door that leads to those mysterious rooms where the hysterical gods are at work with swab and kidney basin.

'After I had waited, soaking up the feel of it, for some fifteen minutes, the narrow door opened and the nurse put her head into the room. She cried winningly: "Mrs Chirk? Is Mrs Chirk here?" and then immediately withdrew her head again like one who knows that though this ritual call must be made, it can never be answered. Then, quite suddenly, the whole place came alive. The door flew open as if pushed by a whirlwind and the lunatic face of an arch-priest flashed on the scene. In a high, cracked voice, he screamed: "Who's next? Who's next for me?"

'A thin, melancholy figure disengaged itself from the circle with a rustling of withdrawing woollens. He spoke no word, only tottered slowly to the open door, where the doctor, his face quivering, seized him by the shoulder, threw him down the passage, and ran after him like a greyhound. The rest of the "Surgery" were pleased by this and began a sort of expanding movement with their buttocks, so that within a few seconds it was impossible to detect the space vacated by the sacrifice. It would not surprise me to learn that when only one patient is left in "Surgery", he, as a result of the tremendous initial compression and subsequent expanding exercises, is able easily to cover all the chairs.

'But scarcely had the door closed when it flew open again and a second, different, medical form forced itself through in wild anxiety, its trembling fingers running through its hair like a grass-fire. "Any more for me?" he cried. "Next, next, for me, next, next, next, come along now, who's next, next?" The sound of gnashing teeth followed his words, and he began passionately to bite his nails.

'There was another tearing sound from a point in the circle and another overcoated figure propelled itself tramp-like over the linoleum. It waved a paper slip, on which the mad doctor bent a malignant eye.

' "If you'd sign this, Dr Burke," the patient muttered. "My cough was only good for last week."

' "No, no, not me!" screamed the doctor, shrinking back as from a leper or a whore. "Nurse will do it; get nurse, nurse. . . . Now, next for me; who's next?"

'The disappointed patient turned to resume his seat, only to find, of course, that nothing softer than a steel wedge could insert itself between his late companions. While he stood there, fretting, the nurse's face, crying faintly "Mrs Chirk? Mrs Chirk?" appeared over the doctor's trembling shoulder; and over *her* shoulder, in turn, loomed up the passionate face of yet another doctor, who shouted: "For me? For me? Next? Next?" And then, realizing that he was not visible to most of the patients, he lowered his voice to a distinctive boom, and shouted: "For Dr Towzer! Who's for Towzer?"

' "For Dr Burke – next, next!" screamed the doctor in front, nettled by his colleague's use of an individual name.

' "Mrs Chirk? Mrs Chirk?" trilled the nurse.'

'Dear me, what bedlam!' said the captain.

' "Pardon me, Dr Burke," murmured the nurse, manoeuvring one hand under his splayed arm and seeking to insert her fingers into the filing cabinet – only to find them closing on the slip of paper which the coughing patient had skilfully insinuated over the top of the cards. "If you'd just sign this, Miss . . ." he suggested.

' "Towzer, Towzer!" bellowed the rearmost physician, flattening himself against the passage wall as Dr Burke began desperately to push one of the patients before him out of the room. "While you're here, Dr Burke, you'd better take your coffee," said the nurse lightly, studying the slip of paper but reaching backwards into a dark recess of the passage with her free hand and vaguely resting a steaming cup on the bent shoulder-blade of Dr Burke's victim. "Mrs Chirk is not here?" she added, raising a pencil on a long string and signing the slip of paper.

'As you see, the field was now left pretty clear for Dr Towzer, who advanced to the very centre of the doorway, brushing spots of Dr Burke's coffee from his suit. The seated patients looked up at him in a friendly way, not resenting his tense and curious glare. The nurse came to his help by suddenly fixing a detective's eye on a woman with two children and asking sharply: "Aren't you for Dr Towzer?"

' "Didn't know it was my turn," said the woman, rising and pressing her children forward.

'All the patients were delighted by this plain, honest reply. But not Dr Towzer, who allowed a look of unbearable irritation to run down the dry furrows of his face. When the rattling and sniffling of his and his patients' progress down the passage had ended at last in a loud crack – whether a slammed door or a snapped bone, I cannot say – the nurse, spotting a group of late-comers hobbling up the surgery path, glanced at her watch and then crossed the room swiftly and pressed down the catch of the Yale lock. This sally was received with smug satisfaction of a most disgraceful kind by those who were safely inside: they reminded me of the favoured drunkards who are allowed to remain secretly on the premises when the landlord cries: "Time, gentlemen, please!"

' "*Now*," said the nurse, placing her hands firmly on her broad hips, "*Is Mrs Chirk not here?*"

'All the patients stared shyly at the ceiling. They were trying to avoid the nurse's accusing eye – for it was clear that even the men suspected that they might be Mrs Chirk. But they also hoped to avoid the appealing faces which the late-comers outside were now pressing, with mingled hope and hostility, against the window pane. After some moments of thus pressing, while feebly twisting the handle of the locked door and giving little knocks, the rejected ones staggered away, hobbling much more than they had before and allowing the gaunt necks of their empty medicine bottles to protrude indignantly from their pockets. As their steps died away, a tired but pleasant-looking woman got up and said: "My name's Mrs *Finch*, Nurse." '

'Capital! Capital!' cried the captain.

' "Well!" exclaimed the nurse: "You *are* a nice one, aren't you? Here I've been calling you all the morning! Come along now at once, and please don't hold the whole queue up like that again."

'I am sure the other patients relished this conclusion to the treasure-hunt: they stared excitedly as the unveiled witch was passed on to the priests wearing an expression of ashamed perplexity. The nurse followed, closing the temple door behind her, and the ante-room became wonderfully peaceful again. In fact, one daring young man lit up a cigarette and said: "Well, they're moving pretty fast this morning."

'What a silly thing to say when you are waiting for something! Everyone in the room, myself included, winced at the young man's provocation of the fates. And sure enough, next moment a thundering noise sounded down the passage, the temple door flew open, and Drs Burke and Towzer, each gripping a black bag and struggling into an overcoat, stormed through the door like Furies and shot out into the street. An instant later we heard the roarings of their new and powerful cars, followed by the painful clashes of clutchs and gear-levers fallen into the hands of madmen. A long sigh passed round the room: only two doctors now remained to assuage whole centuries' accumulation of medical neglect. Everyone relapsed into his other, older self; and even when Mrs Chirk, or Finch, passed through on her way home, she was ignored by her late fellows as a thing belonging to other days, a vision once captured but now escaped again. I felt so sad that I waited no longer, but passed out into the open world again like a visitor emerging from the tunnels of the Great Pyramid.'

'Darling, you have done simply wonderfully!' exclaimed Mrs Mallet. 'I could eat you up!'

'You most certainly deserve the lady's appetite, Beaufort,' agreed the captain. 'A perfect presentation. I make bold to say that when you are old enough to try your hand on a case-history, not another member of the Club will hold a candle to you. But now, to business! What possibilities seemed best to you?'

'Well, obviously the Chirk-Finch woman is ripe for re-identification. Naturally, I don't know her history, but it is clear that she has not grasped herself for many years. It was my good luck to stumble on her just at a moment when, so to speak, the National Health Service was pointing an accusing finger at her suspended identity. There is no question, however, that her original name was Mrs Finch. According to the Electoral Register, which I went on to consult at the Post Office, there is no Mr or Miss Finch in the district, so we may assume she is a widow. She will not demand any great effort from us, poor thing: all she asks for herself is a fixed entity. In fact, the choice is open to us: we can strengthen her waning faith in herself as Finch, or we can follow National Health and recreate her as Chirk. This choice is fortunate for us since Mrs Jellicoe – I mean Miss Paradise – I mean – oh! dear I am confused myself.'

'Gently, boy, gently!' said the captain. 'All is perfectly clear. You refer to our housekeeper, who is Mrs Henry Paradise to herself, Florence to me, and Florrie to your – ah! – stepmother.'

'Exactly. Perhaps Mrs Paradise has known this woman under her obsolescent name of Finch. If so, we can get some idea of whether she is a good domestic. If Mrs Paradise says she is, we will drop the matter for a few days and then tell Mrs P. that Mrs Finch has been unable to come. We will then bring Mrs Finch to the house as another applicant, named Mrs Chirk.'

'The other way round,' said the captain. 'We inform Mrs Paradise of an applicant named Chirk, who is new to these parts, and then we produce Mrs Finch, under the name of Chirk. Mrs P., who will have been feeling nervous at the thought of a strange domestic coming here, will be relieved to find that Mrs Chirk resembles closely a trustworthy female whose name she had forgotten but which she thinks was something like Finch. And yet, on the whole, I think there's no doubt that the important thing is to establish Finch *as* Finch – to give her the feeling that no matter what National Health may think, *she knows best who she is*. If we confirm her as Finch, she will soon feel that this is the one place in the world where she has no reason to doubt her existence. In this respect, of course, she is quite the opposite of Mrs Paradise, who has needed to be totally re-identified in order to make the most of herself. ... Well, what else have you brought from your fruitful "Surgery"?'

'I think it clear that *all* three doctors have already lost almost all sense of personal distinctiveness. Dr Burke's gestures and panting suggested a man bursting with emigration tendencies: only half his mind is chained to "Surgery"; the other half is already wearing pongee in Buenos Aires or helicoptering with a beard between Australian sheep-stations. I am not sure that we could allay this lust for a new beginning simply by bringing him here – unless, of course, we were able to convince him that he had spent his life in Australia and that this was the free, cultured world he had always dreamed of as the only way of realizing himself.'

'Rule him out,' said the captain. 'Restless types are too full of grudges. What about Towzer?'

'*Most* interesting. His is the insanity of the phlegmatic, Britain-can-take-it type. He has gone on taking it for so long that he no longer knows exactly what it is he is taking. With every pore wide open, he absorbs this unknown infliction, squeezing away his identity in order to give room to the stranger. By now, only his way of life remains true to his departed self: he continues to utter sounds that he vaguely associates with his proper status and character. At heart, of course, he has not the slightest idea of what that character and status are; nor does he dare pause to ask, for fear of finding them changed out of recognition. Provided a room full of despondent people between eight and ten a.m. daily, he would settle down anywhere.'

'We could introduce morning-prayers every day at eight-thirty,' said Mrs Mallet.

'An excellent idea,' said the captain. 'You will play the harmonium. Beaufort will always be late, and flushed, and, unseen by Mrs Finch, will wink at Florrie. Why, I am beginning to see a pattern already! Oh, joy, joy! But tell me, Beau, to what use shall we put Towzer? Something in the open-air, poor man, I presume?'

'I thought something in the garden. A hideously neglected bed of roses grows outside his house: I am sure he loved them before his face became so corrugated. He needs a beard, of course.'

'Very well. We'll try Towzer, though I must say I am a little shy of tampering with country doctors. They are accustomed either to being extravagantly praised or savagely denounced. They lack the poise and *laisser-aller* of the Harley Street man: I mean, they are sensitive to people and circumstances, and they expect to fight against odds and suffer. Well, if he is not the father of ten, which he may well be, bring him along, my boy. And now, what about the nurse – that vague lady who so ruthlessly plays fast-and-loose with human names? Nurses are a very distinct type, in my experience; the present does not exist for them at all; though absolutely practical in their daily behaviour, their minds are entirely concentrated upon the future – that is to say, upon the day when they marry a doctor. This is why they become so terrifyingly real when, instead of becoming doctors' wives, they become head-nurses: it is a frightful shock to the nervous system, comparable to a man setting out to walk to Cuba and after years of trudging finding himself in Siberia. Could this particular nurse not help Towzer in the garden? We could give her those old cord breeches of Jellicoe's to wear and, if she's a good girl, a small tractor. While Towzer chops and clips, she can spray and syringe: it will be just like hospital. And who knows – after rubbing shoulders with Towzer in the open air for a few months, she may cause his disbudded instinct to burst forth again? Yes, we must insist on Towzer's beard. Though lecherous, nurses are a *nesting* type – true cuckoos, one might say, in every respect, including monotony.'

'What about their names, sir?'

'Towzer may as well keep his, both as an adjunct to his beard and a foil to his inoffensiveness. So she, of course, will become Miss Tray – Miss Blanche Tray.'

'You don't think that old memories of class differences will keep them apart?'

'If there is one good thing to be said of the medical profession it is that their promiscuousness makes class-distinction impossible. Left to themselves, they would breed a classless world in one generation.'

'Then I shall try and bring both Tray and Towzer,' said Beaufort, rising enthusiastically.

'Don't overdo yourself, darling,' said Mrs Mallet.

'No fear of that . . . I say, who *is* that murky, lurking, furtive figure lounging about in the park? This is the second time I've seen him.'

'Ask him peremptorily what he wants,' said the captain.

Beaufort threw open the window, stepped on to the terrace and shouted in a bull-like voice: 'What are you doing here! Don't you know you're trespassing?'

A sheepish cry came back.

'Something about looking for his uncle,' said Beaufort.

'Tell him his uncle won't be back until the day after tomorrow,' said the captain. 'Suggest he come back then. After all, we may want him.'

Beaufort obeyed. 'I wonder if he's a Paradise relation,' he said, stepping in again and closing the window.

'Time will tell. Off you go, now.'

'I see you are feeling more relaxed,' said Mrs Mallet, when Beaufort had gone.

'Well, it *is* a strain isn't it, that first day or two – assailed by doubts, hating the responsibility? It was I who proposed having the Summer Session in the country; I who assured the Club that a place could be staffed and set in order. But I stand by what I said then: that this will be a broadening experience for all of us. Why, do you know that Orfe and Shubunkin have not once been outside London since childhood? Even the President admits that it is forty years since he saw a hedge. Oh, I am glad to be busy again! And glad to see you and young Beaufort so happy together. It makes me regret my own single state. I have not really been the same man, you know, since they deported poor Becky.'

'To the outsider, if you have changed at all, it is for the better. I mean that your best faculties are better than I have ever known them.'

'Thank you for saying so, dear. It's true, of course, that life with Becky was a terrible strain, and I will even confess that when I watched her being walked away by two policemen, though I could hardly see for tears, I did feel relieved. But what an old-fashioned man I am, at heart! No sooner do I get the peace I've always prayed for than I begin to feel ashamed of it. Celibacy makes one so neat and tidy and prim, a sort of hermaphrodite; all that saves me from hating myself is the thought that the work I am doing will be enjoyed by others – that I do it not for myself alone but for the Club.'

'Someone is knocking on the window,' said Mrs Mallet.

The captain went to the terrace door and threw it open. 'Who are you, may I ask?' he said.

'Paradise, my name, sir.'

'Indeed! Are you in search of something?'

'Thought you might have seen my uncle – and aunt.'

'And why, pray,' asked Mrs Mallet in a high, aristocratic voice, 'should my husband have seen your uncle – and your aunt?'

'You had better come in, anyway,' said the captain. 'And stop shuffling like that.'

'I always do that,' said Lolly, breaking into a broad smile and looking at the captain with admiring surprise, as if astonished that so personal a trait could be detected.

'Well, sit down and keep still,' said the captain. 'When did you last see your uncle?'

'Just the other day. I mean: it wasn't him I saw; but I saw Auntie and she told me.'

'Just what did Auntie tell you?' cried Mrs Mallet coldly. 'Surely not that as a result of seeing her you had seen him?'

'You misunderstand, dear,' said the captain. 'Mr Paradise means that as a consequence of seeing his aunt he was able to envisage his uncle.'

'That's right,' said Lolly.

'It is *Greek* to me,' said Mrs Mallet, taking up some sewing and looking coldly away. 'Unless uncle and aunt so closely resemble one another that even their nephew cannot distinguish between them.'

'Well, if they're not here, I'd better be off,' said Lolly, beginning to shuffle again.

'If you have no objection, dear,' said the captain timidly, 'I will try and help the young man by asking one or two questions.'

Mrs Mallet gave a high laugh, and started to sew.

'Do your uncle and aunt normally reside near these premises?' asked the captain.

'Down at the lodge,' said Lolly.

'*Our* lodge?'

'Why, yes, that's right,' said Lolly. 'But they're away, or something. Milk bottles left outside.'

'On which *we* have paid a heavy subsidy,' said Mrs Mallet.

'You know them, do you?' asked Lolly hopefully.

'They sound like the couple we evicted,' said the captain. 'I suppose, in their panic, they forgot to stop the milk.'

'Evicted?' repeated Lolly with faint surprise.

'Well, what else could we do with them?'

'I didn't . . .' Lolly began, and then stopped.

'*Finish* the sentence, *finish* it!' cried Mrs Mallet sharply.

'I just mean,' said Lolly nervously, 'I didn't know anyone had the right to do that.'

'Good heavens! What an extraordinary idea!' said the captain, laughing. 'Who would prevent us?'

Lolly looked vague and dismal. At last, he said: 'Then they've gone, eh?'

'Unless, in the shape of identical twins, they are haunting the park in spirit form,' said Mrs Mallet.

'Were you greatly attached to them?' asked the captain. 'Because if you were, I could probably find their new address. You see, my agent handles all such affairs – dismissals, evictions, claims, lawsuits. I never see the actual people, because they tell such distressing stories, and I don't want them on my conscience. I have to do it that way, otherwise nothing would ever get done. In fact, as far as I'm concerned, personally, your uncle and aunt just don't exist.'

'They always stayed quiet,' Lolly admitted.

'Well, anyway, I expect you have other relations to step into their shoes.'

'No, sir, they're my only ones.'

'Why not ask the police?' said Mrs Mallet in a nasty voice.

Lolly looked shocked and began to shuffle. 'I don't ask *them* things,' he explained.

'And, pray, why not?' cried Mrs Mallet. 'Is your character not above suspicion? Does some vein of petty crime run though your family? How are you employed, may I ask?'

'Well, I'd better be going,' replied Lolly, edging towards the terrace.

'Come again, in a few days, if you like,' said the captain, opening the terrace door. 'We might have news for you.'

'Oh, that's all right.'

'May I add?' cried Mrs Mallet, 'that if your uncle and aunt had wished you to know their new address they would have taken care to supply you with it?'

'That's right,' said Lolly agreeably, 'so I'll say good morning.'

'You are too gracious,' said Mrs Mallet, with another high laugh.

Lolly ambled down the drive. 'An odd fish,' said the captain. 'I must say he took me by surprise, or I would have kept him. But what could we use him for? I don't want to tackle anything too complicated at this stage. Well, we'll see, next time he comes.'

'You think he'll come again?'

'Don't you? He came this time out of curiosity and because a visit might be to his advantage. But at some moment in the next few days it is going to dawn on him suddenly that he really *has* lost something. A draught will play on his life. He will even get worried, feel unsettled. Like me, when Becky went.'

'Poor dear! You have Becky on your mind today.'

'Well, as I say, she left me in peace.'

There was a knock on the door and Jellicoe entered. 'There is a suspicious character in the park, sir,' he said.

'Do you suggest we loose the dogs, Jellicoe?' asked Mrs Mallet, giving Jellicoe a warm smile to show that she was not being unkindly sarcastic.

'We have already ordered him off, Jellicoe,' said the captain. 'But you were quite right to be alarmed.'

'Jellicoe looks tired,' said Mrs Mallet. 'I think you are working too hard, Jellicoe.'

'It's moving the furniture, madam. Some of it is very heavy. British Railways has just brought a fresh lot.'

'You mustn't try and rush it, Jellicoe. Do it slowly, piece by piece, and you will not feel the strain so much.'

'Yes, madam. I've prepared a bit of luncheon. Rather a scrap one, I must say.'

'Well, you will be glad to hear, Jellicoe,' said the captain, 'that Florence will shortly be with you again. So that will take the cooking off your hands. I hope there will soon be a maid-of-all-work too. And a gardener and an assistant. That will mean a staff of five. Then you will have no complaints.'

'I'm not complaining, sir, I hope I never complain.'

'No, I don't think you do. Still, we must watch your health. We don't want you to break down. Is the dining-room ready yet?'

'I'm afraid not, sir. It's getting the big carpet up the stairs that's holding me back. It's fifty feet long, sir. But I've managed the under-felt.'

'Well, that's the easy part, isn't it? Couldn't you rig up some sort of pulley?'

'Or a slide of some kind, Jellicoe?' suggested Mrs Mallet.

'I could try a slide, madam. But it's up, not down.'

'The *principle* remains the same, Jellicoe.'

*

Mrs Paradise slowly descended the back stairs, grasping on each step to intensify her feeling of self-sacrifice. She had just reached a corner and given vent to a loud 'A-a-ah!' when Beaufort sprang out on her with a loud 'Boo!' Seeing her scream and stagger, he caught her lightly round the waist, gave her a wet kiss, and said: 'Got you that time Florrie!'

'Don't you ever do that again!' she gasped.

'Why, Florrie, from the way you talk one would think I'd never done it to you before!'

'You're a man now, not a little boy.'

'But you still think I'm a little boy, don't you, Florrie? You still look at my ears and knees as if they needed washing, just as you always did. Where are you going now? Come and talk to me. Tell me stories about when I was a child. Or are you going to flirt with wicked old Jellicoe?'

'That's quite enough, Master Beau. I'm going to work, and it would much improve you to do the same.'

'D'you know there are secrets in Jellicoe's past, Florrie? I know all about them. Before he came here he used to seduce women under a fake name and embezzle their money. I'm still trying to find out his alias. But one of the women ran away with all his savings, so he decided to reform.'

'What a terrible way to talk! I would be ashamed to let such an accusation pass my lips.'

'Why are you always so *good*, Florrie?' he asked, escorting her down the stairs in gigantic jumps. 'Do naughty memories suddenly come into your head and make you say: "Surely that was never *me*?" I'm watching you, too, you know. I pick up all sorts of things. For instance, when Mrs Finch, or Miss Chirk, or whatever her name is, came yesterday to apply for housemaid, she said you used to look a treat long ago, walking the fields with ribbons in your hair, singing: "There's nae luck aboot the hoose wi' Jellicoe awa'." '

'I remember no such rubbish,' said Mrs Paradise, seizing the brilliant memory and tucking it away. 'Nor do I remember any Mrs Chinch.'

'*Chirk* or *Finch*, Florrie, I said.'

'Not them either.'

'Well, you'll have to interview one or both of them, whichever they are, this morning, because I'm going to fetch her in the car.'

'There's a car coming now, I hear.'

'That's the doctor's measured tread.'

'What doctor?'

'How do I know, Florrie? You know I never bother with names. He's coming to see Mama. Papa's agog.'

'What's the matter with your poor stepmother?'

'Only a mushroom growth at the base of the spine. We hope it's not malignant. If it's benign, Mama's going to have a little green collar made for it and take it with her everywhere.'

'Oh, dear, what rubbish you do talk! And to jest even about a step-mother's health! And to a widow! What's that roaring noise?'

'Only the doctor mounting the front stairs like the wind on the heath. I say, what a bonzer car he's got! Look, you can see through the loop-hole. I wish *we* had one like that. How we'd show off at the big June house-party! Oh, do you know we're getting a brand-new gardener? They've just come off the ration. The old one wore out. When we took him to pieces we felt it was a miracle he'd stayed together at all – his shins were down to the thinness of pencil leads and the whole pelvic basin was crumbled to bone-meal. It's pretty good, you know; we bought him at twenty-two and six a week in 1889. The new one has a beard, but no one has dared to lift it yet and see what Nature meant. He's bringing a Land Girl with him. His name's Towzer, hers is Tray. They're going to sleep together on mats in the west greenhouse. She's *so* pretty, Florrie, such lovely red cheeks and she does give herself airs.'

'She'd better not round me. Now you go away and fetch that other Chirk woman or I'll never get this house to rights.'

'All I really wanted to say, Florrie, was that it's heavenly to have you up again.'

'Well, you're a sweet boy underneath, and I've always known it, if no one else has.'

'Do you think I've got charm, Florrie?'

'You know quite well you have. But it's not charm that takes a man through life.'

'No, you have to have some money, too.'

'And it's not money either I mean. It's faith.'

'But isn't charm a kind of faith, Florrie?'

'Now, we're downstairs, so stop your prattling and go away. I must speak to Mr Jellicoe.'

Beaufort vanished, and Mrs Paradise entered the huge kitchen. The very sight of its incredible filth and disorder stopped her heart, but she marched bravely through to one of the back passages where she heard a rumbling noise and saw a huge Indian cabinet edging towards her. 'Mr Jellicoe!' she cried.

His head appeared over the back of the cabinet. 'Thank God you're back, Mrs Paradise,' he said. 'I'm at the end of my tether.'

'I didn't expect to find furniture being pushed through my kitchen,' she replied, looking distastefully at his dirty face. 'Nor did I expect to see my kitchen like a pigsty.'

'I've done my best, Mrs Paradise. No one has heard me complain.'

'I should hope not.'

'All this furniture down from the town-house. They want it for the house-party. I've moved every ton of it with these two hands. It's nearly broken my constitution.'

'Well, Mr Jellicoe, if I may say so, the past always revenges itself. We dissipate in youth what we should be glad to draw on in middle-age.'

He blushed. 'You have not come back in a very friendly mood, Mrs Paradise,' he said. 'Only the thought of the loss you have sustained keeps me from retorting with the rough side of my tongue.'

'I hope we are not going to resume relations with bitterness, quarrel-ling, and personal remarks,' replied Mrs Paradise. 'I am really still too ill to be about, and only poor Mrs Mallet's illness has brought me down at all.'

'Is her condition grave?'

'That is for the doctors to decide, Mr Jellicoe. It is for us to stick to our lasts.'

'I have had to couple my duties with yours, Mrs Paradise. It is not surprising if I have fallen between two stools. I trust some new staff will be arriving shortly. Two months alone is a long time.'

'Surely it has not been as long as that?'

'I believe it has. But I have not been in much state to judge. There have been moments when I have quite lost my head.'

'Talking won't find it again, Mr Jellicoe. At least you have got the stove going for me, I see. Now, will you kindly get that heavy thing of yours through my kitchen so I can start work?'

'Gladly,' he said, bending out of sight behind the cabinet, and push-ing. The little castors began to chatter over the stone floor and as Jellicoe passed by, doubled up like a bow, a light shone in his bloodshot eye. 'You could say any words you liked to me, Mrs Paradise,' he panted; 'and still just the sight of you would put me in heaven. I have dreamt of your return for nights on end, and from this moment I am a new man, starting a new life.'

'Thank you, Mr Jellicoe,' she answered coldly, and began slowly and grimly to roll up her sleeves.

*

'*This* passage, doctor,' said the captain. 'No, no, turn round, down here, another turn – that's better; now, pray, follow me.'

'Which *door*, which *door*?' cried Dr Towzer, racing down the long corridor. His bag was in his left hand, his right winked eager fingers at every passing knob. He was in a sweat; his eyes were ready to fly from their sockets like marbles from a cupped fist.

'Patience, my dear sir,' begged the captain: 'The room is not in this passage at all. I brought you this way because the carpet has not yet been laid on the shorter route.'

Dr Towzer gave a loud neigh. 'Do you think I notice dust or carpets, sir, in this day and age?' he cried. 'I have twelve more patients to see before midday. The whole nation, sir, is on its last legs. Or rather, on its doctors'!' He gave a shriek of laughter.

'Left here and up these little stairs,' said the captain.

'Are we nearly there?'

'We are getting warm.'

'Surely this is where we began?'

'Quite another place. Doctor, if I may say so, you need a holiday.'

'Where is the door?' begged the doctor, giving a dreadful groan.

'My dear sir, we are in sight of it. It is the last on the left.'

The doctor broke into a canter, storming down the corridor like a mad race-horse. 'You would not first like a glass of Madeira and a slice of dry cake?' cried the captain, keeping to a trot.

'No, no, no! Here?'

'Permit me,' said the captain. Tapping softly on the door he opened it a crack and murmured: 'Milly, Milly. I have a little surprise. You'll never guess. Don't be cross. I felt I really ought to.'

A faint scream came from inside. 'A doctor! Let me put on my shawl!'

'We will give her just a *moment*,' said the captain, giving Dr Towzer a man-to-man look. 'Tell us when you are ready, darling.'

'Sir, you seem to come from another planet!' panted the doctor, stamping his feet. 'These winsome approaches are not made nowadays. Little delicacies are become monstrous obstacles. The *looks* of patients are not so much as noticed. Why, sir, I shall come away from here scarcely knowing to what sex your wife belongs.'

'In this little backwater . . . ' began the captain apologetically. But he was interrupted by a musical cry from within: 'You may come in now!'

Mrs Mallet's bed was large and lavish. A pink eiderdown two feet thick foamed over it with herself rising from one end.

'Dr Towzer, dearest,' said the captain. 'Like yourself, a lover of roses.'

'So, doctor?' she piped, giving him a fragrant smile.

'I used to be. Good morning.' He made for the bed like a horse at a manger.

'*Used* to be, doctor? But how can that be? I think you never loved them if you no longer do.'

'No *time* now, madam, I mean,' he barked. 'What is the trouble?'

'But you must *make* time, naughty man,' she said, wagging a cross finger. 'Or your life will become quite empty.'

He gave a prolonged, hysterical cackle, ending by chewing savagely at his lips. Dropping his bag with a clash of instruments he held out his hands so that his ten fingers quivered like antennae. In a panting voice, he said: 'Chair-chair-chair?'

'Why bless my soul,' said the captain, smiling ruefully. 'Where are my wits? Of course you must have a chair. Which sort shall it be? stiff, low, high, easy?'

'Any chair; just chair-chair.'

'From here one hears the trains,' said Mrs Mallet. 'But few of them stop.'

Dr Towzer gave another neigh and suddenly exclaimed: 'Life quite empty – he-he-he!'

'Here is a promising chair, Towzer,' said the captain, re-entering from the passage. 'Or is it, in your estimation, too hard?'

'No. It will do,' said the doctor, his voice suddenly slow and faint. 'All chairs are now as one to me.'

'When you have examined me, Doctor Brewster,' said Mrs Mallet, 'you must tell me what varieties you particularly loved, and we will compare notes.'

'Then you think this one will be all right?' said the captain, pushing the chair slowly across the room.

'I think it will be excellent,' answered the doctor, his voice becoming absolutely level.

'I hope soon to be among my beloved standards again,' said Mrs Mallet. 'They become obstreperous without me.'

'What she really needs is a good nurse,' said the captain.

'For God's sake, madam!' cried the doctor, abruptly recovering both his high tone and his hysteria: 'tell me what is the matter with you.'

'On that point, doctor,' said the captain, 'I think I should have a word with you in private. We could withdraw to the dressing-room.'

'Ignore him, doctor,' said Mrs Mallet. 'He always looks on the dark side, and would only pour poison into your ear. To me, even sickness can be a part of happiness if we know how to make it so.'

'Now, do seat yourself, Dr Benson,' said the captain, pressing the chair seat against the back of the doctor's knees. 'I see you are under stress.'

'If the lady will kindly begin . . .'

'From the very beginning, doctor?' she asked. 'Or merely the present symptoms?'

'What you call the present symptoms will do, madam,' he answered, suddenly hanging his head again. He went on, in the dull tones of an old man recalling some text learnt in youth: 'Though it is not for us to cure symptoms. We merely appraise them. It is their origin we pursue.'

'By Jove, that's well put!' said the captain. 'It shows medicine in quite another light.'

'Begin, madam,' said the doctor, raising a pair of dog-like eyes to hers.

She responded by fixing on him the intense, horrified gaze of a revelationist. Her breast rose and fell rapidly. The words began to tumble from her mouth:

'A sort of trembling, doctor, every morning when I wake up – as though I was somehow anticipating the *worst*. At first, snug in my warm bed, I am puzzled – why, I ask myself dreamily, should I feel afraid? Suddenly it dawns on me – oh, heavens! this is morning and I am *me*! I am *myself*, and nothing I can do will mitigate the horror of this fact. This realization – which is too agonizing to describe – is followed by a "Hah-hah-hah-hah" sort of panting, like that of a sheep caught by its horns in a thicket.'

'Omit sheep and thickets, madam, for God's sake!' cried the doctor, turning white. 'We are not a Bible class.'

' . . . Then everything abruptly becomes denser and more tangled; my every limb gets wrapped in strands of millions of encircling tendrils – horrid, tough tendrils that quickly rise and pinion my head. And at this moment, as if at a signal, everything in the room begins to revolve, at first quite slowly, so that I am able to tell myself that if I can stop it now I will escape the *worst*. For a second, indeed, I do succeed in rendering the scene static once more – at which, as if enraged by my interference, it instantly starts to whirl again, and this time at lunatic speed – crockery, furniture, walls, doors, husband, night-light – all whizzing round like checkered lightning – and even this I could bear were it not that gradually I feel myself *pulled into* the circular tow. I scream, scream, but I am caught in the heart of it, suffocated, dumb, the pillow now-over-now-under what once was my head. I have no *option*, doctor, no *option* at all, nor any sense of direction other than circular; all I feel by then is the horror of realizing that the bed, too, my very foundation and root, has been dragged up from under me and that, even while spinning madly, we are also rising higher every second to meet the wheeling, intangible ceiling. Now I am turned on my side, my toes chilled to frangible ice, my gorge rising, my hair streaming out behind me so far that it is caught in my pursuing open mouth – a decisive moment, because at once my taut head begins to strain at its trunk and, failing to break away there, splits brusquely in half with a ripping noise, and the two halves, cloven, chase each other at a distance like mad half-moons, I trying my utmost to recapture and reassemble them. But how can one grasp anything when one has no foothold? "Is this hysteria?" I ask myself – and though my voice is inaudible it is nonetheless the only solid object within reach, so I attempt to clutch it, but cannot place its whereabouts. I strive to *imagine* its sound, so that I may track it down and thus find some clue to myself, but all I hear is the note of a trip-hammer ringing on my ear-drums as on an anvil – thus, what with speed reducing everything to a blur, and sound and vision endeavouring to split this blur into a thousand slivers, I am simultaneously beaten and smothered into the likeness of a jelly and yet fired through the centre of myself like hard machine-gun bullets. I am far beyond screaming by now; and yet questions, hard as rocks and written in black, appear like print across the centre of my cloven mind: *Who am I? Who are you?* At which there is a chuckling, dancing mixture of sound and movement inside me, and a burst of words such as: Only rend, tear, compress, slaughter, dismember, and yet hammer eternally compact!'

At this point Dr Towzer, whose eyes had been glistening for some time, gave a loud shriek and fell with a crash against the back of the chair.

'My dear, *what* a diagnosis!' exclaimed the captain admiringly, hurrying forward and laying his fingers on the doctor's pulse. 'A veritable *bonfire*; I felt quite trembly myself.' He laid his lips close to the doctor's nearest ear and said in a strong, curt voice: 'Now, Towzer, we have had quite enough of your stoic tantrums! You have driven us too far. We are exasperated. It is time for you to reform. A fundamental change, please! Henceforth, sir, you will kindly regurgitate those senses, those fires, that you have so disgracefully swallowed down and banked. From now on, you will remember that it is *roses, roses, all the way*. Those two poignant names, Towzer and rose, are no longer poles apart. They are linked into one – man conjoined once more with vegetable nature. Do you understand me, sir? In place of your repugnant stoutness, breeding such evil nonentity throughout the globe, you will set the most delicate responses to the queen of flowers. Assume and love her soft petals, Towzer; brush gently across her tender sides the soft fringe of your abundant beard; touch her soft lips, and never part. Oh, Towzer, reborn Towzer, take up a new spade in behalf of the rose – that apostle of peace, that loving fire in which steeled hearts first look soft as wax and then firm afresh in the substance of naked gold! All your road now, Towzer, till life's very end, is beds of roses – roses dewy, roses dungy, roses sprayed with draughts of health-giving soap and nicotine:

> 'Polyantha, hybrid tea,
> Pernetiana, pray for me!
> Ah, perpetual delight!
> Ah, the open, sunny site!
> Roses, roses all the day,
> Seed of Towzer and his Tray.
> Nevermore will Towzer walk
> Where the earnest microbes stalk;
> Aphid, black-spot, now his cure,
> Scurf of mildew his allure.
> Slide at last the sick-bed back,
> Blanket down the baggèd quack.

In the gizzard of the rose
Hairy Towzer finds repose.'

'And where do we put him while his beard's growing?' asked Mrs Mallet, stepping from the bed and smoothing down her wrinkled tweed.

'In the Paradise cottage, my dear.'

'I hope you can make him walk. Poor darling, we came just in time. Another month and he'd have been *carried* out.'

'I am sure he will walk anywhere, provided it's not in the direction of the surgery . . . Towzer, my man, do you feel at peace?'

'I feel that with time and proper attention he may be on his way to it,' replied the doctor.

'Well, we have made sure that he will get all that. We are returning him to private practice. His intruder has gone for ever. He was not us. He was only a scoundrel who pretended to be.'

'Thank God for that!'

'Yes. He leaves us to our roses. Let us move towards those roses. Let us stand up, take three steps back and turn to the right.'

'To the right,' groaned the doctor, sluggishly obeying.

Beaufort came in at that moment and said: 'I say, you *have* been quick. He looks another man already. It's a good thing, because I've got Tray and Finch downstairs.'

'Then fetch my curved briar, the psychiatric one, and velvet smoking-jacket, like a good boy,' said the captain, pushing Dr Towzer slowly to the door. 'I'll take Tray first, while I'm still fresh. And for *this* man, a shiny-bottomed pair of dark blue trousers – *not* corduroys, remember – some boots, a clean jacket, a shining watch-chain and a hat, with waistcoat and stiffish collar to match – and don't get too clever by stuffing the pockets with tarred string, Old Moore, and foul handkerchiefs – true gardeners respect Nature far too much to be slovenly in her presence. You'll find all you want in the big chest . . . Now, Towzer, march! Onward to rosy peace!'

'To posy wreath!' cried the doctor.

'To union with the sluggish infinite!'

'T'union!'

'Tray is none too easy' said Beaufort, as the procession moved slowly down the long corridor. 'She was relieved, though, when she saw Towzer's car, and remarked with a giggle: "Now I know Dr Towzer really asked for me and I've not been abducted!" '

'Vulgar little tart!' said the captain. 'I suppose you drove like mad, as usual.'

'Well, yes, I did rather. Finch was in the back seat, you see, and I felt she would benefit from a terrific shaking. Tray said just the right thing to her: "Oh, you're the person who doesn't know who she is, aren't you?" I then left Finch with Florrie, who also opened-up on exactly the right note: "Well, Miss Chinch, or whatever you are, I've been waiting to hear your name, or whatever it is, all the morning." "It's Finch," said Tray, "It's Chirk," I said. We sounded like a trio of canaries.'

'Well, hurry up and fetch those things for me,' said the captain, impatiently fitting the doctor's legs to the first steps of the back stairs.

'Give him to me, dear,' said Mrs Mallet.

'Never swap horses while crossing a stream.'

'But you are getting testy.'

'I think I know my business, don't I?' cried the captain.

'He was *my* business until a moment ago, unless I dreamt it all,' said Mrs Mallet sharply.

'My apologies,' said the captain suddenly, propping the doctor against the wall and giving Mrs Mallet a ceremonious bow. 'My head is so full of ideas, there's no room for sense. Take him by all means. And Beaufort, after you have brought me those clothes, do just glance over the ones Jellicoe arrived in and see if they wouldn't be just the thing for Tray.'

*

She was fidgeting in the breakfast-room when the captain swept in breezily, dressed in a frogged jacket and swinging a curved pipe between his teeth like a vane. 'And what can I do for you, Miss Tray?' he asked briskly.

'Pardon?'

'I said, what brings you here, my dear young lady – on what errand, to what end, to which entity? Though it is perfectly splendid to see you.'

'I thought you said Tray.'

61

'*Miss* Tray, my dear, *Miss* Tray.'

'But then I am not the one you want?'

'Who is to say that? To be unwanted is no fate to impose upon a charming visitor.'

'Oh, never mind who I am, then. Where's the doctor, please?'

'Doctor?'

'The *doctor* – who wanted me.'

'What doctor wanted you, my dear?' asked the captain gently, reflectively pulling the pipe from his mouth and squinting at the nurse over the looping stem. 'Is something the matter with someone?' he inquired, moving a little closer to her.

'Dr Towzer!' she exclaimed. 'He summoned me. There's his car outside.'

'We do have a Towzer here,' he answered, puzzled; 'but he never hinted that he was a doctor.'

'Then why on earth did he come?'

'For roses, of course. He has done so for years. Are you sure we are talking of the same Towzer?'

'No, I am not. Though I do know the doctor likes roses. I have sometimes cut him some.'

Suddenly the captain waved his pipe in the air. 'Dear me, I am very dense this morning!' he exclaimed. 'I have only just realized who you are and why you are here. Tell me, now, if I may start with a personal question: are you often in the mood of feeling wanted by doctors? You don't have to answer, of course; I ask only as a psychiatrist.'

'I think there must be some mistake,' she answered, turning pale when she heard his last, forbidding word. 'I am the nurse from the surgery.'

'Why, of course! Had you thought yourself to be some other?'

'Certainly not. Why should I?'

'Oh, never mind. Let's answer that another time.' The captain replaced his pipe, swung it through a few arcs and then asked: 'Who brought you here, may I ask?'

'A young man in a sports car.'

This was too much for the captain, and he quite failed to hide a knowing smile. 'A young man in a sports car, was it?' he asked gently. 'Did he drive you very fast?'

'We came up the drive at seventy-five.'

'Dear me! What a speed for a respectable young lady to travel at! I assume you were alone in the car with this young man?'

'No. A Mrs Chirk was in the back seat.'

'In the *back* seat?' repeated the captain curiously. 'Now, I wonder what she was doing there. At least, she did not interpose herself between you and the young dare-devil at the wheel?'

'Why should she? She was frightened to death.'

'And you?'

'I like going fast.'

'Ah-hah! Well, we can't deny that you boldly took your seat beside dashing youth and left timid age in the dickey.'

'He opened the front door and I got in. What could be more natural?'

'Why nothing, my dear. It is a perfectly intelligible reversal of roles. By the way, have you met this Mrs Chirk before?'

'I've seen her at surgery.'

'Oh yes. Surgery is where doctors collect, is it not? We don't have it in psychiatry, you see. I suppose you often have quite long chats with the doctors at this so-called surgery?'

'I'm much too busy to talk, I assure you.'

'Indeed. And while you and the doctors are *busying* yourselves, may I ask what Mrs Chirk does?'

'She keeps her seat, of course. Until I call her.'

'Ah-hah. A back-seat?'

'Any seat she can get. Like all the others, she moves gradually to the front.'

'Dear me, how trying! Tell me, is she *always* Mrs Chirk?'

'Sometimes she answers to Finch,' confessed the nurse, blushing.

'And you resist that, do you? You balk at Finch?'

'Well, records are records, aren't they? What's Chirk can't be Finch.'

'That's a point, of course. Excuse me, but may I ask what was your mother's name?'

'The same as mine, doctor.'

'Why, yes, no doubt. But it meant something different, did it not? I mean, when you think of your mother's name you don't automatically feel: "That's me too".'

'Certainly not.'

'In other words, despite the surface likeness, your name is not the same as your mother's?'

'I suppose it isn't, yet I had never seen the question that way.'

'Well, it's not too late. Tell me, did this name of your mother's in any way resemble Finch? Was it Lynch or Tench for instance?'

'Not at all. She was a Mrs Hamilton.'

'And her maiden name?'

'Theobald.'

'In short, a complete disguise.'

'I don't quite understand.'

'It's quite simple, really. Say, for instance – just say – you identified your mother with Mrs Finch. Naturally, you would not wish to do so too openly, would you? We none of us like guilt-feelings, do we? So we put mama at three removes, so to speak; we start her as Theobald, transform her into Hamilton, mask her as Chirk, and finally make everything absolutely safe by thinking of her as interchangeable only with Finch. In my profession, we describe that as "fantasy of the nominal exit". On the other hand, of course, if your mother's name had been Lynch, Tench, or even Hawk or Sparrow, the identification with Finch would have been equally clear. That is what is so satisfying about the psychological method; we get you disguised, we get you plain. Your mother is dead, I presume? Was her departure a happy release?'

'In a way, yes. But I loved her very much.'

'Don't we all, my dear? Nevertheless, we like them to keep in the back seat, do we not?'

The nurse gave a wan smile.

'I see you are an intelligent girl, Miss Tray, and know how to put two and two together. I hope we all do nowadays, because life seems to have lost all its threes. Well, we have gone a long way in this short chat – or rather, *you* have gone a long way: I have merely followed where you led. That is what I like about your case – the fact that you were moving so rapidly in the right direction long before you met me. It was you, not me, who relegated Mrs Grundy to the boot, thus taking the first, decisive step to independence, creativeness, fulfilment of suppressed desires and other things we consider desirable today. And yet, I believe I can help you a few stages further. After all, we don't want this interfering old lady in our lives, do we? If we are

chummy with a doctor or out for a spin with a gay blade, we *would*
prefer, I think, not to have her even in the dickey. Let me make a
suggestion, Miss Tray. This is a friendly, quiet house. Mrs Finch works
here. If you stayed here, too, you would see her every day. This might
suggest that you would be getting the opposite of what you want –
to expel her from your life forever. But the contrary is true: it always
is in the higher reaches. Escapist tactics would be impossible. It might
be painful at first, but one day we would wake up and discover that
she has ceased to matter.'

'But what about my job, doctor?'

'Dr Burke assures me that the last thing the surgery wants is to lose
your services. Let me read what he says,' and the captain took a paper
from his pocket. ' "Our one aim in sending her to *you*," he writes,
"is to make her full talents available to us." That's quite clear, isn't it?
He goes on: "Her stream of unconsciousness is swift and fed by many
a promising tributary: it is only the guilty boulders and insanitary
blockages of decayed repression-tissue that prevent it coursing in full
flood toward . . . etc. etc." He seems to think that you are also anxious
and worried.'

'Well, think of the state of the world, doctor.'

'Of course, Miss Tray. But we know, don't we, that many an atom
bomb is merely a Mrs Finch? Think of her as a piece of film, wedged
deep in the unconscious. We cannot eject her, so we place behind her
the powerful light of guilty evasiveness, which projects her upon the
screen of the outer world, distorted into the likeness of a bomb. Thus
we rid ourselves of an internal mother, by transforming her into an
external explosive.'

'Then the atom bomb does not exist?'

'Some of my colleagues say that it doesn't: they lump it in with all
the other internal problems, like road-accidents, industrial injuries,
cancer, death, and so on. Personally, I'm a middle-of-the-road sort of
man: I believe that machinery, and motor-cars in particular, are
intrinsically dangerous. I even claim that they have the power of
moving quite often in a direction opposite to the one demanded by
their victim's neurosis. But be good enough not to repeat my remark
in the presence of any of my colleagues: any rehabilitation of the
external world injures them far more than could the heaviest motor-
lorry.'

'I have much to learn, doctor.'

'Not nearly as much as you suppose. It depends on your attitude to what I tell you. What often makes things arduous in my profession is the patient's insistence on arguing about everything. It is astonishing how few people realize that there is no longer room for argument, and even blame the poor analyst for prolonging the agony. Everything will happen at breathtaking speed if you once get clear in your mind that the theory by which I work is unalterably complete. It was made watertight many years before *you* came along, and there is simply no argument you can raise which has not been anticipated and answered. Try and imagine this theory as a big hall, in which you find yourself. Unwilling to remain, you walk to the nearest exit, only to find a huge sentry barring your way with a friendly smile. Well, our theory has such a sentry posted at every possible exit, including the skylight and the main drain. The sentries are infallible; they never sleep, they know no error. They were awaiting you many years before you entered the hall, they already know by heart every word of the pleadings and tearful briberies that you will use against them. They are the perfect servants of a perfected theory – by which I mean, a theory which no conflict with experience can ever alter or revise.'

'I'd love to know which one is your theory, doctor.'

'I don't think it would help you, to know. There are so many nowadays, and all divided and subdivided into groups, splinter-groups, and even chips off the old splinter-groups. As they are one and all infallible, despite being utterly different, there's little point in describing the differences. What does it matter to you, after all, whether you are diagnosed on a principle of ancestry, heredity, environment, instinct, the lavatory, or genetics? Nothing you can say is going to make the slightest difference to the outcome.'

'Will I have to give up my surgery?'

'Dr Burke thinks so. So do I. We want to extract your surgery-image, like a decayed tooth, sluice Mrs Finch out of it, and then give it a few new screws and a lick of fresh paint before we put it back.'

'How will I occupy myself?'

'I suggest you help Towzer in the garden. We can give you the proper corduroys. Towzer is a shy, charming, bearded man, and you could share the gardener's cottage with him.'

'Would that be proper, doctor?'

'At this stage of treatment it might be invaluable. Incidentally, he has temporarily lost his beard as a result of illness, and you may think he resembles someone you once knew. If you do, don't be alarmed; it is a common illusion in the Finch stage of neurosis. After all, we only see what we think, don't we? Gradually, as we change your apparatus of thought, you will find yourself with a brand-new set of images.'

'It sounds quite exciting, doctor. Shall I tell the other Towzer, the Dr Towzer, while he's here? Oh, I see his car's gone. It *was* here, wasn't it? *Didn't* I see it?'

The captain gave a broad, very human smile. 'What a little sight-seer it is!' he exclaimed, wagging his forefinger. 'Not content with mother and surgery images, it must have car and doctor images to boot – and all in a single morning.'

'Oh, doctor, somehow I want to cry!'

'That's just joy, my dear: you see the broad new path ahead. We'll chat about it together nearly every day. It won't be a lengthy business. I am not a believer in the analysis that goes on for ever. It makes the psychiatrist so dependent upon the incoming image of his patient that when, after ten or twenty years, the patient fails to show up, the analyst feels like the victim of an optical levy. No, Miss Tray; by all means let me be your father, but not your grandfather.'

'You are so kind,' she said, sighing; 'and if you keep calling me Miss Tray, I suppose you must have good grounds.'

'They will emerge as we proceed, my dear . . . Ah, splendid! Here comes my intern with your corduroys.'

*

'The place is beginning to feel like a home already,' said Mrs Mallet at dinner a few days later. 'Bitterness, rivalry, and questions of dignity are apparent everywhere. Florence is being sweet to old Mrs Finch, to stop her becoming an ally of Jellicoe. She has taken also a wine jelly to Towzer, much to Tray's annoyance. Beau, dear, you are eating like a pig; what has come over you?'

'I've had such a frightfully busy day. Being boyish with so many people is a dreadful strain.'

'We must give them all some money,' said the captain. 'There's nothing like it for giving people a *settled* feeling.'

'The garage is offering £750 for Towzer's car,' said Beaufort.

'That's two hundred below the market price; but that's because it will need licence plates.'

'They were quite amiable about it, were they?' asked the captain, unbuttoning the top of his trousers and sitting back.

'Lord, yes! They said if I stumbled on another, do bring it. They're sending a man up with new plates tonight. He'll bring the money in pound notes and take the car away.'

'Those awful heaps of notes from garages,' said Mrs Mallet, shuddering; 'tattered, oily, so *depreciated*. And on the watermark of each one, made with a ball-point pen, the cyphers and hieroglyphs of a hundred unscrupulous strangers. As lamp-posts to a host of dogs. I hate to tender them at a decent shop.'

'And I hate to think of throwing away a good car like that,' said the captain. 'I am sure the Club would like it. Beaufort, just in case, I shall go and put on my big-business suit. If the garage emissary looks at all promising, bring him up. Take the money first, of course.'

'Very well. And may I be rather more grown-up, just for a change? I don't want to grumble, yet I do find it wéaring to have to spring about so much and show my teeth in those incessant grins. I am almost running out of old-fashioned slang, too. Luckily, I recently remembered "bonzer".'

'Oh, yes; dear "bonzer"!' said Mrs Mallet. 'How long ago it seems! I shall not admit to remembering it.'

'By the way,' said the captain, reaching into his pocket, 'would either of you like to see the rough Session schedule? It came this morning.'

Beaufort and Mrs Mallet gave cries of excitement and snatched at the paper.

'I thought I'd keep it under my hat,' said the captain apologetically, 'knowing what a busy day we were going to have.'

'Dr *Gluber* to open?' cried Mrs Mallet, scanning the paper. 'Why such a Russo-German start?'

'I imagine to get pure theory out of the way as soon as possible,' said the captain. 'It's better to depress people at the beginning than at the end.'

'And Arthur Murray Stanstead second! *Identity in the Middle West.*'

'That's wise, too. First theory, then statistics. Only then, chaos.'

'But where's the Old Guard?' cried Beaufort, peering over Mrs Mallet's shoulder.

'Look, darling,' she said, 'here they all are – Orfe, Shubunkin, Musk – dear me, how exciting!'

'I'll leave you to gloat,' said the captain, rising: 'I must do our first report to the President.'

As the captain went out, Beaufort began to pace the floor so restlessly that Mrs Mallet said: 'What on earth are you so desperate about?'

'I'm sick and tired of being *young*.'

She burst out laughing and put her arms round his neck.

'I mean it,' he said angrily. 'You two are like people in another world. You do your work professionally. You stay so calm. There is such polish in the cases you handle. I feel clumsy and ridiculous.'

'What silly ingratitude! Everyone showers love and compliments on you. Everyone is astonished by the grasp you have of your work – and what's more they *tell* you how astonished they are. You are terribly spoiled, you know.'

'I'm loved because I'm not grown up.'

'You're loved because you're so disgracefully talented.'

'Then when am I to be trusted with something more adult?'

'Be thankful for what you've got. Do you think *he* doesn't wish he could still be Prince Charming? Do you think *I* don't wish I could be the one who gives and gets all the love and tenderness, instead of just the respect and politeness?'

'Well, whatever you say, I'm going to be different with the garage man tonight. I shall be aloof and mature.'

'You'll be, I know, what the situation demands – what the Club, and I, expect of you.'

'Only if you promise to be passionately loving afterwards. I want a simply enormous reward.'

'But I might not feel in a very rewarding mood.'

'I shall make love to you with immense dignity and sternness. When you look up, you will see the worn visage of an elderly bureaucrat, wearing an expensive black hat.'

'You will be the loser. You will find nothing in your arms but a Permanent Undersecretary.'

*

Out of the dark park came a sibilant whistling. Footsteps shuffled over the cobbles of the yard.

'So it's you, is it,' said Beaufort. 'Fancy that! Found your uncle and aunt yet?'

'Oh, no,' said Lolly, giving a weary smile as if to suggest that he had long since reached the limits of search. 'Nice car,' he said, peering at the sports model. 'Nice car,' he said, turning to Dr Towzer's. 'Which one?'

'The M.D.'

Lolly sighed, and untied some half-rotted string at the foot of his trouser-legs. Out of each leg slid a licence-plate. 'And Mr Brown said this was for you,' he said, handing Beaufort a small sack designated as self-raising flour.

'Thank you. Do thank him.'

Lolly studied the doctor's car for some moments and then said: 'The old plates are still on.'

'That's right. You have to take them off before you put the new ones on.'

'If you had some wire, I could just tie the new ones over the top of the old ones.'

'Certainly not.'

'Oh, all right. Got a hammer and chisel?'

'Here's a spanner. You undo the nuts.'

'Takes longer.'

'Works better.'

Beaufort left the garage and paced the courtyard for a few minutes. When he returned, Lolly was inspecting his work on the rear plate.

'If I were a policeman,' said Beaufort, 'I should feel a dry suspicion that someone had tampered with that car.'

'Think so?'

'And now how do you attach the new one?' asked Beaufort, studying Lolly with deep professional interest.

'Nothing like wire,' said Lolly. He bound on the new plate at a raffish angle. 'See? Now I'll do the same in front.' He moved off slowly.

When he had finished, Beaufort said: 'You know, you remind me of a chap I used to know named Stapleton. He had one of these huge red moustaches.'

'R.A.F.?'

'That's right. If you had one, you'd be the image of him. Like you, he loved machinery. Do come in and meet my father. He owns a huge car firm. He'd give you an important position.'

'Why?'

'Because he loves people who have a natural bent.'

'Well, all right.'

'If he calls you Stapleton, be sure to play up, won't you?'

'Why?'

'Well, he never forgets a face, or thinks he doesn't, so it's wiser not to contradict him. He has hundreds of total strangers working for him under faces he thinks he remembers them by. I have often known him to turn an old friend down for a job on the grounds that he is already employing him. I'll go ahead and make sure he's free.'

He soon came back and led Lolly to the breakfast-room. The captain was invisible behind the *Economist*, above which he rose slowly like a model of big industry from the sea of popular imagination: his brows sourly knit, his eyes well-trained to fire bullets at balloons of pure theory. A downward bend at the corners of his lips suggested a man who wrests Nature's secrets from her depths and, at small profit to himself, hurls them broadcast to the world's needy. A thoroughly aggrieved expression covered his whole face, as if his life had been an endless struggle against slander and taxation. A cigar-lighter shaped like a Canberra bomber stood at his elbow.

'Stapleton!' he barked at once, snapping his fingers. 'I never forget a face. Whiskers or no whiskers.'

'He's known as Lolly Paradise in these parts, father,' said Beaufort. 'Nephew of the old couple who were at the lodge in the old days.'

'Huh. They're both in the north now, my lad.'

'Oh, did you find places for them, dear?' asked Mrs Mallet, from a game of patience. 'A seedy trespasser, you remember, was asking about them the other day.'

'Me,' said Lolly with a rather proud smile.

'Nonsense, Stapleton!' said the captain. 'How could it have been you? As to your uncle and aunt, they were fine people, but in a rut.'

'That's right,' said Lolly appreciatively.

'You don't get a union-card by wearing riding-breeches and listening to cuckoo clocks,' continued the captain.

Lolly was greatly amused by this remark: he had been used to thinking of himself, rather than his relatives, as the one whose life was lacking in purpose. The captain thrust a cigar at him, played on its tip a ferocious burst of flame from the bomber, and said: 'Sit down, Stapleton. You are ready to go to London immediately, I understand?'

'How?' said Lolly, with a faint start.

'In that car, of course.'

'I'm supposed to take it to Mr Brown.'

'What on earth difference does *that* make?'

'Well, he'll think I've pinched it, won't he?'

The three Mallets burst into roars of laughter, continuing for so long that Lolly looked bewildered.

'Stop, now!' said the captain sharply, suddenly turning grave. 'The lad means it. He sees a hitch. He's not a fool. Now, Stapleton, just tell me what you're driving at. Be frank and open. I like a man who thinks.'

Lolly turned red. He was not embarrassed, but he found it a strain to marshal his thoughts. After some struggle, he said: 'Doesn't the car belong to Mr Brown? Didn't he just buy it?'

'What if he did?' asked the captain with astonishment.

Lolly scratched his head. His mind was being driven into reaches that it scarcely knew: he was terribly at sea.

'Do you really think, my boy,' said the captain earnestly, 'that if you don't return with that car, Brown will think you've stolen it?'

'I think he might,' said Lolly. 'He's a cute bloke.'

'Oh, Father,' said Beaufort, in a drawling voice; 'let's drop the whole business. He's probably afraid of the police, or can't drive, or something.'

'I'm sure you are wrong, Beaufort,' said Mrs Mallet, looking at Lolly with the affection of a mother for an oddity. 'It seems that Mr Stapleton is trying to be *fair* and *honest*.'

'That's right,' said Lolly gratefully. 'Fair and honest.' He repeated these words with some awe.

The captain dropped into his chair. 'I am baffled,' he said.

'Me too,' said Beaufort.

They both stared at Lolly.

'It's like this, I think,' said Mrs Mallet gently. 'Mr Stapleton is trying to say – but he's not very good at words – that since Mr Brown is paying him to fetch this car *and* has given him the money for it, it would not seem *right* for Mr Stapleton to hand it over to someone *else*.'

'I only get more confused,' said the captain, waggling his fingers crossly. 'I don't know what all these words *mean*. What would "not seem right" for instance? There's nothing *wrong* with the car, is there? If there is, we must put it right. Or is the money counterfeit?'

'Forget it father,' said Beaufort with a yawn. 'Stapleton's not interested.'

'But I am!' cried Lolly.

'You don't *show* much interest,' said the captain.

'I think you two should be more tolerant,' said Mrs Mallet. 'You mustn't shut your minds to all ideas except your own. Mr Stapleton has a perfectly sound point of view.'

'What is it, then?' cried the captain.

'What I explained to you, dear.'

'But that didn't make any sense.'

'I'll say it again, then. Mr Stapleton has the car in *trust,* for Mr Brown. Mr Brown has given us a large sum of money for it. He would not think it honourable of Mr Stapleton to dispose of the car elsewhere.'

'What on earth has all that got to do with it?' exclaimed the captain. 'I am trying to perform the simple, direct sort of business transaction that I do a dozen times a day. All I hear from you and Stapleton is some purely personal opinion about trust and honour. I cannot see that there is the slightest connexion.'

'Well, that's quite true, of course, Mr Stapleton,' said Mrs Mallet. 'I'm afraid we can't deny that. You are bringing what we call "value judgements" into a simple business matter, aren't you?'

When Lolly only looked desperately puzzled, the captain said: 'Look here, my boy; if you're *afraid* of Brown, that's soon settled. I can have him beaten up at once.'

'I wouldn't want that,' said Lolly, looking horrified.

'And why not, pray?'

'He'd get hurt,' said Lolly.

At this, the captain and Beaufort looked absolutely stunned. They stared at Lolly with stupefaction.

'I must say, Mr Stapleton,' said Mrs Mallet, 'that you are pushing things a *little* far. After all, there *is* a National Health Service to look after Mr Brown's injuries. Even if he died, his relations would not have to pay for burying him. You must try and be a *little* more practical.'

'I'm afraid we'll have to call the whole thing off,' said the captain.

'I'm going to try again to explain to Mr Stapleton, so be patient a little longer,' said Mrs Mallet. 'Come and sit here beside me, Mr Stapleton, will you?'

He obeyed. Looking at him with a smile, she said gently: 'Now, it's like this. All our lives are divided into two parts. One part of us is the things we were taught when we were little, by our mother and father and the clergyman. They told us what it was to be good, honest, hardworking, and kind to others – and we needed .to be told these things or we would never have known about them. Now, the other part of our lives is *doing* things – making dolls and aeroplanes when we are very small, doing business when we grow up. Now these two parts are quite different. The first one is a personal feeling that we would hate to be without. The second one is a public duty that we perform so as to keep ourselves and the rest of the world well-fed and properly dressed. This second part is very complicated and scientific nowadays: it is very difficult to learn it. But think how much more difficult it becomes if we start muddling it up with the first part of ourselves! And that's what you've done. Instead of having two separate selves, like any normal person, you've tried to squash them into one. That means that whenever you want to *do* anything, you have to stop and ask if it's *right*. And how *can* it be right? Is it ever?'

'Well, not often,' said Lolly.

'Don't look so guilty, Mr Stapleton.'

'I bet he's had trouble with the police,' said the captain sympathetically.

'That's right,' said Lolly, sighing.

'It could hardly be otherwise, Mr Stapleton,' said Mrs Mallet gently. 'Once you start muddling your two identities, you quickly begin to muddle everything else. The police find out at once: that's what they are there for.'

'I like Mr Brown,' said Lolly suddenly. 'He's a friend.'

'Oh, well, then that settles it,' said the captain, walking briskly to the door. 'If he's going to bring friendship into the transaction, I wash my hands of it.'

'You have missed a wonderful opportunity, Mr Stapleton,' said Mrs Mallet sadly.

'The man's nothing but an idealist,' said Beaufort.

'You've no right to call me names,' said Lolly.

'Stop it, Beau!' called the captain from the door. 'Say good-bye politely to Stapleton.'

'Oh, all right!' cried Lolly, greatly humiliated. 'I'll do it.'

'Don't trust him, father!' exclaimed Beaufort. 'The next thing we know, he'll have taken the car straight to the police.'

'Not me!' cried Lolly.

'Stapleton,' said the captain, returning from the door: 'my son is hot-headed. He has no experience of men. I have. I believe you when you say that you would avoid the police. Now, since you don't understand normal language, I'm going to make you a proposition. You take the car to London tonight, and tomorrow morning I'll go and see Brown myself and explain the whole matter. I'll tell him quite frankly that everything was rather confused, and that on the whole we think it better to keep the car in dry dock for a few more months.'

'What about the money?' asked Lolly.

'Well, I'll pay you twenty-five pounds to drive it up to my London manager and he'll give you a good job, starting as of last week. How's that?'

'I mean, *Brown's* money,' said Lolly.

He saw the same old look of stupefaction creeping into their faces; it was more than he could bear. He said: 'All right, all right, never mind: I know I'm barmy.'

The captain sighed, opened the bag of self-raising flour, and handed Lolly twenty-five pounds. 'I'm taking a frightful risk, trusting a shaky fellow like you,' he said. 'I'm going to tell my manager that he'll have to put you through a stiff course.'

'I could go up with him, father,' suggested Beaufort, 'if it would ease your mind.'

'I back Stapleton absolutely,' said the captain, scribbling on a paper. 'Now, here's the address. It's a club. You ring the bell, and when a man comes, you say: "The Captain sent me to the President." That's all. It's a code. Do you understand?'

'Yes, sir,' said Lolly.

'It'll be a couple of months before we see you again, Stapleton. I hope we shall hardly recognize you. You will be another person.'

'I have a feeling we shall all be very proud of you, Mr Stapleton,' said Mrs Mallet.

'He'll look down his nose at us, if I'm any judge,' said Beaufort.

'I'm not that sort,' said Lolly. He buttoned up his greasy leather jacket.

'You'll find this more suitable for driving,' said the captain, opening a huge chest and producing an overcoat with a fur collar.

'Thanks,' said Lolly, donning it with much surprise.

'And here's a hat,' said the captain, placing a black Homburg on Lolly's head.

'Oh dear! *I* meant to wear that tonight,' said Beaufort.

'There's only one other thing,' said Lolly. 'About me being named Stapleton . . .'

'I've explained all that in the letter. The President will know all about you. He deals with that sort of thing all the time.'

'Oh, come on, father,' said Beaufort. 'I'll go up with him. He probably doesn't even know the way.'

'I know it very well,' said Lolly. 'And I'll take it alone.'

*

'Today is pay-day,' said the captain a few weeks later, pulling the bell-rope and crossing over to his desk. 'I have told the staff that now all the furniture is in position we can resume our old friendly customs and rituals. Today, for instance, they will all come in by turn, to get their money and exchange a few words with the master, as they have done for many years. It may interest you to know that we won't have to draw on Club funds at all. Jellicoe and Mrs Paradise, I find' – and the captain held up a passbook – 'have enough to pay their own wages for some years, and Mrs Chirk's, Tray's, and Towzer's to boot. So that's one weight off my mind. Not that I approve of living off capital; but then, I'm old-fashioned.'

There was a knock and Mrs Paradise entered, smoothing her skirt.

'Take that chair, Florence,' said the captain, putting on spectacles. 'Well, pay-day is here again – that dear, distant day we so despair of seeing. What is the general tone of the house, Florence?'

'On the upsurge, sir, now that all is ship-shape.'

'Had there been *grumbling,* Florence?'

'There were murmurs, sir.'

'Indeed! How is Mrs Chirk settling down?'

'She seems a kindly, willing body, sir, but a bit flutter-headed.'

'You have taken her under your wing, I hope?'

'Oh yes, sir. But she is still a little bewildered by the greatness of the house, and her place in it.'

'Well, it's the heart that matters most, Florence, is it not? Now, here are your wages. I am sorry the paper money is so oily and tattered, but the Bank was short of sovereigns.'

'Thank you, sir,' said Mrs Paradise, receiving a neat, cream envelope backed with the Mallet motto: *Ja'y Donné Ma Pledge.*

'I know that I have asked you this question every pay-day for twenty years, Florence, but I will ask it again. Do you still want to continue our old arrangement, under which I put 60 per cent of the wage in your envelope and invest the remainder at 5½ per cent, tax-free?'

'I do, sir.'

'I think you are wise. Just sign the usual form, will you . . . Thank you. You know, if you go on saving like this, Florence, you are going to be comfortably off, eventually. I was totting it all up the other day, adding in, of course, the money left you by your husband. The total quite made my eyes sparkle.'

'Don't tell it to me, please, sir, I like to feel I must go on and on working as hard as ever I can, because there's nothing between me and the workhouse.'

'I wish there were more like you, Florence. If it would please you, I could deduct still more from your envelope and put it in one of those Government Social Security schemes that are so popular nowadays.'

'No thank you, sir. The word "security" only makes my heart flutter. It's not a natural word, sir. We must struggle on like animals, sir, and those of us who fail must crawl under a bush and die.'

'That is a splended sentiment, Florence. Without it you would not be where you are. Now, Florence, I hope you will keep everyone up to the mark, because the time is drawing closer every minute. Only three weeks and our great house-party begins: some of the most distinguished men in England will be here. The affair will last about two and a half weeks, as usual, after which . . . '

'We will return to our quiet everyday life, sir.'

'Something of that nature, Florence. I shan't bother to give you instructions: after twenty years, you know all about our house-parties. But last year's party was a model: if you follow that, you can't go wrong.'

'Will many of the same gentlemen be coming, sir?'

'Almost all of them. You will see many a familiar face ... Very well.'
Mrs Paradise left, and Jellicoe came in.

'Sit down, Jellicoe. Have you any complaints?'

'I never complain, sir.'

'Have you any doubts?'

'I never doubt, sir.'

'Any worries?'

'They are for me to stomach, sir.'

'Well, that sounds very healthy, Jellicoe. I am glad of your re-assurance, because I had thought I noticed a restrained sourness.'

'I think I was only tired, sir.'

'Why would that be?'

'The furniture, sir. There seemed to be no end to it.'

'Would you expect there to be, in a house of this size?'

'No, sir. Now the work is done, I am proud of it and feel every minute was well spent.'

'Well, don't get smug about it. One of our most common failings is to make such a fuss about a very ordinary matter that we draw some extraordinary moral from it. And remember: most disorganization and struggle, even with such things as furniture, are at bottom only a reflection of a disordered personality ... Now, here is your wage. You will find it a *little* more than usual – that is my appreciation of your extra duties during Mrs Paradise's collapse.'

'I am deeply grateful, sir.'

'Not too deeply, because the appreciation does not amount to much, and I have had to deduct some of it to cover furniture chipped and scratched by you in recent weeks. There is also the usual child-maintenance and bastardy-arrears deductions, and I have, as always, kept back half the total to put in the usual 7 per cent Argentine Preferred ... Tell me, by the way, how long have you been with us, now – or should I say: how long have we consented to keep you?'

'Jellicoe came the morning after little Beau broke his finger in the Long Paddock,' said Mrs Mallet. 'That was on Easter Monday, 1928.'

'I remember it well,' said Beaufort. 'Until then I had thought life was all joy and kindness. On that day, I realized it was full of knocks.'

'That is quite right, Master Beaufort,' said Jellicoe warmly.

'Then for more than twenty-three years,' continued the captain, 'you have been investing in these Argentines, Jellicoe. I wonder if you

78

would like a change? A friend-of mine in the City has a sound stock which pays $9\frac{1}{2}$. Would you like to try it?'

At the mention of $9\frac{1}{2}$ per cent a fierce light boiled in the butler's tepid eyes, and he struggled with himself for some moments before answering: 'I think I'll keep to the old, safe ways, sir. Greed and adventurousness only lead to disaster. Those Argentines have been good friends to me for many a year: in my old age they will be my staff and comforter.'

'Very well, Jellicoe. Under your nervous, hypochondriacal skin, there is a heart of old oak. I hope some of it will be visible when our friends arrive for the house-party.'

'How many are expected, sir?'

'About the same as in previous years. Perhaps a dozen more.'

'Are there any special instructions, sir?'

'Only the usual ones.'

'Very good, sir.'

Jellicoe left, and Mrs Chirk came in.

'Come and sit down here,' said the captain. 'I expect all this is quite new to you and makes you feel strange. We have only had you a few years, have we not?'

'Not even that long, sir, I think.'

'Well, well... Now, this is the day, every month, when you receive your wages, make any complaints that may have crossed your mind, ask permission to marry, give notice, and so on. But first, I think I must ask: what *is* your name? We have been very patient about it, you know, but if all the staff were as reticent as you we should find ourselves living in a state of suspended anonymity.'

'If I knew my name, sir, I would feel more myself than I seem to feel.'

'Surely it is written on your ration-book and identity-card?'

'I've never thought to look, sir. What's come my way, I've eaten and been grateful for, with no thought to spare for the name that's brought it. Now, when I'd like to know, I can't find the dratted books.'

'It is not an edifying story, you know. You might just as well have put the food in the larder. Tell me, is there any name that would appeal to you particularly?'

'Pardon?'

'Can you think of anyone you would like to be known as? Some famous character in history? Your older sister? The doctor's wife?'

'It's all the same to me, sir. I only want to work and be at peace with the world. I don't need no name for that.'

'But you said you were puzzled without one?'

'It's the having of my attention distracted to it that puzzles me, sir. I do all right if people don't keep nagging at me for a name.'

'Then we shall have to call you Mrs Chirk. Master Beaufort will make you out a new ration-book and identity-card in that name . . . Now, Mrs Chirk – for that is your name – I want to talk to you very seriously. We have been taking a grave risk in continuing to employ a person who has no sense of nominal responsibility. Try and get into your head that though your friends and employers may find your name immaterial, the Government refuse to take such a lax view. They insist that everyone has an identity, however slight, and people who will not admit to themselves are often sent to prison. That is what will happen to you, if you continue to pursue this vague course. You must try and understand that the old days are over – the days when you could take your identity for granted. Nowadays, all the old means of self-recognition have been swept away, leaving even the best people in a state of personal dubiety. Even dispossession, the surest means of bringing home the naked identity, has disappeared. Very wisely, governments all over the world have sought to stop this rot before the entire human population has been reduced to anonymous grains. They give you cards, on which they inscribe in capital letters the name which your fading memory supplies before it is too late. It is their hope that by continually reading and re-reading your *name*, you will be able to keep your hold on a past that no longer exists, and thus bring an illusion of self into the present. As you see, the authorities have been obliged to reverse the normal procedure – which is, of course, first to create a world and *then* to name the things that inhabit it. Now, by doing the naming first, they hope creation will follow as a result of association and suggestion. This, as you know, is the method followed by women who want to have babies.

'This method has its dangers, of course; we all know mothers who have dreamed-up an Agnes and, on being delivered of a Horace, have stubbornly brought him up as Agnes; and something of the same kind may result from the authorities' efforts at present. But that is not my point at the moment. What I want to emphasize is: don't lose your name again, Mrs Chirk. Don't, at least, lose the cards on which that name is written. Not only would you yourself be left nameless, but people have been known to pick up such lost cards, put them in a wallet with their own, and start a hopeless tangle of selves that spreads like a bush fire. Even people in very high places today, men whose names are being printed and spoken aloud repeatedly, are often so foreign to their selves that they become involved in the most extraordinary identical lapses. Here, for instance, in this morning's paper, is a letter written by someone who believes himself to be named Sir Arthur Trotter. He is addressing the Minister of Mines and Places, and he writes as follows:

'My dear Minister,
You will recall that on 28th September of last year you invited me to luncheon at the Dorchester at 1.15 p.m. After the *hors d'œuvres* you invited me to become a member of the nationalized Cobalt and Sundries Corporation, at a salary of £5,000 a year. When I replied that I knew little of cobalt and less of sundries, you urged me at least to "have a whack at it". Over the sweet, I agreed. Now, after fifteen and a half months of intensive effort, I find that I am being shifted, without prior consultation, to the post of Warden of Stoke University. As I cannot see how this can be considered advantageous to the national interest, and still less to cobalt or Stoke, I have no recourse but reluctantly to resign from either and both offices. May I publish this letter?

' "My dear Trotter," replies the minister, "Of course you may publish your letter, though I do feel that letters such as yours are taking up a lot of space in the papers nowadays. I am astonished to hear that you have changed your mind about Stoke, since your appointment to the vacant Wardenship was made solely at your own request last Thursday. Surely I am not indulging in fantasy when I say that on that day you visited me in my office and *asked* for Stoke, saying that the lower salary was 'neither here nor there'? Surely you remember my trying to persuade you that cobalt was more vital to the nation than were the humanities? And while I am correcting this matter, may I add that until you came to see me on Thursday, to ask for Stoke, I had never set eyes on you, and had appointed you, sight unseen, to the

Cobalt Board, solely because I had heard you were well up in the subject. I have not been to the Dorchester since 1932. I never eat luncheon. Are you sure you are not confusing cobalt with some other mineral, or me with some other minister? Needless to say, if you are going to publish your letter, I shall be forced to do the same with mine."

'So you see, Mrs Chirk,' said the captain, laying down the paper, 'you can hardly be too careful. If two such highly-placed officials both appear, both to themselves and to one another, to be totally different persons, sharing no common recollections and enjoying no tenable identity – well, clearly, at least one of the two identities has been left in a cloakroom somewhere and never picked up again. This sort of thing is becoming so common nowadays that it would not surprise me to hear that both the letters I have just read were written by the same person, sincerely assuming in each letter an identity he hoped was his own. Is all this quite clear to you?'

'Well, I understand it, sir, though I couldn't say what it means.'

'At least you recognize it as a warning?'

'I'd rather not dwell on it too much, sir. My poor head is spinning as it is. I only ask for peace.'

'As you please, Mrs Chirk. Here is your wage and your new ration-book and identity-card. You keep the wage and the card and give the book to Mrs Paradise. Kindly ask Tray and Towzer to come up, will you? Good morning, and try not to forget yourself again.'

'Poor soul!' said Mrs Mallet. 'I wonder when she last knew herself?'

'Probably never,' said the captain. 'She may vaguely have known her parents, but that's always much easier. One would probably have to go back to her grandfather to find an identity that really made an impression on her.'

Mrs Mallet took Beaufort's hand off her knee, made a fist of it, and measured the foot of the sock she was knitting him. 'I don't, of course, remember when I joined the Club,' she said, 'but it must have been ages ago. And yet, with all my experience, I still wonder what on earth *other people* think when they come to see Mrs Chirk, or Tray, or Towzer and find the house empty, the old friend gone. What if I went to see their old neighbours, and asked to whom that empty place belonged, who had lived there, and so on?'

'You know very well what would happen,' said the captain. 'You know as well as I do the haunted, hunted look that comes into people's eyes when they try to urge their exhausted minds along a path they have long since abandoned. The first point they reach in such a struggle is, of course, the point when such a question made sense: thus, they would easily tell you who was living in the house in 1911. After a good deal of struggle, they would recall the name of some party who'd taken it in the 20s – "she had tulips in that corner," they'd say. Then they would start following the departed tulips; a haze would come over their eyes; even if they spoke the name of Chirk it would be a hollow sound, too recent to have any significance, come too late to matter.'

'It makes me want to cry. What terrible emptiness! Why do people so rebuff the present? Why, if one day Beau disappeared, *how* I would take on! I would search for him in every house in England; whenever I saw a man I would go up as close as possible to him and stare into his eyes, listen to his voice, study his walk and ways! I would sound alarms all through the country, and never rest until I found the man in whom Beau was hidden. Has Towzer no woman to do as much for him? Has Tray no lover who would die rather than think her lost forever?'

There was a knock at the door, and the captain cried: 'Come in!' adding: 'Well, let us find the exact answer.'

Miss Tray entered, pretty in her breeches. 'Ah, good morning,' said the captain. 'You are looking very well. Do sit down. Someone has been calling to see you, and telephoning. I was not able to catch the name. Do you know who it might be?'

'I can't think,' said Miss Tray, a look of astonishment crossing her face. 'Who would want to see me?'

'Perhaps relatives or friends?'

'Oh, no.'

'Did you not tell me that you had a gentleman friend?'

'Well, there *have* been gentlemen friends sometimes, doctor, but not the kind that would make a fuss.'

'Come, come, Miss Tray! Surely gentlemen friends *always* make a fuss!'

'I've never encouraged *that* type, doctor.'

'May I ask why?'

'They get me disturbed. I want to live my own life, not to be reminded of the things that would upset me.'

'What kind of things are those, Miss Tray?'

'The things men like.'

'Then you never intend to marry and have children, Miss Tray?'

'Oh, yes. I would like a husband who goes to work every day. But a man is something quite different. Of course, I don't mind the ones who just come and go, the ones who drop in casually. And I like sick ones.'

'Very well, Miss Tray. If there are any more phone calls, I shall just say you are not here and we have no idea where you may be.'

'Anything like that, doctor. It would seem the same as ever to them.'

'Have you settled down all right?'

'Oh, yes. It's all become such a routine already, I'm hardly aware of myself at all.'

'You rub along with Towzer, do you?'

'Oh, yes. I'd hardly know he was there.'

'You mustn't become too isolated, you know.'

'No fear, doctor. I'm too jolly and natural for that. And my dream life is full of excitement.'

'Very well. Here are your wages. Will you ask Towzer to come in?'

'He says he can't be bothered. "People, people, people!" is all he says. He's really very sweet. Only the soil matters to him. I love teasing him, because he never notices. So it's like a dream.'

'I advise you to be careful, Miss Tray. One day he *may* notice, and then your dream will suddenly come true. You won't like that, I'm sure.'

'Oh, there's no danger of that, doctor. Whenever a dream threatens to come true, I change to a new one.'

'One day when I have more time you must tell me about your dreams. Would you like to become a nurse?'

'Oh, no. Too familiar.'

'Then here are Towzer's wages. Is he clean and healthy?'

'I sometimes dream he is.'

'Well, we won't pursue that, Miss Tray. But I am glad to see your life is so full. Good morning.'

'Dear me,' said Beaufort, when Miss Tray had gone: 'I must say she leaves me very puzzled.'

84

'She lives in a state of chronic potentiality, that's all,' explained the captain. 'The future is, to her, what the past is to Mrs Paradise. Every morning is a thrilling anticipation of what the following morning may bring. She builds the superstructure today in hope of laying the foundation-stone tomorrow.'

'I have never really been well-up in the chronological side of identity,' said Beaufort. 'I can see the identity lost in relation to people, but when it is lost in time, I am easily confused.'

'Well, here is a simple story that will amuse you. My old teacher, when I first joined the Club, used to tell me: "You must listen for the echo, and try to tell if it comes before or after the sound." And one day, when I was studying the identity of judges, I realized what he meant. The judge in question, despite the fact that he was already buried in the past, invariably acted as if that past were some distant, future goal that he despaired of reaching, for all his loquacity. A summing-up by him would be hardly under way when court was adjourned for the day; when it resumed, he never went on from where he had left off, he recapitulated what he had said on the previous day, intending to go forward from there. But, as the recapitulation took him much further back than, in its original form, it had carried him forward, the business of the court advanced in a regular sequence of retreats, each of which overlapped, in backwardness, its predecessor of the day before. Thus as the days moved on, with the judge receding ever further into the previous weeks, one had the eerie feeling not that time was standing still – that would have been tolerable – but that it was growing younger in proportion as it became older, and that the judge, far from proceeding to a verdict, was struggling to revert to a prediction. I was young in those days, no older than you, and like you I was not really able to grasp the full implications of an identity whose sense of immediacy depends on a state of temporal abeyance. But I did grasp, of course, that where the basic character is moving in reverse, the minor characteristics are bound to follow. This judge, for instance, only knew who he was when he saw himself set among laws that had long ceased to exist; consequently, he never was able to sentence a man to death without remarking that at one time he would have had him drawn and quartered too: or if the sentence was ten years, he would point out that it would have been death a hundred years earlier, and so on. What made this habit even prettier was the fact that his language was likewise a struggle to go backwards: he set the speech of his boyhood in the context of archaic dignity, as if this were the only way he could express his shock and disappointment at being alive at all today. "What a horrid thing was that to do!" he would say, or: "To call you a bad hat is not enough: rotter is better." "Was this not a beastly way to behave?" he once exclaimed, of a man who had cracked a woman's skull with a chopper; adding: "Most especially in view of the trust she had always reposed in him." But I loved best to see him when he was behaving humbly – which was often the case, because judges are the only people nowadays who have the power, indeed, the duty, to slander and defame the characters of others. This tends to make them meek, as if they were thanking God for too great an honour, and they become increasingly apologetic as their brutality intensifies. This one used to say, with genuine distress: "I am really very sorry I cannot have you flogged. The law, unfortunately, no longer permits it. The best I can do is sentence you to five years at hard labour, and hope that you will find this adequate to your needs." Oh, and those expressions! When he pursed his lips, the whole court was sucked in, and dragged down through time into Norman-English. And how the women loved him – for his hatred of men! Poor soul; he was weakened when corporal punishment went, but with the threat of abolition of the death penalty he lost his last grip on self and became a mere child again, toddling from place to place, lisping baby-talk. Well, it's all long ago now, but I still feel that if the Club had got hold of him in time they could have transformed him into something useful and up-to-date.'

'We've done some good work here,' said Beaufort proudly.

'It's not too bad,' said the captain, surveying the comfortable room. 'But the President's eye is very keen, you know. He misses nothing. Do you remember the dreadful day Gluber claimed to have transformed a Logical Positivist into a lover of Dante?'

'Don't speak of it!' said Mrs Mallet, shuddering.

'I shall do some more work on Tray,' said the Captain. 'The others have set very well. I can hardly wait to see the President trying them. Without so much as a glance at their histories, he will ask them exactly the right questions.'

'He *is* getting just a *little* old, isn't he?' asked Beaufort, rather timidly.

'I must go and write to him,' replied the captain, leaving the room.

'Darling,' said Mrs Mallet to Beaufort, 'I shouldn't put such questions if I were you. No matter how apologetically.'

'But he's going to be the *next* President, isn't he?' said Beaufort stubbornly. 'That time is so almost here that I can feel it in my bones already. So can he. His whole manner is becoming more Olympian every day. He is getting that intensely calm, grave look that goes with presidencies. Do you think he knows it? Do you think the President will sense it?'

Mrs Mallet looked away and made no reply.

*

Family prayers. The captain, beautifully shaved and pink, with a morsel of soap foam on his left ear, has taken his place at his pine rostrum and is fingering the old prayer-books, stamped in gilt with the Mallet arms. Mrs Mallet, fresh and beautiful, walks across to the harmonium and delicately scans the lid for dust before opening it. The servants file into their pew like happy convicts; the captain clears his throat and reads the prayer. From outside comes a clattering noise of boots storming down stairs; and just as Mrs Mallet plays the first notes of the hymn, the chapel door is opened furtively, and Beaufort slinks into his place. The marks of a comb run straight from his brow to the back of his head; on each side of this track is a jungle of tow. His tie is half done, his eyes bleary, his pyjama trousers are visible below the turn-ups of his grey flannels. The captain sighs and looks away; Mrs Mallet raises her eyes from the keys and gives Beaufort a sorrowful look, to which he replies with frantic explanatory grimaces. Mrs Paradise's heart is melted by the spectacle, which occurs every morning and gives her day the warm sense of tragic beauty that is the principal feature of her life. Mrs Mallet has chosen her favourite evening hymn for this morning, and they all sing:

> O, give me Samuel's ear,
> The open ear, O Lord!

and while they are all at it the captain surveys them with the care of a ship's master wondering if his little crew will be sturdy enough to meet all storm and stress – for tomorrow the Club is arriving for the Summer Session and every nerve of Hyde's Mortimer is tense with cleanliness and excitement. Mrs Paradise is fat and flustered: she sings with the others, but her thoughts are whirling madly from one room to another, accompanied by a frantic duster. Beside her, Mrs Chirk is all skin-and-bone – poor, aimless, unidentifiable thing, she is resolved to rub and rub until the few threadbare veins in her pale nose are excited to a positive redness. How different is Jellicoe – his face alive with suffering, his eyes filled with that burning dignity which only a life-long addiction to punishment, alcohol, and rebuke can give. Beside him is Towzer – a heavy, gnarled man whose grizzly beard brushes the page of his hymn-book: he peers at the lines through steel spectacles and follows each one with a forefinger as crusted and gnarled as a stump. He still looks old, but he is getting younger every day. Tray is close beside him, as usual; her lips are barely moving because, as always, she is absolutely wrapped up in some ridiculous fantasy: she alone is totally unexcited by the prospect of a horde of distinguished people arriving tomorrow: life is becoming more and more a hilarious joke to her: only a profoundly-confident feeling that one day she will marry Towzer saves the feather-brained little fool from becoming quite hysterical. So, from time to time, she turns a half-affectionate, half-satirical glance at the bearded, burly figure at her side, and positively shakes with laughter when she thinks of how completely ignorant he is, poor man, of what lies in store for him when he has knocked another ten years off his life.

The captain sees all this and understands every bit of it, from the jumping tic in Jellicoe's left cheek (the nearest to Mrs Paradise) to the occasional flash of understanding in Towzer's right eye (the nearest to Miss Tray). He is touched by the thought that each of these people now enjoys a full and passionate identity which each regards as the great, human axle round which the turning world has been built. He is more touched when he looks first at Mrs Mallet, playing the harmonium with such beautiful restraint, and then, at Beaufort's protruding pyjamas; these two companions of his have shown throughout these months a skill and ardour that fill him with admiration. Indeed, he is deeply affected by the whole scene: he feels there is something most beautiful about it: it is far finer than a painting or a piece of music because all the characters in it are actually alive. Formerly, he thinks to himself, an artist took real people and transformed them into painted ones: how much finer and more satisfying is the modern method of assuming that people are not real at all, only self-painted, and of proceeding to make them real by giving them new selves based on the best-available theories of human nature. When he looks at stout Mrs Paradise and thinks of the thin fantasy she was only a few months ago he can hardly believe his eyes: it is incredible to think how well the open ear responds to a little love and chronological falsification. And all these people are his own creation (with all due respect to help received from Mrs Mallet and Beaufort); and as he looks at them now he can hardly believe that in a few more weeks they will all have vanished again. He begins to wonder if, when they return to their old dead forms, they will carry with them any vestige, or sign, of their present identity: it is his experience that such people rarely do, but he never has learned quite not to hope that a little of it may stick. So when the harmonium ceases and it is time for him to take up the book again, he reads the prayer with unusual attentiveness and finds the words far more apt and sensible than usual.

PART TWO

ONE hears much about cavalry, tanks, or guardsmen collecting for a charge; but can these really compare in impressiveness to a body of thinkers collecting for a conference? Their cars storm up the drive, firing gravel all over the lawns, where the blades of the mower will pick it up again and dash it in Miss Tray's face. Row upon row of teeth, false and natural, yellow and black, glisten in smiles behind the car windows as Club members see the captain, Mrs Mallet, and Beaufort waving welcome from the stone stairs. The car doors swing open and everyone begins to tumble out; but before examining the rank-and-file of members it is good to take a close look at the President.

One cannot do so immediately because it is the duty of a president always to be so placed that at least a score of people must move before he can be made visible. In this case, disciple after disciple scrambles out and each, instead of proceeding into the house, stands at the open back door of the largest limousine and peers into it anxiously. Has the President survived the journey or will he be found to have been crushed? Does he know he has reached his goal, or should someone tell him? – presidents are not aware of passages. At last, as if brought into existence by these uncertainties, a shadow in the depths of the limousine is heard to grunt and an unmistakable presidential leg is poked through the door. A disciple at once seizes it by the ankle and presses it in the direction of the ground; others go round to the other side of the car and push the body in the direction of the leg. In a trice, the job is done: the President is not only out of the car but standing up.

He stands for a moment smoothing his little beard and casting his little eyes on his surroundings with good-humoured irony. Like anyone who has been buried under heaps of followers for twenty years and sandwiched between their rancours in a thousand debates, he is a small thin man, and, as befits his rank, messy-looking. His clothes exude, in a refined sort of way, the stench of congested thought; although he has been infinitely pressed, his suit has not. His sophistication is so great that he has long since reached its limits and started all over again at the very beginning, seeing everything with wonder. It is with tolerant astonishment, like an old hand in a new whore house, that he surveys the fresh, strange beauties offered him by Mother Nature – those massive oaks down there; or are they elms or beeches? who shall say? all trees are oaks to presidents; that June stretch of what is unmistakably close-trimmed grass; and, heavens! surely those are *bushes* blooming in that large vacancy over there; how colourful they are, but how bizarre that a bush should behave as if it were a flower! His followers study his puzzled face with satisfaction; though each has extremes of one kind or another, none is capable of carrying bewilderment so far into total innocence. Every gesture of the President is a joy to see; turning now from the landscape to himself, as if to establish a relation, he finds on his waistcoat a quantity of cigar-ash that was unnoticeable in the city, and brushes it off with hesitant fingers. His eyes following, he even notices a run of extraordinary stains down his front, ranging from deep soup and gamboge egg to the dulled brilliance of red ink and mucilage. His lungs are simply abashed by the great quantity of *air* in this place; it seems to stretch for miles, unbroken by chimneys and exhaust-fumes; surely a little *much* for so few people? He is none too steady on his feet because the surface of the earth is so unusually *uneven*: every nerve in his soles impinges upon a Matterhorn of pebbles, rendering him clumsy: walking must be an odd affair, here, he thinks. And what a *wind* there seems to be, even though it is a still day of perfect sunshine: presumably it is the prevalence of air that gives such a breezy illusion. Well, well, well; it is all very peculiar indeed, this so-called natural life of which he has heard so much, with the sun seeming to shine on a man from all sides, unbroken by any city geometry; he is not sure that so much exposure is good. It relieves him to think that shortly he will be at a *desk* again, with *walls* all round him, and that in time to come this brilliant scene will recur only in an occasional, presidential dream, flying through his mind's grey enclosure like a kingfisher through Liverpool Street Station.

But the important thing about the President is that, were he not so stained, abashed, and teetering, he would not be a president at all. Every member of the Club knows that this formidable man has no option but to suggest the immensity of his real strength by parading all his frailties. They know that from the time he was an infant he had a presiding identity, and that it could never have occurred to him to have anything else. When he was quite small, someone must have told him that he was 'every inch a little president', or something of the kind, and from that moment he knew himself to be a president, with no further problem but that of growing-up and finding a corpus and theory good enough for him to preside upon. If he has, while waiting for a suitable vacancy, specialized in this or that aspect of identity, the marks are no longer visible: he has long symbolized unity, totality, globality, the snake with its head in its mouth. His urbanity is staggering; he is so charming and natural that no one would dream he had a brain in his head. In spite and malice he is a match for all the members put together, but no one can imagine him sitting up at night mixing poisons for his darts. He can roll his eyes, twinkle them, scratch his nose, smile with imbecile amiability – but only because he has reached such a state of elevation that if he got down on all fours and crawled, he would still seem to be presiding.

How different are the other members of the Club! They are all perfectly decent people, as people go, but it is not *their* function to coin presidential selves. These competent men have priceless identities of their own; each is quite preoccupied with leaving no doubt in anyone's mind (particularly his own) as to what that identity is. The impressive thing about each of them is not that he specializes in a particular subject, but that he specializes in being himself – that is to say, in being the type of man who goes with the subject he has chosen to specialize in.

Take Mr Harris, for instance, the man who brought Beaufort into the Club and trained him – not to be like himself, of course, but to be as recognizably Beaufort as possible. Harris is an immensely grave man: one day, at school, he wrote an essay that was so dull that one of the masters described it as 'classical'. This was all young Harris needed; until that moment he had wavered, as boys do, among numerous selves, but at that instant his became a classical identity – short, austere, clear, without a trace of gush. The Club looks to him for case-histories that speak for themselves in dry, uninsistent language; they love his efforts to put sobriety into the most intoxicating themes. All this is immediately evident in his face and posture: when Beaufort waves frantically to him, Harris responds with a faint glow in one eye (the other, unfortunately, is glass) and the faintest suggestion of a smile: this, as everyone knows, is Harris's way not only of showing warmth but of making himself recognizable as Harris.

But now consider the man beside him, Dr Alexander Shubunkin. It

93

is his smile that strikes one first, a smile that breaks out at the slightest pretext, splits his face in two and makes his jaw hang like a corpse's. It is the smile of a man who probes so sharply into the characters of others that without it he might be thought unkind. Nonetheless, he cannot give the impression that he is *all* smiles; he has somehow to convey his analytical thrust; so he has decided to express this with his nose, eyes, and forehead, which are all pulled and puckered together to express vigilance and concentration. Lest anyone fail to recognize these confluctions, Dr Shubunkin has arranged for dozens of seams and grooves to serve as clues to his riddle: when his eyes flash with analytical interest, all the lines become illuminated and run to the centre of his face, pointing. It is probable that he got this idea from the electric map system of the Paris Métro.

In sum, his face adds up to a most interesting whole – two opposing parts welded horizontally into one, with each part taking its turn to draw the spectator's attention away from the other. But there are drawbacks to it. Because the whole urge, or dynamic, of Dr Shubunkin is channelled exclusively into his conflicting face he is quite shapeless and unidentifiable from the chin down. Furthermore, anyone who chooses to keep his face in two parts, and to spend every second of his life pushing one part forward or back, according to the situation, is bound to be tense, like a signal box on a busy line, and thus Dr Shubunkin is one of those people for whom the shakes must be the unifying principle; tics and tremors interweave his disparate parts, adding a third aspect to what is already double. More-ordinary Club members take off their hats to Shubunkin; well they know what a grid of energy and nervous concentration goes into the upkeep of his face, which, triple though it may appear to be, is as much a united whole as the United Kingdom, the Magi, or a three-piece bedroom suite.

Dr Shubunkin stands at one extreme of club life; at the other stands Mr Harcourt, whose identity consists – and no less strongly at that – in his conviction that he has no identity at all. No one knows exactly when he decided that absolute negation was the best form of self-assertion, but it must have been many years ago because he does it so well. Like all Club members, he once pursued a particular aspect of the great theory of identity, but at some time or other he found the pace too hot, the competition too intense. Forgetting any dreams he may have had of becoming a poet or a magnate or an authority on hydraulic brakes, he decided to become the average man – one of the most difficult roles because it is such a curb, or drain, on a man's abilities. But he has pulled it off – so well, in fact, that his fellow members often scratch their heads and wonder how on earth he got into the Club without being black-balled. Not only does he disclaim possession of any identity but backs this up by seeming never to know where he is or what is happening. He has never missed a case-history in his life, but speak to him about the Great Theory and he will stare perplexedly, as if the word identity were totally strange to him. It is no exaggeration to say that if the Club decided to dedicate itself to motor-racing, Mr Harcourt would not be aware of any change, even on corners at high speeds. He is a friendly man, but rather a grumbler.

Between the extremes of Harcourt and Shubunkin are all the types necessary to fill a club. One might, briefly, mention Father Orfe, an ascetic who is a heavy drinker and has fixed his point of self-recognition precisely midway between religious faith and the hip-flask: this is a modern tendency among devout priests. There is Mr Jamesworth, whose self consists in a never-failing conviction that other people are always missing the point and spends all his effort, in a debate, trying to change the subject into something more fundamental. There is young Dr Bitterling, an authority on symbols: he is often at odds with Jamesworth but admires Orfe. But as there are many members, each absolutely distinct in his self-creation, and set in his ways by now, there is room to mention only one more. This is young Stapleton, the youngest member.

He is a pale, hollow-eyed youth with a huge reddish moustache and a passionately-excited look: he can't keep still for a minute, so eager is he to get down to business and change the world. It is clear that he has not been in the Club very long, because he looks at everything with such excitement: he has the identity of a reforming zealot at the moment, and manages it very well; but there is every chance that in the next few years he will stumble on some special aspect of life which, after first concentrating his powers in its direction, will then withdraw and permit him to give his whole attention to building up the self that best goes with the bent in question. Thereafter, even if he sometimes forgets what the bent is, he will never be in danger of forgetting himself. Until then, however, he will see self-forgetfulness as his aim in life. He is a wounded veteran of the last war and walks with a limp.

This is also an interesting moment in which to see Captain Mallet afresh: suddenly one sees with clarity why he decided to be a captain. All the Club members are standing on the gravel sharing the President's discomfort and staring apprehensively into the emptiness – and down the stone stairs trips the captain, a picture of smiling ease, a confident leader stretching out his hand to raise doubters from the waves. With careless shouts he beckons them to the stairs; they obey reluctantly, sadly watching their empty cars sweep away. Mrs Mallet and Beaufort stand side by side at the stair-head, also giving welcoming cries: but the members are not in a mood to climb boldly to safety. And so they stand, adamant and tense, at various levels of the stairs, raising their arms heartily but in a doomed way, like figures in a war memorial. The President alone can exorcize their fears, and he cries in his high, querulous little voice:

'What a delightful place for our Session, my good Mallet; but surely a little close to the *sea*? What? No sea for miles! I can hardly believe it. I really do not recognize the atmosphere at all: everything appears so *suspended*; nothing has anything *behind* it; what few solids there are seem quite left to their own devices. Does one feel equally at sea when one is actually *in* the house?'

The members manage to smile, on seeing their skeletons thus made to dance, though young Stapleton, who is every bit as frightened as the rest, sniffs rather snobbishly at the President's words: he is too young to approve of fear. But the captain takes the President's cue, and says understandingly:

'I assure you; once inside, with the curtains drawn, you will hardly know you have left London. *Some* oddness persists, of course; even inside, one has the feeling of living at an unnaturally low temperature in spaces abnormally vacant.'

'Well, well, we must take the plunge,' replies the President, and he boldly sets his old feet going and climbs all the way to the top, treating each step as if it were a dangerous parody of a real one. 'Come on, Harris!' he cries. 'You next! Stapleton! Come on, my boy!' And soon, those who are safely inside the breakfast-room are peering out of the windows at the falterers, and crying heartily: 'Come on! It's better in than out; you'll see!'

Jellicoe enters with a silver tray. The captain closes the tall french windows behind the last Club member. At once, a more homely feeling comes over the city visitors; with their fingers tight on the stem of a glass they can watch the oaks tremble through the window with less apprehension. 'Such a threat to the self!' the President murmurs, as if they had all scraped through a dangerous sortie. He takes an armchair that has its back to the window; at which Stapleton, though he is shaking like a leaf, deliberately chooses one that faces the dangerous landscape.

Now occurs a very pretty, indeed brilliant incident, illustrating the ability of brave men to rise to an occasion even when they are sick with fear. Dr Musk, one of the finest brains in the Club, walks straight up to Jellicoe and says: 'How excellent to see you again! I hope your health has improved since we met last. You were very shaky on your pins, if I remember rightly.' To which Jellicoe, delighted at being recognized, answers: 'It was my hope, sir, that your familiar face would be here again. My health, though of course no better, is a small matter, sir, I assure you.'

When Jellicoe has left the room, the President bows his head respectfully and says: 'What a *finish* you give to your people, Mallet! That man is like an old inlay.'

A murmur of agreement runs through the members: despite their fear, they have one and all studied Jellicoe intently, without once seeming to have looked at him.

'So *untouched*,' says Father Orfe, draining his third glass and looking ascetically at the ceiling. 'Not a *finger*-mark. You would think it had been done by waving a wand.'

'I hope he is really settled *at bottom*,' says Mr Jamesworth.

'He looked like a butler to me,' says Mr Harcourt. 'But then, so do all butlers.'

'I hope,' says Dr Shubunkin, working his signal-box until every inch of his visage becomes a local train, 'that we will soon have a chance to see some other jobs of yours.'

The captain blushes, as a modest captain should. He knows that not another man in the Club, the President included, can make an identity with quite his skill. He would like to rush them all out of the room and show them his other trophies – Miss Paradise, Tray, Towzer, and the sublime Chirk – but he checks himself because he notices that the members are suddenly feeling comfortably at home. The few words of shop that have been spoken have brought back their sense of *vocation*;

they are again conscious of being dedicated persons: simultaneously, they all begin to talk at once, at the tops of their voices, each man expanding, as it were, to his full self. Though each is too preoccupied to hear what any other says, all are united by an identity greater even than their separate own – the identity of the group, or body, devoted in plural ways to a singular aim. No one who has smelt this atmosphere of a congress, or gang, of learned people can ever forget it: to these men, the problem of human identity not only surpasses but embraces all other problems; there is nothing on the face of the earth which they cannot reduce, in no more than three steps at most, to a matter of identity. Moreover, since each man specializes in a special aspect of the special matter of identity, they stand like spokes running to a central hub, as if they were the wheel of life itself. In other rooms, in other houses, all over the world, other bodies devoted to sex, or compost, or holism, or Marxism, are forming thousands of similar wheels: but what makes these other wheels so fatally different from the one now running at Hyde's Mortimer is the fact that all the others are running in wrong directions.

So the captain stands to one side, drinking in the buzz of sound that rings true only when one belongs to a circle which has at last identified absolute truth. But he has a duty to perform; so when the President shouts: 'I am sure your two colleagues played a substantial part,' he bellows back: 'They were pearls without price, Mr President. He (indicating Beaufort) is developing a sensitivity of response that I have never known in such a young member, while she...' – but Mrs Mallet is not in the room at the moment.

At the word 'she', the members fall silent, and the captain continues in a lower voice: 'As we know, she is the only woman member of the Club simply because any other would be superfluous. It takes all sorts to make a man, but one is quite enough to make a woman. Oh, gentlemen, I wish you could have seen our chosen lady in action recently – a veritable dream of female identity! Tears coursing down her cheeks from a reservoir that is yet eternally full; inclinations of the head alone which are enough to give fixity to this amorphous life.'

At this they all take out clean white handkerchiefs and press them gently to their eyes, causing Mrs Mallet to remark as she enters with a tray of sandwiches: 'You dear things! I suspect you have been talking about me.'

One by one they come up and shake her hand, blurt out their compliments, and resume the dabbing of their eyes. Mrs Mallet, who only weeps in the service of her vocation, has a kind word for each of them, enough to make them feel that their lives have been enriched from an important source. Stapleton alone remains aloof; not only has he never seen Mrs Mallet before, but, at heart, the young prig disapproves of having *any* woman in the Club. The President has really done a very interesting job on him.

Taking the captain to the quietest corner, the President now shouts: 'Psychologically, Mallet, which would be better: to let them have lunch first and *then* go over the premises, or vice versa?'

'Get it all over!' the captain shouts back. 'The sherry has steadied them nicely; lunch would only make them sluggish.'

So the President turns and squeaks for silence. 'Gentlemen!' he cries: 'we are going to make a tour of the house and grounds . . . No, be so good as to stop looking so miserable: it *has* to be done. Captain Mallet will first say a few words, after which he will answer questions. Captain Mallet.'

The captain steps forward and rests three fingers on a table. He performs this simple act of self-identification so artistically that a light clapping runs round the room. He bows, and says quietly:

'Gentlemen, this is an historic moment for the Identity Club. For more years than I can remember we have spent our lives in the seclusion of our London quarters toiling at the great theory which is the unifying factor of our lives. It was ever our belief that this theory could be perfected best in isolation: we have known from experience that once a theory is exposed to the knockabout of daily life it loses the bloom on which its beauty depends. Most clubs – and there are many nowadays – ignore this precaution; they pitch their theory into the outside world and back it against all rivals, thus leaving it dependent upon nothing but the hysterical pugnacity of its supporters. This is all very well, but it has always seemed to us that as all clubs are closed circles, permitting no deviations whatever, it is senseless to expose loyal members to the rough-and-tumble of debate. Why argue with a member from another club when you know that both he and you are so inextricably identified with opposing theories that for either to yield a point is like losing an arm or leg? No, gentlemen, since it is the aim of every club to be the only club and of every theory to be the only theory, the way of *our* club is surely the best. We actually do live in isolation from the world – which is to say that we live in exactly the same way as all other clubs except that we do so more comfortably and don't have to pretend that we have open minds. Our beloved theory, the only true one in the world, is the only one we want to hear about. Identity is the answer to everything. There is nothing that cannot be seen in terms of identity. We are not going to pretend that there is the slightest argument about *that*.'

There was loud applause.

'Nonetheless,' the captain continued, 'there are times when even *we* find it necessary to put ourselves in contact with the outside world. This session is one of those times. We have come here for a little change, to see objects, human and otherwise, that we do not see in our club quarters. We expect to translate them all into the terms of our theory, but we shall enjoy having something fresh to translate. It will make next year's case-histories more interesting. It will broaden our minds without changing them in the slightest.

'This sort of house was once a heart and centre of the national identity. A whole world lived in relation to it. Millions knew who they were by reference to it. Hundreds of thousands look back to it, and not only grieve for its passing but still depend on it, non-existent though it is, to tell them who they are. Thousands who never knew it are taught every day to cherish its memory and to believe that without it no man will be able to tell his whereabouts again. It hangs on men's necks like a millstone of memory; carrying it, and looking back on its associations, they stumble indignantly backwards into the future, confident that man's self-knowledge is gone forever. How appropriate it is that these forlorn barracks, these harbours of human nostalgia, should now be in use once more solely as meeting places for bodies such as ours! How right that we should assemble this summer in one of the last relics of an age of established identities! Today, when it is rare to find any man who can be said to know his self, it is clubs such as ours which tell these sufferers who they are. That each club tells him he is something quite different is beside the point. We of this club excel all other clubs in that we give our patients the identities they can use best. We can make all sorts of identities, from Freudian and Teddy Boy to Marxist and Christian. We are thus the idea behind the idea, the theory at the root of theory. And what we like about ourselves is the frank way we go about our work. Other clubs stubbornly deny that they try to supply their patients with new identities. They insist that they merely reveal an identity which has been pushed out of sight. Thank God, gentlemen, we shall never be like them! We are proud to know that we are in the very van of modern development, that we can transform any unknown quantity into a fixed self, and that we need never fall back on the hypocrisy of pretending that we are mere un-coverers.

'Let me say a word about the domestic staff of this establishment. I think that I and my two colleagues have done a good job of fixing these fluid entities. We have given them exactly the selves which they deserved, as well as temporary names which mean a great deal to them. Do not be afraid to call on them for any service you need. If you are too lenient with them, or worry because they seem overworked, kindly show no concern. We have gone to much trouble to return them to their favourite era of injustice and drudgery and any attempt to lighten their burdens will not only distress them but may wreck their tenuous grasp of self.

'Now, as to your own selves. I hope I shall not tread on any corns if I say that many of you will feel that this archaic environment is a menace to your identities. Let me assure you, there is no ground for terror. There is nothing here, nothing whatever, that has any vestige of life left in it. It is a warehouse of distorted memories and nothing else. One evidence of this is that whereas in the old days many curious visitors would have interrupted our Session by paying calls and leaving cards on us, today hardly anyone will even notice that there are living people in the house. The few who do notice will detest the very idea of burdening their lives with new acquaintances, of exposing their broken identities and bad consciences to strangers. Only parasites pay calls today – and our kitchen has already given two of *them* an appropriate welcome.

'Outside these walls, in the open air, many of you may feel a certain sense of *exposure*. The best answer to that is pipes, cigars, and cigarettes which leave a familiar mark upon the void. The wearing of a hat is also helpful: I do not have to remind you of the late Dr Black Planorbis's superb paper on the relation between modern hatlessness and loss of identity. But the greatest help of all is the handling of strictly con-temporary objects, such as ration-books, identity-cards, very small pieces of meat and butter, and objects that have been obtained a little dishonestly. And if these, too, fail, let me advise you to fall back on a dodge that I have found highly successful – carry some money in your pocket and wrap your fingers round it. Often, in the last two months, I have overcome a sense of identical disintegration simply by leafing through my cheque-book.'

There was a chorus of claps, and the President stepped forward. 'These have been wise words, gentlemen, so let us be off and change our clothes – taking good care not to take off the underclothing that is so much a part of us. Let us also follow Mallet's suggestion and transfer plenty of loose silver from the old trousers to the new. We meet here again in fifteen minutes.'

*

When the Club reassembled there was a great improvement evident. The President looked relaxed in a loud check suit: he carried a shooting-stick. Some members were in plus-fours; Dr Shubunkin wore a cap smattered with fishing-flies. All this caused a lot of friendly teasing; but all members noted with relief that, though their companions were totally disguised, their identities – seen, as it were, simply in new frames – stood out even more prominently than before.

'As a special treat,' cries the President, 'I am going to ask Mallet to show us the human occupants of this pile first of all. There is nothing duller than being shown over another person's property, but there is nothing more stimulating than being shown over his cases.'

No one, of course, is more delighted than the captain to hear this and soon the whole company is streaming through the great kitchen door.

Mrs Paradise stands bowing inside. Behind her are great tables sticky with damp flour, dough, and poultry in undress. Her sleeves are rolled up, showing her prime forearms. The Club studies her with interest: there is a flutter of note-books and requests for loans of pencils.

'Good morning, Florence,' says the captain. 'I have brought our guests to see your admirable establishment. Some of them are old friends of yours and it is they who have insisted on showing you off to the others.'

'Admirable, indeed!' cries the President: 'an astonishing place! Tell us, my good woman, do you spend all day in work of this kind?'

'Oh, yes, sir,' replies Mrs Paradise, at once falling in love with this bearded old man's childlike, upper-class innocence. She has not met him before, but almost feels she has.

'I recognize a bird, do I not?' says the President triumphantly, pointing his shooting-stick.

'That is a turkey, sir, in preparation for the table.'

'It looks different without its feathers, doesn't it? You have no difficulty in knowing it for what it is? You never think it a goose?'

'Oh, never, sir. They are far from one bird.'

'It must all be very difficult. To know *what* everything is when it no longer has any resemblance to itself; to know *where* you have put it when you want it; to know *what* to do with it when you have found it. Do you never lose your head?'

'Never, sir. I am at home here, you see. Everything is familiar.'

'You never have the feeling that you are being swept away by powers beyond your control?'

Mrs Paradise smiles and loves him more than ever. She answers: 'Not if we are given ample warning that guests are expected, sir.'

'Of course. I had not thought of that. Everything has to be conclusively identified before a certain fixed hour.'

'That is correct, sir.'

'And how many are you?'

'We are myself, Mrs Chirk, and Jellicoe, sir. Three in all.'

'And you can look after all these guests for three weeks without getting tired?'

'Oh, yes, sir. We work in shifts, you see. During the day we cook and wash-up, and then, when night comes and the gentlemen are in bed, we have a chance to go through the living-rooms. We are rarely in bed before three a.m., and then we are up again at six. We are proud to think that we manage so economically.'

'Yes, it is not half bad,' said the captain.

'I imagine that prayer is a great help, too,' said the President. 'If you have time to squeeze some in.'

'Prayer has never failed me yet, sir.'

'I am glad to hear it. So many people nowadays have simply dropped it. Who is that woman in the corner with red eyes? Would that be Mrs Jellicoe?'

'Her name is Mrs Chirk, sir. People always seem to have trouble with her name.'

103

'Good morning, Mrs Burke. So you work here, too?'

'Yes, sir, I do – as best I can.'

'Do you enjoy your work?'

'I hardly pause to think, sir, but I doubt I would be doing it if there were not enjoyment.'

'Do you get very good wages? That is always a help.'

'The family is very generous, sir. I often find an extra coin in my envelope.'

'How do you like this modern life?'

'I am sure my parents' days were better, sir. We worked harder then, but we were much happier. And the shops were so full of good things. Even though we couldn't afford to buy them, it was a pleasure to think what happiness they brought to others.'

'Nonetheless, you are content with the present? It doesn't bewilder you with its intricacies and swiftness? All these trains, and so on.'

'Only if I pause to ask, sir.'

'I see. You find stability in momentum; identity in thoughtless self-propulsion.'

'I couldn't answer that, sir.'

'You get happiness from thinking that your parents were happy and that your children will be happy too? So the present – yourself – is neither here nor there?'

'Not a scrap, sir, if I just keep going and going.'

'Well, thank you very much, Mrs Jellicoe and Mrs Paradise. We must move on. We are going to shoot, or something, I think. Thank you a thousand times and good luck to you.'

Jellicoe welcomed them at the butler's pantry.

'Why!' cried the President, 'you are the man who brought us the sherry!'

'Yes, indeed, sir. This is where I bring it from.'

'Is that not a long way?'

'Eight hundred and sixty-four steps, sir.'

'Well, if you have time to count up to 864, you are not as hard-pressed as I thought.'

'But I am, sir, if I may say so. It is just that I feel the pain more exactly if I give it a number.'

'Oh. You have a sort of rough-and-ready philosophy, have you?'

'Only a very simple one, sir. I hold that life is intensely painful but that the good man does not complain.'

'I suppose you read that in a book?'

'No, sir. It struck me quite personally.'

'Then your idea of perfect happiness is to meet the maximum of pain with the minimum of complaint?'

'Exactly that, sir. I despise the softness of modern life.'

'Well, you look well enough on your philosophy, I must say. And you never feel the want of a more up-to-date establishment than this one? A gaslight in the pantry, for instance?'

'Gaslight is only an illusion; it is no help to the soul, sir.'

'You are a devout man?'

'Unfortunately, no, sir. Although I deeply respect those . . .'

'Yes, yes, yes; I've heard that one before. I must say, you seem to have chosen the worst of both worlds. Surely you should try and have either a God or a gas-fitting? To reject *both* seems foolhardy.'

'Not according to my philosophy, sir.'

'That's true, of course. Without serious deprivation you would hardly know yourself.'

'Exactly, sir. Pain is the spur.'

'And do you expect no reward for all this?'

'I feel that a reward would spoil everything, sir. I am bitterly ashamed of my good fortune, as it is. I have so much to make up for in my past.'

'Well, you are certainly going about it the right way. Good morning.'

'Good morning, sir, and thank you for your sympathy.'

'Not at all. The whole fun of pain is in the sharing of it.'

Out of earshot the President said: 'That Jellicoe and Mrs Paradise – I suspect they are brother and sister.'

'You are in wonderful form this morning, sir,' said the captain. 'Your guess is absolutely correct.'

Stapleton is immensely impressed. He stares at the President as at a god.

'They have exactly the same hideous ears,' says the President.

Stapleton groans. He had hoped for something far more profound than comparable ears. If ever he becomes a great man he will see to it that truth is given the tortuous capture it deserves.

'Well, gentlemen!' cried the President, 'let me inspect *you*! I hope you are all in good heart, because we are now going to examine the gardener and gardenee.'

He throws open the outer door. Every man hastily lights up pipe or cigarette and reaches in his pocket for his money: they pass into the lime avenue in a column of smoke to a jingling of silver. They see Towzer and Tray in a rose-bed, and the President boldly makes for them. Towzer is bent over the base of a tall rose, grubbing for suckers. Tray is forcefully syringing the same rose, leaving a foam of dripping suds on Towzer's head.

'This is the President of the Royal Medical Society,' says the captain. Tray puts up her syringe and giggles.

'He wants to see how Towzer is getting on,' continues the captain.

'Something has caught my eye!' cries the President. 'Why does every rose have a little tag tied to it?'

'That's the rose's *name*, sir,' answers Tray, giggling louder.

'But why? It won't run away, will it? It's not a dog.'

'To identify it, sir. Roses are all different colours and sorts.'

'You mean, you have to know the name before you can tell the colour? Well, there are parallels in medicine, I must say. And what about that bent gentleman at your feet, my dear? What is *he* for?'

'He's the one you wanted to inspect, sir.'

'I can't if he keeps that crouching position. Can't you haul him up a little?'

Thrusting two soapy fingers into Towzer's matted hair, she tugs his face into view. 'Here's a nice gentleman to talk to you,' she says. 'Try and be sweet and sensible, to please me.'

His bloodshot eyes roll painfully in the sunlight. The pathetic sight is heartening to members of the club because by comparison with Towzer they are healthy giants. They reach for their notebooks and pencils; their vapid, jittery expressions become fixed in the rocky lineaments of professional men. Dr Shubunkin, who has a certain talent, makes a quick sketch of Towzer's back-bent head – the huge yellow teeth, the dense beard, the awful furrows of the ploughed face.

'Dear me!' says the President, 'he *has* been through a lot. How would you like to tell me a little of your history, my man? Don't feel nervous; we are all doctors.'

Tray bursts out laughing and Towzer angrily tugs his hair out of her fingers and returns to his grubbing.

'You'll never get a word out of him, sir,' Tray says.

'Why? Is he a hopeless case? Or has he an unconscious resentment of doctors?'

'He is determined to go his own way, sir. He imagines everyone is trying to change him.'

'When did he first get this suspicion? It is not easy to cure. We find it nowadays in patient after patient.'

'He's much better than he used to be, sir. At first, he wouldn't even speak to *me*.'

'And now?'

'Now, he trusts me.'

'Why? Are you a trained nurse?'

Tray goes into convulsions. 'Of course not!' she screams. 'I'm a Land Girl.'

'Then why are you so interested?'

'*Because*,' says Tray tartly, blushing.

'Surely you don't ever expect him to become *marriageable*, do you?'

'And why not?'

'But, my dear, he's just like an animal. How could a pretty little frigate like you think of marriage with such a sunken wreck? I think I can guess, as a matter of fact. You believe that he is not what he appears to be. You think that deep inside there is quite another Towzer. I wonder what it's like. Something rather *soigné*, d'you think?'

Tray blushes.

'I must say, if his nose were wet I'd think him a dog.'

'I'm afraid I spoil him like one.'

'Is he grateful?'

'Not a bit. He's a real man.'

'Perhaps he knows you're trying to change him.'

'But I'm not. I only want him to be himself.'

'Yes, dear, I know, but there are always two views on what that is. And is he not rather *old*?'

'Good heavens, no!'

'How do you tell? By looking at his teeth? Or does he have annual rings?'

'He's only *playing* old, sir. He's sharp as a young fox underneath.'

'Give me an instance.'

'Well, the other evening, he did his sums so well that I gave him a big kiss and showed him how pleased I was. Next morning, he came down to breakfast wearing his pants on his head.'

'What did he mean? "Keep off the Grass"?'

'He was afraid I'd found out who he really was. When I said, "There's only one man in the world who would come down like that," he whipped off the pants in a flash.'

'So. Well, you'll get him tagged yet, I don't doubt. Does he know you belong to another sex?'

'He knows I don't belong to his, but that's as much as he'll admit.'

'Have you tried tears on him?'

'It would be water off a duck's back, sir. He hasn't got his guilt back yet.'

'Well, I don't think I have any useful advice to give you. You seem to have the case well in hand. I only wish that we of the medical profession had more of the enterprise of you young women. You seem to understand your male cases so much better. Just one more question: do you have any idea what identity will emerge from him?'

'I've only noticed one or two suggestive things, sir. He winces at the sound of a bell. He is never punctual. He hates to have things neatly laid out. He doesn't mind short jobs, but if they get long or complicated he throws up his hands and walks out.'

'That sounds like a plumber.'

'Oh dear! I couldn't have that. I want it more intellectual. Some sort of civil servant, I thought.'

'I don't think the symptoms are suitable.'

'Then I probably imagined them.'

'Yes. I am sure that if you persevere you will find ones that are more in harmony with your hopes. We often find that, in our work. Tell me quite frankly now: what do you *most* hope to find he is evading? What figure do you dream is concealed in this shaggy marble?'

'I would be the happiest woman in the world, sir, if he turned out to be a matinee idol, trying to escape from it all.'

'Well, why not? Has he any bent suggestive of the stage? Apart from his love of flowers, of course.'

'He takes readily to poetry, sir. Anything with a beat and no exact meaning excites him.'

'Why not try him in a play, then? I am sure Dr Mallet would have no objection.'

'None whatever,' says the captain. 'Like all doctors, I always regret that I am so busy with serious matters that I have no time for art.'

'If I could persuade the kitchen staff to help . . .' says Tray excitedly.

'I'm sure there are many volumes of Shakespeare in the library,' says the captain. 'I assume Shakespeare would be your choice.'

'So there you are, young lady,' says the President. 'The rest is up to you.'

They move on and leave her quite delighted. The members, too, are impressed and happy with the interview. Each has already set the great organ of his brain to work on the case and found how neatly it may be tooled to his speciality. The President takes Stapleton's left ear and gives it a napoleonic tweak. 'And what did *you* think?' he asks.

'I thought it very *sad*, sir,' says Stapleton frankly.

'Sad, eh? And what was sad?'

'Just the whole situation, sir. It seems so – so – *irremediable*.'

The members chuckle. 'We shall have to cheer you up,' says the President. 'Put your wits to work. Who do you think that man was, or is, or will prove to be?'

'I suppose that's in the lap of Tray, sir.'

'Quite so. So our question really is: who is Tray?'

'I think she is a nurse, sir.'

'Indeed? Why?'

'She wasn't syringing that rose at all. She was washing his hair. And her duplicity was so ruthless. Although her lip had a tremulous quaver, her forearm was like iron. I felt I was back in that R.A.F. hospital.' He shudders at the memory.

'I think you are cheating, my boy. You saw the words St Thomas's Hospital Nurses Hockey Team written on her belt.'

'Now you are teasing me, sir.'

'Perhaps I am. But let us assume you are right. What victim would arouse such ardour in a nurse?'

For a moment Stapleton is puzzled; then suddenly he cries: 'Oh, of course, now I see! How blind I am!'

'Are we right, Mallet?' asks the President.

'Absolutely right. We got him at the local surgery.'

They all give Stapleton a hearty clap, and he beams and blushes all over, quite delighted. He strides ahead of the others to enjoy his triumph alone, and when, a moment later, he relives the scene at the rose-bed, all the sadness has departed from it. It has become quite a brilliant scene, in fact, with all the roses in full bloom and himself rising high like a lily in the centre of them.

Father Orfe walks ahead and catches Stapleton up. He puts a paternal arm on his shoulder and starts a conversation. Suddenly the same idea strikes Dr Shubunkin and Mr Jamesworth, and they, too, hurry forward and lay their arms affectionately around Stapleton's remaining vacant spaces.

'That boy will go far,' murmurs the captain to the President, as they watch Stapleton being moved forward on eight legs.

'It would seem so. May I have a word with you in private?'

'Of course, sir. Club trouble?'

'As usual.'

'I am sorry to hear it. Of course, they are always frisky when case-histories are in the air.' He signs to Beaufort to take over the duties of host, and conducts the President to the breakfast-room.

*

The old fellow is out of sorts. He peers through the key hole to see if anyone is in the passage. He takes a chair between two windows. He says, 'I'm afraid I am not myself, Mallet. The fact is, the Club has been most restless lately. Young Stapleton is not being embraced by his elders for nothing.'

'Surely we expect that, sir? Every club has its factions. Every faction goes recruiting.'

'Let me tell you something. Father Orfe has taken to blasphemy.'

'*Blasphemy!* But when he is not drunk, he is the most pious of men.'

'No more. I take for granted that every cistern in the Club should be blocked with a priest's empties and that dead men should be found in rows every time his mattress is turned. Priests must have some way of showing how dependent we all are on grace. But to become an atheist as well . . .'

'Have you discussed it with him, sir?'

'A month ago I called him in and had a sharp talk. I said I had nothing against his drinking, but the atheism was quite unnecessary. I reminded him that a priest must have *some* religious side and that he was becoming top-heavy by taking up still another opposite.'

'What was his answer?'

'He accused me, in the blandest way, of being old-fashioned. He tells me proudly that in addition to drinking and blaspheming he is contemplating suicide. He insists that all this has made him vastly more redeemable than he used to be.'

'One sees his point, of course.'

'Does one? I didn't. I simply summoned a Rules Committee. I thought it best to choose a chairman who was not – well – not *too* symphathetic to the Orfe faction, if you know. . . .'

'Quite, quite; one has to do that.'

'I chose Shubunkin. He, as you well know, is our sex member: there is nothing, from a rise in the bank rate to a fishing-smack, which he cannot sexually explain. For years, he has analysed Orfe's asceticism in language that I would rather not repeat. I was confident that for once he would make a good chairman. Indeed, frankly, I hoped that he would give Orfe such a drubbing that the two of them would become more deadly factional than ever – always so much easier for a president, you know.

'Judge of my horror when Shubunkin read his committee's report. They gave Orfe a clean slate and even commended him. Moreover, Shubunkin let fall a hint that the Orfe method might well be followed by others. Surveying the Orfe territory, Shubunkin declared that it was now a well-known fact that atheism and alcoholism were primary evidences of a Christian society. He saw no reason why suicide should not be equally desirable, as a means of emphasizing the sacred nature of human life. He concluded with a *most* disturbing passage. Applying the Orfe method to his own speciality, he concluded that sexual intercourse was the primary element in chastity and virginity. No, I have that wrong. It was the other way round. Chastity and virginity were forms of sexual intercourse. He hinted that he intended to follow up this fruitful line – in other words, that he was damned if he was going to let sex lag behind Christianity. The whole Club is seething with it, and I am most upset.'

'Have you tackled Shubunkin, sir?'

'I could hardly do so when I had myself selected him to tackle Orfe. The whole business dumbfounds me: never would I have imagined an alliance between the club ascetic and the club sexualist. We have had members who despaired of maintaining a clear-cut identity and who were helped to choose new ones more in keeping with their abilities.

III

We have had members who dallied with the temptation to be their own opposites and were consequently more than ever true to type. But this new development is something different. It is anarchy. Imagine its being taken up by the whole club! We would all become unrecognizable.'

'It is not an idea that spreads easily, sir. Most members would see it as a diminution of the chosen self.'

'Alas! it will not be presented to them as that. It is Orfe's contention that one is never *more* oneself than when one is *not being* oneself. This absurd idea has struck him like a ray of light. He is enveloped by it. What you don't seem to understand, Mallet, is that once such an idea emerges, *all* the factions are bound to take it up. They simply can't afford to be backward in an intellectual advance. If the identity is to be recognizable only by its paradoxical opposite, well then, every faction is going to start playing opposites. You know where *that* will lead. Members will begin to feel *guilty*. And I refuse absolutely to preside over a *guilty club*.'

'You don't think they are just a little bored, sir?'

'But they are Tories to a man, Mallet – the more so because they think themselves pioneers. What they love about our great theory is that it is absolutely unchangeable.'

'Perhaps you can joke them out of it.'

'I am much too old for that. I am going to be iron-handed with them. If I joke, it will be to pain, not please. A faintly bored urbanity has been my usual means of self-expression, but I see no reason why a president should not be exceedingly sharp, canny, and unpleasant. Do you?'

'I would only warn against your fighting their paradoxes with one of your own.'

'I am very angry about this. After many battles, I had looked forward to a comfortable last decade in the presidential chair.'

'That is a typically presidential hope, is it not, sir?'

'It is. I am sure my predecessor held it strongly, poor fellow. The trouble was, he was unable to rise to the last, decisive battle. Well, I must leave you or they will think I have been talking behind their backs.'

'I see there has been a change in our schedule.'

'Yes. None of our foreign members this year. Only ourselves.'

'That seems odd.'

'The Americans have written a very vague letter saying that they are having to testify before some committee and think it wiser not to ask for passports. Apparently there is some new movement afoot over there, according to which no change in identity is permissible after a certain age. One of our members was a bar-tender at the age of twenty-three, and it appears that he must remain a twenty-three-year-old bar-tender, despite the fact that he is now fifty-four and vice-president of a shoe company. . . . As for the French members, they say they would rather not leave the country because they may be called upon at any moment to form a *government*. It sounds too ridiculous. Either I am getting old or the world is getting very odd. Why, when I first became a member of this club, each man's identity was absolutely clear. The two clergy members were unmistakable clergymen: I never even saw them drunk. Our statistician lived only for statistics; our brigadier-general was quite uninterested in art, as was our Marxist. No one ever saw the Club economist playing the violin, or the literary critic gardening. I was the first to welcome the amusing notion of opposing tendencies and have always taken for granted that the heart should be gnawed by that which it has removed. But look at what it has all led to – this tolerance! Between you and me, Mallet, we should never have allowed Orfe to start drinking.'

*

Four days pass before the Club session begins because there is much preliminary work to be done. The session would be pretty empty if it consisted of nothing but the transmission of ideas: something must be added to relieve the tedium, and this is supplied by a collection of devices which keeps every member of the Club so passionately active that he forgets the end to which it is all directed. Committees are set up to deal with stenography, catering, hours, schedules, rules of procedure, etc. Each committee must have a secretary; each secretary must have an assistant; each assistant must have a typewriter; each typewriter must have something to type. As the Club is a small one, most members are obliged to serve on more than one committee: this means that the secretary of one committee is frequently the assistant to the secretary of another committee; or the typewriter of, say, the Catering Committee can be used by this body only at hours when the Hours Committee has not designated it for use by the Rules Committee. All this leads to misapprehension and quarrelling, and there is no doubt that none of the Committee-men would carry on the struggle at all if they were not conscious of the presence, in the bedrooms overhead, of the Club intellects straining every brain-fibre to produce histories of attenuated merit. And the histories will not, of course, merely be read aloud and then forgotten: on the contrary, each will be read aloud a second time in French, by a member of the Translation Committee, after which it will be mimeographed, in both versions, by the Duplication Committee and copies handed round for all members to explore a third time. Information on all matters must not only be handed in pamphlet form to each member (including those who wrote the pamphlet) but be pinned to a cork board in the hall and given *in advance* to all committees so as to avoid schedular confusion. To youngsters like Stapleton, who are pining for the bilious thrills of intellectual dispute, much of this subsidiary work seems dull and even unnecessary. But even Stapleton has to confess what a *difference* four days of scurrying makes to the *atmosphere*: it is impossible to say that nothing is happening when every member of the Club has mimeographed sheets sticking out of all his pockets, and at every meal every cruet supports some fresh order or rule that every man must study if his letters are to be posted, his slop-pail emptied, his history read, his Ovaltine brought to his night-table. At all hours of the day, a little cluster of members is round the bulletin board; and there is no more disappointing sight in human life than that of an ardent man running to read the latest bulletin and finding only the few score old ones that he knows by heart.

But the main importance of all this work is that it makes every man-jack of the Club discover anew that he is *identified* with the Club and, without it, would probably have no identity at all. Each time he reads a fresh bulletin he has the impression that he is reading his autobiography. Moreover, he is secretly convinced that he himself is the mainspring of the Club, that it is round his identity that the Club's identity is built. If he is one of the intellectuals, he takes for granted that the history which he is now dragging-out is what makes the Club the brilliant thing it is. If he is merely a stupid secretary, he believes that without the innumerable orders, rules, and schedules that he is promulgating, the high-brows upstairs would soon be in a pickle. It is in this way that great bodies of men act in concert to move mountains:

though few have seen a mountain, all are capable of movement. Their identities become manifold: each man is magnified, first, by his identification with the Club; second, by his membership in a faction of the Club; third, by his pivotal position in being the one on whom everything depends; fourth, by the stimulating increase in sense-of-identity that is generated by the other three causes all working hysterically together. No wonder that after only four days every member feels that he has lived at Hyde's Mortimer all his life. Not even in nightmare does he hear the roar of the angry, winter sea and imagine its castellated waves sweeping him and his friends off the face of the earth for ever.

*

That all the struggle, suffering, and self-discipline is worthwhile is evident on the morning of the fifth day. The parquet floor of the old hall is covered by lines of wooden chairs joined together at the top, so that if one member shifts forward in his seat he carries, if he is able, a dozen with him. The intellectual members are already drooped in these chairs, their faces white and fallen, their finger-tips brushing the floor, evidence of the efforts they have put out and the benzedrine they have taken in. A few, like Stapleton, are quivering on the edges of their seats reading sheaves and sheaves of mimeography over and over for the umpteenth time: they are the children who will go completely mad if the party doesn't start soon. The older members, with records of twenty annual sessions, enter the hall with the utmost calm, and gravely press past the knees of those who are already seated, to chairs which experience has shown them are the best. Others stand by the wall, talking in low voices and sometimes smiling, and it is here that one notices particularly the secretaries of the various committees. Like the intellectuals, they are in a state of exhaustion, but they show by their tense expressions that they are not yet able to relax. Only when the first speaker has gone to the rostrum and intoned the first words of his depressing message to humanity will these devoted harbingers of thought drop suddenly into their chairs and let the bowstrings of their minds so slacken that they could not fire even a dart of inked paper.

The President is heard to cough in an adjacent corridor, at which the rest of the Club makes haste to take its seats. He enters the hall, mounts the rostrum, and, rubbing his white hands together, addresses the Club as follows:

'Lady and gentlemen. This is our fortieth annual session, which means that for forty years, at great expense of time *and money*, we have gathered annually to hear speeches from those of us who believe they have something to say. Forty years – it is really a long time, as you will see if you calculate the money spent on a single session, and then multiply by forty. I was doing this in bed last night, and the total made my mouth water. I am sure it has been worth it, though I must say that when I look back over the thirty sessions I have attended, all I can remember of them is the funny bits. I cannot recall a single word spoken in gravity and mimeographed in solemnity. Nonetheless, the mere fact of having endured these agonies assures me that for thirty years I have enjoyed a continuing identity. Surely this is the purpose of an intellectual session – not to exchange views but to reaffirm our self-conceptions?

'There was a time when our patients served the same purpose. When I first joined this club our great theory was in a fluid condition. So, in consequence, was my identity. We had to build both our case-histories and autobiographies upon patients who showed promise of corroboration. But as the theory grew stronger, so did the patient become more and more superfluous. We began to think it intolerable that we should be expected to spend years ploughing a single patient under. We rebelled against servitude to men and women whose condition had been diagnosed to perfection years before they ever entered our consulting-rooms. Often a full twelve-month passed before a patient would even *dream* in a manner worthy of the great theory on which he was stretched – and this despite the fact that he had been assured repeatedly that he was the son of the theoretician. It is my private view that this let-me-be-your-father approach was a most unhappy, academic mistake: if there is one person to whom no one in his right mind admits his shortcomings, it is his papa. How short and relatively painless the history of psychiatry would be today if, beginning in the first couch, the analyst had pretended to be his patient's mistress!

'I could talk endlessly about the *nuisance* of patients. We all felt like dentists who had created plates or bridges of pure gold to the most cunning designs and were obliged to sit and wait for the appropriate jaws to come in. We were as judges who had already pronounced sentence; only the criminal remained at a distance. I have myself often been obliged to sit on a completed case for years, simply for want of a suitable person. Moreover, there was the problem of what to do with a patient after he had been used. I have known Club-members who kept-on their used patients for ten and more years, purely out of kindness, for they were of no value to anyone. They had been restored to health many years before, as a glance at their now-dusty histories proved. They had a perfect grasp of themselves and of what had been missing from them before. And yet they were eternally dissatisfied. They seemed to have no idea what to do. They lacked all sense of direction. One had constantly to remind them that they were fit to make their own decisions and lead active, useful lives.

'Our first step to freedom was to depersonalize the patient by calling him Mr X. or Miss Y. There is nothing like algebra in this respect. It really gives the brain a chance. But it was no final solution: our equation still had to wait for an X or Y before it could be printed in a book. So, in the end, we got rid of the patient altogether. We keep only enough to bring us in a small income and solve the servant-problem. We write our case-histories with a purity of invention and ingenuity impossible in the days when someone was always coming into the room. But this is where I wish to make my warning. I must remind you that liberty must not breed laziness. I expect the histories we are about to hear to be of a high order. They must be plausible. The invented patients must sound like real people. Any personal whims must be properly contained, not only within the theory but within the bounds of possibility. Absurd paradoxes of human behaviour, for example, must be brilliantly presented if they are to be effective. Patients who have three or more personalities, all ambiguous, must be at least six times more real than patients with only a single, undivided personality. All neuroses must be traced back to infantile origins of a truly -childlike kind and not give the impression of having been found in a library by a Red Indian at his wits' end. This is the challenge, gentlemen. I shall be sharp with any reader who fails to meet it.'

Members had barely had time to conceal their resentment when Dr Bitterling, author of the opening history, sprang to his feet and read loudly from a manuscript. 'I was the third of eight children,' he exclaimed, 'born into an upper-middle-class milieu. My father was prone to tantrums; my mother slept in an elm-coffin. I mention elm because . . .'

'Dr Bitterling!' cried the President, 'you don't imagine we are going to sit patiently through *that*? I see you have one finger tucked into your manuscript some hundred pages further on. Kindly start again at the top of that page.'

The doctor gnashed his teeth.

'Come on, now!' cried the President.

' . . . came back from the war, my four aunts were unrecognizable,' read Dr Bitterling sulkily.

'Much, much more promising,' said the President. 'Any fool can fill in the usual preamble.'

'I hate to waste a whole hundred pages,' complained Dr Bitterling. 'They represent many tedious hours of invention.'

'That is what we fear. By the way, *which* war was it he is coming back from? No, no, don't tell me; never mind. They're all the same.'

Dr Bitterling began again:

The Case of the Co-Warden of the Badgeries

By H. M. Bitterling, M.A.

. . . aunts were unrecognizable. You, who have just heard in detail about my sensitive nature and the many years I had lived abroad, can imagine that the transmogrification of aunts would be the last straw. So often in the expatriate years I had pictured them as I knew them to be – four faded tweed skirts, seen from behind bent over like a row of beer barrels with their heads invisible among beds of flowers. Thus remembered, they were a symbol of the England I loved: it was these tumulous postures I had gone to war to maintain. And now, it was as if these barrels had rolled over, risen up, turned their faces towards me and revealed their true identities for the first time.

You have heard what the loss of Priscilla meant to me. I had only just got over it when I saw my aunts afresh. In view of my agony over Priscilla, you may think that the change in aunts was an anti-climax. You are wrong. The metamorphosis of an aunt hits a man far harder than the immorality of a fiancée. An aunt is more than a relation; she is part of the background by which a man identifies himself. One slightly-modified aunt is enough to disturb the pattern of a nephew: a total alteration in four aunts robs him of virtually every means of self-appraisal. When we are small we are stood against a particular door and, year by year, our increase in stature is defined upon it. The day comes when we find the door has been removed, taking our definition with it. My four aunts were that door.

They had all become chain-smokers. Their tufted, leathery skins, once lovable in their goatish simplicity, had become like hams hung in a chimney, and in the looser parts quite corrugated in a reptilian way. Tender remarks fell dead to the ground on striking these tanned hides. Their teeth were yellower and more jagged than ever, and though they claimed to have National Health sets in the offing, some sixth· sense told me that these would remain forever unclaimed. They greeted me, the returned soldier, with the utmost casualness, like old campaigners acknowledging the return of a playboy. They were all reading catalogues of an auction sale, apparently their only interest in life. When I said: 'So you're not living at lovely old Rose Close any more? What has happened to the old place?' one of them swivelled her fag to a corner of her mouth and asked the others: 'Who *has* got it now, anyway? Broadbent got rid of it to Fowler. Tench tells me that Fowler's sounding out McCready.' At this they all laughed uproariously, and then looked me up and down like hags from the netherworld, bursting with revolting secrets. When I asked after my four uncles, their husbands, they said: 'Somewhere in the *garden,* I expect,' with contempt in their voices: and indeed, I found two of them in the borders, replacing the beloved old perennials with what they called 'labour-saving shrubs', and the other two in the kitchen, washing and drying-up. I would have stayed with these crushed, defeated men, gladly exchanging with them laments for the old days, were it not that my aunts' signatures were essential to my new job: ' . . . also of four Gentlewomen of decent habits' said the old Badgeries' application-form. So I got into the Land-Rover with my aunts and we went rushing off to the auction – down beech-avenues which no longer existed, past houses which regularly changed hands once a year and sometimes twice in twenty-four hours. At all such things my aunts cast quick, calculating looks and bellowed to each other the probable rise or fall in value since the last sale. Where once they had toiled to beautify the landscape, they now laboured to estimate its commercial worth. One of them, Aunt Mildred, seeing the disgust on my face, screamed at me: 'We're not going down with the ship *this* time! No gentility! We're all tradesmen now!' At this, they all cackled hideously, and one of them bellowed: 'No devaluation of *our* war loans *this* time!' and a third shouted: 'Dead or live stock, *we* don't care!' The fourth screamed: 'No compost for us: let the dead bury the dead – and that means the men!'

The Corn Exchange was filled to bursting. My aunts fell into Indian file and walked straight to the auctioneer's table, crushing scores of feet, bruising a hundred ribs in their ruthless passage. They removed from a Sheraton side-table a pile of hideous jugs, basins, and lamp-shades, and sat on top of it. It made a dreadful crackling noise. Aunt Mildred inserted a powerful finger-nail under a corner of the veneer and contemptuously prized it off. The other three rested their heels on its brasswork, shifting to other edges when a piece snapped.

I had always loved an auction, but this one was strange to me. I cannot describe to you the intensity of feeling that filled the hall – the grimness, the unshakeable determination. The pallor of the young post-war husbands, out to furnish the hard-won cottage or flat, was in no way as terrifying as the cold-steel ferocity in the faces of their wives. Every chair, sofa, cabinet, table – some 300 lots in all – was occupied by bodies: at least a hundred women sat silently knitting: I think they were there just for the sake of company and excitement, as at a public execution. Above them all, raised behind a kitchen table, sat the auctioneer; and at his elbow sat his assistant – calm, quiet, and beautiful, her eyes following each bid with detached precision. I fell in love with her on the spot: how can anyone resist a creature so hard-boiled that she resembles a statue of purity? Her cleanliness alone assured me that she was incapable of passion; but it made no difference. I only looked round the hall for some object I could buy, and thus make friends with her.

'Lot 97,' said the auctioneer, 'is an Axminster carpet of blue and red design with a yellow cruciform centre. It measures 13 by 10 and is in excellent condition. Now, ladies and gentlemen, you know as well as I do that such a carpet will reach thirty pounds. Don't, I beg you, oblige me to begin with bids of two pounds ten and that sort of thing. Start me at least at twenty, ladies and gentlemen, and then we'll all be able to go home and mow our lawns and cook our hubbys' suppers.'

My aunts roared with laughter and drummed their heels. The auctioneer raised his ivory hammer and directed upon his audience the keen look of a retriever. They looked back at him in square silence; my aunts whinnied cynically.

'Very well, ladies and gentlemen,' he said crossly: 'if you are going to be stubborn, it's your funeral. Who will start me at ten?'

'*Shillings!*' cried a firm voice. Roars of laughter and clapping rang through the hall.

'Very well,' said the auctioneer, 'we won't bother with this lot, ladies and gentlemen. We will go on to Lot 98. Jenkins, remove 97.'

Not even an adept Jenkins can remove quickly a 13 by 10 Axminster with five adults, a baby, and two dogs on it. Out of sympathy for Jenkins, therefore, a dealer cried chirpily 'Three pounds!' – and turned away as if that completely disposed of the matter.

'Three!' groaned the auctioneer. 'I am bid three pounds, ladies and gentlemen. Very well. Leave it, Jenkins. We will take the long, slow, uphill road. Who gives me five? You, sir? Five, I have – six – seven – eight – nine – ten – eleven – twelve – thirteen – fourteen – fifteen – sixteen – seventeen – eighteen – nineteen – twenty – oh, ladies and gentlemen, how much time we would save if you were a little more sensible! – twenty-one – guineas – twenty-one guineas I have, twenty-two – twenty-three – twenty-four – we are still in guineas – twenty-five – twenty-six – any advance on twenty-six guineas? Twenty-seven – twenty-eight – twenty-nine . . . I am stopped at twenty-nine. I am stopped. I am stopped. Stopped, stopped, stopped. No advance on twenty-nine guineas? No advance? I am stopped in twenty-nine guineas . . . Last chance. . . . '

All this time I had been watching the bidders with immense interest. Human nature is so nonsensical that it entangles even the simplest act in ridiculous complications. Thus, at an auction, the main idea is to bid without seeming to do so, on the grounds that if one is not actually seen bidding, no one will notice that any interest is being taken in the lot, whose evident steady increase in value is then attributed to supernatural causes. At the best auctions everyone sits in their best clothes and never shows the least interest; as if they were in church: only a change from red to amber in one eye indicates that another thousand pounds is going down the drain. But at vulgar, provincial auctions the disguise is more crude. All the dealers, for instance, pretend they are tramps and imbeciles. They lean against bits of furniture with their mouths wide open, their stubbled chins dropped in innocent vacancy. Each cultivates an identity which has no bearing whatever on the matter in hand: like most of the furniture in the auction, it is simply a professional fabrication whose whole aim is to pretend to be what it is not. Thus, one dealer bids by seeming to burst into tears; another uses his left shoulder, which works up and down like a pump; a third allows a brief convulsion to electrify his frame; a fourth uses nothing but his winged nostrils; a fifth, who learnt to wiggle his ears in boyhood, now finds that each ear is capable of elevating a pound sterling. All these ludicrous tricks, which deceive nobody, are imitated by the general public, much as laymen who have read newspapers and listened to politicians become accustomed to expressing themselves in meaningless terms. My aunts' bidding methods, for example, were totally ridiculous: they twitched and shrugged, made secret, obscene motions with their dirty thumbs, and managed in the twinkling of an eye to run their faces through all the manifold expressions of four men shaving in a hurry. Since I have met Dr Bitterling, I understand that all such nonsense has nothing whatever to do with commerce and is simply a means of 'telling yourself who you are' – to use his wise words. But when one has stood a short while in a large hall packed with human beings all going through a twitching charade – oh! then, what a joy it is to hear an honest, desperate cry, the screamed bid of some simpleton who genuinely wants the object that is being auctioned and who fears that if both arms are not raised and the clenched catalogue furiously waved the auctioneer will be deaf and blind to the appeal!

All this was running through my mind as the auctioneer was crying with feigned misery: 'I am stopped in twenty-nine guineas! I am stopped! Last chance, ladies and gentlemen. . . . '

I took another quick glance at his assistant, and screamed:

'Thirty pounds!'

What a bellow of laughter went up! 'We are in *guineas*, sir!' cried the auctioneer, joining heartily in the laughter: 'Where is your arithmetic, sir? You must bid thirty-one pounds to advance. Do you give me thirty-one in pounds? You do? Then I am in pounds again, ladies and gentlemen; thirty-one pounds: any advance on thirty-one? . . . Who will return me to guineas . . . ?'

Nobody would. The hammer fell: the carpet was mine. It was not my bid but my bad arithmetic that won me the carpet: nobody wanted to start twitching again after laughing so much. But how ashamed I was of my innocence – and how furious were my aunts! I had disgraced the family, and as I sheepishly met my aunts' indignant eyes, I realized how greatly the standards of the gentry had changed during my absence abroad. They stared at me as if I had broken every one of the old moral rules – cheating, lying, disloyalty, kissing-and-telling. It would have made it worse for me to excuse my mistake by saying that it wasn't the carpet I had bid for but the auctioneer's assistant: they would have expected me to get *her* for nothing. I now glanced furtively and saw that she was looking at me in quite an amused way, as if she had found a tortoise in her bedroom or a kitten in her shoe. Thank God, I said to myself, for women's mercy: if I had just twitched my bid like a real man, that gentleness would never be in her eyes!

I pressed forward and told her my name: she noted it delicately in her big book. 'I am not very used to auctions,' I said humbly, writing out a cheque. She smiled in a kindly way, so I pressed on, despite the din of Lot 98, and said: 'In fact, I'm afraid I'm an awful simpleton where money is concerned.' This is not true, of course; but my idea was, as Dr Bitterling has since explained in his clear way, 'to press upon her an identity to which she had already shown herself receptive'. He calls this 'limp seduction' and says that it is usually the best way to approach emancipated women. 'One does not take a tin-opener to frozen vegetables,' he explains.

'Are there many more of these compliments to you, Dr Bitterling?' asked the President.

'Quite a lot. I thought it would be dishonest to take them out.'

'Well, turn over half a dozen honest pages and go on from there.'

' . . . back to London breathless and exhausted. I found Vinson slumped in a chair and told him I had the signatures. I also told him about my aunts.

'I found exactly the same thing,' he said: 'The whole cat's cradle has fallen apart. I could forgive them if they'd died while we were away; but the fact is that they have remained studiously alive. In the old days there was never any question as to who one was: our names alone identified us, and where there was any doubt, one always had correct pronunciation to fall back on. One was related to *everything* – even oddities like Roman Catholics. Why, I remember that if I'd forgotten how to pronounce a word, I used often to have to take the opposite side in an argument, in order to avoid mispronouncing the truth.'

'Yes,' I said, 'I knew a man in the war who was asked by an artilleryman to name a certain unpronounceable objective, and he felt obliged to give the name of quite another village rather than be a traitor to his class.'

'Exactly. And it's that spirit that's been destroyed. One comes home with the keys and finds all the locks have been changed. All the initials have gone from inside the bowler hats. All the value's gone out of the currency. There's no meaning in the church bells, no punch left in the hyphens of surnames. I don't like it at all. If I don't get an identity soon I shall start looking as helpless and vacant as everyone else.'

'They had a difficult time, of course.'

'That's no excuse. I can forgive them for giving up their houses and utterly smashing the whole geographical web of family relationships, but I'll not forgive them for throwing away all the old phrases they brought us up on. "What's so nice about him," they always used to say of a gardener or a shopkeeper, "is that you can be nice to him without his ever becoming familiar." Today, they'd be begging him to buy their windfalls. All the furtive pretences for which we fought have been thrown away out of boredom.'

When I looked at his drawn face I felt great pity for him – a man who now had nothing but his own resources to save him from total obscurity. 'Why,' he said bitterly, 'I think I have reached the point where I am not even embarrassed at speaking my name aloud. That shows how meaningless it has become.'

'When do we see Channing?'

'We'll go now,' he said, reaching for his hat.

'Are you going to go on wearing a hat? People don't any more.'

'It's the last ditch. Aut hat, aut nihil.'

Old Channing received us gently in his rooms at the Armoury. It heartened Vinson to be met at the door by a pikeman crying some old warning dating back to the twelfth century and to be taken upstairs by a servant in the jet livery of the Coffiners. 'I am surprised,' said Channing, 'to find that you have not changed your minds. Many well-bred young men nowadays would feel the Badgeries was a waste of time. Have you your ladies' signatures?'

'We have,' said Vinson. 'Though why a signature should remain valid when its author hasn't, is more than I can say.'

'And the eighteen peppercorns? No, don't give them to me: you hand them in a calico bag to the Master of the Bowmen on Lady Day. Remind me to remind the *Times* photographer.'

'When do we start work?' asked Vinson. 'We are both very anxious to identify ourselves with the real England.'

'Well, I don't know that you'll find very much *work* to do,' said Channing. 'The point is to capture the *spirit* of the thing.'

'That's exactly what we intend to do,' said Vinson.

'Well, it's not difficult,' said Channing. 'Centuries ago, the Co-Wardens held every badger in the land and they still do, technically, but with no badgers involved any more. It is up to you two to create, as it were, within yourselves, a sense of duty and responsibility to badgers which no longer exist. You have the livery, which is always a help, and there is a tradition of 800 years standing shoulder to shoulder with you.'

'Is there no immediate badger whatever?' demanded Vinson. 'An occasional glimpse of one would serve as a foundation, though I admit that invisibility is a higher and more splendid challenge.'

'There is a token badger, but according to tradition it is maintained by the Yeomen of Hertford Forest. It is a stuffed one, of course.'

'I suppose they let us take it on ceremonial occasions.'

'Not the actual, token badger, except on the death of the Lord Royal. Normally, you get a clip of artificial fur set in an osier staff. This is an emblem of the token. Thus you retain your technical right to the token badger, and, thereby, to all the living badgers in the country. On the other hand, your osier staff is the symbol of your having waived this prerogative. There is much philology involved, I'm afraid, but the office is ancient and the nation would be poorer without it. That is why you are not paid for it – except for the symbolic dog-rose presented to you annually by the Knights of Egham.'

'In short,' said Vinson, 'what is not symbolic is emblematic?'

'Except where it is token,' agreed Channing. 'Then, it is stuffed.'

'Quite so. Which of these – token, symbolical, or emblematical – applies to our annual ritual of Easing the Badger?'

'I think all three elements are involved. The stuffed, or token, boar-badger is inserted into a symbolic den and then eased out with your official emblem, a symbolical gold spade. In this way, there is no need actually to disturb any living badger: the whole ceremony is performed quietly in London. But I am not *quite* sure; you will have to swot it up. In addition to the Badgeries, I am responsible for the Coffiners, the Datcheries, the Portators, the Body of Threshers, the Royal Key Holders, the Cushion Fashioners, and many other such bodies. It is difficult to remember who does what, when, where, and why. And many of the office-holders are honorary members of some of the other bodies. During the war, in fact, when so many people went abroad, we often had cases of an office-holder assuming the livery of one identity in order to deliver some annual token, and then quickly changing into the livery of the recipient identity in order to receive it. But we try to avoid that sort of thing. Once you start letting your symbolic acts overlap, each tends to deny the significance of the other. That's what's wrong with the Health Service, of course. One minute people think they're getting it free, the next that it is an intolerable burden. They don't know if they're giving or receiving – and if you don't know that it's only a step to manic-depression. That is why these old offices of ours, such as the Badgeries, are so important – much more important as rituals than they were as realities. When you've got a grip on something that really exists and is comprehensible, you don't have to bother with symbols. But once the reality begins to fade, the symbol is needed to recapture it. If all barristers had brains, there would be no need for wigs. Our rituals exist to reassure people that no serious defects are possible, and I hope we will never wake up to find that the life has departed from beneath these symbols, like peas from under thimbles. One can put oneself at too many removes from reality: for instance, it's quite all right to replace a lost material thing with a spiritual symbol, but once you go on to charging that spiritual symbol with a material significance, you get into deep water. So I urge you to hang on to the abstract aspects of the Badgeries. Like old churches, they are nostalgic, photogenic, and give a sense of security to those who hurry past them.'

'It is exactly what I hoped,' said Vinson dreamily. 'By the way, what about the chambers that go with the job? I understand the Wardens have a sort of flat.'

'They used to,' said Channing, 'but the L.C.C. is in it at present and it would be hard to dislodge them.'

Vinson's character, in this painful moment, conquered his disappointment. 'Technically it is still ours?' he asked.

'Certainly. The office of the Badgeries is inseparable from the occupancy of its chambers. So unless you assume that you are living in them, it will be impossible for you to be Co-Wardens. Is that clear?'

'Perfectly clear. The whole thing is a superb challenge to empirical dogma. By the way, in view of the power shortage, are we not also entitled to some kind of fuel?'

'You have sole right to the faggots of Holborn Common. Fleet Street now occupies the site, but if you wish to assert your claim, not Beaverbrook himself can stop you.'

'The claim is warmth enough for me,' said Vinson spiritedly.

'And I,' I cried, 'have bought a *real* carpet!'

'Well, I shall have to boot you out now,' said Channing, getting up. 'I have a few traditional ceremonies to perform.'

'What did you think of him?' Vinson asked me, as the jet Coffiner passed us on to the purple Pikeman.

'He seemed a nice old fellow. Very well up in the subject.'

'You didn't feel he was an opportunist?'

'I think he enjoys the glamour.'

'That's what I mean. The outward trappings matter to him. They don't to me. Even if they took away our hauberks and velveteens I would still be clothed by the essential spirit.'

'What a zealot you are! How are you going to exist?'

'It's quite straightforward. We must both get jobs and a place to live in. We will do our work perfunctorily but punctiliously. The rest of the twenty-four hours we'll devote to our real identities, as Co-Wardens.'

'That's what most people do, isn't it, nowadays?'

'Except that even their real identities are based on material things – hobbies like goldfish and budgerigars. We have something totally abstract.'

'There is no danger of schizophrenia?'

'Schizophrenia indeed! Are you still living in the thirties?'

'Well, a confusion of aims, double identities at cross-purposes?'

'Quite impossible. On the material side we shall have no identities whatever. No aims, no purposes.'

'Will our employers like that?'

'How on earth will they know?'

'They might have a feeling we were insensitive to the firm's needs.'

'You're much too pre-war. People aren't like that any more. How can an employer suspect my identity when he doesn't know his own?'

'There could be a sort of blind-man's bluff. For instance, we know that people who are shy often express it in the most ferocious way. Similarly, people with no identity might well insist on it in their employees.'

'You are absolutely out of touch with the mood of the times. You assume that people still take up certain attitudes, definite selves.'

'Surely we aren't the only two in the whole country who know who we are?'

'Who said we knew? We don't know. We hope to be reborn and find out. We are in a state of becoming. So are all the best people. Everywhere you look in decent circles you see the glow of suspended reanimation.'

'But surely we should know who we are *now*, before we start on a rebirth? I like to know what I'm changing *from*. Here we are, our present selves quite unknown, seeking rebirth in a new identity by means of a vocation consisting solely of symbols. At what point will we impinge upon reality?'

'At the moment when we are apparently most remote from it I can feel a few real twinges already, just by thinking about it. What about you? Don't you already feel a certain inner security?'

'Yes, but I always do when something's been definitely arranged. What upsets me is to discover later that there actually was nothing to arrange. You seem to take so much on trust.'

'It's an answer to materialism. It's a reaffirmation of spiritual, moral, and ethical values.'

*

'So far, so good, Dr Bitterling,' said the President, 'but this is all very heady stuff, you know. I suggest we adjourn for lunch, and that when we resume you stress the love-interest of the history a little more.'

'By all means,' replied Dr Bitterling with a proud blush.

*

'. . . my rapture.'

'I must say,' she replied, smoothing her hair rather pettishly, 'that if

I had known you were going to be so ardent I would never have admitted you to the store-room.' She added curiously: 'What did you say your job was?'

I told her briefly of the Badgeries.

'It sounds like a sort of spiv thing.' For the first time, a note of admiration was in her voice.

We were lying on Lot 41, and I raised myself awkwardly from its dusty cushions. Around us, in the waning light, tier upon tier of bric-à-brac awaited tomorrow's auction.

'My brother's like you,' she said. 'He's got a steady job too, but does his real business on the quiet. But you're the first one I ever met who did it in such high society. Have you got a partner?'

'Oh, Lord, yes. He's the go-ahead one. I knew him in the Army.'

'It's always that way, isn't it? Someone you know you can trust. But where does the money really come from?'

'We have rights in Holborn. And a flat goes with the job, of course.'

'A *flat* ?' Her breath came a little faster. She put her hand on my arm and asked in a mere whisper: 'Vacant possession?'

'There's someone in it now, to tell the truth. But we could claim any time.'

'Most people I know have to get homes the hard way – go on and on looking and looking, studying and studying the faces of old tenants to guess how soon they'll die. My brother judges by the fit of their teeth. The looser they get, the closer the vacancy.'

'Teeth are emblems of freehold.'

'But isn't it funny the way old people cling to life? As my brother says: they've had their time and are ready to go, but instead of getting out of the house and giving the younger people a chance, they persist. And they know very well how impatient we are to see them go.'

'A watched pot never boils. Perhaps there is something about your brother's look which makes every crone resolve to live:

> *There's something in your eyes, chérie,*
> *That makes me sympathize with vie.'*

'How strangely you talk!'

'You should hear my partner.'

'Would he like me?'

'I don't think so. He's too wrapped up in the Badgeries.'

'Who looks after your rooms, then?'

'No one. We give a token scrub occasionally.'

'Is it full of badgers?'

'It's haunted by them. My partner actually sees them.'

'Could I meet him one day? He sounds so interesting.'

'He isn't. There are thousands exactly like him all over the country.'

'Have you quarrelled with him?'

'There's nothing to quarrel about.'

'Don't you sometimes have words?'

'We have little else.'

'About the work?'

'There isn't any work.'

'What *is* there, then?'

'Nothing at all.'

'Aren't you fur-dealers?'

'Yes. But there's no fur.'

She burst into tears.

'Don't cry. If you want to meet Vinson, I'll arrange it.'

*

He was practising the ritual of Easing the Badger. Crossing the room with an incredibly sanctimonious expression, he dropped suddenly on one knee and pressed his Biro into our new carpet. 'Meanwhile, you ease it from behind,' he said.

I went opposite, and gracefully cupping my hands lifted the badger into the air by the buttocks. Vinson rose with both hands outstretched, took it under the forelegs and cried *'Le broc se garde!'* Then he passed it to a Yeoman who took it away to Hertford Forest.

'Better,' he said, 'but still not letter-perfect. We'll know we've got it right when we can actually *feel* the badger.'

'I've found a very nice young girl for the May Day ceremony.'

'What sort of girl?'

'She's an auctioneer's assistant.'

'Are you going to bring filth like that into the Badgeries? She stands for everything in modern life we are being reborn against. What are her qualifications? Is she a well-born virgin?'

'No, she isn't. Don't be a snob about her. According to all I hear, there was a close, familiar tie between classes *in medieval times.*'

'That was because they kept apart. It's one of the simpler paradoxes. There won't be any spiritual and cultural rebirth until the peasant is back in his sty and the gentleman in his library. Your lady friend would do very well for a maypole ceremony, but she's got no business butting in on the Badgeries.'

'I thought we could behave as if.'

'As if what?'

'Surely you know about "as if"?'

'Oh, that.'

'I feel she would give more point than ever to the ceremony if we regarded her as if.'

Vinson was tempted. 'You mean,' he said, 'that it would add yet another symbol to those we already have?'

'More than that. By choosing a woman who is absolutely unsuitable, we would show our scorn for mere physical values.'

'You'll have to clear it with Channing. I can't take the responsibility.'

Channing was most tolerant. 'Use her by all means,' he said. 'It's the spirit that matters. We can't be fussy about the flesh nowadays.'

*

Their first meeting interested me greatly. In Vinson's eyes she was already transformed into a queen of purity; while Vinson, in hers, already represented the prince of wide boys. And yet, these two identities, each so incorrectly shaped in the mind of the other, shared their mutual misunderstanding as happily as if they had known one another for years. The more abstract Vinson became, the more impressed she was by his grasp of what appeared to be high finance. The more excited she became as a result of this, the more Vinson was impressed by her spiritual enthusiasm. He said to her: 'I see, of course, that you are only in your present job in order to make a living. Well, my partner and I are in exactly the same boat. We have to have a job in order to live. But our aspirations are of a very different kind.'

'And so are mine,' she replied warmly.

Later, he said to me: 'About your relations with her. I think you should break off any physical contacts you may have had. For some reason, whenever I start thinking about her symbolical properties, certain properties of yours keep intruding.'

'All we perform is a physical act, Vinson. Were it a ritual one you would have good cause for alarm.'

No doubt you are wondering why I ever introduced her to Vinson in the first place. . . .

'Indeed we are, Dr Bitterling!' exclaimed the President. 'If you can fiddle *that* one, you have a great future.'

. . . and yet there is a very simple answer. Disillusionment in love, with some men, only makes itself felt after a long period of union with the beloved. Sometimes, it is a full thirty years or more before a husband takes a sudden, second look at his wife and says to himself: 'Was this a wise step?' Other men become disillusioned in a matter of months or weeks: but I am one of those persons in whom disillusion begins at the very moment the illusion comes into focus. Even as my pulse begins to race – as it did when I first saw her at the auction – my stomach starts to flag. I see ahead of me those tedious, drawn-out days of courtship, and, beyond them, the indefinite weeks of unmitigated intimacy. My friendship with Vinson was based largely on the difference between us in this respect. Where I was immediately aware of the awful reality of union, Vinson thought only in terms of magic un- reality. He strongly disapproved of my conduct with women, which he considered crude and immature. No sooner had I made a conquest than he arrived on the battlefield and rescued her. This has happened with all the eighteen women who have been in my life, except Priscilla, and it has suited the two of us very well. Vinson loves the slow, uphill pull, the incessant misunderstandings, the effort required to make a normal woman think in terms of pure abstraction. Once he has succeeded, a certain lethargy creeps over him: he has refined the lady to such an extent that she no longer has any reality. Eager to be free, he brusquely reverts to incredible crudity and offers her money to clear out, or introduces her to some other man who, he explains, will suit her much better. I take care to be absent on such occasions: Vinson usually has to visit the local surgery next day with some trumped-up story of a blackberrying accident. Dr Bitterling has since explained to me that both Vinson and I have been immature in our attitudes to women. But that is another story. . . .

On hearing this masterly explanation, the whole Club applauded, and there were shouts of: 'Damned neat, that!'; '*Very* pretty!'; 'What a figure-of-eight!' Flushing happily, Dr Bitterling proceeded:

. . . another story. I will only add a curious point: in retrospect, I think of these eighteen misused women as fairy creatures, symbolic of all that is sublime in womanhood: Vinson, on the other hand, always recalls them as nasty little gold-diggers. What the women think of us, I cannot say, but I imagine that we are what they have in mind when they use the word 'men' with an inflection of hostility.

*

He was very cocky now, going off to bars with his admiring Heloise and showing her off to other men who were seeking rebirth in various ways. At our favourite pub, 'The Coat and Cymbals', we met a fine cross-section of those who nowadays find unusual means of spiritual recapitulation. A number of them, for instance, went in for various kinds of medieval calligraphy, puzzling the postmen with their renascent addresses. All wore hats; but some wore small, curved, bowler hats and arrived at the pub, whatever the weather, in touring cars that had been built in the 1920s: they drank their beer out of old moustache-cups. Many were gardeners, and would grow only roses which had not been seen for some centuries: they were on good terms with those who collect old florins and grew grapes on clay soils. I cannot give a detailed account of all the types: I will only observe that the charm of 'The Coat and Cymbals' lay in the fact that it covered all periods from Thomist to Edwardian, and rejected nothing but the malaise of the present. Vinson was very much at home with these zealots, but he was proud to think that we, as Co-Wardens, existed on an even higher level of renascence. 'A cursive script,' he said, 'is an admirable thing; I have taken it up myself. I also intend to buy a tricycled steam-car, when I can afford one, and a really cursive bowler with raised initials. When I have a garden I shall grow only, and always in compost, Rosa Mundi, Centifolia, and Damascena. But in all such desirable regressions, I shall be dealing with tangible objects. They may be archaic, but they are still real. The glory of the Badgeries is that there is not a single reality left in it: every implement employed in its ceremonies is purely symbolic; every act performed has no pertinence whatever. It is thus an idea wrapped in a tradition; a spiritual nothing existing in a void. One could not ask for more.'

*

A week before May Day, we put on our uniforms for the first time, and I must confess that of the three of us Vinson most represented the spirit of English history and institutions. In his velvet trunks and King of Diamonds blouse, carrying his token spade and looking confidently into the future, he stood for everything whose demise was beyond dispute. We were rehearsing the peppercorn ritual when there was a ring at the bell and a telegram was handed in. It was signed by the Chief Yeoman of Hertford and said: ARRIVING IMMEDIATELY WITH BADGER.

'What's this?' said Vinson angrily. 'May Day doesn't need the badger. It's only paraded at the funeral of the Lord Royal.'

More practical than he, I sprang to the radio and switched it on. Instead of the scheduled talk on insect life there was absolute silence. It was broken soon after by an elegy, or eulogy, I forget which, by Elgar. This could mean but one thing: the Lord Royal *was* dead. Even as we looked out of the window messenger-boys were hurrying by with letters to *The Times*.

Vinson had not known the Lord Royal – a stately, chamberlain-like figure with walrus moustaches – but he knew his finest hour when he saw it. Dashing his peppercorns to the carpet, he flew to the telephone. It was a long time before he could get Channing, who was being phoned, of course, by every symbolic body in the country. On the connexion being made, he saluted Vinson in the Norman-French phrase of grief that is used on this occasion and Vinson replied suitably in broken Saxon. Having thus, as it were, *established* the situation, Channing went on to clarify it. 'There's going to be a frightful scramble,' he said, 'and it's much too early to tell you where you will be in the funeral procession. I am not sure if you have any right to be in it at all, since you have not yet received your Egham rose and will not now be able to do so until after the funeral. But I think we can rush you through a token act of homage and proceed from there on "as if". You know about "as if"?'

'Certainly. We were going to use it for May Day.'

'Of course! I'm sorry to be so forgetful, but the telephone hasn't stopped ringing all day. . . . Anyway, the previous Co-Wardens have

both emigrated to Rhodesia, so there's little doubt about your cred-
entials. And these old institutions of ours are very elastic; one can shove
a fiddle in at any point if necessary. That's an art the Bourbons never
learnt.'

'This is a very solemn occasion,' replied Vinson coldly, 'and we
should like to know the schedule as soon as possible.'

'My dear boy, I am one with you. But it has first to be drafted, then
typed, and then transcribed by hand on to parchment. Only then will
we know what it is, and even then much of the detail will be obscure,
as it will be in Latin – even names like Edgware Road and Cannon
Street.'

'Then we will occupy the interim period pondering the exact *meaning* of the occasion. It has nothing, *au fond,* to do with the Lord Royal's
actual death. That is merely the physical precipitant. It is what his
passing symbolizes in the badger sense that will engage our attention.'

'I'm sure you're right. I'll have to ring off though, I'm afraid.'

Vinson turned and faced us. 'Well,' he said slowly, 'I am going to
have to put my heart and soul into this.'

'Oh, Vinson, darling!' she cried: 'I know you will. And what is *my*
part? I'm *so* thrilled!'

'What d'you mean, *your* part?' he answered crossly. '*You* don't have
a part. This is a funeral. Who ever heard of a connexion between death
and virginity?'

'Come, come, Vinson,' I said, my heart touched by her dismay. 'The
poets have frequently and forcibly likened the two.'

'Only as consubstantial within the frame of a single body. But nothing even remotely connecting the Badgeries with the Lord Royal.
How can you employ a virgin to symbolize a passing? It's a denial of
the whole *sense* of the thing.'

'Then what will I do?' she cried.

'You'd better get back to your auctioneering,' he said. 'It's a good
living, isn't it? If you're short of cash, tell me.'

She pressed her lips together with such terrible vehemence that
when the door-bell rang I thought her mouth had done it. Vinson, who
had already totally forgotten her existence except for a suspicion that
she had just touched him for money, hurried to the door and came
back with a Yeoman – a young man of such attenuation that he seemed
to have been drawn in a single strip from steel rollers.

'I won't stay,' he said, setting down what looked like a gigantic leather hat-box. 'We hardly know which way to turn, everything's such a balls-up. You'll let us have him back after the funeral, won't you? He's wonderfully fit. Here's the transfer pledge.'

Vinson reached for his broad-nib and cursively signed. He stared at the hat-box like a child on Christmas morning.

'Have you got a taxi out there?' she asked the Yeoman. 'I'll share it, if you don't mind.' Women are remarkably quick, sometimes: there was her suitcase, neatly packed, in her hand.

They drove off together and Vinson reverently undid the leather straps. Inside, the badger rested in a neat, wooden scaffolding. Vinson gently eased him and put him in the middle of the carpet.

I have never in my life seen anything more life-like than that badger. How old he was when the Yeoman trapped him in the woods, how long ago he was disembowelled and stuffed, how many centuries of dust had been denied his coat – these questions I cannot answer. I only knew that in modern times we have developed techniques of preservation that would have dumbfounded our forefathers; and that where formerly some priceless relic, animate or inanimate, would have been thrown on the dust-heap, we moderns have so devoted the resources of our science to taxidermy that there is now virtually nothing that is not considerably more lively after death than it was before. Our token badger, who had recently been completely refurnished by a firm which specialized in this kind of work, was a case in point. His fawn-grey hairs, which gave off the most delicate scent of rosemary, honeysuckle, and shampoo, were of such exuberance and vitality that each stood out from its fellows and could be fingered separately. His eyes were velvet masterpieces: one of them, directed to the left, sounded the call of the wild; the other, down-turned to the right, seemed about to weep for the death of its patron and protector. The white badge on his forehead shone with such brilliance that it resembled an antique carving chiselled from a block of snow. Vinson glanced into the box and drew out a silver bowl, one half filled with artificial water, the other with token corn. There was also a real gilt comb, an ivory brush, a box of Qwickit's Dry Shampoo, and some flea-powder – this last a truly significant measure, indicating man's modern ability to make his nostalgia deceptive even to vermin.

When Vinson saw these things, he began to weep; nor can I blame him. For one whose deepest dreams and highest purposes were con-joined in the ecstasy of life-in-death, for one whose only moments of despair came when he trained his telescope on the future and cried: 'I cannot see the symbols!' – for such a man, this perpetuated stuffed corpse stood for more, far more, than the mere office of the Badgeries; it seemed to hold in its mounted paws the fate and destiny of the whole nation.

As I watched, Vinson suddenly stiffened his limbs and groaned; his eyes rolled upwards and he began to twitch with convulsive shudders. I said gently, but with excitement: 'Vinson! Are you being reborn?'

He nodded tersely, reluctant to be distracted, and reached his hands backwards as if grasping a pair of bed-posts. A few seconds later he again groaned, shuddered, slapped himself sharply on the buttocks and let out a high wail. Then, all at once, he became himself again, and lit a Craven A.

I was a little disappointed in his new identity. It was exactly the same as the old one, except that there seemed to be more of it. Sensing my disappointment, he said: 'I suppose you expected a completely exterior transformation. That's not at all what happens. It all takes place within.'

'Are you conscious of the new identity?'

'Certainly. But don't think of it in physical images – as a substance entering and filling an empty space. The old emptiness is still there, but it has been intangibly elucidated.'

'I can't follow that.'

'Of course you can't,' he replied, his voice containing all its old contempt for materialism, but now more forceful and decisive. 'You must *know* it.'

I saw that he had reached that area of inner experience at whose gates language and logic shiver like starvelings. I felt a sharp and hostile envy, and yet I persisted in demanding further explanation.

He laid one hand gently on the badger's head and said: 'The nearest I can get to defining the new identity is to say that the one I lacked previously is now lacking on a much higher level. It's as if with a single leap I had mounted a full flight closer to the Realization of Nothing-ness. But it's silly to try and put these things into words.'

*

The whole life of the nation was suspended for the following week. It is true that auction sales continued in all parts of the country, but no one *spoke* of such continuances, so great was the general absorption in the Lord Royal's discontinuance. As Vinson said: 'It is not his death as a man which counts; it is his procession into an embodiment of that which demands reverence.' It vexed him that the B.B.C., far from emphasizing this crucial aspect of the affair, concentrated on the opposite side: apart from Elgars and elegies they transmitted nothing but eulogies, saying nothing whatever of the new career on which the Lord Royal had now entered. Fortunately, as the days passed, even the wireless was excited by the popular enthusiasm for the funeral, and we heard less and less of the Lord Royal and more and more of his procession.

I think, myself, that there is no greater thrill in life than to see maps of a really big funeral appear in the newspapers. There, before one's eyes, are the drab old streets and avenues of commonplace, everyday life suddenly electrified by the twisting black arrow of death. And when to this human enthusiasm is added the thrill of knowing that one will oneself be following that sombre emblem of direction, that one is already a selected pin-point in that marching host – well, there is not much to live for after that. Vinson and I went about our preparations with a gravity so deep as to be ecstatic: his, of course, being on a higher level of experience than mine, was correspondingly deeper.

The night before the funeral he got stage-fright. We had set the badger up on its gilt trolley, to draw behind us on ropes of silk: we had oiled the wheels and tried on our uniforms with their mourning sashes of sable and saffron. Vinson began to breathe heavily and sweat; twice he got up, consulted the dictionary, shook his head, went out and bought another dictionary, repeated the process, and so on. 'I know it seems completely ridiculous,' he admitted at last, 'but the *sense* of what we are about to do has suddenly escaped me.'

I answered, rather shocked: 'You think it *nonsense*, Vinson?'

'No, no: you misunderstand, as usual. I mean sense in the sense of emotional significance. I cannot adjust my heart to the mood; the inspired nature of the matter escapes me. Moreover, when I decided to withdraw temporarily to the merely commonsense aspect of the matter, even that proved elusive: I was unable to recapture the difference between a symbol and an emblem. The dictionaries have made it worse: they define a symbol as an emblem and an emblem as a symbol, a shameless tautology. Believe me, when one is accustomed to the high fringes of non-lingual mysticism, it is horrifying suddenly to find oneself crawling in the lowest reaches of literal definition. To-morrow will come and I shall have lost my whole hard-won identity: I shall be a puppet in a meaningless ceremony.'

To cheer him up, I laughed and said: 'Every film-star and after-dinner speaker feels as you do at this particular moment. All will be remembered when the curtain rises.'

'I don't like the comparison,' he replied, 'but I know you wish me well. I shall not sleep tonight, of course.'

'Why?'

'I can't explain why, in words.'

*

Of course, he was himself again, next morning. Channing had arranged for a London barracks to be set aside as a tiring-room for the symbolic bodies and we proceeded there immediately after breakfast, with the badger and the trolley and our livery.

A barracks is not the best place for some two hundred men to dress for a death-march. Soldiers, who wear such dress all the time, counter-act it by surrounding themselves with extreme emblems of life. Much of the wall was covered with indecent pictures, and the very boards had an air of rankness – that special flavour created by the clash between sexuality and military discipline. So it was the more marvellous to see the finesse and sweetness with which our two hundred marchers divested themselves of their bowler-hats and black suits and tired themselves in the magnificent costumes of their bodyhoods. They spoke very little: from time to time one would hear someone ask: 'Have you the sprig of tansy?' or, in a more worried tone: 'I think they sent the wrong hemlock.' But that was all. I think I most admired the very old men – the ones with long white moustaches who could stand erect in nothing but their underclothes and still look perfectly emble-matic. But I had an eye, too, for their sons, the young men who would carry on after their fathers had gone and who hoped, in time, to resemble them exactly. Except, as I have said, for the printed map of a funeral procession, I think there is no sight more beautiful than that of an old man dressed in the clothes of an earlier generation accompanied by a son who, though a trifle more up-to-date in appearance, is otherwise papa's replica. There is the father, still leaning backwards towards the world of *his* father, and beside him a son following exactly the same bent. They are thus together recreating the identity of the young man's grandfather and binding the vague present to an identifiable past.

When we were all ready, Channing gave us a brief inspection and arranged us in order of march. We of the Badgeries were to be preceded by a company of Pikemen and followed by a platoon of Coffiners. Barely an hour after the scheduled time we slowly moved out into the street and took up our positions.

When Vinson and I had been alone in our dingy rooms, the antiquity of our uniforms had been pronounced. It had become less so in the tiring-room, where we competed for anachronistic effect with a score of brilliant costumes. But, dear me, when we got into the street what a lesson in humility awaited us! The total length of the cortège was four and a quarter miles, of which we were able to see only a quarter in front and as much behind, due to bends in the street, statues, traffic lights, islands, etc. But what a spectacle was that half-mile of pageantry! Every colour under the sun – and there was a brilliant sun, what's more – was laid out in stripes, blotches, and bands, and cut and sewed into the most fantastic forms of blouse, trouser, breech, stocking, and headpiece. Silver and gold, silk and lace, polished steel and shampooed feather – we could see nothing else behind and before and it was only with an effort that I convinced myself that I was a part of this splendour. And how strange the contrast between us superb death-marchers and the living onlookers who crowded the pavements! There they stood, gaping in their gloomy rows, with their shabby suits and abominable footwear, staring dumbfounded at the unreeling of so much obsolescence. Before I became sophisticated, as a result of knowing Vinson, it would have seemed to me that the contrast was the opposite of what it should be; I would have thought that those who attend on life would look alive, and death's attendants dead. I know better now; I know that the onlooker sees us as lucky men marching in procession towards the past, and weeps drably to think that he is tied to the ever-miserable present.

I heard a trumpet blow. A voice in the crowd exclaimed: 'They're off!' and sure enough the farthermost ranks began to move like the first stanza in an epic. It was about a quarter of an hour before this advance slid backwards to us, and then, we too began our intrepid crawl.

To indicate grief we held our heads bent slightly down, which meant that we could see nothing in front of us above the level of our predecessor's knees. It was not long before this unchanging spectacle of Pikemen's moving calves, in plum stockings with orange rosettes, began to affect me: my heart started to pump; I felt like one of those people who find rebirth nowadays on the Mediterranean sea-bed, glimpsing fleeting archaisms through watery goggles. Behind, I heard the tramp of the Coffiners and the wheet-wheet of the badger's concealed pneumatic tyres.

I knew it was going to be hard sledding when, at intervals, my low vision caught a stretcher being carried briskly to the rear by St John's Ambulance men, and lying on it some utterly collapsed processional figure, his velvet doublet open at the neck, his unbooted toes sticking plaintively into the higher air. Moreover, the farther we tramped, the more vulgarly excited the crowd became. When the head of the cortège was passing them they were, I am sure, reverent and silent; but after a mile or two of it had pageanted by they were spoilt and out of hand, interested only in *what was coming next*. The sight of the badger on his silken tow-ropes was irresistible by a crowd of animal-lovers; long before we actually reached a particular point we would hear high screams of delight: 'Look, Archie, at the pretty dog!' 'Oh, isn't he sweet!' 'He'd be alive if only his tongue hung out.' Much as I detested these excited remarks, I hated more the comments that invariably followed, made by elderly men of the kind who like to show off their knowledge. 'That's no fox, you silly, that's an otter. What they had on Granny's farm;' 'It don't look like an otter to me. More the colour of a beaver.' And once, of course, the loud, dry voice of the man who *really* knows, saying in lordly tones: 'Madam, that is neither a Yorkshire terrier nor a mink. It is what is known as a *cami-leopard*.'

After an eternity of this I raised my swimming eyes, though still keeping my head inclined. This gave me the look and posture of a man who comes back from the pub on a dark night and cranes hopefully in the direction of the nail on which his door-key hangs. To my horror I recognized the sign of The Jolly Waggoners in Kelmscott Way, a mere mile from our starting-point. Three miles to go, and already I was having to recite to myself snatches of poems by character-building authors! I glanced at Vinson.

He was not an athletic type; pacing a room or bar-parlour was his limit. Now, in the high, hard, leather boots of the Badgeries he was suffering torture. But how can I describe his expression as he hobbled along, towing away at the whispering badger? Though his eyes were swirling round and round he never for a second raised them or unbent his head from the painful angle of reverence. It was enough for him to know that he was pursuing a symbol while drawing a token. He paid not the slightest heed to his surroundings: even when the stretchers with their limp bodies began to flit past like dead leaves from some enormous oak, Vinson hobbled on. So strong were his principles that if at that moment he had heard a scream for help from the lips of a loved one, he would only have set his teeth and pressed ahead.

Soho Square is a one-way roundabout and as we trudged round it my annoyance was relieved by the sudden arrival of my second wind. With two miles to go I suddenly was light-headed and relaxed and as we crossed over Oxford Street and headed up gloomy Rathbone Place all my confidence came back. The authorities had chosen this narrow thoroughfare for the procession because most of Oxford Street and Tottenham Court Road were being relaid at the moment of the Lord Royal's death – though, to be fair to the Lord Royal, I must say that it is a rare moment when they are *not* being relaid. But somebody had miscalculated the amplitude of obsolescence, and one of the coaches of Dukes' Provender, filled with emblems of bread, had encircled a hydrant with its leather spring, and overturned. The coach was being followed in the procession by a unit of artillery marching backwards with reversed brass cannon, symbolizing a famous siege in which, the gun-breeches having over-heated, the charges were laid in the muzzles, giving rise to the famous command: 'Men! Backs to the enemy!' Bread, coach, cannon, and gunners were now hideously involved, making a taut bottle-neck for the tail of the procession which was wound-up in a snarl of symbols all the way back to Old Compton Street, where the whores were out in full strength. Efforts were being made to move the blockage from the narrow street; meanwhile, we were being detoured around it. The jam was appalling: crowds three deep filled the pavements; and what with policemen, grunting workmen, and frantic cats, we had no more than six feet of passageway. Moreover, we could see ahead the luckier members of the procession moving smoothly ahead towards Euston station: the thought of being *left behind* on the way to the grave caused considerable panic. Indeed, Vinson was the only marcher who paid no attention whatever until, without warning, he found himself marching reverently into a large heap of synthetic bread surmounted by a fainted gunner. This conjunction was too much, even for Vinson. He raised his eyes to see what was happening in the material world.

If he had not done so, if he had stuck to his symbols through thick and thin, I might never have met Dr Bitterling. As it was, I saw a look of horror come into his eyes, which were fixed on something in the pressing crowd. He shouted: 'No, no! Not that!' and following his eyes I saw *her*, of all people, standing in a rear rank of the crowd with a small bomb clutched in her raised hand.

Vinson was not afraid of death. On the contrary, as we have seen, he was greatly attached to it, and to have been fatally bombed during a distinguished funeral was all he could have asked of life. What he saw, quicker than I did, was that the bomb was a stink-bomb and that she was aiming it *not at him but at the badger*.

Oh, Gods, are there any limitations to the ingenuity of a woman's revenge? This particular one was planned on at least three levels of cynical rage: first, the normal one of punishing a man by harming not him but that which he most loves; second, the highly-intellectual one of reducing the pure, token badger to the revolting status of a stinking real one; third, the ironic one of showing Vinson how well she had profited by his tuition in symbolism. I understood none of this, of course, at the moment itself, but Vinson grasped the revenge on all three levels in the space of as many seconds. And then, seeing his duty, he did it instantly. Stretching his arms wide apart, he fell flat over backwards, intending to shield the danger with his body. But this was the moment when one of the Pikemen, pushed behind us, had chosen to lay his weapon in rest. The back of Vinson's head landed on its point with a splintery crack.

She was through the crowd in a second, screaming: 'Vinson, my darling, what have they done to you?' As in a dream, I saw policemen pulling her off and Vinson being carried away with the bread. I was alone; but processions, once started, never stop. The badger was undamaged. So was I. On we marched, to Euston and the grave.

*

Today, it is I who sit at the auctioneer's raised table, holding in my hand the ivory emblem of the market-place. And it is she, my darling wife, who sits at my elbow, her slim fingers quickly noting the final bid, her eyes alert for the twitched ear, the flared nostril, the jumping shoulder. And below us, more often than not, sit my four aunts, gazing up at us with expressions of permanent astonishment.

My wife and I look down from our table with secret contempt. Thanks to her having kept the books for my predecessor, we have managed to divert most of his custom to ourselves and we make a very good living from it. But a living is all it is: once the last dirty note has been handed in for the last dirty lot, we lay aside our books and hammer and enter a very different world – the world bequeathed to us by Vinson. His photograph is everywhere in our house, and behind a curtain in the living-room is a full-length oil-painting of him, in the full-dress of Co-Warden of the Badgeries.

Our marriage was inevitable. Far from regarding her as Vinson's murderer, I think of her as the only person who really understood his teachings. When he died, he took my old identity with him, and my irresponsible attitude to women was part of it. Until his death, I had been able to be promiscuous because I had known that he, with his immovable firmness, was at my side. Once he went, a panic emptiness came over me: I looked frantically for something solid to replace him.

Who should this be but she, my wife? When a woman loses the great love of her life, she marries, if she possibly can, his closest friend. In this way she is able to continue loving the dead man and to build her marriage strongly on a symbolic foundation. This man, she reasons, as she looks curiously at her husband, is a poor fish. But he is the nearest I can get to the big one that got away.

Does this sound as if I had had a rather poor deal in my marriage? I think not. If you consider my reason for marrying her side by side with her reason for marrying me, I think you will find we come out about quits. Dr Bitterling thinks so, anyway, and he is not a man who says silly things.

In the evenings, when our work is done, we explore Vinson's world. I am still a lazy man and my study of symbolism would soon falter were it not for the ardour of my wife. Like many other women she has a merciful faculty for forgetting things which would plague the conscience of a man. She can, for instance, describe in full detail – and how frequently she does so! – how Vinson looked as he came marching up Rathbone Place: no detail of the carnage of coach, bread, gunner, and pike has been forgotten. But she has absolutely no re-collection of the immediate cause of his death. She believes that he stepped on something slippery at about the time he came abreast of her and that his heart, weakened by over-exertion, gave out at the same moment. Consequently, it is Channing she blames for having killed Vinson – and, through Channing, the whole structure of our present-day society. 'If the whole world were not rotten for want of abstract and spiritual values,' she puts it, 'it would not have been necessary to heap on the shoulders of one devoted man a burden that should be shared by millions.' I am aware that from a purely factual point-of-view she has not described Vinson's death accurately; but viewed from the higher levels of thought, her interpretation is pretty fair. I am the only man who saw her raised arm and the stink-bomb in her hand, and already, after a few years of higher thought, the image is becoming vaguer. I now see only what looks like a birch rod with a knob at the end: in a few more years it will have become a tendril bearing a flower. Dr Bitterling says this is quite normal, and that this is an age, thank goodness, when *angst* and guilt are slowly being enveloped by the healing arms of an infinite symbolism.

My wife and I are now applying for membership in the Identity Club for the following reason. Throughout our working day we have no identity whatever. From our dais we look down on the pushing mob of hysterical buyers with a disgust too great for words. If we did not detach ourselves utterly from the spectacle below we could not go on living at all. So great is our contempt that we do not hesitate to be pretty sharp in our dealings: the bidder who tries too eagerly to catch my eye pays dear for his imprudence. And this, we feel, is the proper fate for greedy materialists: it is we who have higher interests and more-devoted principles who glean the pennies from the dirty pockets of the average man.

So once the money is in the bank and my wife and I are at home again, we take up our true identities. Together, we read a passage from some one of Vinson's favourite books, after which we discuss it and

145

try to ascertain what he might have concluded from it. Then comes a brief supper off celluloid plates, quickly over. After that, we read again and make notes in our journals. At eleven, we go to bed: that was Vinson's hour. At the turn of the moon we fill a cow's horn with an essence of boiled herbs and bury it in the compost-heap. Twice a week we copy out passages from Vinson's letters in Italianate script. About once a month we secretly abstract, and read, one another's journals; this is always a painful experience.

And so it goes. We love our way of life but we would like to spread our identities farther afield. We know that there are people like ourselves springing up all over the nation today, that rebirth into symbolic identities is one of the new spiritual values of the times. In your Club we would hope to find dedicated men who, like ourselves and Dr Bitterling, have tried, like Vinson, to put as great a distance as possible between how they live and what they believe. There was a time, they say, when men loved their work and gave their best to it. But those days are gone. We are glad they are gone. Dr Bitterling says we are right to be glad. *And Dr Bitterling is never wrong.*

*

'How,' cried the President, above the applause, 'we love the beginnings of orations – the expectant silence, the promise, so rarely kept, of novelty! But how much more we love orations' ends! Like prisoners at last released, we wander free in the world of our own thoughts. We see the speaker resume his seat, and as his last words fade into the past, never to be recalled, we start forward in our chairs, burning to press on him, in the disguise of questions, the ideas with which we have consoled ourselves throughout his address. We applaud him not because he has brought his own history to a close but because he has at last brought our own closer to a beginning. Moreover, there are to be other speakers after him, and the sight of him reseating himself is a sign that their number has been mercifully reduced by one. So I am sure we are all grateful to Dr Bitterling for his address, which, when you come to think of it – if so you ever do – might have been much longer. Has anybody any further compliments to pay?'

'Obviously,' said Dr Shubunkin, 'he worked his fingers to the bone. Well, not quite to the bone; down to the second skin, say. Had he but gone a shade deeper he would have uncovered a perfectly obvious sexual situation and seen this badger of his in a very different light. Yes, a very different light indeed.'

'Symbolism is more my field than his,' said Father Orfe, rising with a hiccup, 'so I am not speaking lightly when I say I admired the way he got his false teeth into it. Unfortunately, owing to the eminent split in my personality, I was either too drunk or too exalted to follow the history closely.'

'I liked the part about the auction,' said Dr Musk. 'But then one is always excited by description of money changing hands. It's much more fundamental than sex.'

'The descriptive passages were good, in their way,' said Mr Harris, 'and I say that as one who detests *all* descriptive passages. It was, on the whole, a healthy rebuke of the romantic ideal, though I am bound to say that the best part of it was wasted. I refer, of course, to the aunts – those noble Roman matrons round whom the whole history should rightly have revolved.'

'I was sorry to see no real *centre* to the corpus,' said Mr Jamesworth. 'I cannot deny the *embroidery*.'

'As an average man,' said Mr Harcourt, 'I found the whole thing quite above my head. I have no doubt that people do carry hobbies, such as badgers, to an extreme, but I'm not sure I want to *hear* about such people. Still, an average man is always proud to think that he has sat patiently through a lecture of which he has hardly understood a word.'

'I thought it was a wonderful address,' said Stapleton, blushing furiously. 'It gave a new horizon to the vision. It added a new dimension to the thought. It put another foundation under the ground we stand on; it raised the ceiling above our heads.'

'I should like to ask Bitterling,' said Mr Jamesworth, 'what relative importance, if any, he attaches to aunts? Or were his aunts merely thrown in, *faute de mieux?*'

'Certainly not,' answered Dr Bitterling. 'I would have made much more of them if I had not found that they obstructed the narrative flow. I was quite taken with them when I began writing the early part of the history, but when I found the story taking an unexpected turn there was nothing to do but change them into symbols. I mean that when, as is common nowadays, a man has betrayed his mother, killed his father, divorced three wives, and lost all contact with his children, his aunts are the only fixed points of reference left. Thus, in a sense, my whole history was of the tragedy which overtakes a man when his very aunts shift like sand.'

'Were you aware of this, Dr Bitterling, when you were actually speaking?' asked the President. 'Or is this aunt-symbolism something that has just occurred to you?'

'It was formerly in my unconscious mind,' said Dr Bitterling. 'Now, it is risen to the surface, like corn in a grain-elevator. I thus claim original brilliance on two counts, in two regions.'

'I see. More questions?'

'Does the speaker,' asked Dr Shubunkin, 'intend to make a scape-goat of aunts? I mean, long ago we had wicked stepmothers and villainous uncles and are only now emerging from a period of intoler-able fathers. Is Dr Bitterling now attempting to concentrate man's hostility upon his aunts?'

'I think not,' said Dr Bitterling. 'The function of an aunt has always been to be distressed by the negligence of the mother, her sister, and, in compensation, to make handsome presents to the mistreated nieces and nephews. I am not inclined to deprive aunts of this enjoyable role, nor nephews and nieces of its fruits.'

'Does the speaker not realize the danger of leaving such a vacuum in the sphere of blame?' asked Dr Shubunkin. 'Surely it is his responsi-bility, as a man of thought, to give the man-in-the-street some idea of whom he may fashionably blame for his shortcomings? Since fathers became innocuous, the situation has become desperate. A few more years and people will start blaming themselves. The human conscience will resemble an ingrowing toe-nail.'

'I think we need have no fear of that,' replied Dr Bitterling. 'The wonderful thing about human progress is that when a moral situation becomes intolerable something always turns up. It would be foolish, in my opinion, to force aunts to be answerable at a time when pro-miscuity is providing far better solutions. The obvious key to blame in the modern world is "ex". Most up-to-date people can point to at least one ex-wife or ex-husband who has ruined them permanently. There are men alive at this very moment who can point to four and even five ruinous ex-mothers-in-law. There are children growing up who have known nothing but ex-parents. You may be sure that in a world where ex is so abundant it would be idle to press for aunts.'

'Has the speaker given any thought to the relation between ex and grasp-of-self?' inquired Dr Musk. 'Clearly, any man who has been parcelled out among five women, each of whom has taken *his very name,* is going to feel uncertain of what, precisely, remains to him. Will he be, for instance, but one-fifth of his former self?'

'That is rather outside the subject of my paper,' replied Dr Bitterling, 'but I will say that experience leads me to believe that he retains all five-fifths. He says: "With Shelia, I was quite a gay dog, but with Betty I sobered up considerably. When Angela came along I was rather of two minds, but Cynthia soon put a stop to that. Thanks to Sybil, however, I now see how immature it all was." '

'I must call a halt,' said the President. 'Questions of ex are not pertinent to the case-history of a man who laid down his life for a badger.'

'I'd like to mention just one more ex,' said Mr Jamesworth. 'I refer to the ex-alimony relation, which leads ex-wives who have re-married to say: "I was much better off divorced from Hugo than married to Paul." And also, now I come to think of it, the relation of ex-children. Do these have any claim to aunts whose validity has been liquidated by the remarriage of the parents?'

'The motion,' said the President, 'is that we are moving out of an era of sex into a period of ex. All those . . . What is it, Mr Stapleton?'

'I wished only to raise a human point,' said Stapleton. 'The history concluded with an application by the patients for membership in our club. Do we intend to admit them?'

An awful silence collected about his standing figure and spread to every corner of the room. In a moment, every eye was fixed accusingly on the President, who could not hide a guilty look. Dr Shubunkin said: 'I think this most irregular.'

'In all my years in this club,' said Dr Musk, 'I cannot recall such a situation.'

'Mr Stapleton,' said the President firmly. 'In spite of what I said before Bitterling began, you are under the illusion that these patients exist. They do not – and even if they did they would not have the vaguest resemblance to themselves as represented by a man of Dr Bitterling's ingenuity.'

'Poor Stapleton is a complete novice,' said Dr Shubunkin, 'and cannot be blamed for his stupidity. Whoever instructed him in the great theory must take the blame.'

'That is certainly the root of the matter,' said Mr Jamesworth.

'It would also be the classical ruling,' said Mr Harris.

'Symbolically,' said Dr Musk, 'one would depict the error in the image of the teacher. The actual perpetrator would get off scot-free.'

'It is all above my head,' said Mr Harcourt, 'but a little bird tells me there has been a mistake.'

'That is perfectly correct,' said the President. 'However, it is not for presidents to make apologies for blunders made by them in their teaching roles. I am sure this idea will be supported by those of you who believe that a man can have more than one personality.'

'If that refers to me,' said Father Orfe, 'I shall be happy to defend myself, if I can find my feet.'

'I suggest you reserve your defence, Orfe,' said Dr Shubunkin. 'He has only challenged you in the hope of changing the subject.'

'I think that's jolly clever,' said Mr Harcourt. 'Such a stratagem would never occur to *me*.'

'I think we should have more respect for the excellent Bitterling, gentlemen,' said the President. 'He has delivered one of the most brilliant papers ever heard in this Club and will not, I am sure, wish to see it pushed aside merely because I failed to impress something upon Mr Stapleton.'

'That is entirely correct,' said Dr Bitterling. 'The president's calibre is of no interest to me, except that I am pleased to see that he has un-expectedly developed a warm, unselfish side.'

'I am sorry to see Bitterling fall into such an obvious trap,' said Dr Musk.

'I would hardly call it a trap,' said Dr Bitterling urbanely. 'It is more a happy coincidence of interests.'

'I am bound to say,' said the President, 'that if this squabbling con-tinues, I shall have to declare the session closed. This will make Bitterling furious – and not with *me*.'

'I must say,' said Mr Jamesworth, 'that when one's venom has been distracted in the direction of another victim, it is hard to direct it back on the original one. I had many spiteful criticisms to make of Bitter-ling's paper; by now I have forgotten what they were.'

'Then, clearly,' said the President, 'Bitterling must read his paper again.'

'Gladly, gladly,' said the doctor, reassembling his manuscript.

'I am sure we would all like to hear it again,' said the President. 'If there is anyone who would *not*, will he kindly stand up and say so?'

There was gloomy silence. At last, Dr Shubunkin said: 'There is nothing I would enjoy more than a second reading. But is it wise? Bitterling is one of our most talented members. We must guard his health.'

'That's the essence,' said Mr Jamesworth. 'He's a delicate instrument.'

'Gentlemen, I could do it three times if necessary,' said Dr Bitterling. 'After all, I *am* the author.'

'In that case,' said the President, 'I will ask you, in this reading, to include the hundred pages on adolescence which you forwent in the previous one.'

'Gladly,' said the doctor. 'East, west, adolescence is best.'

'And should you, Orfe,' added the President, 'need to fortify yourself against the second reading, will you kindly do so quietly? The gurgling of your hip-flask spoilt much of the first reading.'

'Since when,' cried Mr Harcourt, 'has Orfe taken to drink? I thought he was a *priest*.'

There was general laughter, under cover of which, like a goose rising from swaying reeds, Dr Bitterling began again: 'I was the third of eight children, born into an upper-middle-class milieu. . . . '

*

'Surely, Mr Jellicoe, they are not *still* talking?' asked Mrs Paradise. 'What *about*? And what about their *tea*?'

'It's badgers, Mrs Paradise.'

'Badgers!'

'Yes. A funny thing happened. A couple of hours ago I paused at the keyhole and heard the words "badger on its silken cords". A couple of *minutes* ago, I again paused at the keyhole and heard *the same words in the same voice*. What do you think of that? It took me a moment to remember that that sort of thing often happens. You return to a place where something has occurred and it seems to occur again. I remember in the Navy – '

'Please, Mr Jellicoe, *not* one of your Navy stories. I know you are ashamed of your past, but remember that I am still wearing black for a very dear memory of my own.'

'There is no woman in *this* anecdote, Mrs Paradise. It was all between men.'

'I distrust it the more, Mr Jellicoe. Kindly tell me instead *why* the gentlemen are on about badgers.'

'They are *sportsmen*, Mrs Paradise. I expect they are framing new rules against gin-traps. You mark my words: what they decide today will be what everyone will be thinking tomorrow. That's how the world works. To me and you, and to millions like us, a badger is a mystery. But tomorrow, thanks to what is going on upstairs, we shall know all there is to know about badgers. It fills me with pride to think that I polish the shoes of men who lead the way into the unknown.'

'Even when it's only for badgers?'

'I don't care what it's *for*. The shining shoe doesn't ask what for, and nor do I. It's being led that matters. You lose your head if people aren't sitting on it.'

'You are too excitable, Mr Jellicoe. You tire yourself out with your passion for thought.'

'I *am* rather tired. There seems to be so much *work*. Somehow there seem to be more gentlemen this year.'

'Just twice the usual number.'

'Are you quite sure? You are not imagining it? If you are right, I shall feel much happier, with a fixed number to grasp.'

'Actually, if my memory serves me right, it is not *exactly* twice as many. There is one odd.'

'More or less?'

'More.'

'Thank God! I shall enjoy calling it twice as many and then enjoy the little extra pleasure that comes from knowing that the total pain is actually a shade greater. Say what you like, Mrs Paradise; I'd rather have a thing with a number than even a thing with a name, if I'm going to really know myself.'

'You don't find it makes you complain?'

'On the contrary. The other day, I tried to think when exactly I last complained. I went back over the years and couldn't find a single occasion, though I was able to revel in a thousand episodes which would have justified complaint. Would you not find the same hardiness in your life?'

'Certainly. But I never dwell on the past. Instead, it hangs on me. *You* are making-up for a wicked past. *I* am trying to forget a beautiful one, shared with a blameless partner.'

'That's what makes you such an unusual woman, Mrs Paradise. Now, my former wife, poor Phyllis, *constantly* dwelt on the past. Once, in a single day, I counted 86 dwellings. Now, 86 is not a number to carry about comfortably, so I provoked her very slightly and she at once produced another four. I have never forgotten that 90 – particularly as I prefer the 90s to 100 any day. Something meaningless creeps in after 99. One shrugs one's shoulders and loses interest. Perhaps it would be the same in dealing with sums of money. But as I have never had any money I cannot say.'

'I am like you, Mr Jellicoe. I am the happier for being penniless.'

'I must say I grieve for your happiness, Mrs Paradise. I should have thought that after so many years of thrifty service, plus possibly something inherited from your late husband, you would be quite comfortably *un*happy.'

'He spent it all on good works, Mr Jellicoe. And most of mine, too. It costs a lot, to buy a sacred memory.'

'I hope you have wisely invested what little his memory did not require.'

'It goes on flowers for his grave.'

'Was he buried nearby?'

'No; in Nottingham. The florists have a weekly standing order.'

'What a very expensive death! All *I* ask, after a life of sin and penance, is a plain slab with the name "Henry Jellicoe". Not that I would seriously protest if some kind friend added just a word or two of explanation.'

'I never knew your Christian name was Henry.'

'Oh Lord, yes!'

'For me, it has strong associations.'

'I rather take it for granted. Its only association is with me.'

'You think you are the only Henry in the world?'

'I am the only Henry who means Henry to me.'

'And to me, the only Henry who means Henry has ceased to be Henry.'

There was a brisk knock on the door and Miss Tray burst in – all corduroy, leggings, flush, and excitement. 'I have come to throw myself on your mercies!' she cried. 'Here is the situation. When I was a young girl – i.e. younger than I am now – '

'Is this going to be a long story, Miss Tray?' asked Mrs Paradise. 'We are very busy.'

'It's terribly important. It will change my whole life. So I have to start it rather far back or you wouldn't see why. When I was a young girl, i.e. . . . '

They looked her square in the face, as is the habit of listeners who have no intention of listening. Their minds were far away, turning over the mysteries of death, the Navy, and an occasional badger. From time to time, a stray word or phrase of Miss Tray's stole into their minds through a back door which the breeze blew ajar and floated aimlessly above their thoughts like a feather over a crowded sink. In short, by the time they paid attention to Miss Tray, their only clues to her topic were, in Jellicoe's case, the words 'Royal Academy' and 'Imagine my grief', and, in Mrs Paradise's, 'taxed to the utmost' and 'a poor sort of hero'. But many a listener has entered conversation, and even controversy, with much less.

'At last,' said Miss Tray, 'my mother consented. I was enrolled. *He* was one of the teachers there, and it was he who taught me to enunciate Shakespeare.'

'You were still in the Royal Academy then?' said Jellicoe.

'I am just entering it now,' said Miss Tray.

'That is what I meant. I was puzzled by the reference to Shakespeare.'

'But that's *why* it's called the Royal Academy of Stagecraft, Mr Jellicoe.'

'I agree that gives the matter another complexion.'

'Neither of us,' continued Miss Tray, 'had much in the way of physique or voice. But he showed me how, by a sort of special agitation of the larynx, one can give an audience the feeling that they are living in a robust Elizabethan atmosphere. These were the loudest and happiest years of my life.'

'It seems ungrateful, then,' said Mrs Paradise, 'to call him a poor sort of hero.'

'Or to imagine your grief,' said Jellicoe. 'I think you were a most fortunate young woman.'

'Others besides you were being taxed to the utmost,' said Mrs Paradise.

Miss Tray began to cry. 'I thought I would find you more understanding,' she sobbed.

Mrs Paradise, touched, patted Miss Tray's shoulder. 'You will find us *most* understanding, dear,' she said, 'if you will only not get so emotional. Try and speak more clearly, more slowly, more frankly.'

'You don't seem to have grasped . . .'

'We have grasped *everything*. Now, dry your eyes, dear, and go on.'

'Promise me, though, that you favour the *idea*?'

'It is all right in its way, but I am not quite sure that it is any concern of mine.'

'But that's what I've explained, isn't it?'

'I must say, at this point,' said Jellicoe, 'that all through those years, I was at sea.'

'Mr Jellicoe!' cried Miss Tray. 'Why did you not say so before?'

'He has said so repeatedly,' said Mrs Paradise. 'And in *your* hearing.'

'I am ashamed,' said Miss Tray. 'I must have been wool-gathering.'

'Mind you,' said Jellicoe, 'it was not my first intention. My parents never thought much of me; I was a diffused child. One day, they saw me floating matchboxes in a puddle. "Oho!" said my father, "so it's *water* he likes, is it?" I didn't like to say it was matchboxes. Next week, they bought me a sailor-suit and told all the neighbours. When I saw that suddenly everyone recognized me, I didn't want to argue and become a stranger again. So I joined the Navy. On the other hand, my brother, who worshipped naval things, was somehow seen to be a chartered accountant.'

'Yes, Mr Jellicoe had an honourable naval career,' said Mrs Paradise. 'He's not easily influenced by heart-rending stories.'

'But you said you would do it!' cried Miss Tray.

'I said nothing of the kind,' said Mrs Paradise.

'But I heard you say "Um".'

'You heard me say "Hm-m".'

'Then you won't do it?'

'I don't say we *definitely* won't,' replied Mrs Paradise.

'I can show you your parts this very evening. We'll all have to take more than one, of course. I don't know what Mrs Chirk will think.'

She began to cry again.

'Come, come, now,' said Mrs Paradise, 'you can be sure Mr Jellicoe and I will do our best for you. But you *must* try and speak more honestly.'

'It makes it worse to know that Mr Jellicoe is an ex-seaman,' sobbed Miss Tray, 'because that's the most important part. It needs a man who has felt the spray. You know that as well as I do.'

'I imagine we do,' said Mrs Paradise.

'And perhaps Mrs Chirk could help with the disguises.'

'You would have to speak to her.'

'There are one or two places where, if we are all two or more persons, we would find ourselves talking to ourselves, and in more than one disguise at that. But we can snip out the bits where things get *too* muddled. And the doctor has been *so* sweet about it. What's more, he's sure the other doctors are going to love it.'

'You can't always be sure with doctors,' said Jellicoe.

'No, indeed,' said Mrs Paradise. 'In my own recent illness they were proved totally wrong.'

'Nor do I see why you should suddenly be so full of doctoring, Miss Tray,' said Jellicoe. 'By nature, you are a jolly girl with few serious interests.'

'That's only my mask, Mr Jellicoe. Now that I have warmed to my theme, I am quite naked. The doctor is very pleased.'

'What puzzles me,' said Jellicoe, 'is that you should find so many doctors available when the house is full of sportsmen. Perhaps some of them are vets.'

'I think not,' said Miss Tray. 'It is exclusively a medical conference for people.'

Here, Mrs Paradise gave Jellicoe a warning look, as if begging him not to press the poor girl. So Jellicoe, who had already noticed many odd things about Miss Tray's picture of the real world, merely said tactfully: 'Of course, the captain's acquaintances cover a wide range of types.'

'Then, you know the part, Mr Jellicoe?' cried Miss Tray.

'Hardly as well as I used to,' he said carefully.

'The title is so misleading, of course. The Prince is not the hero at all. The Captain *is*. I remember his explaining that to me once.'

156

'Who explaining what to you?' demanded Mrs Paradise.

'The teacher I was so in love with.'

'Oh, I see.'

'I must go about my duties,' said Jellicoe, rising naturally. 'Thanks to the badgers I shall have to carry up their tea. Miss Tray, Mrs Paradise will tell me what conclusion you reach. I am sure I shall be in agreement.'

'If you two say yes, then everything will hinge on Mrs Chirk,' said Miss Tray.

'It would seem so,' said Jellicoe, leaving the room.

'Perhaps you could persuade her, Mrs Paradise?' said Miss Tray pleadingly. 'You would do it so much better than me. If you will be both Hermione and the Queen, she can be the minor women and I can dress up as the man.'

'This is all rather a surprise, Miss Tray.'

'I know, but you do see the situation, don't you?'

'Of course. But I'm not sure I like it any the better.'

'Have you had *any* stage experience, Mrs Paradise?'

'What do you mean – stage-experience?'

'I mean, have you done it before?'

'Yes and no. It all depended on the situation.'

'But you have *agreed*, haven't you? You're not going to go back on your word.'

'I don't like being pushed, young lady.'

'I'm not pushing, Mrs Paradise, I promise. That's my natural expression. Oh, Mrs Paradise! Who will be the Queen if you change your mind?'

'You want me to be a queen?'

'*The* Queen. There's only one. You have *such* poise, *such* dignity.'

'You make it all sound like a play.'

'But isn't that exactly what it is?'

'Certainly. I meant the excited way you were saying it . . . I can't imagine what Mr Jellicoe is going to think. The stage won't fit with his penance.'

'But he'll be the *real* hero. Mr Towzer can be the Prince.'

'Well, on the whole I think you are a good-hearted girl, Miss Tray,' said Mrs Paradise, giving her a hug. 'And if you want us to become actors I suppose we can't very well refuse. Mrs Chirk can start work on the Queen's clothes immediately.'

'Will she agree to be Radegund?'

'Mrs Chirk will agree to be *anyone*, dear.'

'Or I could be Radegund, and she Catriona.'

'As long as she is told clearly, that is all she asks.'

'There is something I feel I should confess to you, Mrs Paradise. Not *everything* I said at the beginning was *quite* true. About my life and that man.'

'You needn't tell me that, dear. My instinct told me at once.'

'But it *was* a white lie, wasn't it? The truth is that the play is going to be an act of occupational therapy for Mr Towzer.'

'That is pretty much what I guessed.'

'But it was a *white* lie, wasn't it?'

'White or black, you run along now. This has been a *most* peculiar afternoon for me. Everything has seemed out of place. What with badgers above and plays below, and poor Mrs Chirk in a perpetual flutter, and Mr Jellicoe doing all that arithmetic, and *my* memories... ! Dear me! Sometimes one wonders who one is.'

'That's what *The Prince of Antioch* says, isn't it?'

'What's the prince of *what*?'

'The title of our *play*, Mrs Paradise.'

'Don't shout, dear; I know that.'

'It will do *me* good, too, Mrs Paradise. It will force me closer to reality. If Mrs Chirk plays Radegund, I shall view my mother quite differently. Which is what the doctor ordered.'

'If that's your aim, dear, why not let Mrs Chirk take one of the male parts?'

'Mrs Paradise!' cried Miss Tray: 'what a simply wonderful idea! But would it work? I already have a father, you see, in the doctor.'

'She could be like a brother.'

'*Too* risky, dear Mrs Paradise. We are not playing *Antigone*. And my movement must be *away*, not *to*.'

'Please yourself. Only make up your mind. Mrs Chirk is willing, but she cannot bear suspense.'

*

Midnight found the captain still at work. He had made the rounds of the big house, encouraging Mrs Paradise and Mrs Chirk with a kind word, Jellicoe with a sharp reproach. Now, dressed in his pyjamas and gold-tasselled dressing-gown, genuinely smoking his curved pipe, he sat quietly in his tower-bedroom, examining committee reports and looking exactly what he was – a well-dressed adjutant off duty.

The door opened and the President entered. He, too, was in pyjamas and dressing-gown and bedroom slippers, but all of a sloppy, ill-fitting, presidential kind, like an old windmill.

'I am sorry to disturb you, Mallet,' he said, 'but I would like your opinion. Do you feel the Club has settled down?'

'Why, sir, as well as clubs ever do.'

'You sense no *restlessness*? No *mystery*? Why is Shubunkin in Musk's bedroom? Why is Orfe giving syrup to Bitterling for laryngitis? Why has Harris promised to read-over Jamesworth's statistics on the domestic accident-rate?'

'Why, sir, surely such connivances are an everyday thing in a president's life?'

'You don't think they are plotting against *me*?'

'They have only themselves and you, sir, to plot against. It could hardly be otherwise, could it?'

'It should be one another they detest. Particularly after that lick of discipline I gave them this afternoon.'

'It seems to have boomeranged, sir.'

'Was I to know that Bitterling would lose his voice? I meant him to be an instrument of punishment. He has become an object of sympathy. Why? I have used the second-reading technique of discipline for years: never before has the speaker's larynx exploded in my face. Why has it suddenly changed from an interminable trumpet to a broken reed? We can rule out immediately the notion that it was a physical collapse. We can also rule out, as absurd, the notion that a man like Bitterling would *want* to be left speechless.'

'What, then, do you conclude, sir?'

'Why, that it is all a *plot*. They are trying to force me out. What *is* a larynx? It is that which speaks. What am I? I am the Club spokesman. Therefore, a shut larynx is an impotent president. Why, it's clear as text-book. Bitterling is but the bearer of the hostile message – a reed, a pipe, a mere Hermes.'

'It is not to be denied, sir. I had reached precisely that conclusion.'

'My only hope is that the plotters are not yet conscious of their plot. It has shaped itself deep down in the subterranean darkness of their despicable psyches. Like hot air rising, it will endeavour to struggle to the surface. Its creators will do their utmost to keep it down – quite unconsciously, of course – in order to avoid guilt. If it is too strong for them and pokes its periscope above the surface, they will hasten to disguise it as something inoffensive – say, a jar of marmalade. That will be my opportunity. Fully conscious of what *I* am doing, I shall throw a disguise of my own over their disguise. That will fox them.'

'What kind of disguise, sir?'

'The text-book one. I shall accuse them of attacking *me*. They will then conclude that though I was the overt object of their hostility, Bitterling was really the man they were out to get. I am sorry to have to sacrifice Bitterling, but the Club needs me much more than it needs him.'

'Of course, sir, a session invariably releases the worst in them.'

'A stab in the back will release the best in me.'

'Yes, indeed, sir; it is not a thing to be objective about.'

'I would enjoy it in a case-history, you understand? On paper, I have no objection whatever to these infinitely-concealed manifestations of unconsciousness travelling up and down from bargain-basement to attic with surreptitious stops on all floors. It does the boys good to have so many buttons to press and to keep poor Mr X floating up and down on his greasy cables. But I flatly refuse to become personally involved – to let myself be included as their victim. Once agree to be Mr X today and tomorrow you become X marks the spot . . . What puzzles me is *why* they should be behaving so badly?'

'Obviously, sir, they are in need of authority.'

'Am I not supplying it? Am I not an absolute *image* of authority? Could I be *more* a president?'

'Sir, I well remember your predecessor. . . .'

'What! Poor old Planorbis? My good Mallet, you are not comparing me to *him*? Why, he was utterly decrepit, totally broken-down! He had the *manner* of a president to the last, but he was a mere shell, Mallet, a husk, nonentity in presidential disguise. But I – I am in my prime, a bare seventy-five years old. For twenty years I have piqued them, squashed them, resurrected them, at will. I have dumbfounded them with my intuitions, sat on them with my logic. Where their interpretations of human behaviour have been ingenious, mine have been labyrinthal. Often, I have penetrated so far behind the scenes that they have never expected me to re-emerge. As to the great theory, no sooner has the smallest leak appeared than my thumb has stopped it. I have urged-on the younger members, showered undeserved congratulations on the older ones. They have laid a thousand traps for me and I have not only escaped every one but trounced their setters. Is this leadership or is it not? Could more be asked of authority?'

'Only that it be *recognized*, sir.'

'But they cannot help recognizing it, Mallet. It is indisputably *there. I am every inch a president.* . . . Come now, you yourself are a man of presidential timber. Is there any doubt in *your* mind as to the reality of my identity?'

'Sir, it is not for *me* to doubt. I am a loyal officer.'

'Oh, Mallet, this is no time for scruples! You need only answer my question.'

'Sir, I am not a flexible type, except in dealing with patients. It would undermine me absolutely.'

'Oh, very well! I shall go and do some more spying. Do you know that Orfe is getting his whisky from Jellicoe?'

'It would be in the tradition of these great houses, sir.'

'Give me the old Club premises any day. I shall be thankful when all this junketing is over. The very keyholes give me earache.'

He opened the door cautiously. As he closed it behind him a segment of his dressing-gown, faded and full of moth-holes, remained in its clasp. There was a sharp tearing sound as the President padded away without it.

Beaufort picked it up a few minutes later when he opened the door. 'Good evening,' he said. 'I say, what's this?'

'A piece of the President's dressing-gown,' said the captain.

'Is it a symblem or an embol? Does it mean he has cast his mantle upon your shoulders? Is he afraid you may step in a puddle? And all those moth-holes. I expect they token a parting of the ways.'

'Thank God for your high spirits!' said the captain. 'I was far down in the dumps. Why was our lady-member not at the session today?'

'Headache. She chose to lie down. Here she comes . . . It was only a *woman's* headache, you know. No pain in the head, or anything like that – just buckled despair in the legs and blue rings round the eyes. Is this a spinet? May I play it?'

'What a very good mood you are in! Good evening, dear! Do sit down. We missed you.'

'I simply couldn't face a Bitterling,' explained Mrs Mallet. 'I thought a shaded room would be much better.'

'But all is well now,' cried Beaufort, vigorously playing a theme. 'The shadow has passed. We had feared that I was going to become a father.'

'Good heavens! Have you two been keeping this tormenting fear to yourself – for days, weeks?'

'It's not something one talks about, you know,' said Beaufort, 'even to one's best friend.'

'It would have been the first time since '21,' said the captain. 'Dr Reingold and Miss Y.'

'My despair was terrible,' said Beaufort, turning from the spinet. 'I can't tell you what I have gone through. Like any expectant father, I first thought of all the things I would have to sacrifice to send it to a public school. That alone was enough to reduce me to tears. Then I thought of all the horrors that would henceforth accompany me through life – the crushing responsibilities, the slow but steady increase in torpor, the decline of the critical and adventurous faculties. It was like the end of the world.'

'And you spared no thought for the wonderful woman who was the principal sufferer in this?' asked the captain.

'I tried, but it was no use. There was nothing to spare.'

'His selfishness was rocklike,' said Mrs Mallet, sighing. 'It bound me to him like cement.'

'Another awful thing about it,' continued Beaufort, 'was what the members would have said. I could already hear Shubunkin explaining it all in terms of mysticism.'

'You mean Orfe, do you not?'

'No, Shubunkin. Sex is the only thing that he does not interpret sexually. Orfe, on the other hand, would have blamed it *all* on sex.'

'We thought Mr Jamesworth would see its statistical necessity, too,' said Mrs Mallet. 'After all, charts must rise and fall.'

'And I did *not* relish the reproach of my old teacher, Mr Harris,' said

Beaufort, 'who would have blamed me most severely for construing hetaira as matron.'

'It is a pity, really, Beaufort,' said the captain. 'You cannot postpone your maturity indefinitely, you know. Sometime in the next year or two you are going to have to give your wonderful talents a decisive bent.'

'I shall see which way the wind blows. I can feel it blowing pretty hard already.'

'Indeed?'

'Come on, now,' said Beaufort, laying a hand on the captain's arm. 'Tell us what's happening. We're *dying* to know. Is the President . . . ?'

'I am afraid so,' replied the captain.

'Soon?'

'It cannot be long, now.'

'How miserable! I shall miss him horribly.'

'Why? I thought you were much too irresponsible and carefree.'

'I am. It makes me very fond of old people. He's such an old dear . . . Well, you've quite spoilt the happiness I felt at my own reprieve.'

'You think there is no hope at all?' asked Mrs Mallet.

'I'm afraid not,' said the captain. 'The symptoms are unmistakable. Explanations, protestations, insistence that he is totally unlike any previous president - it's all there. I'm afraid Nature is going to take her course.'

'We couldn't keep him as emeritus, or something like that?' asked Beaufort.

'Don't be silly,' said the captain.

They sat in silence for some time. Eventually, the captain said: 'I count on you two to keep very steady heads. That's why I've told you. We can't have the staff disorganized, and events of this kind are soon felt downstairs.'

'They seem peaceable enough at the moment,' said Mrs Mallet. 'Quite engrossed in themselves. This play of theirs has greatly excited them, too. The thought of *acting*, of being other than what they *really* are, seems to thrill them inordinately.'

'Do you think we may have to leave here earlier than we planned?' asked Beaufort.

'It would not surprise me,' said the captain.

'What a shame! After all our hard work. . . . Tell me, did you see this coming?'

'Only now, when I look back. And don't grieve for the work we put in here. It will take its place in the chain of events. Nothing is ever wasted. The course is always predetermined.'

*

All the bells began to ring, the light on the bulletin board, as arranged by the Electrical Committee, flashed on and off, alternately illuminating and extinguishing the large words typed beneath:

DOG's WAY: *A Case of Multiple Sexual Misidentity*

by

Dr Alexander Shubunkin

A stream of members poured down the corridors; but only when most of them were in their seats did a sort of cortège conspicuously appear, leading, or bearing, yesterday's victim, Dr Bitterling. It was clear from the way they towed and coaxed him into a seat that they intended to take the fullest advantage of his injury: their expressions were those of devoted friends suddenly possessed of a most-grindable axe. The doctor, for his part, played his active, though supine role to perfection: unable to speak, he worked his lips with passionate intent and bestowed thankful pats on his helpers. Around his neck they hung a sheaf of blank paper and a pencil on a string: he was thus attired when the President raced in and assumed his dais.

So loudly did he bang his gavel that all talk ceased abruptly. Only Mr Harcourt, slower of response than his colleagues, was trapped with the end of a sentence ringing through the silence.

'Did you say something, Mr Harcourt?' demanded the President, looking straight over the top of Dr Bitterling's head.

'Not above a whisper,' said Mr Harcourt.

'Then why are you blushing?'

The members, who couldn't resist feeling better when one of their number was shown to be worse, forgot about poor Dr Bitterling and stared at Mr Harcourt. He, unfortunate man, had actually turned quite pale; but as a result of the President's words the blood was now rising slowly over the brink of his pate.

'A damned good start!' the captain whispered to Beaufort. 'I take my hat off.'

The President continued: 'I heard the word "string", did I not, Mr Harcourt? What have you to tell us about string? Are you an authority on string?'

'It was strings, not string,' said Mr Harcourt.

'The plural is of even greater interest. The word that goes with it is "pulling", is it not?'

'Not always,' said Mr Jamesworth, smiling winsomely. The denial made him Mr Harcourt's champion; the smile provided him, he hoped, with a means of dismounting if the battle were too hot. 'There's also tangled, multi-coloured, and knotted,' he said.

'Indeed, Jamesworth?' replied the President, baring his own teeth in a full-dress smile. 'You think, then, that Harcourt's very ordinary mind shares with yours associations of an involved and brilliant kind?'

The members, delighted to have a second and better victim, laughed most heartily and looked at the President with respect. Mr Jamesworth fell back on the worst and most-degrading phrase: 'I only said . . .' he said.

'Jamesworth only said,' cried Mr Harcourt desperately, 'that there was something . . . that I had a feeling . . .'

'About what did you, of all people, have a *feeling*?' asked the President, raising another laugh.

'It was only a very trifling one. I just said, in quite a low voice and without any confidence, that I had a feeling about this house – a feeling that someone or something was . . .'

'Pulling strings?'

'Well, frankly, yes.'

'Do you still have this feeling?'

'Oh, Lord, no. It came and went like a flying-saucer.'

'We are glad to hear that, Mr Harcourt. It is not a feeling we encourage in this Club, is it?'

'Certainly not.'

'We don't want trails of disquiet left by mysterious projectiles, do we?'

'Indeed we don't.'

'I imagine, sir, that it was a simple case of evasion,' said Mr James-worth, hoping to recoup favour. 'Harcourt got one of his nervous spasms and tried to project it on the house.'

'You are very talkative this morning, Jamesworth,' observed the President. 'Perhaps you would like to ask Dr Shubunkin to put aside the history on which he has worked for so long in order that you may address the session impromptu?'

This was well received by members, and above all by Dr Shubunkin. Both Beaufort and the Captain were impressed and looked at the wiry, confident President with affectionate respect.

'It had been my intention to start this session off with a few words of praise for you all,' said the President, pacing the dais. 'Despite interruption, it remains my intention. A week ago, you were a pretty sorry sight, gentlemen. You were pale, tremulous, excitable, utterly at sea in this place. Today, you are a ruddy, capable body of men, at ease with yourselves, and perfectly at home. The change in your condition is all the more marked in that it is not shared by yesterday's speaker, who has clearly lacked the stuff and stamina that distinguish the rest of you. However, none of us worries very much about him, any more than we do about the man who fumbles idly with the gas-cock or points a revolver at his head with the safety-catch on. Such a feigned suicide, we know, is a mere gesture, no more than a passing glance through a dark window. And so, gentlemen, I ignore this crippled trifle and press on to congratulate *you*. I am proud to preside over so stout a body. We have now only to clap upon the strings of Mr Harcourt a mute borrowed from Mr Jamesworth, and all will be well indeed.'

Clapping and laughter followed. All eyes were fixed admiringly on the President, who strode his elevation like a mannequin in sables.

'Let us now,' he said, 'proceed to business. I have only a few more words to say and they are as follows . . . Last night I lay awake and thought about Dr Shubunkin. I recalled his previous histories. I recaptured as best I could their characteristics – their beautiful naturalness, their marvellous economy, their amazing penetration into the minds of others. Then, I was about to go to sleep when it suddenly occurred to me that by dwelling on these aspects of Shubunkin I had blinded myself to the *man*. With shame, I recalled that this wise and brilliant doctor was also a most lovable and admirable human being –

the type we often saw in our younger days on the cinema-screen – devoted, dutiful, and handsome. If we have not always realized this, it is because Dr Shubunkin's field is human nature at its most sordid. Sex, a subject which most of us are only too happy to avoid, has been quietly and scrupulously taken over by this gentle, modest scientist. Daily, he plunges his hands into the sulphurous pit and brings them out as white as snow. Only the dedicated are permitted to do this – and Shubunkin has paid for his dedication. We watch him run through his manifold tics, which break from his nervous system much as sparks break in erratic order from aligned combustion units. We note his singular habit of scraping his left eye-tooth with the bloodstone of his signet-ring; we hear his tinny laugh and shrink from his grin. But these, we know, are not the real Shubunkin, who lives beneath these configurations like a gold thing beneath a habit of dross. Gentlemen, let us salute Dr Shubunkin, the model investigator of our times, the untarnished road-maker, the throbbing liver encased in chromium-plate, the prober into the Place of the Skull. Without him and others like him, we would be living in a *very* different world.'

The members, having excoriated two, were now in the mood to applaud one, and they hailed Dr Shubunkin with claps and cries. The Shubunkin clique, in particular, went half-mad with enthusiasm and pressed their leader's hands, which had gone soft and damp with astonishment. Indeed, the doctor was so taken aback that he added a score of brand-new twitches to his usual repertoire, ran through them twice like lightning, and, when at last he rose to speak, did so with an amiable look of *hubris oblige*.

DOG'S WAY: *A Case of Multiple Sexual Misidentity*

What fun it was in those dear, bygone days to hear mother and father talk sex! 'Let's always,' my father told her, 'speak frankly about sex before the child, so that we don't give society a maladjusted dwarf.' These words are my earliest recollection: I think I was about three at the time. They impressed me because I hated the thought of becoming a maladjusted dwarf, and it seemed that conversation about sex, whatever that might be, was the one thing that would make me grow. So it was not many years before I believed that spoken sex was the same thing as religious salvation and that though people went to it on Sundays and supplicated it at bedtime and even before rising in the morning, it was not a thing which had anything to do with the body. I think I imagined sex as a kind of doctor sitting on a cloud – one whom my father and mother had known very well and whose memory they were determined to perpetuate.

Some confusion arose, however, when I went to school. We attended church every morning, where I regarded the service as a kind of sex. But in the breaks many odd things were whispered to me which I took to be a secret form of religion. I was puzzled, but decided simply not to think about it too much, because a craze for religion is not a healthy thing in childhood. I didn't say anything to my father and mother either, because when you know your parents treasure something, you hate to disappoint them by saying you don't know what it is. In short, I was just like any other child except that I took for granted that sex was a philosophy invented by a friend of my father's.

My parents did their best to teach me. They walked about stark naked whenever they could: I can remember coming home on a cold winter's day and my dear father divesting himself of every stitch. Yes, there were giants in those days.

When I was being pubescent, both my parents were killed in a railway accident. Dr Shubunkin tells me that this is the railway accident that has carried-off thousands of obtrusive parents ever since Stephenson introduced 'The Rocket': before then, he says, it was done with landslides. I wish he had been present to point this out to me when I looked down on those poor, mutilated bodies, fully-clothed for once. It would have made all the difference to know that these corpses were expressions of an old literary tradition and not my parents at all.

I passed into the care of a minor aunt. At least, I think she was an aunt, though I remember calling her Nunk. I am unsure because it was at this time that I began to treasure the words which were my father's only bequest to me. 'Always remember,' he had said, 'that there is no such thing as pure male or pure female. Some wear skirts and some wear pants, but this is only convention. Every man is stuffed with womanly characteristics, every woman is fraught with man. The gap between the powder-puff and the cavalry moustache appears wide but is really a hair's-breadth. I tell you this so that when you grow up and find yourself behaving oddly, as I trust you will, you will know that it is quite apropos. After all, think of dogs.'

Religion, conversation, and dogs – these were now my idea of the what's-what of sex. I tried occasionally to fit these puzzling pieces together, but in the end decided to wait till I was older. My aunt encouraged me in this. Knowing what my parents' view of sex had been, she had braced herself for shocks. Now, I heard her whistle while she shaved.

She was carried off by consumption, just before the war began. Dr Shubunkin says that this is usually the fate of those who have lost relatives in a railway-accident. There is little point, he explains, in retaining in the flesh one who works much better, from a case-history point-of-view, as a distorted image. The whole world of today, he says, as its painters show, is composed of such ghosts, and the sooner we get rid of actual people the better we feel.

When I filled out the application-form for war service I wrote against the word SEX, 'Church of England'. The kindly sergeant kept insisting that this was an improper statement, but when I stood on my principles and refused to alter it he took me to discuss the matter with a young officer, who did his best to persuade me that my obstinacy obstructed the war-effort. 'You've no idea,' he said, 'how much classifying becomes necessary in a war. I'm sure your father was right about dogs, but that was in peacetime.' When I asked him, caustically, if the behaviour-pattern of dogs underwent a sudden, patriotic change when the drums began to roll, he answered firmly that from an official point-of-view it did. I could, he said, take my choice: be a male or a female for the duration and thereafter be as androgynous as I pleased. 'A pretty pickle we would all be in,' he declared, 'if everyone started putting dog-notions on to application forms. I am fully in *sympathy* with you, because I know how hard it is nowadays to define just what one really is. Our fathers, or mothers, whichever they were, had no such problem to face: it existed, of course, but was not yet recognized. But this is not a defined age, such as theirs was, which means that we who live in it must be all the more definite if we are going to achieve any kind of stability. That is why we have so many forms to fill out, why all the questions seem to have been chosen as a challenge to our ingenuity, and why the world has suddenly become overrun with experts who devote their lives exclusively to defining the indefinable. So if you don't want to decide on a sex yourself, I'll refer you to a competent chap who knows about these things and can take the plunge for you.'

169

I must have looked alarmed at this suggestion, because he added hastily: 'My dear girl, please don't think I'm going to send you for some distressing physical check-up. We live in a wiser England than that, young fellow. You will be defined on wholly immaterial grounds.'

A week later I took my place in an enormous queue and after a few days waiting was shown into the consulting room. The identifier was glancing over my history, and said crossly as I entered: 'Really, I think people should give a little more thought to the consequences of the ideas they propound! Take this dog business, now: in theory it is perfectly correct, but how exactly are human beings supposed to practise it?'

A retort came to my lips, but he waved his hands violently and cried: 'No, don't tell me. Anyway, I'd much rather ask questions than hear answers. I think the best approach to your central difficulty will be an oblique one. For instance, are you accident-prone? There seems to be a leaning to it in your family.'

I recited, as well as I could remember, my blunders with knives, mangles, banana-skins, crockery, slippery stairs, puddles, and so on. I was somewhat ashamed when I had finished, but the identifier merely marked a cypher in a box and said: 'That seems fairly good. Your choice was always a normal one; in fact, I should say rather unenterprising and dull. So don't let's bother with your dreams, which would be as humdrum as your accidents. Tell me some stories about your father: this is the oblique approach again: by telling me about him you in fact tell me about you. I must warn you that anything you say will be taken down and used in evidence.'

I told him all father's ideas about sex. It was father's belief, I said, that a pure male (who did not exist) would want absolutely to dominate a female. A pure female (who did not exist either) would want absolutely to be dominated. In fact, however, such definitions were ridiculous. I drew a chart to show how, in everyone, the male-female elements criss-cross interminably, and how their patch-work is rendered convoluted by the attitude the person takes towards it, so that one finds such interesting paradoxes as women who are relatively hairless in a physical sense but have enormous psychological beards, and men whose excessively-small moustaches proclaim the essential frailty of their masculinity. I then briefly summarized the thousands of in-betweens who fill the extremes from full-beard to hair-line moustache, and demonstrated conclusively that to define anyone as male or female was an affront to the intelligence.

'In brief, then,' he answered, 'it's up to you?'

'It's nothing of the sort,' I replied. 'Anyone who makes a sexual decision is returning us to the Dark Ages.'

'Well, let's try it another way,' he said; 'not so oblique, either. Which sex – assuming such to exist – do you most enjoy flirting with?'

I told him I was not bigoted: my emotions, I said, responded to virtually any mixture, with little preference as to type, colour, build, stature.

He made a sound like a shot-gun going off. 'That's what I wanted,' he said: 'Remember it, next time you loose those dogs of yours. You are a born sailor.' He wrote a huge M on my card and cried: 'Good morning! Next, please!'

So I was to be a man! The very thought brought every female element in me into play: I went straight to bed with a sick-headache, took aspirin, and had a good cry. Soon there was a knock at my door and in came a husky sergeant in the uniform of one of the women's services. 'What's the matter, love?' she said, taking my hand: 'The whole house is shaking with your sobs.' 'I've been classed as a male,' I answered, laying my cheek against her iron paw. 'And what's so awful about that?' she cried in a deep bass voice: 'it seems to me you'd make a sweet little man. And what's wrong with being a man, anyway,' she continued indignantly, as if personally insulted: 'Some of my best girls are men. If you are so full of prejudice when you are hardly out of your teens, you won't be very nice to know at forty.'

'It was not prejudice brought me to this,' I retorted angrily: 'it was standing on my principles.' I then told her about father's teachings and my examination by the identifier, and she patted my shoulder and said: 'If there were more women like your father, this would be a cosier world. But he's past helping, so let's see what we can do for little *you*. The first thing is to find you a nice, friendly unit. And don't worry about your definition. It's nothing to do with you. It's literally a war-measure, a yard-stick the authorities require to get themselves to scale. They feel that if they can place *you*, it won't be long before they grasp *themselves*. Still, it might be a good thing to have you re-identified. You can always appeal, you know. But what good will it do? You don't

171

think you'll shake off your old problems by taking on a new sex, do you? That's escapism.'

'Of course I don't!' I answered, with a fresh burst of tears. 'I only ask to remain neither one nor the other. If *you* won't understand that, who will?' – and letting my mouth fall open with a sort of crab-like quaver, I bent on her that gaze of heart-rending disappointment which has wrung the withers of husbands through the centuries.

To my horror, she received it with a most vulgar guffaw, and folding my face against her rough uniform she said: 'Of course, you are simply too adorable to live! I shall keep you here for my very own. We'll have dressing-up parties and I'll show you to all my friends. But listen. I have to go on duty now, but I'll be back before night. I'm going to put you in my room and while I'm away I'm going to discuss your case with some people I know and see what can be done. Don't worry about your definition: by the time the authorities have fed your sex into the right machine and come out with a unit, we'll have you cosily settled where you'll like it best.' She then yanked me, sniffling, from my bed and dragged me upstairs to her own room, where she made me comfortable in a big chair beside the gasfire. 'Be a good little mannikin while mother's away,' she said, wagging a huge finger at me – 'and *don't let anyone in.*' The door closed behind her and, to my surprise, I heard the key turn in the lock.

No sooner was she out of hearing – half down the street, that is – than I jumped from my chair, dried my eyes and began to explore the premises (sometimes, I must confess, I see myself every inch a woman!). The furnishings were of a rather rough kind – a good deal of leather on the chairs, a pair of buffalo horns, dumb-bells, and heavy curtains, much like a good club. To my surprise, the main decoration was a huge picture of a ferocious man wearing a black beard down to his heavy watch-chain. In one corner of him was the inscription: 'To my own little Violet, from her great, big, loving Papa.' Dear me! how very inappropriate! I thought, and looked closer at what seemed to be a leg of mutton at the side of the picture. It proved to be the shoulder of a woman: obviously Violet's mother, who had been chopped ruthlessly from the picture. Sprigs of rosemary were tied neatly to the four corners of the frame.

More curious than ever, I examined the other photographs on the walls: there was simply no end to them. Some were of school hockey and lacrosse teams, and of the staff with the prefects: Violet appeared in all of them, invariably sitting in the middle and obviously the captain of everything. Then there was a photograph of Violet dressed in a huge leather coat, astride an enormous Matchless double-knocker with a great grin all over her face: there had been a pillion-passenger, it seemed, but she (if she it was) appeared to have suffered the fate of Violet's mother and been savagely scissored from the picture. Indeed, there was hardly a photograph in the room which did not have at least one gaping space with the outline of a human form: I wondered what happened to these poor ghosts; were they mutilated and burnt, and if so, what had they done? Some of them, it seemed, had been chopped out because they were destined for higher things: there were, for example, three photographs of girls which were enlargements made from these chopped-out miniatures: they looked rather silly, vapid girls to me, with round sheep's eyes, tender skins, and beat-me-daddy expressions: I put the tip of my tongue out at all of them. But of all the photographs, none impressed me more than that of Violet with no less than seven six-foot women all standing in Arctic clothes beside a tent in the snow. Underneath was written: 'Everest Expedition 1935.'

Well, young lady (if such you are), I said to myself: you've got into the lion's den all right. I then opened a large wardrobe in the bedroom and was astonished to see hanging from the door-rail a black beard exactly like Violet's father's, with hooks to go over the ears. Equally interesting was a wide range of men's suitings – cut, I must say, with just a touch of effeminacy; but how else, in view of the contours, *can* one cut a man's suit to fit a woman? They ranged from plus-fours to very distinguished evening-dress, including a concertina hat and an opera cloak. There was also a choice of swagger-canes, knobkerries, and blackthorn walking-sticks; and there were shoes without number, mostly the sort of brogues that men nowadays find too heavy.

I might have dallied for hours, fingering these coarse stuffs and these trim appurtenances of a man-about-town, had I not decided to explore the second, smaller wardrobe. I gave such a gasp when I opened the door, because a wave of scent poured out and I found myself staring at a row of expensive dresses and nightdresses, with a bottom rail fairly hidden by sparkling high-heeled shoes, wonderful open-toed sandals, and slippers of every kind, from sleek to furry. It was simply too much for me: without a second thought I whipped off my jacket and trousers and tried on an absolutely ravishing evening-dress.

I say 'tried on'; but put-on would be the better description. For no sooner had I got it over me and was tripping gaily to the long mirror to fall in love with myself (which is what try-on really means) than I heard the terrifying sound of a key turning gently in the living-room door.

I knew it was not Violet: I would have heard her thunderous steps. Who was it, then? I stood, my mouth warbling little moans of terror, the back of one palm pressed against my lips. Infinitely slowly, the door opened; at last, a terrifying feline face was poked cautiously into the room. On seeing me, it gave a scream of rage, burst in, and without a word of explanation ran five sharp finger-nails down each side of my face. 'So you're the one, are you?' it screamed, grasping me by the hair (which fortunately was navy-cut) and attempting to throw me into the fire: 'Oh, what I'll do to you, you sneaking little harpy, you two-timing little chorus-girl, you little female ant, you runty little slip, you smirking snippet off a Chiaparelli march-past! And in *my* dress, *my* own sea-wave taffeta! Oh, oh!' She began to rip it off me, leaving me exposed in my woollen combinations and striped suspenders, the sight of which seemed to add to her rage, causing her to scream: 'Oh, a double-harpy, a witch in man's pants, a little Violet's monkey, a suspendered copy twice removed!' At this, I found my voice – which, much to my surprise, emerged almost in a deep baritone. 'You get out of here, you beastly girl!' I bellowed: 'do you think I can't defend myself? How's that, and that . . . ?' and, oh dear, I gave her a good old one-two with the left and right, and when I had her rocking seized one of Violet's heaviest brogues and went at her with it, roaring like a bull. But next minute she was gone: I heard her squeals ringing down the stairs. For a moment I stood panting, brogue in hand; then in response to an angry cry from an American corporal on the lower floor: 'Hey, you guys! A little less—noise if you don't mind!' I slammed-to the door and fell back into my chair.

Now, my tears began to flow again; I touched my poor scratched cheeks with my palms and lamented my miserable condition. If this is how dogs behave, I thought, I would rather be something else – and I had been saying this to myself, between sobs, for quite half a minute before it dawned on me that for the first time I was questioning a tenet

174

of my father's. At this, guilt rolled over me in waves and I abandoned myself utterly to sobs and groans.

Thus occupied, rolled-up in a cocoon of self-pity and self-accusation, I did not hear the door open – only a man's squeaky voice saying: 'Hullo, dear! *Not* idle tears? *Do* let Harold help you. Harold *loves* to help.'

He was the slimmest thing you ever saw, with blond hair like silk. You could see right through his skin to the bewitching little bones underneath: he would have made a delicious feast at a banquet of cannibal elves. His hands, which he held before him wrist up and fingers down, were limp as cheesecloth, and instinct told me that his purpose in thus displaying them was to let them precede him into a strange place and give advance evidence of his utter harmlessness. I saw at once that I must take a strong masculine line with him, so I stood upright and said sharply: 'What are you doing here, you shrimp? Did Violet not tell you to stay away?'

He giggled like anything and answered: 'No, dear, you know *quite well* she didn't. But of course you are absolutely right to suggest she did. It shows that although you don't know *her* one bit, you do understand *me*. And understanding is *so* much more important than knowledge, I always think.'

This put me on my guard. People who can deliver this sort of talk at a moment's notice are always able to take care of themselves, no matter how limply they may dangle their hands. Clearly, my visitor was disguised. But as what? I couldn't imagine.

'I really think,' he said, looking at me tactfully under his long eyelashes, 'that you should put a little more *on*. But not on my account. On the contrary, if woollen combinations are your preference, nothing, absolutely nothing in the world, would persuade me to utter the smallest criticism, let alone the least *reproach*.'

I was now in a quandary. What, if anything, should I put on? Skirts or trousers? I am no fool, and I saw very quickly that this naughty little fop was attempting to shame me into declaring my sex. So I replied very coolly: 'Thank you, I prefer to remain as nature made me. May I ask your business?'

'Such an *awful* old fright,' he answered, 'isn't he?' and pointed at Violet's father. 'It simply gives me *gooseflesh* to look at him. One can almost *see* him *wielding* the knout. On some bare slave.'

He shuddered, and gave me a very appealing, humorous look. It melted me a little because it suggested that poor buttercups like ourselves do manage to keep up our spirits with little jokes about the boots that crush us. So I asked him: 'Are you a friend of Violet's?'

'I'm not sure that *friend* is quite the word,' he replied fussily, working his little face through a series of grimaces and leaving little lines and wrinkles behind which he carefully smoothed out again with his finger-tips. 'There now, look what you've done: you've given me crows-feet,' he said petulantly, glancing into a little mirror which he drew from his pocket. 'No. I *adore* Violet, but friendship is rather *different*. I never think of Violet at all, never give her a second's thought, until I am feeling dispirited and crushed. Then, I have a sudden vision of those refectory-table legs, those square hips, that crimson face, and that hair like pig's bristles. I rush to her for mother-love. One glance at her is enough to reduce me to sheer jelly. I never leave her without feeling that there is more hope and serenity in the outside world than there was when I fled from it. But this time, oddly enough, I have come to ask her *advice*.'

'It seems odd to me,' I said tartly, 'that you should come for advice to one whom you don't credit with much intelligence.'

'But, dear, she *has* no intelligence. She *lay* on it ages ago, like a *sow*, my dear, and *crushed* it, absolutely *drove* it into the mud of her sty. It made her feel *vulnerable*. After all, let's be *fair* to Violet: what does she *want* with intelligence? *All* she wants is people to prod her respectfully in the hams and say: "There's a prize boar if ever I saw one." That's really the trouble nowadays, you know. God forbid that I should object to the sexes having changed places, but I do think sometimes that the women are going a *little* far. Let them be men by all means; I gladly abdicate *that* exhausting role. But must they be Visigoths? Do they have to *look* so repulsive? Do they have to carry imitation to the point of *parody*? I, for one, am never amused by Violet's famous parlour-trick.'

'To which of them do you refer?' I asked cleverly.

'I mean the one with the policeman. I simply *crawl* under the table ... But never mind. I suppose I'm old-fashioned. Today, I had hoped to consult her about my play. There's a part with two Amazons fighting over a captive. I simply can't imagine what to make one of them say in the heat of a particular moment. Perhaps that depends on the sex of the captive.'

'So you write *plays?*' I asked, rather pleased to have the conversation on a higher level.

'Only *a* play. It's one I've always had.' He sighed. 'It really is going to astonish people when it's performed. It is so entirely new.'

'In what way?'

'Well, you see, it's an interpretation of contemporary life disguised as a tragedy of the age of Pericles. It starts with a porter coming on and saying how corrupt everything is in Athens and that if the king doesn't take propitiatory steps immediately, there's bound to be a seven-years' famine. The chorus takes up this theme and goes on about famine for a long time. At last the king comes on, with his advisers and mother and so-on, and they decide there's simply no doubt any more; they *must* get a directive from the oracle. The chorus are very pleased and chant a long time about the wisdom of this decision, but you can tell by a rather malicious grimness in their tones – you know what choruses *are* – that the king's in for a nasty shock. And *how* right they are, my dear! The oracle looks-up some gizzards and tells him that the only way he can save the city is by sacrificing the first person he meets when he gets outside.'

'Surely there is nothing new in this?' I said. 'I seem to have read it all my life.'

'Oh no you haven't, dear. Who do you think is the first person the king meets on leaving the oracle?'

'Someone he is very fond of, of course.'

'Exactly. Well – *it's his mother.*'

He stared at me with a look of maniacal triumph. But when he saw that I was unmoved, even puzzled, he began to explain desperately: 'You see, she was so worried about what the oracle would say that instead of staying in *bed* as her son told her to do – she has a weak heart, you see – she secretly hobbled to the temple. In fact, she listened at the keyhole. So when he comes out with his sword drawn, she proffers her naked breast. It's going to be *the* most dramatic moment since Oedipus screamed – and *so* much more up-to-date. Every thread of life as we live it today, every vital question, will be drawn, as by invisible wires, to this incredible, unanswerable, unresolvable moment. The king must choose between his mother and Athens: that is to say, between

177

mother and *art*. It's sheer horror! Don't ask me which he plumps for. Every time I think of his agony I cry so much that I can't go on writing. That's why I'm just concentrating on the odd bits *pro tem.*, like the Amazon battle.'

'Is his mother an Amazon?'

'Oh, my dear, *yes*! In her prime she's been *something* – sacrificed and eaten most of her children, castrated Herakles, netted and boiled four husbands. The chorus sings a *complete* account of her career while she has her ear to the keyhole. But I see it's all far above your head. You don't grasp it at all. Not that I do, myself. I would much rather not write the play at all.'

'Then why not drop it?'

'How can I, dear? Don't be *too* obtuse. I must know who I am, mustn't I?'

'Surely your own play isn't going to tell you?'

'Of course not, dear; it's the critics who'll tell me. At the moment I don't exist; I don't even know what to *become*. But once my play's done, I'll know. One critic will say: "Harold Snatogen reveals himself as an embodiment of the fashionable anti-Moon Goddess revival." Another will say: "In Snatogen we see what Hegel called ... " and then he'll tell what Hegel called. After that it will be quite simple: I shall become the most flattering definition. You see, nowadays you can't hope to do *everything* yourself. *You* produce the little boys, as it were, and the critics tell you what you're made of. Once you've been told, you just sail ahead, being yourself. It's the first little boy that matters.'

'So you are another who insists on being defined,' I said angrily. 'I seem to be the last of the liberal humanists. You are nothing but an inverted Philistine.'

'Not *really*?' he exclaimed excitedly, seizing my hands. 'Oh, if only you were an expert in such matters! If only I could trust your judgement! But I need a more authoritative definition than yours. And it has to be *printed*. Speech is *useless*.'

We sat in silence, he sadly stroking away his wrinkles, I plucking ridges in my combies. The gap that separates defined men and women is as nothing to that which stands between two inhabitants of the *demi-monde* who are not agreed on a common centre. I felt that no matter how long we sat there – talking, sympathizing, exchanging views – we would never be anything but strangers, sharing nothing but a common twilight. It was a relief to both of us, I think, to hear Violet's boots clumping up the stairs and the crash of her hips against the banisters.

'I thought,' she said, 'I told you to let nobody in.'

Harold did not wait. With a burst, he shot under her arm and vanished down the stairs.

'Don't blame me,' I replied hotly. 'What about that girl who has a key? Look what she's done to me.'

Violet stepped forward. She looked at the scratches on my face. She ran her eyes down my combinations. She looked at the ripped taffeta on the carpet. Then she drew back her left fist and smote me.

*

I don't know how long I was unconscious. I know I dreamt that I was the king in Harold's play and that when my mother bared her breast, I said: 'I'm dreadfully sorry, mum, but Athens simply *must* come first.' My father, who was present, said later: 'Of course, dear, you were quite right. And anyway, she *was* rather a nuisance, wasn't she?' But he spoke in Harold's squeaky voice and wore a taffeta evening-dress, whereas my mother was laid out for burial in the costume of a Tyrolean mountaineer, with hairy knees. Dr Shubunkin says that one would hardly expect anything else: he interprets my mother's knees as a protest against Violet's father's beard and the Tyrolean costume as a snub to Violet's ascent of Everest.

I had been moved to the bedroom. A party was going on in the room where I'd been hit. Violet was talking to a friend: she said: 'Come and see him if you are curious. He's a dear little thing. If he turns out well, I'm going to have nothing but ones like him in future.' The other woman answered: 'Are you going to have him doctored?' '*Probably* not,' said Violet reflectively, 'I always think a lobotomy is better for excitable types of either sex. The trouble is that nowadays one can never *quite* be sure what one really wants. I think it would be a greater triumph to keep him exactly as he is – but much more *modern*, of course, to do as you suggest. To tell the truth, when he's properly dressed I don't think it will make a hap'orth of difference either way.'

'He *is* a he, then, is he?'

'He, she, or it.'

They came into the bedroom. I kept my eyes closed in the most

179

natural way. I felt myself prodded and pinched: my upper lip was raised and my teeth examined. 'Well,' said the woman after a few minutes, 'You've certainly got something. Just *what* is another matter.' They both laughed. 'There's no accounting for taste,' said the woman, 'but personally I do like to know what's what. I don't look forward to hybrid love-affairs: I like my girls to *be* girls.' 'Then you'll soon find yourself hopelessly left behind,' said Violet: 'we are getting closer to sexual chaos every day and I don't intend to be left at the bottom of the heap. Answer me frankly, now: is there anything about this little thing here that remotely resembles what we mean when we say a man?' 'I admit,' replied the other, 'that it is a dual-purpose creature. But I feel it should be in a museum.' 'I can always put it in the Victoria and Albert when I'm tired of it,' replied Violet: 'meanwhile I see it as a sort of *investment.*' 'What will you *dress* it in?' asked the other. 'I'm not *quite* sure,' said Violet slowly, 'but my plan at the moment is to keep it in the house for a few weeks as a playmate. It can wear a neutral blouse and slacks. After that, I shall dress it like a *sort* of man and marry it to one of my old girls. Little Hilda, for instance, would adore a small husband. I'll make them live close by and then I'll be able to use both of them. I could put them in a cottage and go and share them at weekends.'

After a while the other woman said: 'You know, Violet, all this doubling is going to be the ruin of you. Eventually you're going to forget your own sex and become a hybrid of hybrids yourself. Why not stop while you still know?'

'I can't stop,' said Violet in a strong voice. 'Even if it leads to nonentity, I must go on. I won't be happy till all the men are girls and all the girls are men – and *then* I won't be happy until I've changed them all back again. I won't be happy until no one *knows* a he from a she. I want to be able to *tell* them which they are – which will be what I want them to be at any particular moment. I want them to be infinitely exchangeable and alterable. I want to see doctors advertising rebored, resleeved, reconditioned sexual engines, guaranteed to fit any body. I want utterly to erase the memory of centuries of sexual discrimination by making every human creature a sexual melting-pot. I am going to be sex's first great Nihilist. I know that men, in the past, experimented with being all things to all men and women, but I'm going to go one better: I'm going to make all the men and women be all things to me. When absolute sexual nonentity has been reached, the female principle may be permitted to wither away. Men themselves are already absolutely negligible, but the *idea* of manliness has still to be rooted out. At the same time, people must have a feeling of security in their lives; someone has to rule the roost. It can never be the men again, their moral cowardice and terror where women are concerned has undone them permanently. On the other hand, the women are so utterly conventional that even the ones who use their men like doormats like to pretend that at heart they are gentle, sensitive little things forever in search of a manly bully. So we are in what is always called a transitional period – and nothing disgusts me more than the transitional. It is a world of disguises and fabrications; every lie in the book is acted-out in order to hide the truth . . . Oh, well . . . It's a long story and this little mannikin here is nothing but a tiny episode in it – a little pimple on the face of progress. If I thought there was real stuff in him, I'd turn him over to Sven Ormerod, the plastic surgeon, and have him really done-up. He'd make a handsome woman.'

I *must* have turned pale as I listened to this terrible recital. I could hear my heart racing; I trembled all over; and yet, even in this state of panic, my mind remained normal enough for me to think with amazement of the innocence of my dear father and mother. Like harmless missionaries they had set up their little camp, dogs and all, on the verge of a forest inhabited entirely by wild and savage creatures; daily they had preached their little doctrine, thinking it something tender and new, while only a few yards away the forest was alive with monsters practising it. I am sorry to say that at that moment a trace of cynicism entered my heart and remains there to this day.

I heard a voice say: 'Violet, the policemen are here,' and Violet answer: 'I'm coming. I hope they're bigger than the last two.' 'Absolutely enormous, darling,' was the reply; and then they all moved out and I was alone again. Once more, the key turned in the lock.

I opened my eyes and looked wildly round the room. The only route of escape was through the window, which I raised silently. It opened on a nice flat piece of leaded roof – which, alas, led nowhere. There was the conventional drainpipe, of course, leading down into black nothingness; but not even my dread of falling into the hands of Professor Ormerod could make me trust myself to it. There was always the other conventional way, of knotting sheets together; but one is not tempted to such a course with war-time sheets. No, if I were to escape I must somehow open that locked door, make my way unseen through the crowded living-room and walk away down the stairs.

Now, if there is one thing on which I pride myself it is my ability to recognize the central question in a given problem. In this case, the question was: What kind of protective coloration does one put on in order to pass unnoticed through a room containing twelve lesbians and two policemen? Like many questions facing us today, this is a difficult one to answer; indeed, it raises the more-important question of whether people are not too optimistic when they argue that it is questions, not answers, that are of primary importance. Be that as it may, I found an answer to *my* question almost immediately.

I was still wearing my combinations, a good foundation for the disguise I selected. I opened Violet's wardrobe and with great coolness selected a shaggy pair of tweed trousers and heavy boots. Over all, I drew a heavy overcoat, which I buttoned to the chin. I selected the heaviest walking-stick and found to my delight, a large briar pipe. I put a deer-stalker on my head. Then came the boldest moment: I lifted the black beard from its peg and adjusted it to my chin.

When I looked in the glass I hardly knew myself. I looked so exactly like Violet's father that for a moment I fell into a brown study and allowed my heart to range nostalgically through the century before my birth, when any doubt as to the nature of one's sex was utterly dissipated by the unanswerable character of one's visage. This led me to think of the many men who during and since the war have grown such immense moustaches: poor, simple souls! I thought – too late, too late! Your mettle will never rise to the ferocity of your hairs: face to face with the Violets of this world, your proud handlebars will melt into waxy pigtails, fit only for desiccated mandarins. Your courage, unequalled in battle with other men, has abandoned you in your domestic life. It has entered into your women, which is why I, at this moment of disguise, look every inch a Victorian man but feel myself every inch a modern woman!

I did not feel quite so resolute when I approached the locked door and heard the roar of the savages in the next room. Their hoarse exhortations and drunken cheers told me that Violet was starting her famous policeman trick, whatever that might be. If I were to escape, it must be at the moment when her every thought was centred upon her trick: that is to say, almost immediately.

I took an assegai from the wardrobe and inserted it carefully between the door and the jamb at the level of the keyhole. I heard Violet shout: 'No bending, now, you buttered muffins! Stiff as lamp-posts or I'll take a stick to you!' I heard an answering giggle from what could only, in that room, be one of the policemen. Then, suddenly, absolute silence fell.

I waited a few seconds and then gave the assegai a powerful wrench. The door flew open: I marched straight out.

A most curious scene lay before me. I hardly know whether to describe it vertically or horizontally: on the whole, I think I had better begin at the bottom. This means Violet.

She was on all fours, naked save for a pair of orange shorts and a webbed bra. Her face (fortunately, as it turned out) was towards me, but it was only two feet from the floor, because her legs were straddled wide apart, the muscles bulging like parsnips. Over her shoulders was a small oak table, on which stood no less than four women of immense bulk. Rigid on the floor, on each side of the table, stood two large policemen. Violet, holding each one by the nearest ankle with her left and right hands, was at the moment of my entry beginning to rise to an erect position, taking with her this colossal human load. At the moment I strode in, the four nymphs were almost touching the ceiling and both policemen were some three feet above floor level.

The effect of my entry was, plainly, catastrophic. Violet, whose face had been rich purple and strained to bursting, let out a single scream of 'Father!' and crashed full length upon the floor. She was followed down by the table, the legs of which instantly snapped so that it lay across her back with the four enormous women sprawled on top of it. Both policemen fell inwards and joined the ladies. A howl of horror went up on either side.

I had no need even to raise my stick. With a hard, contemptuous expression on my bearded face I walked coolly round the central obstacle, opened the door, and descended the stairs. I reached the pavement without the least trouble – and there, pacing up and down with an anxious look, was none other than my good little Harold! The very sight of him was enough to break down my masculine pretence, and I called in a desperate, broken voice: 'Oh, Harold, are you waiting for me? Take me home, take me somewhere, take me *anywhere*!'

He raised his head, took one look at my portentous form, and let out a squeal of terror. He then set off into the darkness as fast as he could run, his little round elbows working frantically up and down. I rushed after him crying, 'Harold! Harold! It's me! Don't you know me, Harold?', but as my heavy boots and the roaring of the wind in my Victorian passage began to gain on him, he started to scream desperately: 'No, no! I *couldn't* face it! Leave me alone, you awful man! You visitation, you judgement! I never asked for *you*!' Panic gave strength to his little legs, but not enough: soon, they began to wobble and he fell in a heap. Tearing off my beard, I tore his fingers from his eyes and cried: 'Look, Harold! I am not what you think. I am what I am.' But it was not until I had forcibly pried his mauve eyelids apart that he glimpsed me from the corner of one skewed eyeball and lapsed into a brief faint of relief. I sat and chafed his little hands till he came round – and with what indignation did he at last purse his little mouth and flare his ivory nostrils! 'You have frightened me *totally* out of my wits,' he said angrily, his voice trembling: 'words cannot express my mingled disappointment and *horror*. For the first time I knew what poor Io felt when she saw that *abominable* bull. What are you doing here? Why are you Walt Whitman? Where is Violet?'

'She is under a table, topped by twelve Amazons and two bobbies,' I replied.

'My dear, what a *tableau*! *Too* raffish!' He began to arrange his hair.

'You were waiting for me, Harold?' I asked.

'In a sense, yes.'

By now, I was all woman – old fashioned, soft, weepy, infinitely grateful. I threw my arms about his neck and cried: 'Oh, Harold! you have proved yourself the finest of men! Take me away somewhere! Protect and love me always, your meek, adoring wife!'

He gave a choked scream, and cried: '*Really*, this is too much! It is worse than the beard! Drop me immediately, you indescribable woman!'

I at once obeyed, and adopting as best I could a neuter tone, I said: 'Harold, I promise not to lay a finger of either sex upon you. Only find me some place where I can hide from Violet. She was going to turn me over to a *surgeon*, Harold.'

'So unnecessary,' he answered, with a frown. 'Well, come along then. I have a good place in mind. It was where I was waiting to take you when you first *fell* upon me.'

We got into a taxi and Harold gave the driver an address, saying: 'And drive like *anything.*' He was quite perky by now and pleased with himself, and said at one point in our drive: 'You know, this is going to make *all* the difference to my play. Until an hour ago I was merely toying with the *fringes* of reality, my dear, simply hovering on the extreme *hem.* When I have translated your disguise into terms of classical rape, there won't be a house in London big enough to take in the *flocks.* And, my dear, *the Lord Chamberlain!*'

But I was too unstrung to discuss literature. The taxi drew up, I paid the driver with a half-sovereign from the greatcoat pocket, and Harold rang the bell. The door opened, a shaft of light fell upon me, and I swooned upon the doormat, the beard slipping from my fingers.

*

I awoke, dressed in silk pyjamas and with scent behind my ears, on a lovely painted sofa, set in a room that was filled with light, colour, and flowers. Harold was lying naked under a sun-lamp, rubbing cold-cream into his crow's-feet and turning with his palms the pages of a pornographic volume. In a corner, deftly arranging Michaelmas daisies in a tall vase, stood a plump, well-dressed man. A Philippino manservant was dusting a figure of Adonis with a feather whisk – or so I thought until the figure said: 'That's *quite* enough, Carlo,' and walked lightly from the room.

'Yes,' said the man with the flowers: 'it will be a lesson to you, Harold. I have urged you a hundred times to bring a little daintiness and *order* into your life, and instead you have *courted* turmoil. I was patient when the bosun thrashed you; I hid you when you fled the large Jamaican; I interposed *my own form* when your devious camping turned the sun-porch to a *jungle.* As a result, you have come to believe that my affection for you will always be on *top,* my sword for ever *unsheathed* in your behalf. But this is not the case. What, pray, would you have done, if this bearded monster had proved *real?* How would you have emerged from such a test? Would you have emerged at all? Would you have *wished* to emerge? For that is really the main question. Each time I succour you, I have the feeling that I have *let you down,* *disappointed* you. It is no good your talking of Zeus in the guise of some

185

predatory animal: what are you doing in the *den* at all? What have the *classics* to do with it? It seems to me you have got your identity confused: in the Greek world it is only *heroes* who go out in search of monsters, and there is no trace of the heroic in *you*. Instead, there is some nagging compulsion to *wriggle* yourself – for wriggle is the *only* word – into the very centre of a predicament in which you will be utterly defenceless when the moment comes to *pay the piper.*'

Harold gave a slight scream and went on reading.

'But is that not true? Well, I am going to find out. Next time you find yourself in the clutch of some bar-room Jove, *I shall not be there.*'

Harold screamed again.

'No, I shall not. I shall watch your struggles with complacent negligence. When you are carried from the scene, shrieking, I shall not wind my horn. I shall not whistle-up my *dogs*. We shall see then how you emerge from the *bonfire* which has resulted from your childish obsession with *matches*. If anything *remains* of you thereafter –'

Harold gave a third scream and drummed his ankles.

' – If anything *remains* of you, it will perhaps be a more *orderly* remnant, more discriminating in its choice of *friends*, more *sensible* of *itself*, less ready to cast its *bread* upon the waters, leaving a *better* taste in the mouth than is the case at present.'

'What's the time?' said Harold.

The gentleman consulted his wrist-watch and replied: 'It is exactly eleven twenty-nine.'

'Then I must turn over,' said Harold. He did so. 'I'm sorry I interrupted,' he added, 'do go on.'

'I shall certainly do so. What I see ahead of *you*, Harold, is *middle-age*. No, don't scream. I'm only being cruel to be kind. I was once every inch as slim as you. When I entered a room, I, too, did so like a graceful spinning-top. Like you, I tormented my elders and betters, mocking their sage flesh with fluttering and suggestive glances. Like you, I veiled a heart full of trickery and malice under looks of hapless innocence. Indeed, I know it all so well, that when I look at you now, my glance penetrates you from end to end.'

'I like that,' said Harold.

'Of course. But you won't when you have become impenetrably *fat*. And you are *going* to be fat. You are the type who becomes *exceedingly* fat. You are going to look like a *Queen's Pudding*. The creases

186

that you are at this moment so easily smoothing from your eyes are going to be *gullies*, Harold, deep passages down which your elderly tears will flow between banks of mountainous *tissues*. Your hair will not grey; oh no. It will never know a charming silver. It will fall from your head, as silky hair always does, sliver by sliver, and leave not a wrack behind, only the domed sheen of a moribund chamber-pot. You will be a repulsive sight; your feet flat, hot, and heavy; your gait a rolling wobble; your *knees* – but let us say nothing of *them*. Burnt, indeed, *immolated*, at both ends, your candle will not last the night, if only because there will be no night to give it harbour.'

Harold began to cry. Well-pleased, the gentleman continued: 'In short, you are in mid-passage, Harold. Two more years of your present identity is the *very most* you can expect. Now is the time for you to learn from my experience. What did *I* do when, like you, I saw myself approaching the middle of the journey? Did I press on, oblivious, keeping to the dear, familiar road of beauty, youth, and malice? I did not. I resolved then and there to trim my nails and cut my losses. Before Nature could rob me of my hair, I myself clipped it to the brosse. My shirts of many colours I gave to younger men. My suits became double-breasted and severe; my necktie a firm, simple bow. I learnt to walk stiffly upright; I charged my languorous hands with a chubby firmness suggestive of aesthetic dignity. I voluntarily became tubby before my time; I cleansed my house of the riff-raff which haunted it; substituted for the ever unmade double-bed the refined bust, the well-chosen tea-cup, the select *objet d'art*. . . . And turn that sun-lamp on to some higher part of you or you will be a Botticelli from the waist-up, a Bronzino from waist-down.'

Sniffling, Harold obeyed.

'Let me continue. I saw, even at that early stage of my life, that the reward of age is not wisdom but despotism. I trained myself to be hard, crusty, and ruthless. I made myself feared. I killed the butterfly in me and became a managerial figure. No one knew in what shape I might appear – a tyrannous interior-decorator, an authority on harpsichords, a racing motorist, a designer of winter-gardens and connoisseur of camellias, a royalist historian, a distinguished general. I even made a brief venture into marriage – a condition I would still be in were it not for the fact that my strength of character and ferocity made it impossible for me to stimulate the soft, spineless role of an up-to-date husband. And what has been the consequence of all this? Does anyone regard me in the way they will soon regard you – as a repellent old Micawber whose puffy antics and sloppy ways provoke only derision and boredom? Do I live a lonely, drunken life, cooking myself precious little dishes over a dirty gasfire and obtaining from food the gluttonous joy that I am denied by my fellow-girls? Far from it. I am a well-to-do, revered and powerful figure. That Establishment which we call England has taken me in: I am become her Fortieth article. I sit upon her Boards, I dominate her stage, her museums, her dances, and her costumes; I have an honoured voice in her elected House. To her – and her alone – I bend the knee, and in return for my homage she is gently blind to my small failings, asking only that I indulge them privately. The few who dare to sneer at me, do so well-behind my back, and when I find them out my revenge is subtle, immediate, and deadly. When I look at *you*, Harold, sprawled beneath that lamp like an earthworm on a sunny stone, it is not envy or admiration I feel ... it is *joy* – joy that no one can ever turn *my* stone over and render me a revolting slug, condemned to a dark, wet world of slime and misery. ... What? Weeping again? You do not want the Establishment to seize you, try you, and imprison you, to be considered degraded even by the House of Lords and corrupt even by the evening press? You object to standing in a magistrate's court hearing your psychological oddity explained to three rich grocers and a retired colonel? You don't want every illiterate in town to make you responsible for the fall of the Roman Empire, or to become the victim through whom the Establishment will threaten all who detest it? You do not wish to be sponged upon by golden-haired youths who will spend what they squeeze from you on orgies with others more handsome and robust? Surely you need have no fear of *that*. It is you who will be begging from them – piteously reminding them that you, too, were once comely and exotic. But the young never read the terrible messages that are writ on tombstones, Harold, nor do they throw away good money on *ancient mariners.*'

Poor Harold! I had been sorry to hear that he had been keeping such bad company and that his character, as I had suspected already, was of a weak kind. I was glad, on the other hand, to know that there was some older man to take an interest in his future and explain how worried the Establishment always is about the Roman Empire having lasted only a thousand years. But it did seem to me that he was having it laid on pretty hard. It touched my heart to see him lying there, burnt quite red in some places and merely tinged in others, his eyes red with tears, the cold cream smeared all over his pretty book, his insteps twitching with his sobs. It was to save him from further humiliation that I gave a genteel cough.

At once the older man gave me a most sympathetic smile and started across the room. On reaching Harold, he paused, struck him a sharp blow on the buttocks, and cried: 'Stop!' When Harold, with a yell, burst into more tears, he slapped him again, saying: 'Immediately! This is the last warning!' I was impressed to see that within a few seconds Harold's tears had disappeared and only a silent quivering remained to indicate his distress. The Master switched off the sun-lamp and said: 'Now, go and get dressed at once. You are a horrible sight.' And Harold, sighing, rose to his feet and went obediently to the door. I was sorry to see that though he staggered in an ungainly way at first, by the time he reached the door he was moving in his usual affected way, as if totally unimpressed by the sermon he had just received.

'So you are the bearded lady?' said the Master, sitting beside the sofa with a smile. 'Well, my dear, let us first get one thing *quite* clear. It was purely as an act of humanity that I gave you refuge here, and if you are one of the gang with whom Harold associates when my back is turned, I assure you that you will *leave immediately*.'

I was most offended by such a rude beginning. I was about to say so, in the strongest language, when I took notice of the extreme severity of his face and changed my mind. 'Far from being one of any gang,' I answered simply, 'I am an unhappy, persecuted person who has suffered only misfortune as a result of clinging to the strictest principles.'

'You had better tell me the whole story, then,' he replied, 'And no lies and exaggerations, please. I am *never* fooled.'

'This will be the fourth time I have told "the whole story", in a single week,' I answered, 'and yet it is already ten times as long. Only a few days ago it had a long beginning and no end; now, the beginning is negligible as the end stretches into interminable nightmare. A week ago, I stood firmly upon my past; today, it has disappeared and I am swimming in incomprehensibility. It used to worry me not to know who I was, but I find it far worse not knowing *when* I am.'

I then told him the whole story, weeping vigorously when I reached the moment of my parents' deaths because I knew that from now on they would play no part whatever in my life.

'And so,' he said, when I had finished, 'what is the situation now? In what identity do you intend to face the future? Are you going to choose one of the sexes as your own or are you going to continue on the undetermined course laid down by your parents?'

'I cannot see myself doing either,' I replied. 'It seems that the choice I have to make is quite different from what my parents supposed. It seems that nowadays one must choose between being a woman who behaves like a man, and a man who behaves like a woman. In short, I must choose to be one in order to behave like the other. This is going to be much more difficult: already I can see the confusion that will mark my life; the overlappings of the real and the feigned; the mingled half-bass, half-soprano; the incessant switchings, self-reminders, lapses, and interludes of sexual forgetfulness.'

'Oh, come now,' he said, smiling: 'You make it seem too complicated. Let us suppose you decide to be a sort of Harold. Clearly you will see yourself as a sort of accidental man whose aim is to overcome your handicap as quickly as possible. The first step in this direction is to keep the word "girl" uppermost in your mind. This is a decisive, transitional word, specially contrived to fit your particular difficulty. Once you start thinking of yourself as "girl", you will find yourself quite at home in the feigned role. The important thing is to get the word "woman" out of your mind: you can be a girl-man, if you know what I mean, but not a woman-man. Similarly, if you decide to follow in Violet's footsteps, you can become a man-girl, but not a man-woman. Do you follow?'

'Do you really see me a man-girl like Violet?' I asked, smiling.

'Why not? Don't imagine that all men-girls have to look like oxen. There are many, like you, who are slim and delicate and make up for lack of poundage with a hard, cold power which is a great deal more impressive than sheer weight. No, the great thing to remember about this intermediate zone of ours is that your choice is as wide as it would be in the normal world. You can be a languishing type of man-girl, a ruthless type of girl-man. You can also be anywhere in between; there is no fixed register. Moreover, any time you find your chosen role unsuitable, you can make a complete switch.'

'You mean, decide to be just a man or a woman after all?'

'I am not sure about that. It's the most difficult role of all nowadays. Once you start being the girl-man father of five, with girl-man boy-friends on the side and so on; or a man-girl mother with lady-friends-well, I know it's *done*, but it's a dog's life, believe me. One small marriage, yes, simply to keep the conventions, if you are ambitious. But don't overdo it.'

'Tell me frankly,' I said. 'What would you do in my position?'

'Will you,' he asked, after a little thought, 'think me impossibly dowdy and old fashioned if I suggest that your first decision should be anatomical?'

He must have seen from my face that I was astounded, so he continued quickly: '*First* decision, I said. Whatever you may choose to *do*, you should really start out with – well, how can I put it? – a clear picture of the basic potentialities. Your trouble up to now, as I see it, is that you have been suffering from a grave handicap but have not yet decided on which side of the fence it is, so to speak. In short, are you a deviated woman or an inverted man?'

'I never thought of such a thing,' I answered.

'I could probably tell you in a minute,' he said, with a twinkle.

'But I hardly know you.'

He smiled, and said: 'It was I who popped you into bed.'

My mouth fell open. I looked down at my silk pyjamas and cried: 'You mean, you know already?'

'I'm afraid so,' he answered gently.

I lay for a moment without speaking. Then, setting my teeth and drawing a strong breath, I turned to him and said: 'Tell me.'

'Can you face it?' he asked earnestly.

'Yes, yes!' I cried, beating the sofa with my fists. 'Only, tell me.'

'Very well,' he said, taking my hand in a firm grip. 'You are a . . .'

Alas! at that very moment there was a light rat-tat on the door-knocker and a sound of youthful whistling – the sort of sound one associates with urchins and barrow-boys. That, at any rate, I am sorry to say, was the impression the sounds made upon my host, whose eyes immediately lit up with interest, while he dropped my hand and cocked his ear towards the front door. We heard the Philippino go down the passage and open the door: at once, the voice of a girl-man said: 'I'm dreadfully sorry to intrude at *such* an hour, but Lord Lamprey simply *ordered* me not to pass through London without calling on his *best* friend. I would have come *hours* earlier but I was detained – *forcibly* detained, my dear – by some scandalous people in Wapping.' At this, my host left my bedside instantly and went to the door, calling: 'Come in, come in! How is Lamprey's wound?' Even the stoutest of girl-men, I am afraid, lose their poise where a peer is concerned: to the abnormal vanity of their type, they add the snobbishness of you and me.

He returned with a slim lad in uniform and promptly said to me: 'I can't introduce you because I haven't the least idea who either of you is. Do excuse me if I leave you briefly' – and with that they both left the room.

No sooner were they out of hearing than I sprang off the sofa and cried: 'Harold! Harold! Do come at once, Harold! It's most important!' But I called for five minutes before the door opened and Harold appeared, looking sulky and cross. 'What is it now?' he asked in a high voice. 'If it's more of that *endless* business about your sex I'd rather not hear a *word*. There's muddle enough in a girl's life without your adding your tedious bewilderment. And what *does* it matter, anyway? Who cares what sex anyone is? Who cares about sex, for that matter? Not I.'

'You will when you hear what I have to say,' I replied firmly. 'Harold, that girl-man who has just come in is not a girl-man at all.'

'What do you mean?' he said. 'What else would he be?'

'He's a she, Harold. She's the man-girl who scratched my face. Voilet has sent her as a fifth column.'

He gave a scream and ran from the room. I heard him shrieking and raving up the stairs: a second later the Adonis, still stark-naked, raced through the living-room, closely followed by the Philippino with a broom. An awful tumult began upstairs: roars and shouts, the crash of broken Tanagra. But I hardly heard it. Someone, outside, struck the window of the living-room a sharp blow; a pane fell in, a huge hand pushed the edge of the black-out curtain to one side. Next minute I saw staring at me through the aperture the terrifying face of Violet herself, a Commando knife clutched between her teeth....

*

The next minutes were the most terrifying of my life. Much as I would have enjoyed a good faint, manliness told me this was no moment for it. Instead, I screamed till my lungs gave out – and yet, transfixed by Violet's glare, could not have run from the room had not a happy accident occurred. Upstairs, a window opened and there was a scruffling sound; I heard a feminine scream and the Master's voice saying firmly: 'I'm sorry, dear, but there's *no* alternative. *Push,* Carlo!' Next minute, there was a colossal thud and Violet's face shot backwards into the night. They had thrown the man-girl imposter out of the top window; she had landed on Violet's neck.

However manly I may be in other respects, I am enough of a woman to pity those who are injured in battle. I thought now what a hard day it had been for poor Violet, crushed beneath an oak table under police-officers and Amazons, and then risen only to be struck on the neck by a plummeting girl-friend. But even as my heart softened, my muscles stiffened as an even louder roar came from outside, and the sound of hammer-blows on the back door. I heard Violet bawl: 'Come on, men, one – two – three, altogether,' followed by a shattering crash: at once, the Master came racing down the stairs, crying sharply, to Carlo, Harold, and the Adonis: 'It's a siege, girls! We hold that door to the death!' Outside, Violet shouted in her deep voice: 'If you wish to avert unnecessary bloodshed, hand her over and our forces will withdraw.' To which the Master retorted in cold, high tones: 'Not to every Liza in Lambeth! We've got him and we'll keep him!'

For the next half-hour the battle proceeded with unimaginable fury. Violet and her men seized on everything the little garden could provide – bricks from the path, crazy-paving, sections of concrete, nude statues of Pan, and a bust of Lord Kitchener. The wrought-iron garden-bench was used as a battering-ram. The Master and his girls had no such weapons, and it was with the grim looks of those who destroy the beautiful in order to preserve the system which created it that they scoured the rooms for heavy works of art. The French Impressionists were the first to go, dropped from the upper windows with crushing effect; they were followed by whistling mobiles, immense abstractions and three valuable Picassos. The Master himself wielded a reclining Henry Moore: few men in London, I believe, could have so much as lifted it.

How far we have come, how very far, from the days when my simple parents walked the sitting-rooms of life in amiable nudity and expatiated on dogs' ways! It was clear to me, as I shrank back upon the sofa, that this was no world for such as myself, who hope to be Independent Members in the Parliament of sex. Woe, I cried to myself, to the husband who has thrown aside the beard of his forefathers and built his sexual identity upon the sands of equality and shared authority! Woe to the wife who glories in the destruction of her husband's power and exalts herself upon the pyre of self-immolating emancipation! They shall all, all be utterly consumed, and rise from the ashes true girl-men and men-girls, finding in Violet or the Master the authority and domination for which they crave! I – poor, indecisive me! – am nothing but a forerunner of that which is to come, when the vast, lethargic mass of ambiguous men and women is torn from its rootless desert and forcibly shared between the girls of Marathon and the men of Amazonia. And how close that moment seemed when I heard the Master cry, out of the kitchen: 'Violet! I challenge you to single combat!' and heard Violet roar back: 'I accept your challenge. Expose the prize!'

Oh, the ruthlessness of them! Combatants of both camps seized my quivering, asexual limbs, dragged me into the garden, and stood me on the bird-bath. It was January, and the wind whistled through my blue-silk pyjamas – but the shame was more cruel than the wind: I thought it would kill me. At least, I hope I did. To tell the truth, I must confess that despite the wind and the shame I did feel a *little* proud of being so much in demand and a *little* relieved to think that once the battle was over the question of my sex would be decisively answered. Nor did I care particularly which of my two champions carried me off: there is little to choose between a brutal life and a malicious one. As the supporters of both sides began to cheer, I simply put my hands over my eyes and shivered. . . .

There came a crash like two rhinoceroses meeting head-on. . . .

A bomb had fallen on the house.

*

English obituary notices always make strange reading, if one has known the corpse at all well. Violet's for example, was devoted almost entirely to a discussion of the best kind of boots to wear climbing Everest, as if the obituary-writer had decided that this was the only aspect of her life from which the general public could draw a useful moral. The Master's, similarly, emphasized that though he had had many friends in both Houses of Parliament and was a born curator of museums, his spiritual home had been the Palm House at Kew Gardens. I quite understand why it should be thought necessary to write this sort of obituary; the only thing I have against it is that it causes people to try and read between the lines, with the result that they often suspect the deceased of crimes of which he or she was completely innocent. Thus, it was no surprise to me to hear someone say, some months later, that Violet had been secretly married to a sheik, whom she had poisoned because he had betrayed her with other women; and that the Master had spent a year in prison for importuning women in Shaftesbury Avenue. Such stories are harmful, because they arouse the passions of younger people, who unconsciously model themselves on the legendary identity and, later in life, are found performing acts of crime, such as poisoning and importuning, which they believe to be purely imitative, when in fact they are entirely original.

What (I often think) will the obituary writers have to say of *me*? The mystery of my true sex has never been cleared up and it will intrigue me to the end of my days. As I grow older, my sex, far from becoming more defined, only grows more diffuse: in certain moods I imagine myself a normal husband, crushed underfoot by a contemptuous wife but finding solace in drink and the malice of cocktail-parties; in others, I see myself as this same wife, suffering the horrible agonies of unalleviated power, dreaming nightly of abduction by a male gorilla but incapable, in her waking moments, of regarding the other sex with anything but hatred and resentment. Sometimes I soar above this humdrum and see myself as a rough prototype created hundreds of years too soon – product of some fantastic mating between an inverted man-girl and a perverted girl-man. Like everyone who is not at home in contemporary society, I spin out the most ingenious theories to prove either that everyone was once like me or that everyone will be, in years to come. Harold, who was one of the few survivors of that terrible night and to whom I am now, in a sense, married, simply sticks his pink fingers in his coral ears when I begin to air such views, but at heart I think he envies me the notoriety which my books have brought me and the large increase they have caused in the number of people of undetermined sex: this, thanks to my writings, has now been recognized by Parliament and is enjoying quite a vogue. A healthy vogue, too, even though it has attracted riff-raff like the one who, though sexually registered with the Food Office as 'Undetermined', claimed extra cheese as a nursing mother. Harold never misses a chance to poke fun at me and my sex, but it is my private opinion that he himself would like to climb on the bandwagon and become undetermined instead of inverted. But the years have rolled on; he is an old dog now, and too set in his ways.

*

'*Dogs*, Mr Jellicoe! Surely not! Badgers yesterday, dogs today! What will tomorrow bring? Cats and canaries?'

'Mrs Paradise, I am tired of explaining these things. I explained to you the badgers; it went in one ear and out the other. I shall say *nothing* of the dogs.'

'But Mr Jellicoe, think of the *expense*! A huge house-party with full staff; days and days of consultation; sixteen turkeys eaten already: special clothes and printing machines and the best wines! Surely biscuits and love are all an animal requires?'

'Would you like it better if they talked about human beings?' asked Jellicoe sarcastically.

'Well, why not, Mr Jellicoe? People matter too.'

'What do you think they would have to say on *that* difficult subject, may I ask?'

'Do you have to be so bitter and sarcastic? Why shouldn't they have ideas about people too? They could discuss the importance of honesty and faith and love, couldn't they? And beautiful memories and things of that kind.'

'I expect that's what they are doing, except that it is animals involved. Will you never understand that all our knowledge starts like that, Mrs Paradise? We make tests with beasts, and, if they live, we go on to people, knowing that what we are doing is correct. When they get back to London the gentlemen upstairs will do a pamphlet about dogs and badgers and then the people who read the pamphlet will do it to you and me. The trouble with you, Mrs Paradise, is that you are every inch a woman. Women are only interested in things which are about them, directly; a man's mind is open to anything that is half-way promising.'

'Just as long as all that money isn't being wasted. . . . '

'No fear! If you want proof, just pause outside the door. The shouting! The anger! The indignation! You'd think it was the R.S.P.C.A.'

'They don't actually cut up the dogs and badgers, do they? To see what's inside, and why?'

'No, it's all talk.'

'I'm glad to hear that. Suffering and wasted money give me goose-flesh: I put myself in the animal's place. My husband never went to bed without cleaning his horse.'

'That was so as not to waste money, Mrs Paradise. The horse lasted much longer.'

'You don't think it was just out of love?'

'Well, a sort of far-seeing love, perhaps. I'm sure he never groomed the cat.'

'He always had a kind word for it.'

'I'll not press that point, Mrs Paradise. If my memories were as sacred as yours I would keep them safe from any argument.'

'I don't believe you were quite as wicked as you remember, Mr Jellicoe.'

'I was, Mrs Paradise, *exceedingly* wicked, and nothing hurts me more than to have it questioned.'

'All right, we won't quarrel. Let's rehearse each other our parts.'

'That is what we were doing.'

'*Parts*, Mr Jellicoe, not pasts!'

'Oh, oh! Gladly! Where shall we start?'

'Let's with the Queen in bed.'

'If you don't mind, Mrs Paradise, I'd rather not. Although it's yours, I know it by heart.'

'Then let's do Hermione in her boudoir.'

'Again, it's so familiar. Let's do the King's speech when he swoons at last.'

'Am I in that?'

'How can you be, Mrs Paradise? It wouldn't be a speech if there were two in it.'

'That's what I mean, Mr Jellicoe. You have a whole page without interruption.'

'That's what *I* mean, Mrs Paradise. That's why it's so important.'

'Well, I'll hear you your swoon if you'll promise to hear me my boudoir.'

'Fair enough. I'll start, while you work up your mood.'

When he had finished, she said: 'You do do it wonderfully, Mr Jellicoe! For a man who thinks so much, you put in so much ginger. And all those movements with your arms! Why, even your ears tremble! Now, let me do Hermione. . . . '

'That's *much* better, Mrs Paradise,' he said, when she had done. 'But there are still certain places where you don't seem to know what you are talking about. It's clear that you are very moved, but the cause remains unknown. Listen, and I'll read it myself.'

'No, please don't, Mr Jellicoe. It spoils all the pleasure if another voice chimes in. I'd rather not know than be corrected.'

Miss Tray entered, leading Towzer. 'Good morning all,' she said. 'Well, how d'you think he looks? Hold up your head, Tow, for the lady.'

'I must say he's a transformation,' said Mrs Paradise. 'What's that on his ear?'

'Only egg.'

'Won't it come off?'

'I don't believe in doing things for him. The way to change him is to let him change himself. That's what the doctor says, and I agree. How do you like his new clothes? I have to admit, I *did* choose them for him. But if I'd left the choice to him he'd be wearing nothing but a hank of bast.'

'I think your choice has been on the feminine side,' said Jellicoe, looking Towzer up and down. 'I wouldn't choose a mauve tie and a pale green shirt for myself, especially with a spade-beard and a nigger-brown suit. However, I know nothing about gardening.'

'It looks *very* pretty, Miss Tray,' said Mrs Paradise. 'Don't you listen to Mr Jellicoe. Men are always spoil-sports when it comes to clothes. I think you have sharpened him up wonderfully. I'd never know he was the same person.'

'He only wears it for Shakespeare and best, of course. The doctor had it in the big chest.'

'He is still receiving medical attention, is he?' asked Jellicoe.

'Of course. He wouldn't be here otherwise, would he?'

'I thought he was gardening for the Captain.'

'That's what he thinks too. We're not even going to mention such things in his hearing or try and pin him down in the least. Promise me, will you, that if ever he mentions "the Captain", or some such fantasy, you won't correct him?'

'Why, no,' said Jellicoe, giving her a puzzled look.

'We are simply going to nurse him forward and leave him absolutely free to decide for himself. At the moment, he's still at the stage where he's hoping to escape responsibility . . . Just look at him! He knows we are talking about him.'

'Do you really think he does, Miss Tray?' asked Jellicoe. 'I know dogs do.'

'I am certain of it.'

'Then perhaps we shouldn't do it,' said Mrs Paradise kind-heartedly.

'But we *should*,' said Miss Tray. 'That's how ideas will filter into his head again. The doctor makes a suggestion to me; I make the suggestion in front of Tow, and Tow makes it to himself – we *hope*. By doing it this way, the doctor and I cannot be accused of having forced anything on him. All his changes will be entirely his own.'

'I should like to meet this doctor someday,' said Jellicoe. 'He sounds like the sort of man I could learn something from.'

'I did suggest that to him only yesterday,' said Miss Tray, 'but he suggested postponing it until you were not quite so busy.'

'He is in the house, then?' asked Jellicoe.

'Why, yes, all the time,' said Miss Tray, giving Jellicoe a puzzled look.

'Mr Towzer may *understand* things,' said Mrs Paradise, 'but I must say he doesn't *speak* very much.'

'Not with strangers, Mrs Paradise. He is afraid they may try and persuade him to be different.'

'Strangers, Miss Tray! But he's been with us for years. He was here with my late husband.'

'His breakdown has destroyed all that, Mrs Paradise. You and Mr Jellicoe live entirely in the past. But the past doesn't exist for Tow. Only the present matters – and, fortunately, I am a large part of it.'

'It seems very hard, Miss Tray, that me and Mr Jellicoe should have to renounce all claim to a very dear old acquaintance – that *we* should have to suffer because *he's* forgotten the things we remember. It's particularly hard on me, who treasures memories so much.'

'Well, let's just change the subject,' said Miss Tray. 'May I ask if you are settling into your parts?'

'Very well. Mr Jellicoe is word perfect in all four of his. He even has a different voice for each.'

'It's sea-training does that,' said Jellicoe. 'But what of Mr Towzer? I can't imagine how a man who is speechless in everyday life will enunciate Shakespeare.'

'Well, he's word-perfect too, Mr Jellicoe. Once he realized it was only poetry, he learnt it immediately.'

'Then I'm afraid Mrs Chirk is going to be the weak link in our chain.'

'She's coming now,' said Mrs Paradise, 'so don't be rude in front of her, poor thing. Remember, she's quite uneducated.'

Mrs Chirk came in at breakneck speed, red and panting.

'All done, Mrs Finch?' asked Mrs Paradise chummily.

'Half of them done, Mrs Paradise: I'll get to the Execution wing after dinner. Oh, dear me! I *am* upside down! I don't know my left from my right or my head from my heels! If I sat down even for a second I'd never be able to pick myself up again!'

'I hope you know your *parts*, Mrs Chirk,' said Miss Tray sternly. 'We all know ours and it wouldn't please us to think that you were going to let us down.'

'I can't fix my mind on them, Miss Tray. I tell myself who I'm supposed to be, but after a few minutes my mind's a blank again. And having to be *two* women *and* speak the Prologue doesn't make it any easier. And then there's the washing-up.'

'The washing-up has nothing to do with it, Mrs Chirk. It is entirely separate from acting. I think there must be something hostile to the stage in your character.'

'There's nothing hostile in *me*, Miss. I'm the humblest of creatures.'

'That's what we all think of ourselves, Mrs Finch.'

'I'll do better, Miss, when we have our costumes on. Then I'll only have to glance down to know what I'm up to.'

'Why don't you write your name in big letters on a piece of paper and keep it in front of you?'

'Which name would that be, Miss?'

'Whichever one you're doing, of course.'

'I'll try that, Miss. Just as long as I keep the different pieces separated. If I muddled them, it would be the death of me.'

'Think of it as like your ration-book, Mrs Chirk. Your name, on the cover, represents the whole book, but the various pages represent the different things that go into you.'

'Or think of it as like your work,' suggested Jellicoe. 'One minute you are dusting madly; the next, waxing feverishly; the next, scrubbing frantically. Sometimes you are on hands-and-knees like a dog, sometimes rubbaging like a badger. But always *you*, whatever your posture.'

'It's kindly meant, I'm sure, Mr Jellicoe, but if you don't mind I'll not confuse it worse by being different animals as well. I'm not one for bringing things into my life; my peace comes when I can throw them out.'

'But all things in life are related to each other, Mrs Finch.'

'They may be, Mr Jellicoe, but it's not for me to play Happy Families.'

'Well, since we're all here,' said Miss Tray, 'how about a little rehearsal? Which act do you know best, Mrs Chirk?'

'The first, Miss. I'm not one to forge ahead in search of trouble.'

*

'*Who's* looking for trouble?' asked the President angrily. 'All I said was that by the time Shubunkin had put sex through his upper and nether millstones, I cared little what sex *anyone* was. I also remarked on what seems to me a most interesting fact – that some functions, of which sex is one, are naturally so stimulating that they become dull when put on paper. I may have added something about its being time for lunch.'

'It was a shocking way to receive a work that embodied months of toil and ingenuity,' said Dr Shubunkin furiously.

'That was my point. Naturally, the matter proceeds so rapidly.'

'May I say, with all respect for his office,' said Mr Jamesworth, 'that the President is at the bottom of all this quarrelling?'

'No, sir you may not. It is absurd to open a sentence with all respect and close it with none.'

'I shall not move from this floor,' said Dr Shubunkin, 'until justice has been done to my history.'

'We can always give it a free pardon,' said the President.

'Shame!' cried the doctor's claque.

'I was the first to applaud poor Bitterling's little effort the other day,' said the doctor, 'because I always sympathize with people who have done their best. When that best is my own, my sympathy is bottomless.'

Dr Bitterling feverishly wrote on a piece of paper and held up the words: 'Why *be* a subordinate if there is to be no flattery?'

'Precisely,' said Dr Musk. 'Why be?'

'I can only tell you, gentlemen,' said the President, 'that if you don't reach a friendly conclusion I shall turn the matter over to Mr Harcourt and let him have the last word. None of you will like *that*.'

'Me least of all,' said Mr Harcourt. 'I think it a shame that my opinion should count only when my betters are irreconcilable. People used to say of my elder sister: "You can always depend on her in an emergency." How she hated it! "There's only an emergency every twenty-five years," she used to say: "Who am I supposed to be in the other twenty-four?" '

'Things have come to a pretty pass,' said Dr Musk, 'when the day starts with sex and winds up with Harcourt's sister.'

'The history showed Shubunkin at the very peak of his peculiar zest,' said Father Orfe. 'We religious proselytizers appreciate zest, because a fast car is easier to steer.'

Stapleton got up and said in a trembling voice: 'It is agonizing for me to recall the dreams I had during the war of what peace would be like. I thought everyone would disarm and be the best of friends. Now, I wonder why I was wounded at all.'

'I expect you were the type that always is,' said Dr Shubunkin.

'Mr Stapleton, your *heart* is in the right place . . . ' began the President.

'That's what the fox said to the goose!' cried Dr Musk.

'Gentlemen, we have strayed far from the heart of the matter,' protested Mr Jamesworth.

'Then I shall return to it – decisively,' said Dr Shubunkin, working his face like a shuttle. 'The heart of the matter is: When is a President not a President? And the answer is: When he fails to give his subordinates that mingled discipline and flattery which constitute true leadership. *There!*'

Amid silence the President rose slowly to his feet and looked hard at the doctor. 'Shubunkin,' he said. 'Do you invoke Clause (*a*) of Rule 1?'

Before answering, the doctor glanced quickly round the room to test the moral of his claque. Finding it none to good, in that the gentlemen concerned were all suddenly studying their feet, he replied defensively: 'Well, it's a bit thick, you know.'

The President put on pince-nez, stared closely at the doctor for some moments, and said: 'I can't see from here. Are you eating crow or flying the Jolly Roger?'

'A direct apology would not be in keeping with Shubunkin's distinctive identity,' said Dr Musk. 'Like all sexologists, he must be permitted the fullest ambiguity.'

'His assertion *and* its contradiction must be swallowed as one,' said Father Orfe.

'Though, if he has erred,' cried Mr Harris, 'he must bare his neck to the short sword.'

'I don't know what the quarrel's about,' said Mr Harcourt, 'but I do think it's cruel to make people apologize. To prevent anyone making me, I always hasten to make the apology first.'

'The President is *never* cruel,' said Stapleton. 'He is the perfect healer whose image was so often in my mind when I was in the hands of the R.A.M.C.'

Suddenly, from a back seat, Captain Mallet arose. So impressive was his gradual ascent into common view, so portly the bearing of his head, that all the members, including the President, gave a sharp twitch – except Dr Shubunkin, who gave a score. 'I am only a plain, blunt officer . . .' began the captain, but was silenced by a burst of applause. 'I am only a plain, blunt . . .' he began again, and was once more silenced by loud enthusiasm. 'I am only a plain . . .' he began a third time, and then gave up.

'This is all very well, Mallet!' cried the President in a high, nervous voice, 'but what is your point?'

'He himself is his point!' cried Dr Musk, winking at his claque. They applauded frantically.

'One is abashed,' murmured Mr Harris, 'by the *economy* of such self-assertion.' At which Dr Shubunkin signalled *his* claque and they, too, burst into applause. This put all the other claques on the *qui vive*, so that when Mr Jamesworth rose, they cheered in unison before he could say a word.

At this, the captain, a troubled look on his grave face, rose again and said: 'It was not my intention, gentlemen, to focus attention upon myself.'

'Then you are to be doubly congratulated,' said the President angrily, 'on having done so with such success.'

There were cries of 'Shame!' from all claques and Dr Shubunkin said indignantly: 'That was a most unjust remark! It is Mallet's business to epitomize the ideal of honourable and humble service. To treat him as a rival is to cast doubt on his highest ideals.'

'A *beastly* thing to do!' cried Mrs Mallet in a high voice – and at the sight of her standing there – all *woman*, with flushed face, sparkling eyes, and small fist clenched – the Club again burst into applause. The noise reached its peak when Beaufort, his Adonis head rising high above the intellectual ruck, laid his hand on her arm and proudly dragged her down into her seat.

'I don't, of course, know why,' cried Mr Harcourt abruptly, 'but I am beginning to feel much, much better! My doubts are ebbing away: I suddenly feel *at home* in the world.'

'A *most* important statement!' exclaimed Mr Jamesworth. 'I propose that we proceed to immediate discussion of why Harcourt should so suddenly have become acclimatized.'

'Nothing would please me more,' said the President, who was looking old and pale. 'Unfortunately, Orfe's history is next on the agenda.'

'I'm sure Orfe would gladly sacrifice his paper to the common weal,' said Mr Jamesworth. 'And a discussion would be much more exciting.'

'On the whole I wouldn't,' said Father Orfe, pocketing his flask stoutly. 'Anyone else's paper, yes.'

'I am sure,' said Stapleton, 'that Orfe is not being selfish when he refuses to stand down. I expect he has numerous reasons.'

'I have *one*,' said Father Orfe, 'and it's the best I know.'

'I think it shockingly naïve of Orfe,' said Dr Shubunkin, 'to allow the whole mood and sweep of the Club to be destroyed simply by a foxy appeal to his egotism.'

'It was my religious principles,' replied Father Orfe. '*Après moi le déluge*, i.e., first things first.'

'Before we go to lunch,' said Stapleton, 'could we not shake hands all round?'

'It would take exactly seventeen minutes and thirty-two seconds,' said Mr Jamesworth, half-closing one statistical eye.

*

The secret of Father Golden Orfe – unknown to everyone, including Orfe – was that he would have been a concert pianist had he had any interest in music: only tone-deafness made him instead a student of the soul of man. It was certain, however, that he had at one time had a musical relative, or box, or chair, or something of that nature, because at an impressionable period of his life he was taken to at least one concert, which marked him for life. As is usually the case in such matters, he was not marked by the recital itself but by the extraordinary behaviour of the performer. Just as men who are quite uninterested in food become chefs in order to add a white hat to their stature, so Father Orfe became a pianist in every respect save for the piano.

This is obvious when the Club assembles for the next session. It is set to begin sharp at two thirty, by which time the whole Club is present, including the President. Everyone is chattering away as vigorously as possible, as is natural before a long monologue; but as the minutes pass, members start glancing at their Swiss watches and raise their eyebrows. They sprawl into their seats and make worried faces at each other: 'Where's Orfe?' 'Can't think.' Suddenly, fifteen minutes late, the door opens swiftly and Father Orfe enters at a rapid glide, sober as a judge and moving like a well-tuned mowing-machine. He approaches the President, murmurs: 'So sorry sir; delayed, you know,' and then skates straight to his seat. Where is this seat? Well, it does not exist; what happens is that Orfe arrives at the seat he has decided to choose, seizes it by the back, shakes it, and drops a huge portfolio upon it. He does not realize, it seems (so deep are the preoccupations of musical genius), that the seat is occupied by another member; and anyway, after he has shaken and dropped for a moment or so, this is no longer the case. The Club watches him nervously: they have often seen Orfe make this characteristic entry but have never managed to conquer the terror it arouses in them. They immediately stop talking: only Mr Harcourt's voice is heard, as usual, for a few brief seconds, tailing off in the middle of telling his latest dream to Mr Jamesworth.

Father Orfe is too fine a pianist to notice the absolute silence. With a stupendous frown he opens his enormous portfolio, takes out twenty bound manuscripts, holds them up to the light one by one, peers at them, and grunts at each. Then he puts all the manuscripts back in the portfolio, snaps it shut, grunts generally, and runs through all his pockets as if they were exploratory scales. He finds a lucky penny in his trousers and a cigar-lighter elsewhere: but that is all. His expression becomes exceedingly grave: he stands for a full quarter minute with his hands reaching down as far as his knees, not moving, only thinking. At last, as if to say: 'A thought strikes me,' he opens the portfolio again and instantly produces the lost manuscript. A puff of relief comes from the audience: it has hardly expired before Father Orfe is at work on a new business, clenching the manuscript between his teeth while, with one hand, he tries to close the portfolio, and with the other adjust the chair in relation to the light, set the portfolio behind it and himself in front of it, brush ash off his waistcoat, and so on. He goes on doing this until all the members' nerves are again as tense as barbed wire; suddenly, he concludes it, takes the manuscript out of his mouth, and stands absolutely erect, his hands folded over his top fly-button. He then begins, in the manner of a weather-cock, to turn his head, beginning towards the farthest right-hand quarter of the room. All the members in this area have been silent as the grave until now, but as soon as they feel the death-ray of Orfe's eye they burst into a consumptive roar of coughing, sniffing, and grunting. Orfe continues to stare at them, until they increase their noises to a crescendo and only sink back into silence out of sheer exhaustion. Orfe then waits for the inevitable, single cough that always breaks this silence; after that he waits for the silence itself to become silent. Only then does his expression of a man bitterly insulted ebb slowly away – returning as he turns his eyes to another quarter of the room, where he repeats the whole process. At last, with everyone completely silent he does a sort of flashing, general test-of-the-room-as-a-whole, provoking and crushing fresh coughs in every quarter. After that, as if it were a private Armistice Day, he tests the overall silence for two full minutes before he at last raises his manuscript, clears his own throat with a delicacy which is an example to all, and opens his mouth. Everything is now ready for the first pebble of sound to drop into the pool of silence; but Orfe has a joker up his sleeve. His teeth come together again; he gives the slightest of frowns, lowers his manuscript – and moves his chair one inch to the right. The portfolio falls on its side with a crash. Members would like to gasp, but dare not, for fear everything will start from the beginning again: but this is where Orfe suddenly seems to blaze up into an unexpected fire of majestic tolerance: he gives a light sweep of his white hand, as if to say: 'What do noisy trifles matter to a man of my stature?' and, raising his manuscript, begins to read aloud almost like any normal person:

SECRET AGENT: *Multiple Confessions and Singular Identities*

by

Father Golden Orfe

The monastery bell is striking nine and I must be off to testify before the International Anti-Communist Committee. My eight-cylinder Panther Perfecto, bought with the movie-royalties of my last confession, awaits me in the monastery garage; but I would like to write a few words about myself before driving away today. The nice thing about living in a monastery is that it makes one introspective: each day brings a new and fascinating aspect of oneself to light, arousing so many delightful sensibilities that tears come to my eyes when I must leave them even for a day on television.

First, a word about this monastery. It stands on a hilltop which might be anywhere – a rise of the Sussex downs; a castle-site above a European valley; a slope above the Hudson where that blue, incomparable river nurses the shad in the shade of Sing Sing. As monasteries go, ours is pretty new; but in view of the speed with which newer ones are springing up nowadays, it is soon going to seem quite old. Ours was planned to accommodate fifty ex-Party men, but long before it was finished we had three hundred applications for cells, and there is now a long waiting-list of international distinction.

The land about the monastery is an endless joy. Every year the trees throw off their old leaves and put on new ones: this is God's way of reminding us of how we, too, once shed old selves, old dialectics, old aims, and put on new means dedicated to His ends. There are herds of many wonderful, unthinking beasts, such as cows, sheep, goats, ducks, and hens: it is our joy to serve these witless creatures instead of packing them off to Siberia. Indeed, like all who have fornicated with the cold Whore of Reason, we never tire of praising the beautiful attributes of those who have nothing to think with.

Unlike the old Party days, there is only one brother in each cell. This is a plain, four-square room, with a double coat of whitewash. It contains everything a penitent requires – an iron bed for remorse, a stone floor for prayer, and a writing-table for confessions. We have, of course, an Abbot who wields absolute power and lays down the 'Abbey Line' at regular intervals. We have numerous rules about silence, discipline, punishment, and so on, all delightfully humiliating; and we have the world's finest library of Marxist literature, every volume of which we are theologically confuting in the giant *Encyclopedia Penitentia* which is our principal work. We bring out a revised, up-to-date edition of this once a year, and one of our strictest rules is that if any brother is needed to do some work on the *Encyclopedia* he must immediately put aside his current confession and join the editors in the library.

But I hope you will not think of us as grim men to whom duty is everything and democracy still nothing. On the contrary, our little Abbey is a tolerant place. The outside world is full of ex-Party members who have not found God, and they spend their lives fighting an exhausting battle of suspicion and hatred centring upon the question: 'At what date did *you* break with the Party?' Each heretic believes that he alone broke precisely at the moment when the *eau-de-vie* of Communism changed to the ditch-water of absolutism; those who broke before him he regards as renegades, those who broke after, as charlatans. But in the Abbey, we have none of this. We believe that God is not subject to Party chronology and that His admission to Heaven of the penitent thief is the 'line' He laid down for us to follow. So, to us, those who break at the very last moment, tomorrow, will be as welcome in His midst as those who broke in varying yesterdays. The brother in the cell on my left is a so-called 'Thirty-niner': he went out of the Party with the Stalin-Hitler pact. The brother on my right was 'out in the '45', as we put it; and there are some who made their breaks even later, as well as a few who actually broke with Lenin in the battle of the Mensheviks. Frankly, I think that to make a break *before* an autocracy has even been established is as silly as getting a divorce before one has been married, but I shall not press the point. For here, in the Abbey, we have destroyed the whole prestige chronology of breaking: we argue simply that each of us erred and fell into wickedness and that the exact date of his breakage is no more interesting than the date of his birthday. What *is* important is that he has since made a religious reformation and has reason to believe that his piety is as sincere as his wickedness was.

I would like to stress this point. Many outsiders think that our Abbey is a place where tired radicals go when their rationalism has died; but this is not the case. We have no cell for people who are tired and disappointed; and nor has the general public: who would ever read the confessions of such men? No, our Abbey is for those who could not hope to reach the first stage of Christian humility without Grace abounding. The world of today is one in which religion, if it is to mean anything at all, must seem to have been invented by Bunyan and had teeth put into it by Dostoyevsky. This means that only those who have been indescribably wicked in the past can hope to be religious in the future: indeed, I would go further, and say that the only road to Rome nowadays is via Moscow. There *are* alternative by-ways: many intellectuals, for example, have a soft place in their hearts for drunkenness, moral cowardice, sexual quiddities, and other non-political vices, which, if practised frantically enough, serve, they say, as adequate preliminaries to the religious state. Some of them even argue that the two states are inseparable and that the man most likely to succeed is he who carries prayer in one holster and a really good vice in the other, firing each according to whim. Be that as it may, the fact remains that the old-fashioned notion of religion as a sort of everyday affair in which everyone can join has quite gone out: the only devout ones today are those who really have something to be devout about.

Take Brother Kapotzky, for instance. He cannot bear to kill a chicken for Sunday dinner. If he sees a worm in his path he picks it up, blesses it, and puts it in a safe place. Is this the result of going to Sunday School in childhood? Not a bit. All through the twenties and thirties Kapotzky was an official of the Ogpu and NKVD: thousands went to their death over his loose signature. 'Believe me,' he says, 'it's only when you've liquidated large numbers of people that you appreciate the miracle of life.' In short, we are all converts today, if we are anything at all, and it is only logical to assume that the greater the preliminary sin, the more triumphant the ultimate conversion. The public agrees with this and only listens to prayers made with red hands. I remember one novice in our Abbey exclaiming spontaneously: 'I must say, we are jolly *lucky* to live in an era when sin is considered so very religious.' To which the Abbot replied drily: 'I think, Brother Thomas, that *Providential* would be the better word.'

*

Oh, what a day! The crowds, the press-reporters, the noise, the dirt – and the *questions*! I imagine that when expert brain-specialists, endocrinologists and geologists are called-in to give opinions on heads, glands, and substrata they feel the exasperation I feel when I am cross-examined by the defence on my Marxist past and Christian present. What *does* the layman know about either? Absolutely nothing! 'Is it true,' they ask, 'that you were a Soviet agent in Montreal from 1933 to 1938?' Of course, it is true: it is all down in black-and-white in my confessions: had I not been an agent then would I be an expert on agents now? 'Did you not commit perjury on May 4th 1931 in Ecuador?' they continue – well, of course I did, and well they know it: all they are trying to do is persuade the jury that I am not an honest man. And so they go on, interminably: 'Did you feel no moral scruples?' 'Had you no qualms about incriminating an innocent man?' – really, if it were not that piety enjoins on one a sympathetic attitude to stupid people, I would like to stand them all against a wall and shoot them. Even those who are on my side – the council for the prosecution, the judge, the police, the detectives, the press-reporters – have so little idea of *who I really am* that their misrepresentations are enough to make me scream. Willy-nilly, I find myself back in the old vocabulary and saying to myself: 'Here's a pretty kettle of bourgeois fish! Is there among them a single man who has any conception whatever of the fire that burns in the heart of the Party member and the monk?' I catch the eye of the spy against whom I am testifying and we exchange an invisible wink. Brothers under the skin, and how well we know it! I admire the way he stands up to these oafs. A few cleansing years in jail and he will be ripe for the Abbey.

*

An ugly atmosphere in the refectory. As it was the day of silence I couldn't find out why until I got back to my cell and heard it in Morse over my radiator. It seems that yesterday Brother Herbert finished the first draft of a set of confessions in good time to meet the publisher's deadline (Easter Week). He handed the draft to the Abbot, who, after glancing through it, refused his imprimatur. Why? Nobody knows, but Brother Herbert has been going about with a ghoulish look and won't eat (hunger-strike?).

*

B. Herbert still not eating.

*

B. Herbert was not at Mass this morning. I at once looked at Brother Kapotzky, and sure enough he was wearing the tortured expression he assumes when the Abbot has made him execute someone. At Vespers, Herbert's death from pneumonia was announced, simply and movingly, and the Abbot asked our prayers for the repose of his (Herbert's) soul. We all fell to.

*

The inside story of the Herbert affair turns out to be interesting, but not bizarre. According to Brother Gregory, who is a real Sherlock Holmes in Abbey matters, Herbert was under surveillance throughout Wednesday and Thursday – a precaution the Abbot wisely takes when one of the brothers has had a tiff with him. Apparently, the two brothers who were watching Herbert wondered why he was looking fatter, rather than thinner, in view of his hunger-strike: they concluded that he had concealed the rejected draft of his confessions under his robes. The Abbot ordered it removed: this was done by Brother Nimpy, a clever old servant of God who was a political pickpocket under the Tsar before he became one under the Bolsheviks. Nimpy substituted a brown paper parcel of the same size, and poor Herbert went his way in ignorance. That evening, he was observed flashing his torch from his cell-window; a car drew up and a representative of his publishers came to the foot of the wall, caught the thrown parcel, and sped away. It was too much for the Abbot, who called in Kapotzky at once . . .

It is a sad story, really, because this was Herbert's very first confession, apart from the usual witness-box and Sunday-papers ones, and we all felt he would go a long way. I am dying to know how and why he bungled the draft: he must have made a *complete* hash of it, otherwise the Abbot would merely have edited it in the usual way. It is all the more mysterious, because Herbert's contributions to the *Encyclopedia* had been perfectly 'in line' – in fact, he was sometimes rebuked for lagging behind the switches.

*

Herbert's death has been an irritant. Everybody is going about with a soul-searching look – as if all their confessions had come to nought and would have to be written again. I am not surprised: I share the feeling. Nobody thinks of Herbert as a martyr, but they do feel that he tried to steal a march on the rest of us. Obviously, he confessed things which are not properly confessed, with the result that he leaves the rest of us wondering what they could be and whether any of them might be usable by ourselves. Surely it was enough that he should make us feel small by having pushed ahead, without getting himself killed for it and exciting a spirit of competition in the living?

*

The Abbot preached yesterday (Sunday) about obedience. He showed (you know the argument, I'm sure) that he who is most obedient is most free, in the true sense of the word free, and that he who most respects authority is the least subject to it. He added with a dry smile: 'I hope you will not apply this logic to the wrong things. It does not follow, for example, that he who is most unselfish is the most selfish, or that he who is the most upright is the most cast-down. Or rather, it *does*, depending on how you twist the words about and whether you take them at their face-value or use them so that they mean the opposite of what they suggest. Your spiritual authority – myself – will always be at hand to tell you how far logic may be pressed, and at what point a word, under the leverage of faith, begins to mean its opposite. In a recent case, I am sorry to say, this authority was not respected and a fatal ambiguity resulted. Royalties and fame, let me remind you all, are not everything, and the confession that lies behind the confession should be rendered to God's vicar, not to Caesar. So, brothers, be content with what you have already confessed and do not be so proud as to think that you alone are in duty bound to go your fellows one

212

better. When the world demands a different sort of confession, I will be the first to inform you of the fact.'

Everyone feels much easier as a result of these sensible words. What the Abbot is laying his finger on is the fact that once one begins making confessions, the thing tends to become a disease. After I had confessed in the courts, I could hardly wait to write a book confessing the real truth behind the mere court one. A bare six months after my book was out – and reviewers everywhere applauding the way I had bared myself utterly – I began to have the feeling that I had said nothing at all about *what really mattered*. I sat down and wrote a kind of 'private' confession (it was later published) that sought to go behind its predecessor. Within a year, that, too, struck me as meaningless – indeed, I began to feel that far from stripping myself really naked, each confession only covered me with still another petticoat. I felt terribly at odds with the world: once I had a ridiculous dream in which a night-club audience cried: 'Take it off!' and applauded madly each time I *put on* another rope of pearls. I began to think of confessions in terms of infinite regression – the very act of making one would cause another to pop up behind it. I even began to suspect that the really true confession would not be about my crimes, etc., but about why I was so eager to write confessions.

It was the Abbot who saved me from madness by convincing me that though the object of confession is to tell the truth, only the proud man attempts to decide for himself what the truth is. If all of us, he explained, insisted on being free-lances in truth-telling, the whole edifice of confession, as it exists today, would fall to the ground, leaving the public with nothing to read but detective-stories. We ex-Party men are the examples which the man-in-the-street follows today: it is not for us to deny him salvation in the name of truth.

What would *I* consider true about my life if I were so proud as to disobey the Abbot and my conscience? Would I ever find a real, final confession underlying all the others? This is hard to answer, because the first thing that strikes me about myself (it is one of the main reasons why I have become a monk) is that I have never in my life been able to know when I am telling a lie and when I am telling the truth. On all matters of fact I am perfectly honest: I can state dates, acts of treason, Party-meetings, executions, etc., with absolute veracity. But once I start confessing the why-and-wherefore of my *behaviour* (as one is

213

expected to do in a book), I become so entertained by the personal drama of it all that everything I put down has a wonderful *ring* of truth: I feel myself growing from a particular person into a universal design – much as a musician might set out persistently to play the recorder and find himself always in the organ-loft. It is the *notes* that get the better of me: they have such a heavenly *sound* that I cannot think them false. When I read St Augustine's *Confessions,* I know that he is *telling* the truth; and that there is a great difference.

I don't want to start writing *another* confession, but if ever the Abbot's line changes, in response to public needs, I think I would begin by saying that where I differ from St Augustine is that he confesses to smallness whereas I only confess to sins that increase my bulk. I don't think I could bear to make myself look ridiculous, to confess to having been swayed by petty motives which no organ could amplify into grandeur. I simply have to make the crime fit the confession: it would kill me, I think, to cease to identify myself with a vast historical event and admit that my career resulted from carrying to an extreme the pettiest conceits of the most ordinary man.

Well, I have said it, and I am still alive! The next question then is: for what petty reason did I become a Communist agent? The Abbey line on this is that I was a tortured soul who was carried away by ideal-ism: I have confessed to this repeatedly, but I regret to say that it is totally untrue. I came in contact with Communism soon after I first joined a trade-union – and the only reason why I joined a union was because I had exhausted all other means of drawing my parents' atten-tions to me. I interested myself in Communism only when I noticed that the Communists in my union had advanced a shocking step further. To this day I am able to relive the thrill that went through me when first I sensed the *apartness* of these men – their feigned nonchal-ance, the friendly smile with which they embarrassed normal people, the impression they gave of being the only members of our happy family who knew what skeletons were in the cupboards. I had no sooner become aware of them than I was filled with the conviction that I, too, could look and walk like them – just as, later, when I stumbled on the saints I had no difficulty in adjusting my stride.

I would like to interject here a warning to parents. None of you, I am sure, wants to see your son become first a secret agent of Material-ism and then a public-relations agent of the Incomprehensible. Well, you can prevent this from happening if you will only hold your tongue and stop bragging about the little chap. Whenever I felt lazy or vapid and put on a moon-face, my father always bellowed at the top of his voice: 'Just look at him! With the other children you always know where you are, but you never know what's at the back of *his* mind!' It had not occurred to me before that I *had* a back to my mind, but once this area had been brought to my attention as the place where admiration is found, I took a life-lease of the premises. When my parents said: 'Well, boys, we have a surprise today: we are going to take you to the circus,' I never turned a hair. While my brothers cat-called and hurrahed, I sat with a pudding-face, looking, if anything, more depressed than pleased. My father was enthralled. 'Just look at the little b—!' he would shriek, 'not a squeak out of him! I wonder what's going on *inside* – *at the back*?' My mother would tousle my hair and murmur fondly: 'A mother *always* knows. He's more thrilled than all the rest of them put together – *that's* why he's so quiet.' I would reward her with a coy, inscrutable smile, leave the table, and retire to a position in the garden which was just visible from the dining-room window. There I would stand staring at nothing, until I glimpsed the corner of my father's nose against the edge of the pane and heard his muffled roar: 'Damn my eyes, what's the little devil up to now? If this goes on, there's no saying what he'll be when he's older.'

Oh, my dear parents, I would have loved and honoured you more if you had not forced me to devote the bulk of my childhood to making an unknown quantity. It was you who taught me that mystery commands the greatest respect and that the highest identity is a secret nothing.

You will see from this that when I grew up and looked for a profession to attach my mystery to, Communism was just what I needed. Far from being, as people suppose, a creature which devours the identity, the Party is exactly the contrary: it is the most *special* thing in the world. Everyday life is killing to the identity; Party membership is so thrillingly individual that its rules and rigidities seem merely to be a frame for the self-portrait which one has painted for so long. Who would say billiards was unindividual because it is played on a walled table? Moreover, the Party supplies the thrill of discovering that the game becomes more and more individualistic the further one gets into it: the players become more and more select, the table is set up in a more and more remote room; the face of the scorer grows increasingly grave: one leaves everything that can be described as average further and further behind. I felt I was entering the intimacy of demigods, and it did not take me long to put on the requisite appearance: soon, I could walk into a room with just the right tread, listen to argument with just the right blandness, and make my face suggest that simultaneously everything and nothing was taking place behind it. I also began to swot-up on Dostoyevsky, Nietzsche, and so on; and I must apologize to the public for having confessed that such reading *led* me into Communism. The opposite is true. It is only *after* one has begun to model oneself on selected demi-gods that one asks for the address of their tailor.

I did all this so well that the Communists in my union soon noticed that I was not an ordinary person. To climb, in any organization, one has to study not the theory on which it is based but the moods of those who put the theory into practice. Today, for instance, I can sense almost immediately the Abbot's mood-of-the-moment, and when, without warning, his jesting face suddenly turns sour and he intones some smug, pious reprimand, I am never on the receiving end. I have always stopped joking a split second ahead of him. The great art in this, of course, is not to overdo it: the man who anticipates his superiors *too* consistently gets it where the chicken got the axe. The superior has had to work very hard to become an absolute chameleon, and the wise subordinate does not carry anticipation to the point where it makes the boss look like a mere traffic-light.

I mention this because people believe (as a result of reading our confessions) that hard work and overriding idealism make one a secret agent. Why, I could name dozens of men with these virtues who never got further than the most ordinary position in the Party and wouldn't have been entrusted with the secret blue-prints of a button-hook! What's more, most of them are in prison now, instead of in the Abbey. No, the way to get on is to make the right remark in the presence of the right person, to wear the right face in the right place. It is no different from the way young men get ahead as commercial travellers. The only difference between an insurance agent and a secret agent is that the higher the latter rises, the greater need he has of the former.

The day came when I was *recognized*. I mean, that when my superior gave me some boring chore, I knew instinctively that he knew that I was capable of better things, which he would soon call on me to do. Soon, I found myself meeting Party members who were superior to those on whom I had modelled myself. The backs of their minds were set at even greater remove from the fronts, and their poise was so great that they had perfected the thrilling art of turning the whole method back-to-front: that is to say: they often stated quite frankly what was happening at the *back*, leaving one to wonder whether they kept their secret in the *front*, or if they had a back behind the back. I was an ambitious youth: it was not long before I regarded my old models as very ordinary, humdrum mortals and went to work on the more subtle design of manifold secret drawers. I made my Marxism more abstruse and less obvious: I relegated almost the whole of my real identity to regions which even I found it difficult to locate. This is why, as I have said, I never know when I am telling the truth: a confession which seems to come from the heart usually turns out to have been nesting in my head.

In the presence of these higher equivocators, I occasionally, very humbly, let fall a remark that indicated flights of thought of which my old heroes were quite incapable. My reward came when one of the dignitaries, in my presence, referred to one of these old heroes as 'a good wheel-horse'. It was my first great test since Pa had thrown the circus at my feet! I remember looking back at the speaker with just the right degree of non-expression on my malleable visage: my look suggested that though I was too intelligent to deny the imputation, I was also too unpromoted to concur in it. When you can do that sort of thing with your face alone, imagine what you can do with the brain behind it!

I soon reached that select circle of Communism in which everything of importance is relegated to indefinable areas of the mind and the common-or-garden front has only two functions: (1) to deepen the mystery of the back parts by non-committally grunting at the right moment, and (2) to relax the tension of secrecy and mystery by swapping sneers about the stupidity of the average Party member. I was too young then to know that every élite is rooted in mockery of the tier below it: I thought my laughter was part of the very top-laughter. Today, when I know better, it makes me wince to think that in distant Moscow my little élite was considered so contemptible that it was not even worthy of our masters' jokes. Well, I must confess that we are much the same in our Abbey conversation: we never lack for a joke about the mundane worshippers of this world. Somewhere on high, I don't doubt, there is a Comintern of archangels to whom our great Abbot seems exceedingly comic. God alone doesn't join in such laughter, which is why we self-made men always feel comfortable sitting at His feet. He alone, I know, will never point a calloused finger at the back of my mind, and shout with a loud guffaw: 'What's *that* for? *I* never put it there. You made it yourself!'

When I look back on it all, I see that one of the greatest secrets of the Party was in knowing how to protect its members from ridicule. There is not a single tenet of Marxism about which select Marxists do not make jokes, but they *never* joke about the ways in which the theory is put into practice. The more absurd a practice is, the more solemn they are about it.

Take, for example, the unspeakably childish routine which is inflicted on secret agents. Its only purpose is to make the agent believe that he is somebody who matters very much. One is given half of page 24 of the Sundays Only London-to-Brighton time-table. One is told that on Wednesday the 5th of March at four-thirty p.m. one will walk down Lavender Grove wearing an Edwardian bowler hat and that under the second lamp-post one will see a gentleman in a mackintosh reading *John Bull*. Him one will approach, and murmur the symbolic words 'Can you give me a light?' On his producing his matches, one is to observe in his free hand the other half of the Sundays Only time-table, at which point one is to show one's own half. But this, ladies and gentlemen, is merely the beginning of the ridiculous acquaintance! The mackintoshed man, oneself in pursuit, disappears into the next-to-nearest Underground station, boards a train, changes at Gloucester Road, changes at Baker Street, gets out at Hyde Park, and hires a penny chair – the pursuit of theology itself is not more complicated! You, if you have managed to hang on, then take a chair beside him, and mutter some prearranged nonsense like: 'Wilfrid hopes the bunnies will have fine weather,' to which he earnestly replies: 'Bunnies believe in deeds, not words.' Then, *and only then*, do you hand him the stolen plans of the new rocket.

When I look back on this, I would burst out laughing, were it not that I myself was involved in many such meetings and, though I love penance, I cannot bear to feel absurd. But was there ever such childishness? As I have said, the point of it all was to make the agent feel distinctive, to reassure him that his years of rehearsal were not going to be wasted. Moreover, this charade was *so like the real thing*; it was as if what I have called the back-of-the-mind had been changed into the exciting terms of back-of-the-act. Its object was to make us happy.

But oh, when I look back on my past, I really *am* grateful to God for having taken such episodes out of my life! The number of time-tables, dollar bills, and cigarette packets I have dismembered: the number of *streets* I have walked, from Budapest to New York; the number of dismal *parks* in which I have sat; the number of *trains and platforms* into and on to which I have scurried; the times without number I have kept assignations before the Mona Lisa, the left-hand lion outside Pennsylvania Station, Mozart's statue in Salzburg, the Albert Memorial, the Tombe des Invalides! The awful little cafés I have ended up in; the occasions when I have found a dog vying with my mackintoshed contact for use of the second lamp-post; the trains that have broken apart in tunnels as soon as I boarded them or slid-to their doors at my approach! I think now with sympathy of the English comrade who went quite out of his wits over the whole business. After years of formal spying, such as I have described, he fell to pieces. When he got on the track of something interesting, he would go to a *public telephone* and *call up* his superior! When he stole a document, instead of contacting 'Wilfrid' and awaiting orders for the usual pancake-race, he would put a *post-card* in the *letter-box, addressed* to Wilfrid and saying: 'Dying to see you; lots to show.' And then sign it with his real name! Poor fellow, he only did that once!

But this brings me to the heart of the matter – the real dead-centre of my *true* confession. The reason why we never laughed at our ridiculous antics was that we were all people who are killed by laughter. Had we been asked to drop our information in the letter-box we would soon have begun to lose all sense of backness-of-mind and felt like quite ordinary people. I have told you about the wonderful sense of personal identity that grows stronger and stronger as one grows in invisibility, and how with each stage of Party ascent one becomes more-and-more a select, rare, chosen individual. Well, if you add the elements of scurrying melodrama and utter secrecy to this sense of self, you really begin to get near the condition of uniqueness which is the goal of every agent. This uniqueness was my aim then, as it is now: I am one of the few men in the world who has been first uniquely secret and then Uniquely loved.

The only word for this is conceit, or vanity. But the Abbot does not allow these words in our confessions, because pride is a much meatier word and is more elevating to him who confesses to it. Moreover, if I call it vanity, will you ever grasp its magnitude? Vanity, as I practise it, is hardly conceivable to you; how can you begin to imagine what grandeur and supremacy of self were the reward of me and my comrades? Any one of you has climbed up into a select circle and looked down on the thousands of little figures in the routine below, but few of you can picture how intoxicating this view becomes when the peak on which you stand is invisible, and you yourself an enigma! To know that you are the exact opposite of what nearly everyone thinks you are; to sit in a crowded train, disguised as a passenger, knowing that you are a spy and that no one else in the carriage is aware of it – there's identity for you! You can talk of great actors playing to roars of applause, but that only shows them to be the most ordinary of men. Wait until you have spent most of your adult life playing a leading role in a play that is real, before an audience who, thanks to your skill, is not aware that a play is going on at all! The contrast between their dumb innocence and your own supreme awareness must be experienced to be felt: only mystical experiences are comparable, which is why we of the Abbey have so many. And mystical experiences take place the other way round, of course, with oneself the innocent party for a change. I will only say that the magnificent prayer of Archimedes – 'Give me where to stand and I will move the world' – is granted the secret agent in a golden whisper. Never, never, will I know again the passion of identity that possessed me in the days when, lever and fulcrum in hand, I stood invisible upon the Party heights – and saw the world move!

*

I know this sounds as if we agents were selfish people with no love for human beings; but this is not the case. We have no interest in people when we enter the Party; indeed, we enter it in order to get away from them. But, just as we read Dostoyevsky *after* joining rather than before, so we develop a deep love for humanity once we have reached a point where we need an excuse for our behaviour. The higher we climb, the greater our secret grows and the more we become an unknown menace to ordinary people. It is imposible for us not to feel pity for the innocent friends and relatives who still trust us, and this pity exists side by side with our determination to go on deceiving them. Most of you have experienced something of this kind when you have been betraying your husband or your wife with one of your best friends' husband or wife, but it has only made you feel ashamed. The agent is not ashamed: betrayal of his nearest-and-dearest is his favourite duty, not his sensual whim. He suffers dreadful torments, but they are the blessed agonies of a martyr; the more he suffers, the more admirable he becomes; the more he loves humanity, the more he exalts himself as its dutiful seducer; the more people he executes, the more splendid is his own pain. Often he thinks, as he mixes his poisons in the living-rooms of those who love him, that one day, probably long after he is dead-and-gone, his secret will be told to a revolutionized world and his victims will weep when they think of the misery *he* must have experienced in the course of deceiving *them*. Many agents consider this posthumous worship as a martyr more exciting than the brilliant deception of their lives, particularly if they have a large number of *close* innocent friends, to say nothing of children and a wife. They argue that the supreme secrecy of the career gives them one priceless identity, and the exploding of the secret a second – in short, two bags full, one to enjoy on the spot, the other to imagine in the hands of posterity. Many of them, following the theological example, even reach the point of insisting that the living identity is inferior to the one which will come after death: they rather look down on the comrades who derive their ecstasy solely from being *living* mysteries.

Personally, I am doubtful about trusting posterity too much. The public 'line' of worship is very changeable and the lime-pits of this world are full of unaccepted martyrs. A full public confession while one is still alive is a better idea; not only does it make the martyrdom occur immediately, when one is still alive to enjoy it, but it also takes precedence over the career, which it amply excuses. Moreover, if the joints squeak or the wrong bones rattle in the first edition, they can be replaced in a later one, like a Revised Authorized Version. Personally, I believe that our Abbey will never run short of funds so long as the public keeps its highest favours for those who have plundered it; and there is not likely to be a change of attitude so long as the leading thinkers go on insisting that there is no better Paul than a former Saul, no clergyman more moving than one who is too drunk to stand, no prayer so deep as a hymn of blasphemy, no man more devout than an atheist. There are always periods in history in which everyone stands on his head to stress the importance of his feet: I trust the present one will persist until we maudlin sinners go underground for the last time.

It is the function of our good Abbot to keep an eye on all this. A day may come, for instance, when Communism no longer matters; its agents will then become useless, and converts such as myself totally uninteresting. The Abbot is even now preparing for that grievous day, confident that with God's help he will switch us to another, serviceable line. What is likely to happen is that with their dearest menace removed, people will be driven back on themselves and will need new scapegoats. All the shrewd gentlemen who looked into the hearts of men and found them to consist of warring 'ideas' occurring in a frame of 'history' will hurriedly decide to see real hearts there instead – and will they wallop the public for not having realized this all along! The new emphasis will be on strictly *personal* things; it will be inexcusable to say that one was led astray by an *idea*. Everyone will be expected to examine his conscience, rather than depend on guilt to see him through. This is the moment for which the Abbot is making ready; the moment, perhaps, which Brother Herbert sought to anticipate. We shall all write our confessions anew and they will all be along the lines I have sketched in this brief introduction. We shall confess, as we have so often confessed, that our previous confessions served only to disguise the truth. We shall wallow in little ignominies; the pears which St Augustine stole will become less-than-pears in our case. We will put the public in the place we have just vacated: we will remake ourselves in the form of pygmies. We will substitute a hundred petty vices for our major crimes: we will make ourselves look so humble that the public will feel thoroughly ashamed of its bloatedness. Poor public! I feel sorry for it already. It takes at least a generation for leading ideas to seep into the suburbs, which means that just when we great sinners decide to take up the role of simple bourgeois, they, in turn, will have just started careering off into our old ways of secret charades, drunkenness, and pious blasphemy. What a spectacle it is going to be: the priest, sober as a judge at last and quite able to stand erect in the pulpit, preaching to a congregation that swigs away from hip-flasks and screams aloud the most shocking confessions of murder, incest, suicide, and treason! Oh well, God bless the public anyway, and God bless the newspapers and the Russians: we owe them a debt we shall never repay. And God bless the people who think 'ideas' are so much more important than behaviour that anyone with a large enough theory can confess away with bloody murder. And God bless, above all, that great Thermostat, our good Abbot, who knows which time is ripe for what confession, and which seeds to sow in the wet springtime of a guilty world. Which reminds me – God bless guilt, the thinkers' darling, who, unlike conscience, comes only when the bloody act has been safely performed and ushers in the ecstasies of publicized remorse. May great royalties forever bear his train!

*

P.S. We shall not *always* have an Abbot. Eventually, he will wither away.

*

I had barely written these words when my radiator sang out: 'Caution! Abbot approaching!' I seized my manuscript and stuffed it into the radiator, which has a secret compartment for such trifles. With so much pneumonia about, it is foolish to overheat one's cell.

The Abbot walked in. He was followed by Brother Nimpy and Brother Kapotzky, his bodyguard.

'Always scribble, scribble, scribble, brother!' said the Abbot, smiling. 'And what is it *this* time, may I ask? Not *another* confession, I hope? Have mercy on your poor Abbot whose *nihil obstat* is beginning to look scrawled and jaded.'

'Only a children's book this time, Father,' I replied with a smile, indicating the stooge MS. which is always open on my desk.

'Indeed? Of what nature, pray?'

'A day in the life of a rabbit, Father.'

'How full of possibilities! May I glance at it? I am fond of children's books. And while I'm looking at it, you won't mind if Nimpy and Kapotzky search you?'

'I have nothing to hide, Father,' I replied, thanking God that this was now true.

'Of course not,' he said. 'And nowhere to hide it.'

While Nimpy and Kapotzky frisked me, the Abbot leafed through my manuscript. He ignored the top and bottom pages and rippled through the middle ones, his eyes darting brilliantly from point to point. From time to time he held a page against the light, in search of code pin-pricks. 'It seems perfectly all right,' he said at last, 'but make the rabbit a giraffe, will you?'

'I could make it become one in the course of the tale. Father,' I said. 'It could be transformed.'

'No, from the very beginning, if you don't mind. If you consider the principal feature of the giraffe you will see why it is much more desirable, symbolically, than a rabbit.'

'Nothing to report, Father,' said Nimpy.

'Good,' said the Abbot. 'You two boys can go now. Pray for me.'

Nimpy is a dear old man. He forgets continually *which* monastery he is working in, *which* Abbot he is spying *for*. Now, he gave the Abbot a Hitler salute, genuflected, and withdrew. Kapotzky gave a big grin and followed him out.

When they had gone the Abbot gave a sigh of relief and threw himself into a chair. I say 'threw himself', but that is only a way of speaking. It is not easy to master the art of tossing a heavy, hairy, robe about, and the Abbot does it perfectly. One brisk, coordinated gesture and there he was, a replica in brown of Whistler's 'Mother'. He finessed his profile, and sighed.

'You look tired, Father,' I said.

'I am. Poor Herbert's death has upset me. I don't like pneumonia in the Abbey. It's so *infectious*.' He gave me a sharp look and said: 'You saw a lot of him, didn't you? How are you? No colds? Sore throats? Virus?'

'I am in the pink of health, Father,' I said.

'Do your best to remain so, then. Everything in *moderation*. See?'

I bowed. After a pause, he dropped his stern tone and said in a friendly voice: 'I hope you didn't mind our little search. Pure routine, as you know. Frankly, I wanted your advice on a point that is worrying me. So do wipe all that sweat off your forehead.'

I obeyed. One of the great things about our sort of life is that signs of terror cannot be taken as evidence of guilt. If they could be, we would all have died of pneumonia long ago.

'Would you say?' he asked, 'that you are just about the best man here in the matter of the Divine ontology?'

'God's identity *is* rather my speciality,' I said. 'Brother Thomas is better on its history, but I am the more up-to-date, particularly where the gracious and merciful aspects are concerned.'

'You did mercy for the *Encyclopedia,* did you not?'

'And love, Father.'

'I thought so. Did you run into any trouble?'

'Oh, no, Father. The Scriptures are perfectly in line.' Suddenly curious to the point of audacity, I exclaimed: 'Is there going to be a switch, Father?'

'No, no, no,' he said testily, and added sharply: 'And don't talk like that. Why does everyone here treat me as if I were plotting something?'

I blushed. He asked suddenly: 'What do you know about the Divine *patience?*'

How exactly like him – to drop the crucial question without warning! *'Patience,* Father?' I said. 'Why, there are many references to it.'

'To the *Almighty's* patience? To *ours,* yes. What about *His?* Can you give me, for instance, one powerful, authoritative quotation?'

'There is St John the Divine, Father, " . . . *in the kingdom and patience of Jesus Christ".* But I am not sure that the word had the same meaning in those days.'

'We *never* argue from Revelations, anyway.'

'How about "long-suffering", Father?'

'Now, that's an idea. It means patience, does it not? Is it also incomprehensible and infinite?'

'I would hardly say so. There is no mystery about it, and as it is usually mentioned just before the delivery of some violent punishment, it can't be considered infinite. I could, of course, put up a good argument for its being so, should you need one.'

'No good. The evidence, I know, is all the other way. There comes a time when *His patience snaps.* He has had enough. Love and mercy are both arguably present in the resulting chastisement. But not patience.'

'What is your bent, Father, exactly?'

He hesitated, and then said: 'As you well know, the basis of all our arguments nowadays – all thinking people's, anyway – is that it is not for us miserable sons of men to question His faculties by attempting to define their limits or the nature of their operation. In the last century this argument was popular when people suffered, or when children died. But today we use it, shall I say, much more *actively*. We bestow His mercy on the vile, not on the windows and orphans.'

'*Exactly* what I was writing!' I cried. Oh, egotism, which drags one to the brink of pneumonia itself! Fortunately, the Abbot seemed too interested in himself to hear me.

'I mean,' he said, 'we have been using Him rather *loosely*. When you consider the clear, strict, simple rules He laid down for human behaviour, I am not sure that He approves of our present enthusiasm for His mysteriousness – for His indefinable mercy and unpredictable grace. He may be beginning to feel that we are using His dialectic as a means of avoiding His instructions. I am not sure that He ever intended to be as mysterious as all that.'

'But after all, Father,' I said, 'we have sincerely repented. And there's no doubt that the repentant sinner gets the best breaks.'

'Of course, of course. What worries me is the idea that perhaps we are giving the repentant sinner *all* the breaks. The *general public*, I think, is beçoming to miss Him. I think they are beginning to resent the way He is allowed to operate only in dives, cells, and Africa. And all His gestures are becoming so dramatic!'

'These are dramatic times, Father.'

'That's just it. Isn't He getting too much like ourselves? I do think we must start sharing Him with the relatively-innocent as well as the inordinately-guilty. Sometimes I feel we haven't changed very much since our radical days. Then, we used Marx to beat the bourgeois with; now, we use God. That's why I asked about His patience. Won't He, at some point, begin to feel that we are imposing upon Him? I am sure, here in the Abbey, our slates are *pretty* clean; but even we do rather emphasize that it's not what you do that matters but what you repent of continuing to do. I feel that God may soon begin to resent this. I think we ought to start hinting that His grace is available, to say the least, to quite ordinary people, and not only to psychotics and ex-Party members. I would even go so far as to say that we might hint at a return to His first principles of good behaviour. I mean, we might say quite definitely that it is our intention to start behaving better ourselves. To set an example. After all, He has put up with our inventing a mysterious holdall for our bad behaviour named The Unconscious,

226

but I am sure He is growing indignant at the way we expect Him to dole out forgiveness from an equally-mysterious trunk named Grace. If Heaven's our destination we shouldn't mark *everything* "Not Wanted on the Voyage".'

When I remained silent, he said: 'It struck me that perhaps one or other of us might feel the urge to make a fresh confession, rather along those lines. I want to know if such a poor thing can be made readable; if it has any box office.'

'If you mean me, Father,' I said, 'I am always ready to obey orders.'

'I don't think that is the spirit in which to approach revelation,' he answered, frowning.

'All I mean, Father, is that if my superior so orders I am only too ready to re-examine my conscience.'

'That's much better. And don't be shy about it. See what the dredge brings up. The trouble about this place is that you are all such rabbits. How do you think we are going to compete with the poets and novelists outside if none of you ever has an original idea?'

I was nettled by this, and said: 'Father, we think a great deal more than you imagine.'

'Well, I wish you would confess to a dangerous thought occasionally. There I sit outside that box and never a glimmer of originality comes through the grille. Old Nimpy is the only one who ever makes a gaffe, and that's only because he's in his second childhood. Nonetheless, he's worth the whole lot of you put together.'

Now, I was really angry! To be rated lower than a hack like Nimpy, a man who had never climbed higher than the next man's pocket, was more than I could bear. I was about to expostulate when the Abbot shouted:

'What do you *do* with yourself all day? Do you *ever* use your brain? Do you ever have an idea that is not orthodox?'

'You'd be surprised!' I shouted back.

'Would I? Give me one scrap of evidence – just one!'

'I have nothing on me at the moment. . . .'

'Exactly! None of you ever has. Sometimes I wonder why any of you stays here.'

'We've taken vows, haven't we?'

'Vows, indeed! It's not vows that keep you here. It's the wonderful public appeal of a holy place. As long as you stay here, you are somebody: if you went, you would be a nonentity. Just like the Party!' Observing me grinding my teeth, he went on: 'Well, perhaps I shouldn't pick on you. The point is, my dear boy, that when you came here I had such high hopes of you. Your earliest confessional work had a wonderful simplicity. Even your evasions looked like golden curls. Here, I said to myself, is my successor. Here is a confidant, one who stands above the ruck, a man who could help me draw a good line.'

I was thrilled by these words, and answered: 'Father, I am still that man.'

'No, no. Too late! It was all a dream. "I have nothing on me at the moment": that is what you said. For once, it was true. I must bear the burden alone. I must be solitary on the hilltop.'

'I will prove you mistaken!' I cried.

'You will do nothing of the sort. I flatly forbid it.'

'You have no right to forbid it!'

'Oh yes I have. It is not my duty to encourage normal minds into nervous breakdowns.'

'Normal minds!' Never had I been more insulted! I turned white with rage and my eye flew to the radiator. I raised one trembling hand in the direction of my hidden manuscript.

Suddenly the Abbot began to cry. 'Forgive me, brother!' he exclaimed, 'Pray with me! I am the worst of sinners.' He dropped on his knees.

'No!' I cried, all my anger forgotten; '*I* am the worst!' *I* dropped on *my* knees.

'Far, far the worst!' he groaned, laying his forehead on the floor and punching his breast decisively.

'Yet not so low as I,' I bellowed, rubbing my whole face on the ground.

At this, he flung his legs out behind him, so that he was prostrate overall, and said: 'That's quite enough, brother! I'll trouble you to keep your proper station.'

I obeyed. We prayed.

*

I woke this morning feeling unwell. My stomach was not itself. I thought of calling in the Abbey doctor; but one is always reluctant to take this step. I must confess, though, that even the thought of a fatal illness visiting me did not stop me feeling rather proud. It is not every day that one argues the Abbot on to his face. I went over our little fracas stage by stage, rather enjoying it; I did this a second time; and then a third.

It was on this third round that I suddenly turned white as a sheet. In the two previous replays I had only been repeating our *words*; this third time I was doing our looks and gestures too. Only then did I realize that the Abbot's cry for forgiveness had come a split second after I had gestured in the direction of my hidden manuscript! The dreadful truth broke on me: in that instant he had discovered my secret: his plea for my forgiveness was not, as I had imagined, a purely routine bit of Abbey theatre; it was an absolutely genuine request for something that he was going to need – something which I would shortly be in no position to supply.

It is not nice to know that one is soon going to die, that the impressive edifice one has toiled to build is going to be rubble. Fortunately, for people like me there are many consolations. If we have enough time, we can always write still another confession, something really poignant. If time is too short for this, we can start thinking about death–that is to say, of what we will look like from a dead point-of-view. This is a wonderful occupation: abruptly one realizes that this is *the* great moment. I mean, all about one are millions of living people – and there is one's own dead face staring out of all the morning papers, a thing apart, a secret agent in excelsis, *the* insoluble enigma, *the* end to which one has devoted one's whole energies since childhood.

After thinking on these things and marvelling at the clever way the Abbot had tricked me to them, I rose, went to the radiator, took out this confession, and laid it openly on my table. I then popped 'A Day in the Life of a Rabbit' into the radiator, for Nimpy to steal. This gives me, I reckon, about twenty-four hours' grace.

*

Dear Abbot,

By the time you read this, pneumonia will have carried me off. It simply had no option. I love to think of your sermon; I know it will be a good one – and the first I have ever had which was about nothing but me!

Apropos of my published confessions: a good deal of bickering is still going on between my agent and the Brazilian publishers. *Do* back-up my agent – particularly as I would like the Abbey to have the money. I like to die feeling that you are all under an obligation to me! ! !

As to the confession you are reading now, I do hope it is along the line you mentioned last night. What pleases me is knowing that I have left it in the right hands. You alone will be able to judge when the time is ripe for publication. It will need some editing, of course, but as long as it remains *recognizably me*, I don't worry.

I can't tell you how proud I am to go out like this. It seems to me that I had the best of two worlds while I was alive and am going to have still a third when I am not. My sole aim, now, as always, is uniqueness; and I must say, with all humility, that few others on this planet have come as close to it as I am coming now.

Skipwith and Heilbronner have always treated me very well and have the option on the new book.

Re the Mihailovich case coming up shortly (at which I was to testify) do give the prosecutor the list of names and dates in my drawer. I *think* you might also hint that a two-minute silence in my memory would not be out of place in court.

Let me say again that to be the one who was chosen for liquidation in so great a switch of the line is all a man of my type could possibly ask. What bothers me is the thought of having to share this crown of thorns with Brother Herbert. I don't grudge him *some* prominence, but I would hate to think of sharing the limelight with a second-rater. I depend on you to give me top billing.

Best of luck to you and the Abbey. They were good days and I regret nothing. I hope that when your time comes you, too, will go to God confident that you have written your very last confession!

Yours ever,

'One of the Boys'.

P.S. Don't please be offended by the bit which says that eventually 'the Abbot will wither away'. I only meant it as a little joke. Abbots like you will never wither away as long as there are brothers like me.

*

Silence is golden before and during a recital, but it is not a thing the performer wants to hear at the end of one. So Father Orfe was well pleased to stand bowing left, centre, right, front, back as the shouts and claps resounded through the room: he did this with the dignity that is proper to a male pianist – that is to say, he blew no kisses to the clappers, caught no huge bunches of flowers; he merely *acknowledged* the din by awarding it severe torsal inclinations and permitting his eyelids to become half-hooded. When it had died down somewhat, he raised his manuscript once more and began to read aloud again:

'Here is a tale about our Abbey which I am sure will amuse you. Brother Nimpy is what is known as a "manual type" – that is to say, he is almost illiterate. This means that when he writes his confessions, his publisher's religious-editor has to do the actual writing, imitating what Nimpy's prose might be, had Nimpy prose. Well, Nimpy's confession went up to the Abbot in the usual way and got a *nihil obstat*: but next day the Abbot met him in one of the corridors and said earnestly: "Do you feel well, Nimpy? You look as if you had seen a *ghost*."'

After great laughter and clapping, Father Orfe again raised his hand and said: 'Here's another, equally funny . . .'

'One encore is sufficient, Orfe,' said the President, raising his hand.

'Just this one more,' said Father Orfe.

'Certainly not. It has all been most interesting but it could easily become dull. I have a good many points to make, but as I have not marshalled them yet, I would rather someone else made a stumbling opening. First speaker, please.'

There was no response.

'Come, come, gentlemen,' said the President. 'You are not shy, I know.'

At last Dr Musk rose and said: 'I think members feel that it is the duty of the Abbot to open the discussion of this particular history.'

'Abbot?' cried the President.

'I am sorry. It was a slip of the tongue. I suppose an apology is in order.'

'Not merely in order. For immediate delivery.'

Dr Musk looked sulky. 'It will take a moment to frame one that will not involve too much loss of face,' he said.

'Very well. We will patiently await your self-insurance.'

Everyone watched with interest while Dr Musk raised various phrases in his mind and examined his dignity in their light. At last Father Orfe cried: 'May I point out that the whole *tension* of my history is slipping away?'

231

'That's true enough,' said Mr Jamesworth. 'Just watching Musk's face for three minutes has caused me to forget every word of Orfe.'

'I've got it!' cried Dr Musk. 'No, I haven't after all. Sorry.'

'May I point out,' said Dr Shubunkin, 'that this is the third time in as many histories that an apology to the President has been demanded?'

'I second that point,' said Dr Bitterling. 'In my opinion, a Presidency should not depend upon reiterated apologies.'

'I wish you would all shut up,' said Dr Musk. 'I almost had it then.'

'I rise to propose a motion,' said Father Orfe angrily: 'namely that Rules incorporate a clause giving discussion of a history priority over apology.'

'Come along, now, Musk,' said the President: 'You are making us all very fretful. Just spit it out.'

'All those in favour?' cried Father Orfe furiously.

Most of the Club raised their hands.

'What!' cried the President, and again: 'What! Gentlemen, have you taken leave of your senses? There is no valid motion but that which is intoned from the chair.'

'Intone it then!' cried Dr Shubunkin.

'I shall do nothing of the sort. It is wholly against my interests.'

'I've got it *now*!' cried Dr Musk. 'Here goes . . . ! It's rather long. . . .'

'There is a motion on the floor, Musk,' said Dr Shubunkin, 'so bottle your apology for some other occasion.'

'Or for some other President,' said Mr Jamesworth.

'That is very well put,' said Father Orfe. '*Some other President.*'

'No, no!' cried poor Stapleton, tears running down his face. 'I am sure the President will be only too *happy to explain*!'

'For God's sake, Mr Stapleton, sit down!' exclaimed the President. 'Death is as nothing compared with the horror of your support.'

Stapleton turned white and collapsed in his chair. By tomorrow, he will be a cynic for life. Clearly, his war-veteran identity was nothing but a makeshift.

'Since the President has been frank enough to declare his fate,' said Mr Jamesworth, 'it is proper that we should match it by drawing up a frank indictment.'

'I have had one in my mind for some time,' said Dr Musk, 'and, unlike my apology, can think of it instantly.'

'Are you not proceeding too rapidly, gentlemen?' cried the President.

'We'll not pause for second thoughts, if that's what you mean, you crafty old fox!' cried Dr Shubunkin passionately.

'You flatter me,' said the President, looking rather pleased.

'Recite the indictment, Musk,' ordered Father Orfe.

'Just a minute, what *is* all this?' cried Mr Harcourt. 'I thought we were discussing monasteries.

'You're an intelligent citizen, aren't you?' asked Mr Jamesworth. 'Are you not in favour of the indictment?'

'Yes, I'm sure I am, but I don't know what it is. It's all over my head.'

'*My* head,' said the President.

'Go on quickly, Musk, or he'll wriggle out!' cried Dr Bitterling, abrubtly recovering his voice. 'Where his life's concerned you can't trust him an inch.'

'We, of the Identity Club,' said Dr Musk, 'hereby indict our President for having failed utterly in his duties. It is the task of every leader to give his followers that sense of security and rightness that makes life worth living, and this our President has failed to do. He has allowed members to feel doubt as to the uniqueness of their selves. He has allowed his own image to lapse by utterly misapplying it –failing to drive home at the right moments the rudeness, amiability, satire, benignity which are the marks of leadership. Either as a result of bore-dom or senility he has not lent a sense of passion or urgency to the theory on which this Club is based. He has even given the impression that all theories are pretty much alike as far as he is concerned, and that the Theory of Identity is not only not the only true theory but merely one of the many plausible ideas which are floating about nowadays. His behaviour has resulted in a feeling of grave unease among our members which, if allowed to develop, might result in many of them dropping the whole idea of identity and starting off on quite a new one, such as carrots, vitamins, money, or sex. We therefore believe that it is time to get rid of him and replace him with a President less subject to the eclecticism which is bringing so much ruin on the world. We believe he would make an excellent corpse, and that in fact he has already decided to become one. We agree that in choosing this new identity he has acted wisely and we propose the immediate formation of a committee to discuss the best way of assisting his suicide.'

'May I add a rider?' cried Mr Jamesworth: 'that we feel no good would be obtained by postponing the business in any way?'

'Quite so,' said Father Orfe. 'Nostalgic memories of his prime might stay our hands.'

'We will have more room for grief once he is out of the way,' said Dr Shubunkin. 'So don't let's put the cart before the horse.'

'It begins to sound like a tumbril,' said the President.

'You will be much happier, you know,' said Father Orfe, 'in an identity that really suits you.'

'You don't think that is stretching our theory?' asked the President.

'It seems to me to follow admirably,' said Dr Musk. 'It would be a poor theory if it didn't.'

'It would lack all the qualities of absolute finality that every good theory must have,' said Father Orfe. 'It would leave room for doubt. You wouldn't want that, would you?'

'Why, no, I don't think so,' said the President. 'I had always realized, of course, that every theory must reach a fatal conclusion, but it had not occurred to me that this time the conclusion would be me.'

'I don't think this is a time for jokes,' said Mr Harcourt peevishly. 'If the President intends to resign, as I gather he does, he owes it to the club to do so with dignity.'

'Gentlemen,' said Captain Mallet, rising suddenly, 'let me warn you that in a few minutes the staff play is due to begin and that we cannot put it off.'

'I warmly agree,' said the President.

'Surely that's fiddling while Rome's burning?' said Father Orfe.

'You will hear no objections from Rome,' said the President.

'It is heartening, gentlemen,' said the captain, 'to see our old friend go out with a jest.'

'He has not much option,' said Mr Jamesworth. 'Besides, the tragic vein was never his forte.'

There was a knock on the door and Mrs Paradise appeared. 'We are all ready, sir,' she said, dropping the captain a curtsey.

'And so are we, Florence,' he replied.

'Do all the gentlemen have their programmes, sir?'

'They do, Florence.'

'Then shall I put out the lights?'

'By all means. And draw the curtains.'

The Prince of Antioch

or

An Old Way to New Identity

BY WILLIAM SHAKESPEARE

*

Edited by Miss Blanche Tray

CAST

THE PRINCE OF ANTIOCH	Herbert Towzer
CAPTAIN JACK	Henry Jellicoe
COUNT OF BAALBECK	Mrs Chirk
DUKE OF BURGUNDY	Miss Blanche Tray
KING OF ARTOIS	Herbert Towzer
KING OF ARTOIS' PRIME MINISTER	Henry Jellicoe
TURNKEY	Miss Blanche Tray
GHOSTS	Mrs Chirk
HERMIONE	Mrs Paradise
CATRIONA	Miss Blanche Tray
RADEGUND	Miss Finch
QUEEN OF ARTOIS	Mrs Paradise

Other Dukes, Lords, Counsellors, Courtiers, Pikemen, etc.
played by all members of the staff, according to convenience.

PROLOGUE

Spoken by Mrs Chirk

Thank you, good friends, your welcome warms my heart
(Now, clap ye all, and justify my start).
Retard your orange 'til our acts are sped;
Cast not its blood upon the Prologue's head.

* * *

Before you walks a company of men
That's sad and weary in its acumen.
We ask you: who are you, and what are we ·
That play as riddlers with identity?
Are you our hosts, who pay us for our pains,
Or is it we boards you, and entertains?
Answer me not! Can any answer be?
Can any tie one tight identity?
E'en he that's *Will'd* this play is self-mistaken,
Flitched like a hog to make a *Bacon*:
Is yoked to *Oxford* to conform a *Vere*,
Is skinned and tanned, so *Dyer's* hand appear.
The skeleton that's left, with this all done
Must course a *Derby* e'er his race is run,
Yet still must hear that he was much remiss
In wearing laurel which was pluckt by *Chris*.
Was ever butcher's boy so tricked and baited,
So carved to sirloin – or so well related?
Nay, never was; hence he hath thought it fit
To add to his apportionments, his bit;
T'assuage, in mirth, the sadness of his fame,
Which all acknowledge but decline his name.
Our play's a riddle in which ours display
The guises which your living selves portray;
The many semblances that make one you,
Shall play, through us, the game of who is who.
And play it fair, as players only can
Who've played your play since play and time began.

I.1

Scene: A furious seashore: enter, on spars, the Prince of Antioch, disguised as a common sailor, and a sea-captain.

PRINCE: Fundament! Fundament! Do I find bottom?
CAPT: Aye, zany, anchor thy soles!
  Cut short thy prayers; they're curtly answered.
  Oh, I am froze white as my grandfather's beard!
  Off! Fetch sere sticks;
  We'll build such fire the north star himself
  Will find his ice a-sweat.
PRINCE: Who orders me? Am I one that's ordered?
CAPT *(striking him)*: Sticks, goose, rummage thy bill!
  Waste not my chilled surmise
  On thy peculiar. Art so wet i' the pan
  Thou hast forgot thyself? I'll fetch flint.
            Exit Captain in search of flints.
PRINCE *(picking up sticks)*: He does not see the toity prince,
  Shrouded in sables, hung in gold carats,
  Who lolled the poop, pond'ring an Assyrian theme,
  Barking him orders till his knee-caps creaked
  Much as these woody bones *(breaks a twig)*. Thus, too,
  Was my dear greatness snapped, when that vast storm
  Screaming from northward in a harpy's veil,
  O'er powered the barque in which I was in route
  (From Thule on successful embassy) back
  To my desert throne. A state of caution
  Warned me to this disguise, lest I in turmoil,
  Should be despoilt.
            Takes a handful of rubies from his pocket.
  But now, I'll drop it off and be myself.
  With these I'll bribe the churl to take me home.
            Enter Captain, with flints.
  Here, Captain, precious gems; look, look!
CAPT: Put off your sanguine pebbles! All's now

Grown green; red's but a boiled lobster.
Give me your sticks.

Kindles fire.

PRINCE: This hotty beam exonerates my chills.
CAPT: Stand that the rising flame may cause the sea,
    Hugging its harbourage in your worsted cape,
    To be expelled right out in ghostly steam.
    Thus did I when we foundered off Ragusa,
    Spalato, Joppa, Tenereef, and Ness,
    And many other wrecks of which I shall
    In due course tell you, down
    To the last detail.
PRINCE: So many founderings?
CAPT: Was never a storm,
    Turning uncertain in the seven skies,
    But saw me peaceful in a distant sea
    And chose me for her seat.
PRINCE: Yet thus thou hast escaped men's follies ashore, Captain?
CAPT: Nay, nay, all them too I've had.
PRINCE: What! Treason, revolt, dissent? Landsmen's furies?
CAPT: Never a month absent. They wait me at the port.
PRINCE: Some heaven's protected thee.
CAPT: Ay, some heaven and a cutlass.
PRINCE (*aside*): Through this hard wretch, if I am resolute,
    I may at last draw wisdom from her well,
    For he, salt as a winter bean, may
    Keep ajar a whole philosophy
    To feed a tender prince.
    Off, royal self and panoply! I'll be
    His mate and pupil; thumb his horny book,
    And take fresh wisdom home to Antioch. All my
    Advisers, counsellors, and nobs, I'll
    Rule with tar and salt, a sailor king,
    Shrewd as a flea.

To Captain.

Knowst thou this shore, sir?
CAPT: Your sir is pleasing in my ears; no sound
Has quite the sweetness of the bending spine.

As to this shore, I see upon a dune
A tug of twitch-grass: where that couchie
Grows, Nature dictates the sand of Brittany.
PRINCE: Thrice-cloven Gaul, salute you this triune!
One, a hard Captain, wombed in a canvas gut;
Two, a soft Prince, tutored in all but life;
Three, a poor student, fumbling a new book.
Whence now, sir, captain?
CAPT: Art steamed, clam?
PRINCE: All but my marrow.
CAPT: We'll find a farmhouse: on its fringe, I'll
Hang, spying out the land.
At my demand you'll climb the guardian roost,
Abduct a creamy goose
And hasten back. I'll tend our rear.
PRINCE (*aside*): His methods are not nice nor honourable,
But I'll not question one whose mischief bold
Doubtless conceals a soul as wise as gold.

Exeunt.

I.2

*Scene: A Chamber in the Palace of the Duke of Brittany.
Enter the Duke, Counsellors, and Attendants.*

DUKE: Tedium engrosses me. Another hour,
Another face, all different, all the same.
Is business done?
COUN: A few more peasants ask you justice.
DUKE: Murderous few! Enter, assassins!

Enter 1st Peasant.

1ST P: Most noble Lord, Serene Preponderance –
DUKE: Plea, sir! Law is a mouse-trap,
Sprung in a trice!
1ST P: Your honourable steward hath proclaimed
That I, my flocks, my whole demesne,

And wife and bairns, numbering seventeen,
Are forfeit all to you.
DUKE: Harsh! Harsh! Give him a groat for a new codpiece.
Ha! Ha!

Exit 1st Peasant.
Enter 2nd Peasant.

2ND P: I fished a troutlet from your stream.
Tomorrow I'll be hanged.
DUKE: Good riddance! Hang and be damned!
Wait! Where was the catch?
2ND P: Beneath the sallow, at the gloomy bend
They call Lejeune's.
DUKE: Here's information to dry on a gallows! Give him
A golden livre; appoint him
My Counsellor of Fish.
2ND P: Delicious Duke, protect you God!

Exit 2nd Peasant.

COUN: All done, my lord. Wouldst play at chess?

Arranges board. They play.

DUKE: Ha! I'll chop you a mitre! Ha, Ha!
COUN: My mouth turns dry, but I'll cry check, my Lord.
DUKE: Hounds and cameras; here: take it, take it!

Kicks chess-board into the air.

ATTEND: Hermione is here, my Lord.

Enter Hermione.

DUKE: Come near, Hermione. Rosiest
Of blossoms, Sharon's choicest nut:
Sugar me, sweetmeat; pluck me till my strings
Fret to a gallop.
HERM: I'll take you to my boudoir,
Show you my brushes tortoiseshell;
My charms, my lockets, sprigs, and fairey sprays,
Wind you in pinky silk of bodyguard,
Closet your humour in a secret drawer,
Coddle your langour
Into sharp infamy.
DUKE: She half persuades me. No, no;
'Tis but old nip and tuck

Veiled in a rainbow. Take the old bag away!
                    Exit Hermione.
What now? Where's my new clown?

ATTEND: Clown! Clown!

COUN: The rogue is absent, lord.

DUKE: Find him, old goat!
His oddities delight me. False
As the plover's cry, they hide deep wisdom.
Oh miserable man, unhappy me,
Fixed as an alter, dull as a keystone;
Condemned to duty, as a kitchen knife's
Clenched to a grindstone. To hang,
Promote, and pardon, play on a board,
Fuddle a witch – what fates
This dismal round? I am
Deader than any doornail. Oh, oh!
Where is my clown?
                    Exit Attendants in a flurry, shouting
Clown, Clown!

I.3

Scene: The Ducal goose-roost. Enter the Count of Baalbeck,
disguised as the Duke's clown.

COUNT: Peace, peace at last. Among these furs and feathers,
Beaks, horns, and claws I find a leisure.
The Duke's a bore, his attendants worse –
If worse than bore can be – and I,
Disguiséd through necessity, must play the fool.
How can I cackle, trip, and play the goat
When every item in my senses' book
Sums to the total of Hermione?
This screwy fowl that apprehends my steps,
Resumes the pretty strutting of my love.
This monstrous dunghill, in contingent rank,
Doth but attach me to her vaprous scent.

241

As I a clown, so does she play a whore,
And yet methinks she, too, is somewhat more.
A certain quality beneath her brass
Bespeaks a gentle. I wonder, say,
If she's my sister in disguise;
(That would be odd) or some disfranchised queen?
But whore or paladine I'll never ask! Love
Probes not th'essent nature, hugs in the one enfold
Enclaves of pro and con. Oh! my heart raged
To see him put her off so sharp! Death –
His or mine I know not – clouded the moment's breath.
But hist, whist! Voices, voices; what does?
>*Conceals himself.*

Enter the Prince of Antioch, followed at a distance by the Captain.

PRINCE: What now, sweet mentor?

CAPT: Here's a place for plunder, schoolboy, oh my eye! On, on, there's a spanking roost ahead, filled up, I swear, with host o' drowsy muttering fowls. In, in with you, snatch you a gander. Cosset him close at the neck, snug as a tippet. I'll wait you here, whisp'ring advice.
>*Hides.*

COUNT (*aside*): What! A mariner robbing my pumpkin's roost!

CAPT: Forward, forward; forward is hearty!

PRINCE: Forward, my aspic legs!
>*Enters roost.*

COUNT: Ho! Ho! Guards and securers! Arson! Murder! Help, help! A manikin in my lord's filbert, a second under brush.
>*Lights and alarms.*

PRINCE: What, now? Master, master, inform me, pray, pray!

CAPT: Thou'st muffed it, colt. Put thy legs to the fence or swing 'em on a gibbet!
>*Flees.*

PRINCE: Can a poplar run, rooted?

COUNT (*advancing*): Antioch's voice in Brittany!

PRINCE: Touch me not, fool!

COUNT: No fool but knows his brother. Look, my visage.

PRINCE: What! Two fools o' the same mother?
>*They embrace.*

242

How're you here, dear one?
COUNT: Antioch's lost. Since your depart, Enos,
  That trusted eunuch, hath
  Turned i' the pan, put out poor father's eyes,
  And wound him up a mummy. Your own betrothed,
  The velvety Zenobia, raped by conspiring Turks,
  Which have enslaved our mother. Our sisters now
  All concubines, praying to Mahomet, blood
  Like a million Niles flooding our ancient seat.
PRINCE: Oh, dear, what sorry news! My grief oblates
  In oozy gutturals.
COUNT: Fly, fly, redeem your kingdom, heir of Antioch!
  Or stay and hang, a common poacher.
        Enter Guards, Attendants, with pikes and torches.
PRINCE: Meseems it were too late.
COUNT (*aside*): Thus was he ever. Some disposition
  Peculiar to his temper checked his pace.
  In Antioch, instructed by old Zeno, a
  Sluggard sprite engaged him, made all his homework late.
  Oh, brother, brother! Thou hast hesitated
  For the last time.
        Exeunt Guards with captive Prince, followed by Attendants and Count.

I.4

*Scene: The Duke's Chamber. Enter Guards, Attendants, with
Prince and Captain, manacled, followed by Count.*

1ST COUN: Here's diversion, my Lord! A sailor turned roost-robber,
  caught in the act, and his fellow snatched up two fields distant.
2ND COUN: You'll hang them both, my Lord, with much entrancing
  ceremony.
3RD COUN: 'Twill bright a whole long tedious morning, Lord. Do I
  call the Master of your Ceremonies?
DUKE: I guess so.

1ST COUN: Remit, dear Lord, a public invitation, and delight your
villeins with the spectacle.
DUKE: Why not?
3RD COUN: I'll call the torturers and butchers too. We'll make a
shambles.
DUKE: Thanks, generous friends.
  I see you do conspire
  To silk the silly worsted of my life.
                    Aside.
  All fur and presence, yea or nay according,
  They tread me as their hen, much as these mariners.
                    To Prince.
  Crimer, absolve thy gritty soul.
  Babble thy last excuse.
PRINCE: Hungry, I sought a goose.
DUKE: Peace, hunger; thou'lt seek no more.
                    To Captain.
  Hast, too, a little line, or wilt thy tongue,
  Silent, anticipate the gibbet's purple?
CAPT: 'Twas thus, amazing peer and demi-Caesar:
  I am a man of parts innumerous,
  Cradled in Asia, reared in far Marsaylls,
  Parlaying in Haver, sotto voice in Rome,
  Was gibt's in Hamburg, do-ye-do on Thames,
  Amico, loving, shy, on every land. But,
  On the decks, thwarting the furious surge
  Of Neptune's chariots, another man entire.
  Upon my stance at helm a whole world waits,
  Sighing and fretting, pacing the patio,
  Murmuring: And doth his convoy come? Alas!
  Sometimes, alone with the sea-god, he
  Layeth finger on my thigh, and worsens
  Me. So was it now. Consigned
  By Antioch's king to bear his son,
  I struggled might and main to clench
  My trust, was overborne, tossed brusquely on
  Your sands. There, as I stood, peeling
  Salt rainbows from my eyes, this vagabond

Strides up. Limpid, he cries:
Poor captain, chase with me, let's snatch a dinner,
Behind's rich territory. What! Poach
In Brittany, cried I? For shame, for shame!
Then he, aware my ethic, bends a smile,
Takes out red gems, bribes me to show the way
(For I am wise in ways). I'll lead you
Captive to noble duke, threat I, and follow
Him. He takes the gander; I take
Him – or am about to, when
Your feal guard, blind with sweet ardour,
Snatch rat and cat together.
COUNT: A lie, a lie! Oh, my poor brother,
Hanged
On a cord of lies!
DUKE: Sew up thy lips, fool; we are solemn.
Investigate, my friends, the poacher's pouch,
Duct his red rabbits.
CAPT: Fast in the pocket; there on t'other side!
     Attendants discover the Prince's rubies.
COUNT: Lord, dear Lord; allow me speak!
DUKE: Thou'rt hired to sing, not speak.
COUNT: Then here's a song will save my brother's windpipe!
      Sings.
   When by Ganges they are found,
   India's rubies are quite round.
   China rubies are ellipt,
   Ceylonese are somewhat tipp'd,
   Persian gems are fat and fair,
   But Antioch's alone are square.
   Only princes of the throne
   May enjoy their blunt hedron.
   So, logic says, the miscreant there
   Is mother's son and Antioch's heir!
     Embraces Prince.
DUKE: I see square rubies. Do I see two square princes?
PRINCE: 'Tis true, my lord. I, your poacher, am Prince of Antioch;
 he, your clown, is the Count of Baalbeck, my brother.

245

DUKE: And this fast sailor, what's he? Mahomet himself in a pickle
of salt?

COUNT: A venal rogue, my lord, fit to be hanged over and over: once
were too lax to stop his gullet.

DUKE: We'll hang him twice: once for his own sake; once for your
disguises'.

CAPT: Ah, well! 'Twould have been a good play, had it but served.

DUKE: Thou prince and duke of Allah, welcome,
Who are to me in earthly rank, two brothers.
But what avails, alas, this brotherhood
When, in God's eye thou art abominable?
Guarded, I'll post thee to the diocese
Of Rouen, where the papal axe
Will chop thy heads for Christ. I
Much regret it.

COUNT: Good duke, thy piety is sweet
But vent it not on us. Had I
Not feared its rage, I long before
Had witnessed my true self.
Thou must believe that I, and
Brother dear, took secret dip
In Egypt's font, and clasp the Cross, as you.

DUKE: Then all is fine and fair 'twixt you and me.
Stay, brothers, in my court till your return.
Beguile my stingey hours with florid talk
And we'll all laugh at what the sea threw up.
Tomorrow morn, we'll have a royal show,
Sit in our box and watch the poacher leap,
Thou'lt laugh the louder that it is not you.

PRINCE: Dear brother, Duke of Brittany,
Thy hospice will be sunny to our hearts.
Permit me, though, to crave a lease of life
For this convicted. Wise in the world's
Ways, he is my mentor,
Chos'n upon your sands to armour me
In steely lore of life. Princes
Must learn from scoundrels, or
Their piety, begot in dreams,

Hems in and suffocates the growing craft.
In two short hours this lusty reprobate
Hath run me through the primer of his years.
It were a waste to throttle at the source
A sustenating Nile of savoir faire.

DUKE: Fair words and fair advice, sweet Prince.
Take you the rogue.

COUNT: Oh, brother, brother, loving simpleton! Cheat'st thou the
gallows, that thou mayst hang thyself? Heed him not, good duke.

PRINCE: Nay, nay, 'tis life to learn. Leave ignorance to the grave.

To Duke.

You sunburst cyclamen, august and wary,
Conjoin our rebel.

DUKE: What! What! How so? I, too, strive to become another?

PRINCE: Here's the philosophy. What man
Is happy with the man he is?
Didst choose thy mother, Duke, didst
Seek thy sire? Nay. 'Twas their
Conjunction bred in the dark, occasioning
You, as plotters in a hedge had bred
Conspiracy. 'Tis faint, at start, this
Weakly, others' plot, asks little of
Itself, content to suck, and be,
And trust who made it. At length,
It waxes, growing will and sinew.
And, looking in glass, shrinks back
From him it sees. Now comes
Resolve to be another, to smash
The silly, brittle plan and hew
A better. But where's a form?
Oh, Duke, good Duke, this
Life's astream with forms; we shape
Us how we will. There's Time,
Calling us back to shapes made
Hon'rable by his dark shade, or,
Crying us forward to anticipate
Himself and grow new fangled.
There's Place, which ever asks of us

A man that's other than the man we are.
There's Faith, which bids us hew
Down at the very base our inborn
Root, and climb anew. There's
Reason, Chance Remark, there's
Heroes of now and then, and Circumstance.
We bend them to our make.
COUNT: Or so we try. Like muscled trappers
We bend down the tree; but
Up it flies – and we with it;
Back as we were, not new but hurt.
PRINCE: Aye, brother, the chosen form's
Not always in our clasp.
What wots it? One thing alone
We know: we'll not endure
The foolish shell in which we did begin;
We'll not be lame and sick, timid,
Hunchback'd. Or, if we're strong,
We'll yearn t'attain that weakness
Which woos the love of men.
Hairy, we would be smooth,
Or smooth, become uncouth.
COUNT: Happy, we would woo misery,
Content, find pain in frenzy.
Folly, folly, brother! Duke,
Have none of it! Wouldst take
A sailor's form? Hath not
The world sailors enough
Without dukes float? I
That was Count to start was
Forced a clown, nor chose it.
Now, Count again, I'll stay.
DUKE: And yet, I am engaged, dear Count.
Your princely brother's words are
Sage or silly, do not ask me
Which. But this I know,
The desert that's my life
Dreams to be green, and

Green I'd have it. Good
Prince, I'll follow where you lead
In footsteps of this man,
Sit in his class and
Shape myself anew. What
Shall we name our mentor? Master
Of Horse? Prime Minister? Or
Duke himself?
PRINCE: Duke were the best, for true authority.
DUKE: Duke it shall be! What say you, Captain-Duke?
CAPT: I like the eminence; 'tis above the gallows.
COUNT: I fear a horrid consequence, oh Lord!
DUKE: Now, Count, take up thy silly fears;
 Gather them in a bundle with
 Thy old fool's rig, and heave them
 In the sea that's made four friends.
 Tonight we'll dance roulades with gongs and lays,
 Tomorrow twist our toes to sager ways.
Music

II.1

Scene: A courtyard for jousting, with hurdles. Enter the Prince of Antioch, the Count of Baalbeck, the Duke of Brittany, Captain, and Attendants.

CAPT: Now, smartly hearties; to it, to it: th' next lesson! Stir your-dry joints, 'flect shrewdness in your eyes; supple up. When tutor barks, lazybones get nipped in the hams!

DUKE: Oh my poor legs! Poor cracking meat! Is such the life led by men beneath the throne? Oh, oh! A hundred thrones seem pitched upon my shoulders!

PRINCE: Courage, courage! I too am fazed like a reed, but my swim-ming self is renaissant for sure.

COUNT: There's ought but stillbirth in my poor cradle.

CAPT: Triple chatterers, save breath for acts! Now's a lesson against thievery. Some teachers put it at the head of the book: I like it later, after experience. Suppose the Duke a fat farmer, back from market fatter than 'a went; elbows tight asides to dim the chink of coin. Prince, a slim rogue would pick his pockets, elbows despite. Count, the farmer's friend, and would save him. Now! to it, all three! Strut, Duke, fat farmer! Up sly behind, rogue Prince! Run up distressed, country friend! (*Prince picks Duke's pocket.*) Why, rogue, those paunchy fingers would wake the hibernating bear! Strike him, farmer! (*Duke strikes Prince.*) Now, rogue, run for thy life, or farmer and friend will have thee! Must jump those hedges in the way, or swing! (*Prince runs, followed by Duke and Count.*) Over, beauties, tuck up your calves, leap for the moon! (*Prince, Duke, and Count try to jump the hurdle, fall in a heap with hurdle on top of them.*) Sad, sad! I'll brush you all, dough-legs: white bread and daffodils rise smarter.

PRINCE: My poor backbone is snapt through. Prithee, good Duke, regurge thy champing knee.

DUKE: Knee? I've no knee; 'tis smashed its cap right off. Good Count, reject thy belly from my nose.

COUNT: Good hurdle, depart in peace from off my neck.

CAPT: Next time, thou'lt all know better – pick neater, strike sharper,
tuck up thy toes like hawks fresh up from the wrist.
PRINCE: Teacher's a hard taskmaster and I a poor puffin: nevertheless, it delights me to see wisdom peer through the cracks in my bones.
DUKE: I'll not be laggard; so I'll say that every blue bruise on my poor
flesh is worth a heap of purple.
CAPT: Hast breath to groan and yap, hast breath for the next lesson!
Up, up and read! Now, ye are three scurvy soldiers, dropped by a
flying rearguard, pikes and muskets a foot behind ye. Run, run for
your lives; enemy is fierce on tail, and the first one caught must be
whipped and stripped. Off, off!

Exeunt Prince, Count, and Duke, pursued by Attendants with cudgels.

II.2

*Scene: Hermione's boudoir. Enter Hermione, sewing lace, with
Catriona.*

HERM: *Lente, lente* – I have forgot the rest,
Save that it sadly treats of knights and horses.
CATRI: Glum, Madam?
HERM: Ay, glum to death and farther.
I'd find a cosy convent for retreat,
Were't not that they of late are grown
So fashionable, there's not a cell
That has no tender she. One little week
Of seven tiny days – speak not o' nights –
And I am all flung out. The Duke's
Insipid bride, convoyed from old
Artois, will take his marriage hand,
While I, his whilome ministress, must go,
Leaving my maidenhead
Upon the field I lost it.
CATRI: Courage, lady! Has not good Baalbeck's
Count (like miracle disclosed as more than clown),
Cast orient eyes upon thy bust and

Groaned like smitten peer?

HERM: He hath indeed, but yet I have no rank,
Am nobody, am nothing, pas di too.

CATRI: In fables, Madam, when the sheep-girl sighs,
'Tis found in nick of time she is some queen,
Raised in the mercy of a shepherd's crook
But always by a royal sire forsook.
Or else, what she presents is masquerade
Concealing blood as pure as marmalade.

HERM: No hope that way, I fear.
In latter days, disguise is grown so rife
That it is folly to expect a peer
To credit any more. 'Tis said
So many kings are now abroad
In shape of scullions, so many
Queens, got in whores' clothings, that at taverns
Each looks on each in sharp soliloquy,
And doffèd caps must sure reveal gold crowns.
No, Catriona, I am soon gone out
In smock and clog which hide no more than me.
Yet do I love the Duke and wish him well.
It doth perturb me that his present whim
Is got so boistrous. Bound up
By that bad captain, he's so rough,
So banged and crouchet-up, I
Fear that when his fair bride comes .
He'll ninny at her like a capon'd Jove.

CATRI: Fear not, dear lady.
Methinks the Duke's prime blood
Will summon reassertion at the pinch.
And he, o'erjoyed by manhood, will bestow
A handsome purse to take you your long way.

HERM: Amen, amen. And yet, I would be counterfeit.

CATRI: Why so, Madam?

HERM: Nay, the better to lose him. I'll not miss him if I'm not myself.
'Twill be another he's pushed out.

CATRI: 'Twere better stay thyself, Madam. Thou'lt not love the Duke
in his changed form, and so will be free of him. Shouldst thou

change too, thou mightst do so into a new lady approximative to his new gentleman and then all would be grievous once again.

HERM: Hast experienced these things, Catriona, that thou speak'st so?

CATRI: Aye, Madam, as oft as I have lain with one. I have been mad with love for them until they have left me; thereafter, I have thought them mad, and myself in self-possession once more.

HERM: And didst thou not bewail these sad divisions?

CATRI: Wail, Madam? Why, forsooth, I wailed, that my eyes filled water-butts. But 'twas water, Madam, brook-water, pure as rain; 'twas not the bitter brine which I shed when my hare, Bobby, ate of green pears and was took by Colic the Hunter.

HERM: Fie, Cat! To set a hare above man in the open heart!

CATRI: Ay, and shut it fast up again when the hare was took out.

HERM: What's the advice, then? That I do retain my old self and offer it anew?

CATRI: Surely, Madam, that's the course. Has the Duke declared — outright he will cast you off?

HERM: Nay, not yet. A manly hesitation seals his lips.

CATRI: I know it well, that seal. I beg you, Madam, cast you him quickly, while you are still tied up.

HERM: And knot anew with Baalbeck?

CATRI: Why not, Madam? Baalbeck will love you more, that you have turned to him of your own will, not of compulsion. And the Duke will regret you, in that he has not had the privilege of putting you from him.

HERM: Is not this making a play of love?

CATRI: Ay, Madam, forsooth it is, and to play is a jolly thing – a very breeder of love. Your turn is come, to strike: I beg you, do not leave it to your opponent.

HERM: I'll think on this, Catriona.

CATRI: Ay, Madam, and think well. There's some say thought is fruitless: I have ever found much advantage in it.

II.3

Scene: The Ducal Chamber. Enter Captain, Duke, Prince, Count, and Attendants.

DUKE: A galling, squalid day: thank God 'tis done! If it's thus my peasants live, then heaven's all should occupy their dreams.

PRINCE: See, brother-duke, thou'rt learning piety as well as craft.

DUKE: Piety, too, may be bought too dear. I am smashed like a bowl of choice walnuts. Ah well, lesson's over; I'm duke again for the night. What's for supper?

ATTEND: Venison and Humphrey pasties, my lord, and muted cress in a wine coddle.

DUKE: Ha! Bring it straight: I'm fed to the teeth with suasion, but not so much as a sausage to bite on. (*Attendant brings venison.*) Sit, brother Prince, brother Count, here's rich reward!

CAPT: What, sagged at the knees and greedy? Here's lesson the twenty-fifth – to stay staunch and prime on a belly empty as a consul's conscience.

DUKE: What, blackguard? I may not eat?

CAPT: Bring him black bread and a shrew's-worth of cheap ale. Must suffer for thy own sake, Duke, and I, the diligent doctor, take my fee.

Eats venison. Attendants lay crusts of bread and cheap ale before Duke, Prince, and Count.

PRINCE (*eating*): Like much morality, 'tis bitter bread, meant for the soul not the stomach. Therein is its worth.

DUKE (*eating*): It rankles me: nevertheless, I doubt not but your words are fit and right.

COUNT (*eating*): Yea, right as the passing ding-dong, and fit for a corpse in his shroud.

CAPT: If ye have breath to converse, lesson the twenty-sixth is soon ready at hand.

DUKE: Nay, nay, sweet instructor, we are silent as clay pipes.

CAPT: Must still learn the way with underlings. Unrobe that dais, mount me upon it.

Attendants uncover throne, assist Captain to mount it.

DUKE: What, y'are on my throne, dog?

CAPT: To instruct a play rightly, the forms must be mimicked. I am pretending judge; ye are three varlets must defend thyselves with thy wits. Now I ask pompous: Sirrahs, it is evidented that you did mischievously purloin ten livres from the groom o' the duke's chamber when 'a was fuddled and unstrung. Do I say right, Master Groom?

1ST ATTEN: Ay, Lord Justice, but I was only unstrung; not fuddled, musing on philosophic themes.

CAPT: Thy philosophy snored and had bad breath. Well, accused, didst ravish this stinking philosopher?

DUKE: Nay, good my lord, I but stood there to guard the sleeper from prowling thieves.

PRINCE: And I was not so much as present at all, Lord; but with Tib and Arthur in another town.

COUNT: For me, I never did see these two men before now, nor do I know any groom.

DUKE: My lord, he decoys like a false mushroom, and is an atheist come straight from the galleys.

PRINCE: My lord, these are both young foragers who love a purse; but I am old in purity as I am babe in innocence.

CAPT: Thieves' separate quarrels, mind you well, pupils, indicate conjunctive guilt. Now I order: Mr Serjeant, seize and search these villains! (*Attendants search Duke, Prince, and Count.*) What findings, sir?

1ST ATTEN: On villain Count, a wretchedly scrabbled sonnet to 's mistress.

CAPT: Read it forth

1ST ATTEN: *Under suppression of thine eye's black darts,*
Encircled total by thy lips' red rounds,
I lose possession of my wandering parts
And lifeless drop as Acteon 'fore his hounds.
What, what! cry I, does blood not then resume
When 'tis abducted by the siren's call?
And can I not at all on life presume,
Until Hermione withhold my fall?
How then may I . . .

255

DUKE: Dog, not in play, but truth! Hast flapped cow's eyes at my mistress?

COUNT: Let's stop the play, or further harm be done.

CAPT: Play's must be played out, little ones, or what's a teacher for? A drivelling sonnet's bad evidence; bad, bad, but not to present point. Search the next caitiff. (*Attendants search the Duke, find the ducal seal, keys, and gold, which they hand to the Captain.*) Oh, shocking, shocking, here's the theft itself; ten livres, precious keys, and the ducal warrant! Take them below, dungeon them, Mr Serjeant.

DUKE: Sirrah, what lesson's this? I would now I had swung you!

CAPT: Peace, peace, my lord, 'tis but a pretending end to a pretended day, an interlude serving to teach thee how to sleep on cold stone. Thou'lt laugh and be proud tomorrow, chockfull of hard wisdom.

DUKE: Methinks I have engorged enough. What say you, Antioch?

PRINCE: That peaceably we should go below, and become sage as frogs from observation of damp quarters. 'Twill stand us in good stead if ever we are downset in earnest.

DUKE: It's foul and horrid, but I must not wail. Tedium has left my life.

CAPT: Tomorrow, when the laughing turnkey comes
And bends the intércedent lock 'twixt you and day,
The gentle world will seem so sweet and dear
That thou wilt praise provision of contrast.
And I shall be again a sailor low,
And thou shalt be again a thund'ring duke
And all the world refitted as it was.
What's more delectable than old identity?

PRINCE: Come, brothers, sweet dreams wait below.

DUKE: Sweet as rats' eyes, doubtless; but I'll go.

COUNT: So down with wisdom, folly's on the throne.

Exeunt Prince, Count, and Duke, guarded.

III.1

Scene: The ducal Chamber. Enter Captain and First Attendant.

1ST ATT: Captain, the milkmaids have put up their buckets, the kine is browsing these many hours and we approach a noon sun.

CAPT: Icar showed that to stop the sun were a fool's errand.

1ST ATT: The duke is heated hotter nor any Icar; nay, he is flaming rabid, rattling his bars like a bedlam Joseph.

CAPT: What says the Prince of Antioch?

1ST ATT: He counsels patience, sir.

CAPT: Then take thou heed of his counsel, which is excellent.

Enter Turnkey.

TURN: Sir-Captain, my lord demands that I undo the door.

CAPT: Hast the door's key?

TURN: How may I have what hangs on thy belt?

CAPT: And how mayst thou worry, then, to do that for which thou hast not? (*Exit Turnkey.*) Inform me, sir: what's the Duke do in mornings?

1ST ATT: As the whim takes him: to hunt, if buck have showed; to judge, if judgement's arose; elsewise, to talk, game, be clowned and see his espaliered peaches how they've prospered.

CAPT: So I too. Yet a man who's dressed for the poop must redress if he's to talk to a splayed peach. Fetch me clothes, Privy Counsellor.

1ST ATT: Didst call me Privy Counsellor?

CAPT: Ay, sir: wouldst not be?

1ST ATT: Ay, indeed: 'tis most elevating.

CAPT: Then bid my valets, grooms, and chamberboys dress me a degree higher than myself. And, passing the armoury on thy way, see that the locks are fast, or thou and I may drop like the said Icar.

Exit 1st Attend.

Enter Hermione.

HERM: Where's my lord?

CAPT: About to doff small canvas and put on royalty's whole rig.

HERM: Nay, he's seized and flummoxed.

CAPT: Flummoxed, madam? Does he not stand before you, poised as a line of kings?

HERM: Thou scabby tar! Unhook that crooked elbow from his throne! Blunt, raucous starling; get you to other eaves for your droppings!

CAPT: Have a care, strumpet! E'en monarch's mercy hath an elastic snap!

HERM: Monarch! Algerian goat! Muscovite dissembler! Undo the Duke!

CAPT: Out, bawdy-toy! Here are my cooks will shave and put a fresh apple in my mouth, that I may come to banquet glowing.

Enter Grooms and Valets with clothes and robes, and 1st Attend.

1ST ATT: Do your work, dressers. But first, do ye swear fealty?

GROOMS: We do.

VALETS: If need be, fifty times.

CAPT: Thank you, my Privy Counsel. Where's my court?

1ST ATT: Closeted tight for the most part, fearful of a change in the wind, my lord.

CAPT: They're fully pardoned. Summon them. Remove this frantic whore, lest she blush at sight of a naked man.

Grooms exeunt with Hermione. Valets attire the Captain, assist him to the throne, hand him the Duke's sceptre and a nosegay.

1ST ATT: Now, sire, thou'rt all complete – throne, seal, keys, sceptre, and the little bouquet that gives hard monarchy his sweet touch.

CAPT: Now farewell dangerous sea, and impudence
Of high waves' spray, farewell, farewell!
Power and appearance, twin necessities,
Are grid and mantle to the new-rose peer.
And now my dictive tongue must change its tune,
Forswear its vulgar past, and choppy mode,
Drop finally the coxon's hoy, belay,
The galley mandate and the sailman's curse,
Pronouncing henceforth in prime blank verse.
Ah, how this throne rides neatly in my swell!
How most becoming is this sceptre's spar!
Two little minutes under ermine's flag
Convince my keel 'twas ever over me.
Prick me a genealogy, my Counsellor,
Limn it ablaze with lilies and with crowns,

Plantagenista in a dragoned field
And quarterings of Geoffrey and Capet.
Next week, I'll hear the fierce uproarious tales
Of how my grandsire with his train of knights
Grasped Christ's sweet body from the maudlin Turk
And built thereon this happy, purple world!
1ST ATT: Thyself to be a sirer, good my lord.
For shortly comes thy grand imbroglement
With noble Artois' daughter, Radegund.
CAPT: Sweet Radegund, art thou the unknown dam
Wilt loose my princely spate?
Fertility's expensive, doth she bring
A gorgeous dower?
1ST ATT: Ten thousand livres, my lord.
CAPT: A stingey price. Command my brother,
The lord Artois, to make it twenty.
1ST ATT: He'll be much vext, my lord.
The contracks are all signed, the lawyers drunk.
CAPT: Hereby I them unsign.
Artois must learn, as must
Each duke and princeling in the cope of France,
That Brittan's fields have now a stronger sun.
Send out my couriers and tell the world
That for the nonce I hereby do suspend
All treaties, greements, truces, and allies
Formed antecedent to mine own ascent.
Dickrings and bargains made by simpleton
Shall be dismissed unread by this cold eye;
And so I bid you trumpet on my men
To gallop up and down intelligence
That: 'Brittan's throne is took by Captain Jack;
Old parleys join old clothes in sea's deep wrack!'
                    Trumpets.

III.2

Scene: Hermione's boudoir. Enter Catriona and Hermione.

HERM: Weep, woman, weep; the coup has fell.
  The very throne whereon his elbow leaned
  Doth now uphold his butt.
  Methought the stone, melted by 'pugnant ire,
  Would vomit up and toss him off itself.
  Alas! it stands rock-ribbed, shows no dismay,
  And bears his false impression with aplomb.
CATRI: Deep in its heart, too deep for handkerchief,
  I vow it weeps, poor throne!
HERM: And those the Duke loved well?
  Are they, in whispers, framing dreadful plots
  Will shrill betimes the usurper from his seat?
CATRI: Much otherwise. Within the library
  I saw young Albert, whom the Duke so loved,
  Stitching embroidery upon a gilded frame.
  Strike you no blow for freedom? I inquired.
  To which the pigeon, trimming his needle,
  Remarked that brawls so much upset him
  That any conflict was not to his taste.
  So say they all, some furtive, some unshamed;
  And armoury's lockt as tight as is their hearts.
HERM: When men to wax inmelt at sight of fire,
  Ladies must steel their flesh and take the glint.
  Good Catriona, thou and I are such
  Must sprout a mannish stance and save the realm.
CATRI: Wield halberds, Madam? How?
  I have no craft in cleaving, lopping, chops;
  Even stilettos make my soft womb turn.
  I ne'er have shrunk from any man's embrace,
  But do reject his cannon, out of face.
HERM: I speak of art, not arms.
  Nay, woman-like, we must dissimulate,

Practise for virtue's sake our nastiest vice
And boldly feign to be what we are not.

CATRI: Disguises, Madam?

HERM: Ay, thick as thick. I'll not see Baalbeck founder.

CATRI: Baalbeck, Madam?

HERM: Ay, he's writ me a sonnet, and I love him. In truth, I ever have.
She that loved the Duke was some other: I know her not.

CATRI: Methinks, Madam, thou has been thoughtful, as I advised.

HERM: Nay, I thought not at all, only remained silent; at which, my
heart did speak.

CATRI: I'll not press thy heart, then, Madam, knowing well how tripping is the tongue of my own.

HERM: Well spoken. Let's turn to our disguises. To find what they
should be, we'll ask: What is their purpose? What our mission?

CATRI: Why, marriage, Madam.

HERM: Marriage is no mission, methinks.

CARTI: Is't not, Madam? It were surely a mission to save men from
celibacy. There's but one man may have no wife and that's the Devil
himself.

HERM: Devil or no, our weddings must await. Our mission now must
be to free our friends: we'll bind 'em in due course.

CATRI: And they the riper for it, being under obligation to us and so,
ashamed to spurn the hands which loosed them.

HERM: I am ever shamed by thy blunt speech, Catriona.

CATRI: 'Tis from the heart, Madam, or thereabouts. Let's disguise as
pedlars, and buy entry to the gaol with knick-knacks. Or as vintners,
and regale the turnkey till he snore. Or spinners of yarn that's making a rope of hemp and would try if it fits.

HERM: These are too rough. We cannot feign the too robust.

CATRI: How's piety, Madam, to feign?

HERM: Better, better. Proceed.

CATRI: Once, in a moral play, good ma'am,
I was the part of Lazarian nun.
My eyes so low they bandied with my toes
And all agreed I was the thing herself.
But that's long since, and many a broad moustache
Has rubbaged off the mantle of my bloom. Yet,
I could feign once more.

HERM: Nay, Catriona, nuns are grown naughty.
　At night, when all's asleep, the Abbess
　Rises, and takes a pick and spade in hand.
　Helped by her sisters, emulating moles,
　They tunnel underground for leagues and leagues,
　Come up at last i' the Bishop's cell
　And ravish every friar.
CATRI: Is't so, Madam? Why, when
　I've walked the meadows, I've remarked,
　How, underfoot, the ground springs up and down.
　I'd not believed 'twas all athrob with nuns.
HERM: Catriona, we must be friars.
CATRI: What, Madam? Do friars not tunnel too?
HERM: Nay, 'tis woman's work, sappery.
CATRI: What of our beards, Madam? Can we raise them up,
　And set them to our chins?
HERM: We'll be young friars, in whom the academy
　Hath gaoled the refulgent whisker under skin.
CATRI: And what thereafter, ma'am, when we're made vicars?
HERM: Thereafter comes hereafter, we shall see
　What chance and skill provide. Attend
　The chapel vestry, Catriona, bring two garbs.
CATRI: I'll choose the most becoming,
　Intact with hood and necklace rosary.
　Yet not delay and haver, as it were
　A pedlar's holiday.

III.3

Scene: The Palace Dungeon, with Duke, Prince, and Count.
Enter Turnkey, carrying food.

DUKE: Open, open, foul, dismal, and abominable! I'll have thee on
　the rack, heresiarch, soon as my foot's on stool again!
TURN: 'Tis not a promise doth much coax my key to the lock. Never-
　theless, 'twill help forward thy own limbs to the rack, doubtless.

DUKE: What, rat's guts! Dost threaten me with my own rack?

TURN: Racks, beds, thrones – they, inanimate, agree and accommodate whomsoever may fall into their keep. Now, here's a platter of old tripes will stuff thy gab.

Pushes plate under bars. Duke hurls tripe at Turnkey's head.

DUKE: Like to like! See Master Tripe twine with his brother! So'll a halyard twine soon to Master Mariner.

Exit Turnkey.

PRINCE: Impetuous duke! Prithee, recall 'tis all a play for our improvement; a play played with much subtlety and earnestness, that we may learn, and for which we should tout thanks and not ingratitude.

DUKE: If it's a play, 'tis drawing out so long and miserable that, willynilly, it's grown true to the life and beastly. What say you, Count?

COUNT: That if it's a play, we must make our own words and acts, for they've forgot to give us the book; and that if it's life, similarly we must plot to do what worms and prisoners do – discover a way out. If it's life, then death's coming on the heels of the tripes; if it's play and unrehearsed, then let's meet art with art. Those that have no identity but that which is foisted upon them, must embrace it or create a better.

DUKE: I warrant; if thy brother the Prince had but a bead of thy sagacity in his noddle, he'd still have a crown to set atop it. So, Prince, 'tis a play for our instruction: master has set us a problem and left us to cudgel an answer: he asks us, how do we propose to make exit? Wilt play in this play?

PRINCE: Ay, readily. I had not thought it was so subtle. Now I'm all fire to begin.

COUNT: Good brother, damp the fire somewhat, like a good player, lest thy plot appear in the face to be read before thou'rt ready to disclose it.

DUKE: Ay, try to pretend that thou art truly locked in a dungeon. Now, let's huddle to plot. Insinuous Count, make suggestion.

COUNT: 'Tis known through all the world that mariners
Are superstition cased as fish with scales.
This wicked sailor seated on the throne
May easily put off his salt regail
And stride inpompous on a royal stage:

Yet, in his heart, where valet may not buff,
Must still reside the supernatural quake
Awaiting apparitions of distress.
Could we but find apparel of the mist,
Some chalky-white enclosure for ourselves,
Remove from here and hover round his throne,
We'd throw him in a fit.

DUKE: Design's so sweet and cunning to my thought
That it doth quite transport me to that place.
I see him frothing on his velvet knees
While three inspiréd ghosts do circle him
And moan and gibber him to mental crack.
And yet, and yet, withal my lovely dream,
He's there and we are here.

PRINCE: When all's done, we'll explain 'twas all a jest.

DUKE: An' he survive the jest, ay, explanation will be forthcoming.

PRINCE: We were better witches, brother Duke, meseems.

DUKE: Howso?

PRINCE: In that the ghost is an element which is already resident
within him that observes it.

DUKE: I'd not heard so.

PRINCE: Ay, 'tis the latest discovery among froward alchemists.

DUKE: What say you, Count?

COUNT: That we await the coming of a suitable disguise before we
anticipate the nature thereof. And that we ready ourselves to provide
whatsoever it may be that our enemy is loth to project from within.

DUKE: Excellent man!

PRINCE: Ay, 'tis sage advice, inasmuch as our dear Master, being
innocent, may lack the propulsive guilt which, alone, may fire
forth a destestable apparition.

III.4

Scene: Hermione's room. Enter Hermione and Catriona carrying bundles of disguises.

HERM: Look to the lattice, Cat!

CATRI: Clear, Madam. No peeping Tom!

HERM: Then let's to our mirrors. Oh, I do love the glass which will not give exit to the eye but returns it whence it came!

CATRI: Ay, 'tis ever the brighter vista, yet like a dwelling, a walled self, permitting but one visitor to the single hostess yet never saying which be visitor and which hostess. Oh what a hairy robe is this, Madam! I caution you, divest nothing but lay it straight over much understuff, as it were nettles. But what of our hair, Madam, our ells of sweet honeysuckle?

HERM: We'll be of an order which is sworn ever to be hooded and is thus eternally upbraided. Step about, Cat, that I may examine you.

CATRI: So, Madam.

HERM: Wherefore art thou all crouched, like a curious badger?

CATRI: To be humble, Madam, no?

HERM: Stoop but the head; there's pride's seat. Ay, better, better!

CATRI: How's my buttocks, Madam; for there's the test? 'Tis hard to thwart the roll of a lifetime, and moreover one that's joined to the eyes, making every turn of the keel swing the lanterns of the poop.

HERM: Fair, fair. Now, 'tis my turn to be examined.

CATRI: So soon, Madam? I was but begun.

HERM: Nay, thou'rt blind to thine own needs. And thou would'st reach woman's goal, thou must first and ever bear in mind the state of men.

CATRI: True, Madam. I had clean forgot them, poor souls! in admiration of my new buttocks.

HERM: Watch my gait, dear Cat! Do I walk lowly yet with pride! Am I of reverence, but not offensive? Am I a father that is ever childless withal and elevated by his looking down? How seems my paradox?

CATRI: Madam, thou art the thing himself – same teeth, same eyes, same air, same everything.

III.5

Scene: The Palace Dungeon. Enter Turnkey.

TURN: Oh, oh, what a weight of death! I can never hear the carpenter's merry hammer but think what a deal of good ash must go into a gibbet – all waste, extravagance, pomp, where a penny knife would perform quicker, neater, nicer.

DUKE *(within)*: Ho, ape, dog, dungeon porpentine! What's the clock?

TURN: Not so late that it will not briefly fetch you up.
  (Enter Hermione and Catriona disguised as Friars.)
Good morrow, good clockmakers!

CATRI: Good morrow, good catsguts!

HERM *(aside to Cat.)*: Naughty doll! Hast forgot thou art no longer a woman? *(To Turnkey.)* Sweet servant, we are come to shrive the dead. Admit us to the room.

CATRI: And leave us to incline the tender ear,
The harebell chalice of confesséd dew.

DUKE *(within)*: Oh, oh, what comes!
Meseems we shall in truth change into ghosts
More real and ghostly than our plot designed.

TURN: That man just spoke, 'a calls 'a self a duke
But is a very devil.

HERM: Admit us; we'll expunge him.

TURN *(unlocks gate)*: I'll hover near, as ward.

CATRI: Yet not overnear.

TURN *(shouting)*: Forth, dead! Ye've your emissaries. Forward!

COUNT *(aside)*: That taller friar has elements of face
Which turn my mind to other sorts of grace.
His succ'ring eyes, so soft in innocence,
Are somehow far removed from penitence.
No matter!
                    To Hermione.
Good priest, 'fore any absolution,
We mortal three do make a plea for shrouds,
Shrouds white as lilies, to conduct our clay

From here to thence.

HERM: Shrouds, thou'lt have them, poor soul, three shrouds *in nominem Domini*, shrouds (with a stout saw i' the hem) *pax vobiscum*, shrouds shall carry thee high as Elijah (with a stout rope i' the girdle), shrouds, three soft shrouds (with hard daggers for seams) to ensure *requiescat in pace*.

TURN: This tender scene brims gallons o'er my lids! Shrouds, white shrouds; thus passed my own mother, and my three sucking brothers who never lived one whole turn o' the seasons; countless others all in shrouds, oh, oh!

Weeps.

HERM: Two women which we know will pare these shrouds
And, weeping, press them in our saintly hands.

TURN: Prithee, father, say no more: thy voice is sweet as a choir, so warm it melts manacles. Oh, the littlest of my brothers, his shroud was so small it could better have been used to steam puddings.

HERM: Bless you, good keeper!
To you, tomorrow, we'll confide the shrouds.
Now you, three dead, fold down upon your knees
And glut our ears with expiated slough.
Need'st aught but shrouds?

DUKE: Here's an odd question, damned odd!

COUNT: A little chalk
Shall smooth our way to Heaven.

TURN: Oh, I am quite on the rack! Pity, cruel pity, cease tearing me!

HERM: What more?

COUNT: Why, in case we should sin again meanwhile, let us leave absolution until the shrouds come.

TURN: Now, here's real tragedy, for what sin could such a place as this allow? Prison's prison indeed when even sin lacks room to raise his elbow.

HERM: Here's foretaste of absolution.

Kisses Count.

TURN: Nobly and mercifully done – to kiss a dead dog. Thus kissed my mother when the rest declared me stillborn.

CATRI: Good gaoler: that kiss, ten times compounded, shall be yours
When Heaven dotes upon your limey corse.

TURN: And say you so: and true it is, for lime, they say, doth break and sweeten clay. But say no more; else I'll forget I've duties here and fly off harping on a white cloud. Come, come, fathers, hastily, hastily, or my rackhand itself will turn human-fond.

Exeunt Hermione, Catriona, and Turnkey.

DUKE: I am much bewildered; yet meseems 'tis a tolerably favourable condition.

PRINCE: I think it was a venal sin of us
To confuscate their piety for play.
I trust that in the acts which follow this
Our naughtiness avoids a sanctive kiss.

IV.1

*Scene: Morning. The bedroom of the King of Artois.
King and Queen in bed. Enter Minister, holding a letter.*

KING: What strange conundrums do appear in spring!
   Sixty long winters, sweet, it seemed to me
   Had played tag-harry with my brow and crop,
   And thou also had lately looked to me
   A plaintive ruin of thy former self.
   But, in this April month, the sun has turned
   And goldened all those winters into springs.
   This sudden sun hath glowed upon thee too,
   And where I late did rue a fallen town,
   (Battlements crumpled, arcatures unpierd)
   I see thee in a lovely pride of place,
   Solid and pink as new-chopped porphyry.
QUEEN: Thank you, dear heart, for nice and tender words.
   Though couched in stone they speak a gentle soul.
                   They embrace.
   For my own part, I thank the providence
   Which hath allayed my weak maternal fears
   And, to six upright Christian courts of France,
   Hath brided our six girls.
KING: And has bespoke therewith an easy dower
   That's left our treasury well-stocked despite.
   Six brave alliances we have transpired –
   Matilda, Ingfried, and proud Winifred,
   Cortona, Mary, and dear Radegund –
   With six great nobles at the trifling cost
   Of livres ten thousand multiplied by six.
QUEEN: Yet when I part from Radegund, I'll weep.
   I'll flood the very moat.
KING: Such is thy duty, hen, as mother.
   E'en I, hard cock, shall fling from out my eye
   A tributary gush.

But let's not speak of tears.
I hear a lark cry, and a robin chime.
Let's be ourselves that lark's and robin's tone
And crown the sunshine with a king's duet.

KING (*sings*): When gaffer in his snowy hat
QUEEN (*sings*): And beldame in her strawy flat
KING (*sings*): Do find that in this late attire
QUEEN (*sings*): They yet may with the spring conspire
BOTH (*sing*): Then off flies age and out flies doubt
Then winter's heart is turned about
Then fires burn that were put out
And maypole dons his ribboned clout
In hey the dandy over the rig.
In hey the dandy over the rig.

KING: Why jenny wren, thou sangst it every word as gay as thy cock robin! (*Minister coughs.*) But what's this now? Who called you, Monsieur eavesdropper, into our very bedchamber?

MINIS: Outrageous news impelled me to invade
The sacred privy of thy regal choir.

KING: Give it here, sirrah! (*Takes letter.*) And pray you it is enough outrageous to vindicate your prying! (*Reads.*) Eh, eh, what's this, what's this? 'Brittan's Duke, by Eternal Grace and His own Effort, Lord of this World – doth commence herein his supreme Preamble – doth summon you.' Who shall summon Artois, by God? No sixth son-in-law, by all the Saints! Has plague o' madness reamed Brittany? The Duke's style was never thus; always suave as a ferret, yet indolent and half asleep. (*Reads.*)
'We here denounce that scabrous contrack,
Made unbeknownst to Us twixt thee and We,
In which the princess Radegund was plight
To Us in paltry purse ten thousand livres.
Hereby We slash this parchment with our sword
And munch its ribbons into papery shards,
Demand a moiety above this dower
Paid instantly upon the union's flower.
Five thousand more to linger in Our chest
'Til Radegund's conceived.' Oh, blatent cockerel!
Would doubt my fecund loin?

270

Fetch me my spurs, my sharpest golden ones.
Where are they?
QUEEN: Why, in that closet, Lord, where they've been hung
Since your return with Egbert from crusade.
KING: My mantle, hauberk, two-hand sword, and boots,
My archers, pikemen, and artillery,
My shield inscript with Artois' badger's teeth,
My water-bottle, and five thousand men.
I'll rive bold Brittan 'twixt two poplar trees
And share his moieties with Belle and Beau.
QUEEN: But ever gently, love; in no rash blood.
KING: Rash, say you? I'm crazed to slobbering
And deaf with rage. My aged joints
Crackle like smitten thistles.
Spurs, archers, water-bottle, here, here! To me! to me!
Exit King, furiously.

IV.2

Scene: Brittany. The Ducal Chamber. Enter two Courtiers.

1ST COURT: I promise you, he's mad.
2ND COURT: Hush, prithee: no ruler's safe dubbed mad 'til a's made
his last bow.
1ST COURT: I'll not be squeamish. Mad, mad – 'tis my word! Yesterday, great duffer, he sundered five more alliances – Poitiers, Cognac,
Normandy, Burgoyne, and Charente. I've no mind to find myself
beneath a red heap with five furious dukedoms reared upon my one
belly.
2ND COURT: True, true; 'twould be unbearable.
1ST COURT: Yet such's the sage's fate when eminence
Takes a new master on its vaunting back. Gone's
The old counsellor with his twisted maps,
His gentle cough, his subterfuging trap.
Where craft and bargain weft a knotty tie
Runs in the usurper with his razor eye.

He sights afar the rangéd hornbeam pins
And with one furious bowl makes smitherins.
'Tis ever thus with men too lowly bred,
They stretch their sinew and abase our head.
To me, old men, old ways are ever best
And novelty a most detested guest.

Exeunt.

Enter Captain with Attendants.

CAPT: There's respect wanting here; of me and mine: it roils me, boils me, sirrahs, lessens me. I would see more caps doffed, like a storm of autumn leaves; more knees biased, like hedged limbs; tones more clotty with unction, as dressed salads. As one who's dropped straight as a hailstone from the groins of Alexander of India, Abraham, Platon, and the kings of Jerusalem – to name but a few venerable blooms which dropped seed to my comminglement – can there be a limit to my due homage? I'd see it press me so close I should be perforce upright, and having that incapacity to move which is dignity's mark. Ay me! I recall more awe, more tremulous celerity, when I stood upon the poop – nay, nay, that's wrong; that was not me; I was never to sea; he that was was a certain self once claimed me; an imposter that spoke to another of his strange poops. Poop, poop forsooth! What should it mean and who spake it?

1ST ATT: No man spoke of any such, my lord: 'twere a ridiculous, absurd word and without any vestige of meaning – unless, indeed, the speaker were inspired by thought of King Jason; he that steered to immortality disguised as a seaman.

CAPT: Tell me more of this Jason and where he sailed, the contemptible rascal.

1ST ATT: Why, sire, though he was a priceless king, he sailed to Troy, where he confounded and ripped up an hundred Greek kingdoms and came home to his own seat in robes of gold fleece, and was married to one Dido of Carthage.

2ND ATT: Ay: so 'twas exactly: rare, rare.

CAPT: Was this Jason a Christian king?

1ST ATT: Ay, when age pressed him thus; and so he embraced the Cross despite the protestations of his pagans on Tiber, which he once swam.

CAPT: Mark him then among my ancestors, remarking beside the mark that albeit I disclaim him as a silly voyager, I do inherit him as a hero king and a Christian.

2ND ATT: It shall be writ down straight-faced immediately, my lord, as is ever best with pedigrees.

CAPT: Good, good. Dim the lights, and I'll sleep. (*A couch is brought; he reclines.*) Put out the rabble, lock the doors; a few remain to guard. But, stay. Why needs omnipotence any guard?

1ST ATT: That it may be protected from a dreamy misuse of its own power, my lord: no more than that.

CAPT: Well, well . . .

Sleeps.

1ST ATT: Why, how he snores there like a truffling hog!

2ND ATT: There's a monstrous belly asking a rip from Picardy's sword!

1ST ATT: The salt's still in hard crystal in his beard, and the stink of the hold, overdue in hot weather, clinging to him.

CAPT: Belay, whore's sons, belay! Steward!

2ND ATT: A pretty duke, his crown dropt on his nose-bridge, and he a-wallow in sea-dreams.

Enter Ghost, much devoured by fishes, wearing the legend H.M.S. Dog *on his cap.*

GHOST: Captain Jack, yes, yes; steward's here, sir, at your service.

CAPT: Oh, oh, 'tis you, ragamuffin, conscience demon?

GHOST: Ay, sir, old Dombey still himself, still, at your service, though bedraggled by much immersion since you pleased to drop him out, that black night.

CAPT: Eh, clammy man come to cold-finger me! (*Wakes. Exit ghost.*) Where's he, that wet steward walking on a draught?

1ST ATT: No steward, sir, only a brave bodyguard – and, above, the horned window flap-at-the-catch.

CAPT: Make all fast, for Christ's dear sake! (*Attendant locks window.*) Ow, he looked all rubbery! More like himself in spirit than ever was in flesh. How's that? To be more when thou art less? 'Tis like a sieve, the greater for being fraught with nothings.

2ND ATT: Lie down, dear lord.

CAPT: Ay, 'tis sleepy-time for tiny Jack.

Sleeps.

1ST ATT: Now is the big hog turned little suckling.

2ND ATT: Had I a red asp, I'd stuff it in him for teat.

CAPT: Ma-ma, ma-ma!

Enter Ghost of a much debauched female.

GHOST: No cozzle for thy own mother, sweet Jacky, little Jack! Wouldst sell me for a Portuguèse mark, strumpet thy own milk-weed?

CAPT: Nay, nay, I never did: only that he was passing, and the gold shone in his palm.

GHOST: How salves this my poor heart, that's wandered mizzling so long in Purgation, moaning that its own son made it a trade-stuff? Clip me, little Jack, own Johnny, fast and tight.

Embraces Captain.

CAPT: Oh, trenchant octopus: I'm all strangled: give over my manhood and depart! (*Exit Ghost, sobbing.*) Where's she, the old whore?

2ND ATT: What old whore's that, Duke?

CAPT: My mother, fool!

2ND ATT: The noble dowager, thy mother, mumbles with fan, poodle, and beads in her retired villa.

CAPT: Why, so she does. I've mixed her quite. What's the hour?

1ST ATT: Early for dukes to be astir, sir.

CAPT: Yet I'll sleep no more. My pendulum's unhooked, and clock's face is white, and the steady pointers threat to cease their indications. How do I look?

2ND ATT: Awful, my lord, like Jove.

CAPT: Come, then, we'll turn the galleries.

Exeunt.

IV.3

Scene: The Palace Dungeon, on the same night. Enter Turnkey.

TURN: Peace be with you, poor dead! About this hour your shrouds come, and after that is only a quick axe-fall 'tween you and redemption. I am almost minded to come with you there, carrying my chopped head gently.

COUNT: Three's enough to go to trial together without heads: add a
fourth and the symmetry's too square for judgement.

DUKE: By God, despite it's yet upon my shoulders, I feel the carriage
of my head like a bird-in-hand!

PRINCE: Momentarily I feel affrighted: then stalk up reason and
wisdom to remind me that I am a goose.

DUKE: Ay, with Christmas all but upon you.

COUNT: Gently, gently!

Enter Hermione and Catriona, still as friars, bearing three shrouds.

HERM: Dead souls, how hast thou stirred
Thy master Satan on this murky night?
Aloft, the noble duke doth pace and pace;
A train of sleepy courtiers at his heels,
Two ghosts supporting at his funny bones.

CATRI: Hast thou invoked black Hades to thy part?
Hast charmed stone gargoyles into whited flesh?
Around this place is come a swarm of owls
Bassoonly hooting of remorse to come.

COUNT: Nay, we've done nothing.
If ghosts and owls sooth are abroad tonight
They're flit from crannies in a guilty skull.

HERM: Add not your number to the ghostly crew.
Two ghosts may ring a brainpan till it crack,
But if three more attend, then fear departs,
And haunted man, yielding to numbers,
Declares the world's all ghosts, and quakes no more.

COUNT (*aside*): What admirable sense is here! This friar
Seems to advise me to a change in plan.
Doubtless some holy hand has seized his tongue
And twists its saying to my better fate.
I'll trust this absent hand and press for more.
To Hermione.
Thou say'st, good father, that the dismal night
Has ghosts enough enow. How then
May three more souls disport and still affright?

HERM: There's witchery.

CATRI: Ay: witchery flies by daylight when weary ghosts retire.

COUNT: You would have us witches, then?

HERM: We said nought.

COUNT: Who are ye? I doubt you are the friars ye seem.

HERM: Would we might doubt you are dead prisoners.

DUKE: We'd give thee room for doubt had we but the means of witchery.

HERM: Hush thy loud voice, amiable dead! Here! Take this.

Gives him a shroud. Two hammers, three files, a chisel, fall to the ground.

PRINCE: Ha, ha, ha! 'Tis a brisk game!

CATRI: Oh, Madam, thou art a sorry packer!

TURN (*without*): Ho, what's the clangour?

HERM: Nought but five flows of tears,
Changed straight to ice by sorrow and remorse
And raining down like steel. I fear, should
We remain, our hearts will so complain
They'll shrill like brass.

Gives Duke two more shrouds. Six poinards fall to the ground.

CATRI: Enough, enough. Let's go
Before we wake the dead.

DUKE: We are already much alerted.

Exeunt Hermione and Catriona.

COUNT: Hide quickly these coarse tools of liberty!

DUKE: Douse out the candle;
We'll work i' the spring moon.

COUNT: I'm all agog to fret these rusted bars. Do you snore, piteously, good brother, and mute the file's moan.

PRINCE (*snoring*): Thus?

DUKE: Ay, master will be proud of thee if thou canst snore like a file. I'll drum my heels and dim the hammer-blows.

Count files and hammers, Prince snores, Duke drums.

TURN (*without*): Absolution hast left ye rowdy, meseems.

COUNT: Shall skeletons not rattle?

TURN (*without*): Why so hasty for thy last dance?

DUKE: We would practise, that we may turn our toes well and please the Duke.

COUNT (*aside*): Morning will see us prancing at his door,
Forbidding, neighing females of the heath.

PRINCE: Let us confide all to the good turnkey that he, too, may enjoy the jest.

DUKE: Nay, for he is an ancient man and too much laughter might split his sides.

PRINCE: True, true.

DUKE: And take you heed, when we emerge past him in witches' form, ask him not to delight in the metamorphosis.

PRINCE: Nay, that were to affright him, and fear is a great killer of jests. Ah, how wise I am grown! But I'll not be puffed-up.

DUKE: Well said! There's no end to wisdom, and doubtless further lessons await us.

PRINCE: I pray so. It is excellent comical.

Snores.

Scene: A Gallery. Enter Captain and Attendants, weary.

CAPT: They're still here – off, off, traitors, mummies! (*Brushes his elbows.*) I'll walk without you. Strike 'em away! (*Attendants strike at his elbows with staffs and daggers.*) Here's morning come to my assistance. Oh angel dawn, self-murderer of ghosts!

1ST ATT: Are they gone, my lord, these weird identities?

CAPT: Yea, they've fled suddenly to China, where night's descending to welcome them. I – poor, besieged fort – am granted respite. Sit, gentlemen.

All lie down.

Thus rises morning on a shattered sea
Whereon a storm of night hath played foul havoc:
And beaten sailor on his swinging feet,
The tempest's memory athwart his eyes,
Incredulous regards the softened miles
And round horizon of a wavy wheel
To which he's axis. Alas!
The connective spokes lie bobbing all about,
Ruptured and wreck'd, reminders of the night;
A chest, a jutting spar, a dawdling corpse,
A cage of singing birds the coxswain loved,
A beam of Orient teak, a small child's hand –
All these stream by, confute the morning's peace,
Carry the night into the day's brain pan.
So you, my courtiers, like a score of wrecks,
Surround the haggard ship that floats in me.
Ay, yes, but float we do, and there's the thought
Will properly exclude regret's sad drift
And give us, as we weep, the heart to sleep.

Settles himself. Enter Servant.

SERV: Three witches to see you, my lord.

CAPT: Now, here's naughty mischief! Do I dine ghosts to break fast

278

with witches? Pray them wait for noon: say I'm closeted in stately
business.
SERV: They flat refuse to wait, my lord.
Pent up with message like a bitch with whelps,
Delivery, they scream, is now, now, now!
CAPT: Show them in.
Exit Servant.
The way of Satan is not to dispatch,
But to prolong; 'til prolongation
Itself itself dispatches. Ah, ah!
Enter Prince, Count, Duke in rent shrouds, disguised as witches.
Crones, are ye real and actual?
COUNT: Indeed, my lord, we are, composed of pinched, torn flesh too
quickly horrible for description.
CAPT: No cauldron, brazier, frogs' legs?
COUNT: Nay, to carry your fate already was to overburden us.
DUKE: True, its dismal weight has given us the staggers.
CAPT: Speak, trio of horrors!
PRINCE *(aside)*: Poor soul: he's all haggard in earnest, and we here to
torment him in play! We are cruel boys that hurt our teacher.
COUNT: With goats and arabesques we three had framed
A sunny holiday with Egypt friends.
Scarce seated by the Nile with gipsy Nicks
The whole stream quaked, and turbulent rain
Deluged our hair, rinsed forth our greasy joy:
While through the torrent and black atmosphere,
Hordes of winged rats, vultures, and nimble stoats
(Bound round with gizzards of decaying whales)
Flew rushing northward in a spate of glee.
We asked: Sisters in Satan, what emergency
Doth so propel you from your native sands?
They, cackling and dribbling with a maniac spite,
Answered, they'd nest in Brittany come night.
We asking why, they chorused that a sea
Of depthless blood was washing to this place;
That by the fall of night a carnage heap
Would be their perch for song until their teeth
Had glutted every morsel under claw.

Picardy's up, they howled, and so's Burgoyne,
Normandy, Cognac, lily-strewn Lorraine,
Feeble Artois has waked his sleepy sword,
And the fourth Henry on his London throne
Has heard such tumult that he's spit poor Dick
And turned his pack in fleets across to France.
All say some villain has usurped the world,
Smashed the whole globe to dance among its shards,
They hint of one they'll slaughter through and through;
We gravely do expect that it is you.

CAPT: May I not fly: are not legs for flying?

DUKE: Fly and be damned! Evade the natural sword
And hellish gnomes will speak the ghastly word.

CAPT: Then come, sweet death!

COUNT: Patience, he is on the threshold; a little minute, you'll hear
him knock.

CAPT: Bid him hurry, that I may die aloof from ghosts.

PRINCE (*aside*): I'll play no more: we've hazed him unto death,
Shown we're good pupils at his sad expense.
No more's needed: to prolong were spite.
I'll straight reveal myself.

To Captain.

Good Captain Jack, wipe off thy monstrous sweat,
Fear nothing; nothing's here, and nothing looms.
Thy loving pupil, Prince of Antioch,
Doffs now his witchery and embraces you!

CAPT: Oh, helpless, awful combination!
Under the horrid witch, more horrid ghost
Of dungeon dead! Identity
Hard heaped upon identity! 'Neath each, another.
Remorseless spirit, spurn that ghastly smile
And let me flee!

Exit Captain, running, followed by Prince, Duke, Count, and attendants.

V.2

Scene: A plain in Brittany. Enter Captain, running, pursued by Prince.

PRINCE: Captain, my captain; halt; take conference! My partners in this game are fell behind.

CAPT: Leave me to hell, scurvy hag, ghost, prince, and whatsoever else you be!

Falls.

PRINCE: See, master, I rend my disguise, reveal plain Antioch! Here, touch my doublet and, under straggled hair, fur cap of maintenance. Look, my square rubies!

CAPT: Antioch's doublet, Antioch's rubies and, over all, Antioch's callow voice. (*Rises.*) How dared you, pupil, witch thy teacher thus?

PRINCE: That our play might be match for thy play; two plays coincident and instructive.

CAPT (*aside*): 'Tis past incredible that a creature may so persist in innocence. Let's screw him yet a notch farther. (*To Prince.*) Thou'st played admirably, chicken; master is proud of thee and ready to send thee to 'Sorbonne. Where's thy two confederates?

PRINCE: Scouring the brush for thee, nearby.

CAPT: Then quickly, we'll on to the next lesson – the very last. Hand me thy witchery, take my ducal robes.

PRINCE: Ha, ha! Gladly.

They change clothes.

CAPT: Now, off to our respective businesses; play thou a fleeing Asiatic mariner in a French duke's disguise, forgetting thou art in reality a Syrian prince that feigns to be a witch.

PRINCE: I am much diverted.

Runs away, screaming.

CAPT: I, too; and, praise God, may so be also my enemies!

V.3

Scene: Another part of the plain. Enter King of Artois, Radegund,
and Followers.

KING: This turf is soft and downy underfoot;
  Unlike our rocky Artois as the dove
  Is in caparison remote the rook.
  Here's murdock interfest with eglantine,
  And savage roses pink as little babes.
  There looms the master-castle which we seek,
  Shaped in the river's curved suggestion
  Simply as child within a mothering arm.
  Sad contemplation, that with steely swords
  We'll hack the ducal father into bits!
RADEG: Yet, father, spare to me some vital parts;
  Enough to make a husband of a sort.
KING: What, wench; thou wouldst still marry Brittany?
RADEG: Better for me to wed his leg, his arm,
  His left great-toe – whatever shall remain,
  Than sit secluded on my maidenhead
  While lawyers, counsellors procrastinate,
  Unroll parchments, annotate in ink,
  Negotiate husband this and husband that,
  Melt wax enough to seal a leaking roof
  And sand and polish for a dancing-floor.
  One bit of Brittany to clasp today
  Is fairer than whole husband years away.
KING: Thou art thy mother's child. From me ne'er sprang
  Such heedless, sentimental promptitude.
  It shames me much to dally with your whim,
  Yet shall I struggle to withhold my sword.
  Thus was I ever: woman's gentle voice
  Gave hardest principle a soft distort.
              Enter Captain disguised as a witch.
  Welcome, good hag, if good and hag thou art,

If merely hag, get hence.
I seek the Duke; art thou his toy?
CAPT: Suffice to say I am a stranger here,
    Witness of sights more foreign than myself.
    Christian and prince of Syria, I sought
    Solace and harbour when my úsurp'd throne
    Was torn below me. Alas! here refuged,
    Came new usurper to usurp my peace.
    A dirty seaman so engaged the Duke
    As wholly to offset him and take up
    Cuckoo assumption of the dukely nest.
    Yet God, who sleeps not, speedily dispatched
    Some horrid emissaries retribute,
    And now the usurping wretch runs here about
    With nought but ghosts to claim his nasty soul.
    Two awful witches follow in his train
    And nag the remnants of the ghostly prey.
    Such horrors had I seen that I despaired
    Of tumbling safely from the bath of blood.
    When, suddenly, rode up a blessed envoy
    Which did inform me that my Syrian seat
    Was new restored to me. Thither
    I hurry now, disguised, and glutted up
    With gloomy judgement of the Frankish ways,
    Resolved that Antioch shall never see
    Practices beastly as the ones I flee.
RADEG (*aside*): How sweet and courtierlike he doth appear,
    Yet manly, broad, and muscular withal.
    Would he were my duke!
KING: Poor royal traveller, Antioch's far placed;
    Placed far, meseems, beyond thy straitened means.
CAPT: I've three red stones will buy me to a ship.
    Faith and robustiousness will buy the rest.
KING: Nobly said; yet take these aids also.
              Hands Captain a bag of gold.
    Come happier times, I'll visit Syria,
    And, smiling, ask of thee replenishment.
CAPT: Excellent King, come soon!

Now, go I must, while Antioch remains.
I prithee, shouldst thou meet my brother,
Inform him how I'm gone and whither.
KING: Gladly. Farewell!

Exit Captain.

There goes a royal pound of ounces!
RADEG: Would he were and would weigh him in my arms!

Enter Picardy.

PIC: Artois, thou too! Art here to hunt?
KING: To hunt carrion.

Enter Cognac.

COG: I fear I'm come too late
To rend the cur that's rent my token up.
KING: Spirited Cognac, fear not truancy!
The chase is up, prey sighted, nothing more.
Come, ride with me, and as we ride I'll tell
The tale which lies within this outer frame.
But first, send men-at-arms that will procure
Priests to protect us from the witches' rage.

Exeunt Men.

COG: What, witchery to boot?
KING: Aye, to ghosts' behoof.
Fall in with me; I'll tell you all.
PIC: Lead us, Artois; for thy decrepit rage
Is nicely suited to the work in hand.
Where's England's Henry?
COG: Delayed, they say, by fog.

V.4

Scene: Before the Castle. Alarms and tumults. Enter, running, the Prince of Antioch as Duke; pursued by Count of Baalbeck and Duke of Brittany as witches; Hermione and Catriona as friars; Artois, Cognac, Picardy, men-at-arms, pikemen, and others all as themselves.

DUKE: Excellent, excellent; have at him; on, on!

PRINCE: Oh, oh, life is a hard teacher! I pray 'twill stop short of death,
or wherefore my new self?
COUNT: Hew him hardly; blink not his babble and his ducal guise!
HERM: Heed not his puny cries, strike him to hell!
ARTOIS: Admirable priests, admonish those loud witches! They do
affright our pikemen.
CATRI: Ho, witches, play the man; the chase is done!
Pikemen fall upon the Prince of Antioch.
COG: Oh, good, good, stalwartly slain!
Would that this sword had struck the featly blow!
Remove the horrid corpse.
Men carry away the Prince's body.
Yet do I fear these horrid, anguished hags
Which glare upon the fatal body's course.
Good friars, thank them for their services
And gently ask that they shall now withdraw.
HERM: Instantly.
To Count.
Sweet witch, be shriven afresh by one
Which shrived thee once and would again assume
Herself the bewitching role.
Kisses Count.
PIC: Here's odd conduct in a friar.
COG: They say, in Brittany all's done peculiar.
ARTOIS: I smell some mystery, or even intrigue.
DUKE: Fair Radegund, partner and mate of bliss.
Unworthy husband pleads for thy caress!
Tears off disguise.
RADEG: Brittany - in all one piece!
HERM: Farewell, friar's self!
Tears off disguise.
COUNT (*tearing off disguise*): Vessel of dreams! Feigned furbisher!
Embraces Hermione.
ARTOIS: I am too old for war - yet older far for peace.
This armistice doth weave such strange designs
As shake an agéd brain.
CATRI (*tearing off disguise*): My lord, 'tis simple as the earth itself,
Where all's most right when seeming mostly worst.

ARTOIS: No more!

Swoons.

DUKE: Revive him promptly.

Attendants carry off Artois.

Disguiséd men and ladies, pray restore
Identities, decorum, natural ways.
Put up the sword of war and reassume
The beaky warble of the ring-dove's tune.

COUNT: Where's my poor brother in all this confusion?

RADEG: That stalwart man is even now en route
Back to the desert throne he lately left.
Restored with honour, he's resolved to shape
The Antioch desert into fertile land.

COUNT: I wish him well. Perchance he's learnt a lesson despite. I'll not
pursue to ask.

DUKE: Nay, Baalbeck, stay, and with Hermione
(Who's on this spot created countess)
Double the nuptials of my own fair spouse.

PIC: Triple it rather, for I'll take to wife
That second, jolly witch.

CATRI: Most sweet and unexpected!

Embraces Picardy.

DUKE: We'll celebrate our new, voluptuous parts
With naked selves which blush not for disguise
But for that they have none.
My lesson's learnt, and tedium reigns no more
Though much is back to where it was before.
A throne is saved, a fraud crushed underfoot,
Cannon and ordinance, acclaim and shoot!

Guns.

Wisdom is victor; sennett and tender flute,
Hail right identity with fair salute!

Flutes and sennetts.

THE END

PART THREE

MRS CHIRK had rarely played a flute, nor had Miss Tray large knowledge of the sennett. Even Mr Harcourt's teeth clenched to a fine edge as the last notes climbed an unknown scale on nameless rungs. But as the lights went up it was clear to every member of the Club that their new President was not upset by trifles. So calmly did he rise upon the dais, so naturally did he grasp the official gavel, so nonchalantly did he pass the back of his hand downwards over his chin that even such grave, ambitious men as Orfe and Shubunkin felt obliged to give him a complimentary clap.

'I thank you, gentlemen,' he said, 'for your friendly unanimity in a matter which is of some personal concern to me.'

There was laughter and more clapping, to which he responded with a firm but amiable smile. They noted and greatly appreciated how content he was to stand easily beside the chair and allow the applause to well around him, his expression pleased but indicating that such tribute had been his since childhood and was more an essential part of his environment than a desirable compliment. He gave this impression with such economy of gesture and expression that the Club's clapping became more and more vigorous; he, in turn, responding ever more non-committally to the growing din. Thus do great leaders provoke passion and unswervable loyalty in their followers, allowing their great images to recede so gently that the applause pursues them with ever-growing excitement.

'I imagine,' he continued, 'that most of you would like us to move straight into a discussion of the interesting play we have just seen: there is always so much to say about Shakespeare – what he really meant, what his genius guessed at but was incapable of analysing, and so on. But I would be failing in my duty as your president if I did not insist that this matter be shelved until after lunch. Or should I say after dinner? I have rather lost hold of the exact time.'

The Club greeted this evidence of presidential nonchalance (so unlike, say, a man who identifies himself with a military rank) with affectionate smiles.

'Anyway, after whatever comes next. For the moment, I would like

287

to discuss a matter that suddenly came into my mind as a result of listening to Shakespeare. While thinking of all the problems that beset a man when he begins, slowly, laboriously, and with many checks to build himself a tenable identity, it occurred to me that the plight of the *dead* was much graver. Very famous people, of course, have to die before they achieve their full identity, which is readily supplied by their numerous admirers. But what of those who are not famous? They pass on into nothingness, stripped of every shred of that which they toiled so hard to create. Take, for example, former presidents of this Club. Consider the passionate feuds that revolved around them, the love and hatred they created by sheer imposition on others of their chosen selves. And yet, once gone, all this is forgotten: it is as if they had never been. I remember well, for example, as no doubt do you, my predecessor in this chair, a man of great parts who played his Presidency with diligence and subtlety until age and infirmity removed him from our ranks. It seems a shameful thing to me that apart from the usual Wedgwood plaque in the Club library he will be utterly forgotten – and, indeed, is already virtually forgotten. Perhaps some of you gentlemen could think of a means by which we might perpetuate him for at least a decade or so.'

'As one who remembers him very well indeed,' said Dr Musk, 'I feel that the problem is self-answering. In the course of his life he was a most undesirable character, and I could think of a hundred examples of his brutality, cynicism, egotism, and injustice. Since he has ceased to be our President, however, I have felt a change of view coming over me. I suddenly think of him as a dear, likeable old man – a gentleman in the true sense of the word. He has a place in my heart which I never imagined him being in. Without any disrespect to the present incumbent of the chair, I must say that I shall always think the defunct occupant was the better man. When the present incumbent passes on, I shall proceed to think that *he* was. I consider this perfectly natural. The car we used to have is always the one that started on a cold morning: we have to have a new car to appreciate this fact. The peace we had before the last war is always an excellent period, which is why new wars are desirable at regular intervals – to make us love what we detested. The same, in my opinion, goes for presidents. The memorial to a past president is erected quite automatically by the mere existence of his successor.'

All the members were impressed by Dr Musk's clear exposition, but deemed it safer not to back-up the dead President, until they had better knowledge of the weaknesses of the living one. He, for his part, merely gave the bold doctor a fatherly smile and said:

'Our good Musk has always had the habit of gauging the validity of life by an estimate of death, and of allowing memory to rectify – if that is the word – the bias of his present judgements. Proud as I shall be to represent, in his eyes, the life that always falls short of the death which preceded it, I think I would like to see a rather more *solid* memorial to my predecessor.'

'Surely nostalgia is about as solid as one could wish?' asked Dr Shubunkin.

'I'm afraid it will get swept away,' replied the President. 'As Musk says, the old memory makes a dear ideal, but after a while there arises a general feeling that to dote on it too much is to make oneself seem old-fashioned, and even rather decrepit. I am sure none of you gentlemen, Dr Musk excepted, rejoices in a decrepit self. Shubunkin, for instance, is ever in eager search of that which is new – inventing it where necessary.'

A sharp clash would certainly have followed had Mr Harcourt not exclaimed: 'What's this? Has somebody resigned? Why?'

Amid the loud laughter which followed young Stapleton rose, and resting one elbow on the back of his chair, said sarcastically:

'How about a large vase of fresh flowers in every Club room on the anniversary of his birth or death? Or we could collect his aphorisms and bind them in half-calf. Better still, a cast of his hand, to leave on a table with ashtrays.'

Infuriated, Beaufort sprang to his feet, his face burning red, a living picture of the solid citizen outraged by cynicism. 'Why, you miserable little rotter!' he cried.

The cynical youth responded with what he intended to be a nonchalant shrug of his shoulders: unfortunately, being quite inexperienced in bitterness, he succeeded only in leaving an impression of ignorance and bad manners. The older members studied him with interest, detecting for the first time the little cloud on the horizon that denotes the rise and challenge of a new generation. Indeed, this is an interesting moment for all parties: a new, but well-known figure in authority, a new, untested runner emerging suddenly out of the empty background of nonentity: suddenly the old humdrum pattern, gone with the old President, has readjusted itself, and revolutionary men-like Musk and Shubunkin, challenged from behind, suddenly become conservative. As for Beaufort, it is the end of him as we have known him; the emergence of a tough young rival has cooked his charming and irresponsible goose: overnight he will become a solid, dependable citizen and be married to his mistress as soon as they get to the first registry office. This is sad, in a way, because he was very likeable, but how fortunate it is, in life, that as soon as death creates a vacancy, everybody moves up a seat! How fortunate for the new man in authority that no sooner is he challenged by the old rebels than they are forced to his side by an upstart radicalism which they fear far more than he! It is inspiring to all these worthies to see the President, fresh and strong as a mature lion, fix his hard eye on the young rebel and ask: 'What, pray, Mr Stapleton, does that convulsive movement of yours indicate? I should like an answer immediately.'

But even as he bends inquiringly forward, a nervous knock is heard on the door. Mrs Paradise, still disguised as the future Countess of Baalbeck, enters the room and says with a loud sob: 'There's a police-man would like to speak with you, sir.'

'A *policeman!*' cried Dr Shubunkin.

'A *policeman!*' cried Dr Orfe.

'A *policeman!*' cried Mr Jamesworth.

'Gentlemen, gentlemen!' cried the President. 'Am I the leader of a herd of cows? Florence, what is the reason for this officer's visit?'

'He says, sir, he has reason to believe this house is occupied.'

'Do you burst into tears over such a simple statement of fact?'

'It's the dear old gentleman I'm weeping for, sir. Is he dead?'

The President assumed a bewildered look and surveyed his colleagues as if requesting an explanation.

'I think, sir,' said Beaufort, 'that she is referring to the last scene.'

'*Last scene,*' repeated the President. 'I find this *most* confusing.'

'To be buried under such a heap of gentlemen, sir, at his age!' cried Mrs Paradise.

'She refers, sir,' said Beaufort, smiling, 'to our little casualty.'

'Oh, oh, yes,' exclaimed the President. 'My dear Florence, you are much too emotional. He is lying down. Be assured, he'll be down for dinner. By the way, Florence, do you realize that you are still in disguise? May I ask how you explained your costume to the police-man?'

'I never thought to explain, sir. I was too distressed.'

'Where is the rest of the staff?'

'In the kitchen, sir.'

'And the officer?'

'He is on the doorstep, sir.'

The President reflected for a moment, and said: 'Show him politely into the butler's pantry by the side door, Florence. When I ring, bring him in here. Tell the staff to remain in the kitchen.'

'I hope we have done nothing wrong, sir.'

'Nothing whatever, Florence. It is probably some new tax on amateur theatricals which the officer has come for. Is the staff comfortable?'

'I can't say they are, sir. Mrs Chirk is most hysterical and even Mr Jellicoe is not himself. Why did all the gentlemen rush on to the stage in the last scene?'

'They thought you were rather short of pikemen, Florence. They wanted to help – to make it all more lifelike.'

'But why did they throw the poor old gentleman on the ground? We never dreamt he was at the bottom of the heap until we all got off.'

'He was only winded, Florence. He should have been more careful not to fall down at such a violent moment. Now, off you go and do as I have told you. And stop weeping, immediately. The play was excellently performed.'

Mrs Paradise left the room, holding Hermione's skirt to her eyes.

'Gentlemen,' said the President. 'You will go immediately to your rooms, pack your suitcases, put them in the hall, and *return to this room.* I allow you five minutes for the operation. Beaufort – no, I shall need you elsewhere. Let me see, now.' His eyes ranged over the pale, impractical faces, resting at last on Stapleton. 'Mr Stapleton, something tells me you have a knowledge of cars. You will go to the garages and bring all the cars quietly to the front of the house. You have half an hour.'

Stapleton leaves his seat and walks briskly to the door. His old limp is gone, his new-found arrogance in abeyance. If he is to be admired for springing to the Club's defence in this emergency, the President is still more to be admired for raising him, in the twinkling of an eye, to an act of greatness.

Suddenly Mr Harcourt cries: 'I say, are we *leaving?*'

'Yes Mr Harcourt, we are leaving. Now, gentlemen, here are your instructions . . .'

*

The policeman is surprised, on being shown into the breakfast-room, to see a group of people penned in one corner with a red velvet rope running along the stomachs of the first row. Two men, who appear to be butlers or footmen – or something archaic like that – are standing near the door as he enters; each raises a warning finger to his lips and hisses 'Ssh-sh!' They hiss thus because his lordship, or squire, or duke, or whoever he is (the policeman is too young to know these extinct distinctions of identity) is standing in the middle of the carpet saying:

'. . . not *exactly* an original, but so fine a copy as to excel, in the view of many art-experts, the original itself. The flaking which you may observe in one corner is due to the efforts of a younger son of the house to remove certain Victorian paintings-over of the nude figures: the result of this strife between decency and art is, as is always the case, confusing to the spectator and disproportioning to the nudes. The painting is insured for many thousands of pounds and is known as "The Last of the Great Easel Paintings of the Neo-Dutch School".'

This classifying of the object immediately gives it an importance which cannot be disputed and is received with a flashing of notebooks and pencils. While the scribbling goes on, one of the footmen approaches the duke, who turns and looks at the policeman with surprise and then comes over to the door. He is about to address the policeman when one of the crowd shouts quite shrilly: 'Is that going to the National Trust too?'

'One moment, sir, if you please,' he answers, and says in a low voice to the policeman: 'I am *very* sorry to have kept you. When they said: "An officer to see you," I thought they meant some ordinary Army one.'

The policeman, pleased, replies: 'That's quite all right, sir. I am sorry to have interrupted.'

'We are open to the public, you know, nowadays.'

'So I see, sir.'

'It takes me about twenty-five minutes to show them over. I would be most obliged if you could wait.'

The policeman looks at his watch and decides to be reasonable.

'Why not join the party?' says the duke. 'It is quite an interesting old white elephant.'

He smiles and gives a nod to his footmen. Adroitly, they release one end of the crimson cord and stand like sentries in front of the tourists until the duke has put himself in the van. 'This way, please,' he says, and leads them out.

The policeman follows. He is amused to see the two footmen, thinking they are unobserved, give a hasty dusting to the parquet on which the tourists stood and spray a jet of disinfectant into their vacated air. Ahead, he hears the duke cry: 'We now enter the library,' and the tourists nudge each other and murmur: 'Library. That should be interesting' and 'I'm told it is a famous library'.

A man with a twitching face is sitting at the writing-table near a window. He rises from a heap of papers and gives the tourists a courtly bow. His face is lined, his brow high and furrowed. The footmen run in just in time to corral the tourists with the crimson cord.

'Here is one of the family at work,' explains the duke. 'In the passing of these old houses, nothing is to be more regretted than the loss of the library – and, with it, the sort of occupant you now see. Before we discuss the room, I would like you to look very closely at this individual. His bent shoulders, his pinched and nervous face, his tremulous grasp of his quill pen indicate that he will not be in contemporary society very much longer. I am not *too* well up in these matters, but I am assured that without him and his predecessors we should not have any culture at all. Throughout the centuries, ever since the dissolution of the monasteries, he has written modest commentaries on theology, Greek legend, Stonehenge, and water-divining – none of which is of much interest nowadays and, indeed, never was. He has been to literature what the rock-gardener has been to horticulture. He was never what is called a creative type, but he was always sensitive and tolerant, decently dressed, and came to meals punctually. A dim figure, you may say, but it is precisely dim nonentities which constitute the past for which we yearn. We are so dreadfully harassed ourselves and feel that we are so inadequate to the demands of our day that we love

293

best the image of one who was happy in his mediocrity, never made a fuss, and never got drunk.'

The tourists study Doctor Shubunkin for some time. A few of them make notes, but as the duke has not given the object a definite name, they just put 'Lord X?' 'Hon. Blank?'

'As for the rest of the furniture,' says the duke, 'all the things on the left are Chippendale, all the things on the right Sheraton. The books are pretty much the usual books. That brass thing is for weighing letters – popular, long ago. I think that's about all.

'We now pass down the corridor and enter the dining-room. The table is laid for dinner: I am sorry you cannot see the family actually *eating* their food; it is a human spectacle. Each has his or her butter-ration in the little thing like an ash-tray in front of his place. The sugar is pooled. You will observe that the table is laid precisely as it always was through the centuries: the family take pride in cleaning the silver themselves, despite the fact that they have little use for it. At the other end of the room is the hatch. When the meal is over, one member of the family shoves the broken meats on this side of it and another member goes round behind and drags them through. We take turns with the washing-up. The ceiling of this room was painted by Pagannini in 1882 and has been the finest extant example of a Pagannini ceiling since 1947 – the date of the collapse of a rather better one in the next county. The Adam fireplace is blocked-up with newspaper: we prefer the Valor stove which you see standing in the grate. The tapestry on the left was chopped up and used for polishing for many years before we were told it was a work of art and had it sewn together again. It is known as "The Last Judgement of Paris by the Bordeaux Etalier", and was presented to the family by a close friend of William Morris.'

At this, two or three of the tourists look meaningfully at each other, consult their watches, and sniff. They have been, probably, to hundreds of other decrepit mansions and feel bilked if the antiquities are not up to the highest romantic standards. The duke, who is clearly a proud man and is doing all this only in order to make money, flushes slightly and leads the way out. One of the sniffing tourists is deaf and has to cup his ear when his companion whispers at the top of his voice: 'I'm – say-ing – that – it – looks – mostly – junk – to – me . . . No – junk – jay – you – en – kay. . . . Herbert – asks – do – you – want – to – go – on? We – could – catch – the – five-fifteen.' The other answers: 'What are

294

we doing this for, anyway? I thought we were *leaving* the house. It's all quite over my head.'

The duke does not seem to notice, as he leads the way up the grand stair, that there are now three less in the party. The footmen, too, have fallen behind: no doubt they are thoroughly disinfecting the dining-room. A car is heard starting-up in the drive.

The duke is explaining the series of hunting paintings that climb the stairs. 'The first shows the squire receiving an intimation from his keeper – the stocky, cringing one on the right – that there is game abroad. The second shows him having his boots pulled on, while his little son looks enviously at his father's flint-lock and the spaniels leap with joy. The third shows him leaving the house, fully accoutred, while his wife waves a sympathetic lace hanky from the terrace. Now comes the fun! Picture Four shows the squire aiming at a hare, propped from behind by the faithful keeper. The hare is falling dead, as if in anticipation of the fatal shot. Actually, the poacher, whom you see behind that bush, has fired the shot in question, and Picture Five shows him scurrying off with his booty, pursued by the spaniels. Pictures Six, Seven, and Eight show the hunting of the poacher through various types of lovely countryside, with the squire on horseback and the keeper running beside. Picture Eight, entitled "Cornered At Last", shows the poacher surrounded by spaniels in a gravel-pit; Nine, Ten, Eleven, and Twelve are the usual concluding ones, showing the felon brought before the magistrate, who is a friend of the squire's, and being deported to Australia, while the squire reads a passage from the Bible to his children. *That* brings us to the top of the stairs.'

Some of the tourists have weak hearts. They are still making a pant-ing study of Pictures Six, Seven, and Eight when the duke mounts the last step and breezes off down the nearest corridor. It is doubtful if the stragglers will ever catch up.

'One of the problems of mansion-showing,' says the duke, pausing outside a room, 'is to keep people like yourselves *interested*. Our habit here is to try and give you the past atmosphere of the house by the arrangement of descriptive tableaux. Here is one that will interest you. It is entitled "Discovered!"'

He throws open the door and they crowd in with curiosity. They see a huge four-poster bed with crimson velvet curtains: a man has parted these curtains and stands staring with a look of horror at the occupants of the bed. These are a very handsome young man, looking up in angry surprise, and a woman, her mouth open in a scream, who is about to duck under the bedclothes.

'This,' says the duke in a low voice, 'represents the son of the house caught in commerce with a drab. He has picked her up at a tavern, pressed gold into her hand, and inveigled her up the back stairs. His uncle, who entered the room to ask the young man a question about lithography, has found himself faced by something of another stamp. This is the sort of thing that was always happening in old houses. As the estate is entailed, this objectionable young man is bound to inherit it. He will cut down all the trees to pay his debts and eventually will have to sell the whole place to a nouveau-riche – or, worse, marry the daughter of one. As his morals sink lower, income tax rises higher, reaching the standard nine-and-six just as he is reaching the sink of iniquity. You know the rest.'

The tourists are impressed. It is clear – or seems to be clear – that the actors in the tableau are alive. One can see them breathing, and sometimes their muscles twitch. The uncle holding back the curtain has fits of trembling. On the other hand, these are precisely the signs of life that one would expect to see in a well-conducted hoax. On looking closer one begins to question the naturalness of the figures: the uncle's skin is too deftly pock-marked and tinted to be real and a hip-flask is sticking out of his rear-pocket. The woman's hair is not the colour that goes with her skin; the young man's beauty is a bit put-on. Even the policeman, who took for granted that the figures were alive, now peers more closely, unwilling to look like a fool. After a while, the tourists begin to smile admiringly, and they nod, more or less agreed, when one of the party murmurs: 'You can tell by the eyes. That blank look. And the eyelids and the mouth. Too mechanical. I'd guess it's plastics, wax, and a few small air-pumps.'

The duke smiles and says: 'We have another for you in the next room.' He goes out, but most of the tourists are too fascinated to follow. They seem to have forgotten that they are viewing a bequest to the National Trust and are obsessed with the more fundamental matter of distinguishing between appearance and reality. 'Please do not touch the figures!' the duke calls back.

The next room is not so romantic. The curtains are drawn, everything is half-dark. Four tall candles burn at the corners of a high stately bed on which lies the well-dressed corpse of an old man with a white goatee. Artistically arranged on his breast are the contents of his pockets: a snuff box, a much-worn gold chain with an old gold watch at the end of it, a lucky iron nail, a card of membership in some club, a thin wallet smoothed by years of use, etc., etc.

'Here,' says the duke, 'lies the old squire, his heart broken by the vices of the young heir. The old man asked only one thing of the boy – that he keep his whores where they belonged and not bring them into the house. This reasonable injunction was not, as we have seen, obeyed. What has killed the old man is not, really, grief, but his knowledge that a whore in the home is like a horse in Troy. Once friends of that sort get into the better bedrooms, the so-called vertical structure of society begins to teeter. Any ass can get a woman *into* a house; to get her *out* is a labour of Hercules. There is no surer sign of the degeneration and collapse of an imperial class than the need to bring the vice into the home instead of going out for it.'

The tourists are not very interested in the duke's words because this tableau is rather a let-down, compared with the previous one. Any fool can see that the corpse on the bed is a dummy. A few, just to make sure, slip out of the room to take a comparative glance at the other figures. But the two or three who remain, and who are all that are left of the party, do not hide their contempt: they point to the false beard, made of an old whitewash brush, the pink ears of moulded wax, the clumsily-managed nose, the unnatural straightness and flatness of the legs, the tracery of small veins made by a feather dipped in blue ink. This is not what death looks like, nor is it what an undertaker's job looks like. As the policeman says (to himself): 'Some amateur done that.'

Another car is heard in the drive. The duke says 'Ts-ts!', looks at his watch, and shoots down the corridor again. His voice is heard in the next room talking about gold-leaf mouldings. 'I don't think I'll go on,' says one of the three tourists sourly: 'I expected aristocracy, not Madame Tussauds.' 'My little nipper could mould a better corpse,' says a second. 'When I pay good money,' says the third, 'I expect a natural response.'

The policeman catches up with the duke, who has only just discovered that he has lost his audience. Rather angrily, he questions the policeman, who says frankly that the gentlemen, as far as he could tell, semeed to have lost interest in going on. With an incredulous look, the duke rushes back down the corridor and peers into the corpse's room. Then he tries various doors and even looks behind a curtain. Just at that moment another car is heard starting and the duke lets out a howl of rage. Bellowing: 'They haven't *paid*!' he runs to the grand stair like a madman.

The policeman, left alone, throws an observant eye over the corridor. The carpeting is so frayed and dirty that his wife wouldn't allow it even in an outhouse. The ceiling is filthy. Sympathetic as he is where rank, antiquity, and beauty are concerned, he does feel a certain contempt for the duke. Tableaux are all very well, but they are unable to disguise poverty.

A few minutes pass, and the duke has not returned. The policeman begins to pace the corridor. He thinks he will have a private peep at the couple in the big bed; they will have a more fundamental interest without the duke present to insist on their social significance. But the coverings of the bed have been flung aside; the bending uncle is gone; the room is empty. The policeman is rather impressed: they *were* real, after all. He goes into the corpse's room to look at the dummy again. But it has gone too. This means that it, too, was alive, or that it was a dummy which is taken away and cleaned after each exhibition. The former is the more likely theory.

He does a little more pacing and then begins to feel uneasy. Something is wrong somewhere: what is it? He is a methodical man and has been well-trained in the art of asking the right question. He decides that his uneasiness is caused by the whole set-up of this place: it is not in step with life. It does not belong to the jet-age nor to antiquity; it falls short both of the National Trust and of the export drive. But it is not his business to question the structure of society in working-hours: he has questions to ask the duke and he sets off to find him.

On the grand stair he sees an ancient countess complete with wimple. She is madly dusting the banister. He asks her where the duke is, and she answers: 'In the kitchen.' He does not press her because she seems a bit daft: she looks at him as if he were disguised for a tableau.

He tries the library, but the intellectual 'Hon. Blank' has gone. He roams through various rooms, some of which seem not to have been occupied for years and years. He opens one or two doors and raises his eyebrows at what he sees. He opens the front door and stands on the balustraded terrace, but there are no visitors and all the cars have gone. So he goes down to the servants' quarters and opens the kitchen door.

The words on his lips are: 'Where is the duke?' He doesn't speak to them because he sees that the two men in the kitchen are disguised as *real* dukes and the two women as duchesses. Apparently, they are a part of one of the ordinary duke's tableaux. It all seems rather hopeless: too confused. He smiles and decides to break the ice with a little joke. 'I suppose you're the ones who take away the dummy,' he says. 'May I ask where the governor has got to?'

The older of the two duchesses bursts into tears. One of the dukes pats her shoulder comfortingly. The younger duchess pays absolutely no attention. She is grasping the hand of the other duke, whose beard is all tangled in his ruff and whose eyes are horribly bloodshot. 'Try, darling,' she says, 'try just once more.'

He rolls his red eyes and his voice comes in a croak. He says at last. 'It was a red football. Our team was called "The Merry Dodgers".'

'Try not to go backwards, darling,' she says, pressing his hand more tightly, 'that was *before* you went to school. Aren't there any *pictures* in your mind?'

He says, panting: 'I can see knives and a huge building full of white people.'

The other duke becomes very alert and says: 'That sounds like a colonial memory, Miss Tray. Ask him if he was brought up in Africa.'

'Were you born in India, darling?' she asks.

He shakes his head. The other duchess has a fresh flood of tears. 'I think it's *too* cruel!' she cries. 'It's hurting his poor head. Why can't he be a gardener?'

'Is something wrong?' asks the policeman, stepping up and looking closely at the bearded duke.

'Not really,' says the other duke. 'We're just trying to find out who he is.'

'Who do you think he is?' asks the policeman, becoming vexed. 'Under his costume, d'you mean?'

'Oh! that's nothing!' says the younger duchess. 'We want to know who he was before he was a gardener.'

Now, the policeman *is* vexed. He says sharply: 'Is there a telephone in this house?'

His words have an alarming effect. The bearded duke lets out a shriek and puts both hands to his ears. 'Telephone!' he screams: 'day and night – ring – ring – ring! No peace, never, never!'

'Darling, you're getting warm!' screams the younger duchess.

'He needs a doctor,' growls the policeman.

At this, all four of them throw up their hands and shriek in unison: 'A doctor!' The younger duchess, beside herself, shakes the bearded duke and screams: 'Darling, darling, say it, say it! Were you a doctor?'

He goes limp and says with a terrible groan: 'Yes. I was a doctor. I cannot deny it. Oh, my God!'

The other three sink back with white faces. Then, all at once, an astonishing thing happens. The older duchess raises both fists in the air and screams: 'Where's my money? It was a joint account!' She pauses an instant and screams: 'My brother! Thief! Thief!'

'I think, dear,' says the non-bearded duke, 'that your habit of blaming everything on me has gone too far this time.'

She turns on him furiously. 'Didn't you go to the house?' she demands. 'Did you come back? If not, where *did* you go?'

He replies slowly in a trembling voice: 'I seem to think I went to sea.'

The younger duchess corrects him. 'You were at sea *before* you came to this house, Mr Jellicoe.'

'I think not,' he answers. 'My sister forbade it. So this was my first chance.'

'We'll see about that,' says his sister. 'We'll go straight to the bank.'

'What is all this about a bank?' he asks.

She looks at him with rage. But there is something innocent about his face. Despite his ridiculous costume and make-up, his appearance seems so tidy, so prim, so respectable. One can imagine him a parasite, but not a thief. He looks at his sister with eyes which seem to represent utterly his inmost self. She cannot resist them. Suddenly she throws both arms round his neck and sobs: 'Oh, Henry, Henry! They told me you were dead.'

'You are wetting my clothes, dear,' he answers. 'Why do you always believe what you are told? Why do you always think I have changed?'

The younger duchess makes for the door; the policeman politely stops her. 'Let me go, officer!' she exclaims, 'I must tell the doctor at once. I mean, the *head* doctor.'

'She means the captain,' says the man Henry, giving the policeman a significant wink.

He cannot accept the wink. 'Will you kindly keep your seats,' he says: 'I must ask you a few questions. First, are you the staff of this establishment?'

It is a tactless beginning. Henry's sister puffs up like a pigeon and says sharply: 'Certainly not. I am a woman of independent means. So is my brother.'

The bearded man rises and assumes a certain shaky dignity. 'I think you know me, officer,' he says. 'I am a local doctor.'

'I think not, sir,' replies the policeman firmly.

'Perhaps not in this beard,' says the doctor: 'permit me to remove it.' He pulls, but the beard remains. It is not a false one at all. Irritated, he pulls at his ducal robe. This is certainly false; when it comes away, he is revealed in combinations and a dirty shirt.

'And you're a doctor, are you?' asks the policeman scornfully. 'Do you have an identity card?'

'It is in my car, officer.'

'Your car?'

'My car is outside. My bag, I brought in.'

'I see. May I ask you other ladies and gentlemen for your cards of identity?'

They look confused. 'Well,' says the policeman, 'ration-books, licences – anything like that.'

They fumble in their robes, but nothing comes out except the stub of a ticket for the Old Vic dated April 15, 1934.

'I can identify my *car*, officer,' says the doctor.

'Except it's not there,' says the policeman.

'My partners will identify me. Though, for the moment, I cannot remember their names.'

Now the policeman springs his surprise. 'What do any of you know about the three hundred eggs I saw in the larder? . . . Nothing? And nothing, I suppose, about the two hundred-pound sacks of sugar?'

Suddenly the supposed doctor points to the young duchess and says: 'She's my nurse.'

The young duchess turns white as a sheet. Now, it is her turn to cry. 'Oh, oh, what have I done?' she wails. 'Something too awful!'

The policeman thinks so too. 'You had better all come with me,' he says.

He opens the door and they all rise and slowly follow him out. At the foot of the grand stair they run into the loony countess, still dusting madly. 'And you, too, please,' says the policeman.

'It's only poor Miss Finch,' says the older duchess.

'Only poor Mrs Chirk,' says the younger duchess.

They start off down the drive – a long, dusty walk. It is the policeman's hope that he will be able to get them to the nearest telephone without their costumes attracting too much attention. For the same reason he wishes that he himself were in plain clothes – which, in the long run, always prove to be the best.

LANNAN SELECTIONS

The Lannan Foundation, located in Santa Fe, New Mexico, is a family foundation whose funding focuses on special cultural projects and ideas which promote and protect cultural freedom, diversity, and creativity.

The literary aspect of Lannan's cultural program supports the creation and presentation of exceptional English-language literature and develops a wider audience for poetry, fiction, and nonfiction.

Since 1990, the Lannan Foundation has supported Dalkey Archive Press projects in a variety of ways, including monetary support for authors, audience development programs, and direct funding for the publication of the Press's books.

In the year 2000, the Lannan Selections Series was established to promote both organizations' commitment to the highest expressions of literary creativity. The Foundation supports the publication of this series of books each year, and works closely with the Press to ensure that these books will reach as many readers as possible and achieve a permanent place in literature. Authors whose works have been published as Lannan Selections include: Ishmael Reed, Stanley Elkin, Ann Quin, Nicholas Mosley, William Eastlake, and David Antin, among others.

SELECTED DALKEY ARCHIVE PAPERBACKS

FOR A FULL LIST OF PUBLICATIONS, VISIT:
www.dalkeyarchive.com

SELECTED DALKEY ARCHIVE PAPERBACKS

FOR A FULL LIST OF PUBLICATIONS, VISIT:
www.dalkeyarchive.com